THE RIDINGHOOD GETAWAY

JEANIE DOYLE SINGLER

authorHOUSE

AuthorHouse™
1663 Liberty Drive
Bloomington, IN 47403
www.authorhouse.com
Phone: 833-262-8899

Published by AuthorHouse 08/05/2020

ISBN: 978-1-7283-6760-6 (sc)
ISBN: 978-1-7283-6759-0 (e)

Library of Congress Control Number: 2020912995

Print information available on the last page.

Any people depicted in stock imagery provided by Getty Images are
models, and such images are being used for illustrative purposes only.
Certain stock imagery © Getty Images.

Cover art by Wyatt A. Doyle

This is a work of fiction. All of the characters, names, incidents,
organizations, and dialogue in this novel are either the
products of the author's imagination or are used fictitiously.
The story and setting are not meant to represent any events
or property that now exists or have ever existed.

This book is printed on acid-free paper.

◆CAST OF CHARACTERS◆

Ridinghood Corporation:

Parish Stenopolis - Head Accountant
Ian Moseley – Chief Executive Officer
Tim Hogan – Chief Financial Officer
Slate Ridinghood – President of the Board of Directors and company owner
Midge Melanckton – Head of Human Resources
Odella Whitefeather – Head of Purchasing
Miguel Reyes - Head of Information Technology
Doris Possum – Administrative Assistant to Ian Moseley
Lawrence Manke – IT employee
Sally Stills – HR employee and live-in girlfriend of Lawrence Manke
Bobbi Bennett – Purchasing employee
Connie Evans – Credit & Accounts Receivable employee

Additional Characters:

Blayze Pashasia – IRS Forensic Auditor
Davy Sarkis – Pierce County Sheriff's Detective
Ellen Hogan – Tim Hogan's wife

Annabelle Elliott – Friend of Bobbi Bennett and Connie Evans

Sylvia Elysian - California resident

Luanne Fraser – Attached to the military

Janice Colton – Seattle resident with Ocean Shores property

◆CHAPTER ONE◆

Apprehensive the ship verged on sinking Parish Stenopolis watched Tim Hogan, an officer of the Arthur Ridinghood Corporation, receive a tall trim man in a sleek fitted Hugo Boss suit. Tim was short, broad, and losing the fair hair on top of his head, which emphasized the other man's height. This man with longish, curling dark hair, high cheek bones, and ominous eyebrows made Parish think of the hawk that kept the pigeons hiding in the corner on the roof of her apartment. He carried a briefcase and possessed the purposeful walk of the high executioner. It didn't take much figuring to determine he was the Internal Revenue Service auditor. He looked the part. She thought he appeared imminently appropriate to serve as the assassin who slaughtered the company and sunk her hopes for the future. To make it even worse she was the one who would help him do it.

Tim glanced at her and as he beckoned her direction she moved toward him.

"This is Blayze Pashasia with the Internal Revenue. He will be auditing our tax returns."

She could think of better places for him to spend his time. Placing her small hand in his long-fingered slim one she met his intense gaze from eyes of pale blue.

"Parish will be assisting you.

"Nice to meet you," she lied boldly.

His gaze rested on her a moment as if detecting her untruth.

Tim continued, "I'll leave you with her and if you have any more questions, she can get hold of me." Tim immediately retreated to his office in the executive suite.

"What do you need to see?"

"A place to work. I have your last five years returns. I'll need the supporting documentation."

She pointed to the magnificent oak stairway, one of the splendid features of the historic building the architects and interior designers had left untouched. She led him from the marketing department lobby with its coffee and cream décor into the elegant off-white hallway molded into Romanesque arches from which short halls led to the left and double doors opened to the right. At the second hallway she turned to the left, opened a door and ushered him into the room. "The office here," she explained, "is not used at present. I've had a computer installed. It should give you space to work." She noted the auditor's raised eyebrows.

"Rather eclectic," he commented, glancing around at the warm gray-toned room with off-white and gold trims. A medium oak desk and credenza accompanied a desk chair with brown, beige and white checked upholstery.

She wasn't sure if he referred to the room or the various spaces they had passed through. "This is an architectural and interior design firm," she reminded him.

"What is your position?" He looked as if he thought he ought to pat her on the head.

"Accountant."

His eyes flashed surprise but he merely nodded. "And the man who just left us?"

"Chief Financial Officer."

We're sliding down the scale of credibility, Parish thought ruefully.

After showing Mr. Pashasia to the office set aside for his use she provided him with access to the files he requested. Once he was settled with his task she returned to her own space from where she was subsequently summoned to the company board room.

This was not the executive committee room with the long oval table and thick leather chairs where vice presidents met with the board of directors, but a larger half-circle shaped room with seats arranged facing a white board and pull down screen making videos possible. Tim Hogan stood at the front while various staff members found places to sit. Behind him another row of chairs sat unoccupied.

Acute dread accompanied Parish as she located a seat. She was aware, if only vaguely, that Ian Moseley, Ridinghood's Chief Executive Officer, had been out of the office for close to a month. Unsure what that meant, she figured this meeting wasn't hallelujah-you're-back-let's-all-give-a-cheer.

Once the entire staff had arrived and taken seats a line of older men and women filed into the room to occupy the vacant chairs arranged behind Tim Hogan and the podium. Although unacquainted with these people Parish had seen some of them in the past and read about them in the newspapers and corporate newsletter. They represented the Board of Directors, an even more ominous indication.

Once everyone was seated and a hush had fallen over the assembly, a square man with bushy graying hair rose from the group behind the podium. Tim Hogan introduced him as Slate Ridinghood, Chairman of the Board of Directors. From Parish's knowledge of the company's heritage he was the younger son of Arthur Ridinghood, the founder of the corporation. His father had retired some years previous leaving Slate with primary responsibility for the business.

Contrary to frequent developments with second generation business owners, the let's-enjoy-the-benefits group, Slate had proven as business savvy and dedicated as his father. His appearance, in an excellently tailored gray suit, would have made an appropriate cover for *Forbes*. However, although his countenance betrayed his concern his deep resonant voice expressed compassion not anxiety.

"I've called this meeting in advance of having to confront the press and questions plaguing the company for the past month. I want you to know where we stand and what has happened as far as we can determine prior to hearing the gibberish the press will make of it." He paused visually assessing his audience. "Our Chief Executive Officer, Ian Moseley, as you are aware has been absent from the office for the past month . . . without explanation. As best we can determine he has disappeared.

Employees assimilated this revelation with an undertone of mumbling and hushed expressions of surprise.

Slate continued, "Our first order of business has been to locate him. Thus far we have been singularly unsuccessful. Ian has apparently disappeared without a trace. Before appealing to the police or sounding an alarm, given problems that would cause our business, we hired a private investigator. However, he was also unsuccessful locating Mr. Moseley. We have no reason to believe anything has happened to him but his continued absence without contact leaves us no alternative but to appeal to the authorities for assistance. We feel any other action would be irresponsible on the part of the corporation.

"As it stands I will be temporarily stepping in as Chief Executive Officer. Due to the irregularity of Mr. Moseley's absence his office will be kept closed and locked. We shall continue business as usual. There is no reason to believe this will adversely affect our operations. I hope it is unnecessary for me to caution you about speaking to the press. They are best handled with a simple "no comment". They are adept at taking insignificant remarks and twisting them into fantastic stories bearing no resemblance to reality. These irresponsible articles and rumors can produce significant adverse affects on our business and as a consequence your job and position.

"We all hope this mystery will be shortly resolved and whatever action is necessary become clear, leaving us free to move on. I realize many rumors are circulating, which is natural in the situation. I have spoken with many of you attempting to determine if there is any validity to them, any basis upon which we could formulate a theory or base an investigation. Given some truth can be found in most rumors, even if unutterably inaccurate, I am interested in hearing whatever may be available."

"I realize some people are loath to spread stories and gossip. Nonetheless, I am inviting anyone with any information whatever to come to me. I will keep the source confidential. You need have no fear I will jump to any conclusion or take any rash action based on what I am told. Everything will be given careful scrutiny to determine if it holds any truth that could lead to a solution."

"I must warn you as employees," Slate turned to the group behind him, "and you as directors the police will be conducting an investigation here. At this time we also have the IRS making an audit of our tax accounting. I'm not implying any connection between the two, but it is necessary everyone be as cooperative as possible in both instances. Our greatest hope in getting to the bottom of these problems we will be able to move forward. As a corporation we have prided ourselves on integrity therefore we should have no fear of what the investigation uncovers. If some illegality or corruption has taken place here it is without the consent or indulgence of management and owners. Consequently its discovery and exposure is to our advantage. However, we do wish to keep this within the company and not expose our business to the willful and capricious twisting of the media."

Slate Ridinghood made a few more remarks designed to calm fear and caution staff then dismissed the employees with information the media waited outside the room for a news conference following with the Board of Directors.

Positioning herself behind one of the more extroverted sales managers Parish passed through the swarm of news reporters unnoticed, which was not unusual. She had become so accustomed to being unseen and unnoticed she saw it as an advantage. The sales manager was accosted by an aggressive media tigress whose gaze swept over Parish as if she were empty air. She moved to follow another of the larger male employees as the group moved toward the elevator and stairs. Reporters appeared torn between obtaining interviews with retreating staff and positioning themselves for the conference about to begin.

Returning to her office, she considered the situation regarding the CEO. What options did she have for retaining her position and prospects for the future? How much did it depend on the results of the CEO's disappearance? Was there anything at all she could do where that was concerned?

$$\approx$$

A.Blayze Pashasia frowned at the television screen on the wall at the back of the bar. On the screen he recognized men he had met that afternoon at the offices of Arthur Ridinghood Corporation. The sound was off but Blayze could guess what the broadcast concerned. The company had finally parted with information their Chief Executive Officer had disappeared. In fact, he had been missing for more than a month in which time the institution had carefully maintained an all-is-well front. As a high end architectural and interior design firm it was essential to keep bad news at a minimum for the sake of the business and its investors. His acquaintance with the corporate executives had come as a result of questions relating to their corporate tax return and not thus far related to absence of the executive officer. That fact came to his attention only while waiting to be greeted by the Chief Financial Officer and the accounting team and then only by inference from conversations he heard in passing.

Ridinghood's corporate tax return for the year previous had triggered a red flag which in the course of events produced his summons to audit. Apparently the company had been placed on a watch list for some years as a prior return had alerted the government's tax authority. Ridinghood had successfully dodged an audit at that time by providing information to support their previous returns and questions the IRS had put to them. However, too many questions over the years and the red flag had sealed their fate. Blayze had been assigned the audit.

Interestingly enough no one at the corporate offices had seen fit to inform him of the situation regarding the CEO. Was that suspicious relative to their tax audit or only incidental and irrelevant? From his perspective the month long unexplained absence of the Chief Executive Officer could hardly be considered irrelevant. Yet that appeared the approach being maintained by the remaining staff. Until today, that is.

The next question plaguing Blayze regarded whether this day's revelation amounted to a voluntary admission by the corporation or had it been precipitated by the media's pursuit. Although Blayze had spent the afternoon at the corporation he had not been privy to events ending in the television broadcast. He wondered if his new assistant, Miss Parish Stenopolis had been.

Miss Stenopolis puzzled him. She looked hardly more than a teen-ager, an innocent, naïve teen-ager at that. Her pale blonde hair with bangs to her eyebrows and pastel blue eyes with long sweeping eyelashes behind a pair of dark-rimmed eye glasses gave her an angelic air of femininity. In fact she was devastatingly feminine. However, her manner was entirely professional and competent. She provided him with space to work, answered his questions directly, demonstrating no hesitancy in understanding what he needed or requested.

Although her appearance and behavior constituted the utmost in womanliness she made not a single flirtatious move. Her gaze was direct, her smile friendly but impersonal, her body language gracious but aloof. She amounted to the ultimate untouchable. Although not necessarily attracted to her, Blayze found her imminently interesting. He struggled to align her appearance with her attitude and position.

Though not the kind of man who liberally played the field, Blayze possessed no lack of experience. He knew how to begin and end a relationship. He had to concede a considerably greater proficiency at ending one than maintaining one long-term. Admittedly something eluded him in the matter of long-lived relationships. However, thus far it had only constituted a minor frustration in his life.

The exception being his doctor's comment when he had been released from the hospital a few months previous. "Get married," Dr. Cheung had said. Blayze spent a moment or two occasionally considering the concept but made no moves in that direction. Nor had he even adopted the idea for serious consideration.

The restaurant, one of the popular bar and grill style, offered multiple television screens visible from every angle and table. It served a variety of sandwiches, grilled or barbecued, in addition to soups, salads, and a variety of soft drinks, beers and wines. Furnished in dark cherry wood and leather-like vinyl, the place possessed a casual atmosphere decorated in gold and orange including screens in royal blue with a pinkish lighting. Blayze considered it an assault on the eyeballs.

The television broadcast had moved from the exterior of the corporate headquarters to the interior assembly room. Here the group of men previously addressed by the reporters was arrayed in front. Outside of these people the room appeared filled with the press. Blayze noticed none of the personnel he had encountered that afternoon in his auditing efforts. Undoubtedly this represented the broadcast of portions of the press conference.

Absorbed in concentration on the television screen he failed to notice someone had stopped beside him to observe the same scene until this person addressed him.

"You acquainted with the company?" asked Lieutenant Davy Sarkis.

Blayze turned with surprise to the voice beside him recognizing the police lieutenant from an assignment he had previously completed. "I was there this afternoon."

"Learn anything?" The lieutenant's bright brown eyes peered at him over the top of his spectacles.

"Not about that." He nodded toward the screen.

"That's too bad," Sarkis lamented. "I could use some insights."

"Are you investigating their missing CEO?"

"We've just been called in. Somewhat after the fact," he grumbled running his hand through his reddish brown hair. "You meeting someone?"

Blayze shook his head.

"Care to join me."

He figured the lieutenant was information gathering, but then it wouldn't hurt to be in a position to squeeze him for some later. "Sure."

After turning to look for a table, the lieutenant approached one where a man sat while another took his leave. "How's the religion business?" the lieutenant addressed the seated man.

This man with jarring good looks and brilliant blue eyes grinned. "Probably about as good as the police business." He glanced around then offered the use of his table.

"Don't mind if I do," Lieutenant Sarkis said, adding to Blayze, "This is Pastor Dark Ansgreth." To Dark he said, "This is Blayze Pashasia, IRS."

Blayze followed the lieutenant, taking a seat at the pastor's table.

The pastor stacked his dishes.

"Don't rush off."

"Actually," Dark said, "I could use some advice."

Lieutenant Sarkis hesitated as if concerned about getting involved in some time consuming inquiry. "What's the matter, God quit answering your prayers?"

Ansgreth laughed. "I thought perhaps you were the answer to my prayer."

The lieutenant snorted. After the waitress had taken orders for Blayze and Davy, the lieutenant turned to Dark. "Do you have a missing person?"

"You are the answer to my prayer. The wife of a man in my congregation has been missing over a month now."

Blayze noted the light bulb expression on the lieutenant's face.

"A month?" Davy turned to Blayze. "How long did they say that CEO was gone?"

"A little over a month."

"I've just been handed a missing persons case regarding a corporate CEO. He's been missing a month also."

If the lieutenant considered putting the two together thinking they may have disappeared together; Blayze figured that seemed a little too convenient.

"So what happened to your woman?" Davy asked the pastor.

"Went to Ocean Shores and hasn't been seen since."

"What was she doing in Ocean Shores?"

"According to her husband she was meeting a friend to get away from it all for the weekend."

"Has he talked to the friend?"

"Apparently he has talked to all her friends. The ones she met in Ocean Shores have returned. None of the others were going or have recently been there."

"And his wife hasn't returned?" Davy crossed his arms over his chest and alternated his gaze between Dark and Blayze.

Figuring Sarkis still considered the possibility the two missing people met up, Blayze shook his head. "They said Moseley just walked out of his office and never returned. No mention of Ocean Shores."

"Ah, well." The lieutenant sighed. "Missing persons is some of the most frustrating police work I do."

"I thought you were in homicide," Dark observed.

"Right." The lieutenant bobbed his head. "But when they get a missing persons like this where someone of significance has been gone for an extended period of time they start thinking it might be homicide." He drew a sheet of paper from his pocket and opened it. "I have to confess to a small matter of neglect." He grimaced. "I have another missing person case I was given some weeks ago but haven't given a great deal of attention. Some musician was reported missing by a woman in the band he was part of. I could find nothing to say the guy hadn't gone off simply wishing to get away from it all too."

"You think that's the deal with the Ridinghood Exec?" Blayze questioned the lieutenant.

"We just got that case so I can't speculate, but couldn't an executive just want to get away too?" Davy verified his supposition with his companions.

Ansgreth grimaced. "The problem with that is the individual might just have wanted to get away from it all, but dumped all his or her responsibilities on someone else. He left that person in limbo unable to take action because of his irresponsible attitude. What's this husband supposed to do about his missing wife? Presumably she isn't dead. What does he tell his children? Should he try to find her? What other liabilities is he facing?"

Blayze acknowledged Dark's comment with a nod. "The same for this corporation. They may not care if the executive resigned his position. They'd hire a new CEO and move on. But they've been left in limbo. Whatever they do affects the integrity of their business reputation and hence a lot of innocent people."

"It may be a minor inconvenience for your woman in the band to get another man but these other two situations need to be resolved by locating the missing person." Dark nodded to the waitress who removed his stack of empty dishes.

"What I'm wondering is if there's some common thread in these cases. Something that would lead to finding any one of these people if not all of them?" Davy consulted his companions in turn.

"I can give you what general information I have on the woman in question. I was acquainted with her myself and her husband is amenable to helping in hopes of finding her."

Davy turned to Blayze with lifted eyebrows.

"I'm at Ridinghood to do a tax audit. The CEO was gone before I came."

Sarkis cocked his head. "You wouldn't be interested in keeping your antenna up to see what information might become available?"

Blayze eyed the lieutenant frowning. "I'm not opposed but . . ." He lifted his shoulders. "However," he added, "since they've upped with the announcement of his absence it may create more talk."

"There's something you probably need to know about this woman," Dark addressed Davy, with a glance at Blayze. "She was also employed by Ridinghood Corporation."

The lieutenant glared at Ansgreth. "You're kidding."

Dark shook his head.

Taking out his piece of paper again Davy said, "According to this my other guy is a musician. But it does say that's a part time occupation. What are we going to bet he's also employed by Ridinghood?"

◈CHAPTER TWO◈

Ridinghood's corporate offices occupied a century old building in the historic district of Tacoma. After purchasing the building the corporation had transformed it into its corporate headquarters. Having been there the day before made it possible for Blayze to locate the company without difficulty. In fact his previous couple assignments, close to Tacoma's downtown and his stay at the hotel there had familiarized him with the general vicinity.

He entered the main floor reception area where he had been introduced to his assistant. He recognized the substantial stairway in the midst of the light and dark taupe interior. The building, impressive for its Italianate exterior preserved for a century and a half, gave no indication of its mind boggling interior, an exotic blend of decors. He noted the teal accents of the rug and furnishings in the reception area as he climbed the stairs which he recalled led to the office he had been assigned. On the second floor he turned toward the archway leading out of the immediate area into a hall where he noticed Parish standing by one of the double doors talking with a young man holding a two foot roll of paper. She wore a concerned expression. Glancing at Blayze her expression changed to one of apprehension, an expression with which he was familiar. Most people at most companies viewed him with apprehension, that is, if they knew who he was. Although sometimes being intimidating served his purposes, for the most part he would have preferred to be viewed as any other man might have been.

The head accountant, as he had learned she was, wore a well-fitted a-line skirt, a silky blouse with a ruffle at the neck and a tweed blazer that appeared slightly large for her. She appeared both professional and fragile. After making a comment to the young man, who cast a glance at Blayze, she came to meet him.

"Good morning," she said politely. "Do you recall where you'll be working?

He nodded with some reserve.

She accompanied him further along the hall to his assigned office. "I've brought as much of the supporting documentation as I have available. Most of it is on the computer. My office is there," she pointed over her shoulder to a high steel blue arch from which the door, open now, gave onto another room. "If you need anything, just let me know."

Blayze thanked her then set his briefcase on the desk and removed the papers he had brought with him. After taking a seat in the unusually textured office chair, comfortable though, he successfully logged onto the computer and located the accounting program. He set about his auditing assignment in the traditional fashion while keeping his ears open as he had promised to do. The morning went quickly as he became lost in his assignment.

At noon, Miss Stenopolis appeared in his doorway. "The corporation has a cafeteria. I can show you if you like."

"I'd appreciate that." He slid loose papers into his briefcase and logged off the computer.

Parish took him to an elevator just beyond her office where they ascended one level.

Figuring that getting to know his associate may be strategic, Blayze made an effort to be congenial. Acutely aware his position and employer made him intimidating; he struggled relating to people where he worked. His personality wasn't charismatic making it difficult to lighten the atmosphere. The need to not compromise his authority when it would come to the results of his investigation weighed heavily upon him. Nonetheless, his impression of Miss Stenopolis made him believe he had nothing to fear from her in that line. Her femininity was exceedingly intimidating, but not her gracious handling of the accounting.

"You worked here long?" he asked her.

"Four years," she replied, casting him a sidewise glance. "And no I wasn't still in kindergarten."

He opened his mouth to protest, then laughed. "You also read minds?"

"Sixth sense." She glanced at him, a trace of amusement on her face.

Once out of the elevator she led him down a hall framed by the exposed brick of the building's structure. In a large open area at the end of the hall and to their left was a designer circular staircase. Reaching the top of the stairs they stepped into a room that made Blayze think of secret meeting places for the mafia. Not that he knew anything about the mafia outside of how they are portrayed in film, but this splash of red, black and brass gave him that impression. A glance at Parish told him she was laughing at him.

He nodded, commenting for her. "It's an interior design firm."

Working to pick out elements of function in the room he noted in the center a circular serving area where there appeared a sizeable array of lunch selections. They proceeded immediately to this spot where they each picked up a tray and made selections.

Once seated in plush red chairs at a black granite table for two, he pinned her with his gaze and asked, "When do the guys with machine guns arrive."

She cocked her head. "You don't like it?

Turning he observed the entirely circular room surrounded by windows, flanked by ornamental brass poles and covered in pale gold sheers. Two person tables ran around the periphery and across an expanse of black carpeting with a large white fan-shaped pattern were four person ones. In the center near the food were tables for four that could be moved together to accommodate a larger group. "A surprise attack on the optic nerve?"

"It's a fine dining restaurant at night," she offered by way of explanation. After a moment of quiet, she asked, "How bad is the situation that brings in an IRS auditor?"

He studied her expression briefly. "What concerns you?"

"A scandal that does the company in."

Blayze shook his head. "What I'm doing won't cause that kind of problem." He paused a moment. "A worse one might be your missing CEO." He noted her troubled look. "You concerned about losing your job?"

"It's not that I couldn't get another job, but getting something that pays well and has a future." She made a face. "I have a teen-age son to get through college."

Blayze shot her a shocked glance. She looked like a teen-ager. How could she have a teen-age son? "You know anything about the missing man?"

"Only what we were told at the briefing yesterday." She met his eyes with a guarded expression.

He figured she didn't particularly care for the missing CEO.

"I knew who he was if I saw him. He would have mistaken me for one of the desks. Actually what I've heard of him he probably thought most of the people here were part of the furniture."

"Egomaniac?"

Parish laughed. "King Nebuchadnezzar." She waved her hand. "Into the lion's den if you don't bow down and worship."

Blayze frowned, feeling slightly confused. "Megalomania? People like that are dangerous."

She gave him a quizzical look.

"You disagree?"

"I'm not sure I know enough about it."

"Usually persuasive. If they're charming or good looking," he shook his head, "they sucker people into most anything." He had seen it happen often enough.

"Mr. Moseley isn't good looking." Parish stated flatly her pastel eyes gazing at him through her spectacles. "Or charming."

"Wealthy?"

"Presumably."

"Various things impress people. Egocentrics are all about impressing people. They're bold, convinced they're special, a class above." He recalled his mission to get information. "Is anyone else from the company missing?"

Parish frowned at him.

"I'm told there's a woman gone about a month."

She considered, but after a moment shook her head.

"Maybe I can get a name."

"Was she supposed to have gone with Mr. Moseley?"

Blayze sighed, lifting his shoulders. "Possible, I suppose."

She appeared unconvinced.

❦

Returning to her office after seeing Mr. Pashasia once more ensconced in his space with his auditing, Parish spent a moment considering whether she had heard any gossip regarding someone having gone missing with Ian Moseley. Part of the problem was she never heard Mr. Moseley had gone missing. Most of the employees knew he was absent from the office, but with the executives that could mean anything, a month's vacation, an extended business trip, or a medical issue.

Consequently, she knew nothing about anyone going missing with him, which in itself meant nothing. Any number of rumors could circulate she would not have heard, not being part of the inner crowd, those in the know. Although in truth she doubted how much "those in the know" actually knew. Her perception, they thought they knew more than they actually did. However, they spread gossip as if it were accurate information tried and true.

Now word was out regarding Mr. Moseley's effective disappearance rumors would fly like so many seagulls at the seashore. Separating truth from fiction would be challenging. In such an atmosphere truth, like a penny, was of little value.

However, at this time in Parish's life discovering the truth had become significantly important. Could one in the process of checking rumors find the truth? What was the most effective way of securing accurate information as opposed to wild fantasy? Considering these questions occupied her mind off and on while she worked formulating reports for the executives.

Thinking of her friend who worked in HR, she grabbed her cell phone and tapped her entry for Midge. What might she know about all of this?

"What are you doing after work?" she asked when her friend answered. "Would you have time for coffee?"

Midge giggled. "Would you be free for dinner? You could come to my house. I made lasagna yesterday, too much." She giggled again. "I need help."

Parish ran through her evening commitments. Her son Xavier was staying with a friend from basketball camp. "I can be free."

"Come about six."

Midge Melanckton lived in a small two bedroom cape cod in the northwest part of Tacoma. As summer's end approached the sun rested low in the sky casting a golden glow on the waters of Commencement Bay, visible to Parish off and on as she made her way there. The towering supports of the Narrows Bridge sat etched against the light blue sky. Surrounded by lush greenery, Midge's house, except for the basement, would be smaller than Parish's apartment.

After parking in the driveway to a small detached garage she climbed the stairs to the side door which opened into the kitchen. No one ever used Midge's front door.

Ezekiel, her Pomeranian, yipped sniffing Parish's feet as she handed Midge a bottle of Chianti she had picked up on the way.

Midge cocked her fluffy blonde head. "That bad, huh?"

Parish grimaced. "It could be." She stepped into the tiny kitchen in the center of which sat a round maple table covered with a green and white shamrock cloth, set for dinner. Along one wall stretched an array of cabinets. The refrigerator remained alone against the farther wall.

Midge nodded at the flowers in the center. "I bought them just in case we needed to mourn. Sit down, I'll bring the salad." She went to the refrigerator from which she withdrew two wooden bowls filled with greens. In another trip she brought the dressings.

Parish grabbed two stemmed glasses from the cupboard before being seated. "Do you have an opener?"

Midge was more than fifteen years older than Parish, not surprising given the circumstances in her life gave her more in common with Midge than many people of her own age.

"Do I have an opener?" Midge did a Broadway flourish reaching into a cabinet from which she brought out a metal envelope and withdrew an elaborate contraption. Applying it to the top of the wine bottle she successfully removed the cork with one swift movement. "What do you think of that?"

Impressed, Parish laughed. "Where did you get it?"

"Estate sale."

Midge held the trophy for her estate sales purchases, everything from the wine gadget to the latest in resort fashions. After pouring each of them a glass she took her chair. "So what's the problem?"

"You went to the briefing about Mr. Moseley?"

Midge nodded. "Where do you think he went?" Her gray eyes observed Parish over the rim of her goblet.

Ignoring the question, Parish continued, "According to the IRS auditor I inherited at least one other person from Ridinghood has also disappeared."

Midge peered into her wine glass as if it were a crystal ball.

"I wondered if you know who else is missing."

"As opposed to quitting, on leave of absence, medical leave or vacation?"

"Right." Parish suddenly realized the possibilities for people to be absent from work were so numerous it might be difficult to determine who was gone who shouldn't be.

Midge stared over Parish's shoulder at a small lamp attached to the wall with a retractable arm. "How long would this person have been gone?"

"Well, to have gone with Mr. Moseley it would have to be about a month, right?"

"You know, you are on verge of dashing my hopes to pieces." Assuming a broken-hearted expression, Midge placed her hands on her plump bosom. "I'll tell you who's gone if you promise you won't go looking for her and bring her back."

Parish eyed her with suspicion. "Who?"

"Bobbi Bennett. She's not much of an employee, so I'd be delighted to lose her. Unfortunately she's related in some way to the Ridinghoods or I'd have sent her on an extended only partially paid vacation some time ago."

Laughing, Parish asked, "What department was she in?

"Purchasing. You should check with Odella."

After picking up the salad bowls, Midge removed the lasagna from the oven and placed it on a trivet in the middle of the table then took a spatula from the utensil drawer.

Seated once again, she said, "Something else. Now that I think about it Sally, my assistant, says her boyfriend has disappeared."

Parish frowned. "Does he work for Ridinghood?"

"In IT." Midge sighed. "She's been really worried about him."

"If I mentioned that to this IRS guy would it be a problem?" Parish had no idea what Mr. Pashasia wanted, but it made a place to start.

"What does the IRS care about missing employees?" Midge pinned her with a suspicious squint.

"I don't know, but he asked about them this morning. I'm afraid with what's going on if we don't do something the company is going to take a big hit and we'll lose our jobs."

"That would hit me hard." Midge frowned. "But I think Sally already reported her boyfriend missing to the police."

"Are they taking it serious?"

"I think she did it a while ago and has had no results." Midge lifted her shoulders. "It doesn't bother me if you mention these people to the IRS guy." She leaned forward. "Is he good looking? You could have him come talk to me."

"He looks like an IRS auditor. Formidable."

"Formidable is good. I could find that attractive."

Parish rolled her eyes and shook her head.

◆CHAPTER THREE◆

P roceeding with his auditing process Blayze noticed some consistent oddities. Large sums of money appeared to disappear then return. The money would leave, sent to a bank account he could not identify, then within the quarter return to the main account. In an attempt to determine the exact bank account it traveled to, he could find a number, presumably an account number, but not the name of the bank. If not mistaken he figured the bank's name had been removed from the computer along with any files once the transaction had been completed, making it appear to a casual observer the money had never left the original account at all.

These transactions he realized could have triggered the IRS audit. They would also explain why, when having been red flagged and confronted the corporation was able to prove their innocence. Yet the following year it would trigger another red flag. Blayze was unable to ascertain what trip the money took or what it accomplished during its absence. Given the corporation's other issues this odd short term absence of sizeable sums took on greater significance.

He concluded the first person to confront was his assistant, the head accountant. Ms. Stenopolis had certainly appeared apprehensive when he met her and even today on his arrival at the corporation. Had she become involved in something and was afraid of discovery? He needed to be careful about discounting her based on her innocent, naïve appearance. She had not become head accountant for nothing. However, having reached that position didn't make her automatically suspect either.

Another thought, did this relate to the CEO's disappearance? That was an equally difficult stretch to make. Until he determined how the money spent its time during its absence he could not reasonably speculate on the culprit. Possibly a totally above board explanation existed.

Blayze's cell phone alerted him.

"You have time for coffee?" It was Lieutenant Sarkis.

"Sure. Where?"

"Isn't there a coffee shop on the main floor of your building?"

Continuing his search for banking information he wondered what Sarkis wanted. One day was insufficient time to come up with any answers to the man's questions. He also considered what information he might want to get from the lieutenant. However, he needed to exercise caution. His work remained confidential business information for Ridinghood's eyes only.

Leaving his office, Blayze debated taking the elevator or descending the staircase. Since the stairs were a safer bet he headed for the archway leading there. On the main floor he paused in the reception area, glancing to his right through another arch at the expansive hallway, thinking it probably led to the coffee shop. However, uncertain, he opted for leaving the building and walking around on the sidewalk to the official entrance. A miniature park lay just outside the shop's entrance with a couple wrought iron benches. The lieutenant sat on one of them, his long legs stretched out in front of him, examining a small notebook.

They entered the coffee shop together, one of the independent ones in the local area leasing space from the Ridinghood Corporation. The shop, done in wicker with peach and taupe cushions and tables with marble tops, was nearly empty. Near a window overlooking the little park sat a woman Blayze would have expected to see at the IRS offices, stocky with a square face, short dark hair and intense hazel eyes. A couple teenage girls sat at a table within a short proximity of the counter, bantering with the young barista.

Sarkis began once they were seated. "I reviewed the information I had on the other disappearance. Apparently he's a computer guy as well as a musician. He was reported missing by his girlfriend but at least a couple weeks before the CEO supposedly disappeared. It seems unlikely they had anything to do with one another." The lieutenant sighed. "More's the pity."

"You want them connected?"

"It would save time if the thing were all one big shindig. I wouldn't have to chase a bunch of different clues."

The lieutenant's logic failed to impress Blayze. "I'd think tying them together would make them difficult to follow."

"Not if they all took off together. Or at least for the same reason."

"A computer programmer, a corporate CEO and some guy's wife?" That seemed farfetched. "Where did the wife work?"

"According to Dark she'd had a number of positions with Ridinghood. At the time she left and failed to return she was in purchasing."

"Working her way up the corporate ladder?"

"I got the impression she was in danger of falling off the ladder."

Interesting, Blayze thought. He noticed the girls leaving but the woman still sat with her gaze fixed on the door into the corporate offices as if expecting someone. While he watched the man who had introduced him to Parish joined her.

"Have you learned anything helpful?" Sarkis' clear brown eyes peered at him over the edge of his spectacles.

"My assistant didn't seem to know anything." He sighed. "Not even about the CEO until the announcement."

"So she wasn't associated with him?"

Blayze shook his head. "She did mention he was an egomaniac."

"Hmmmm." The lieutenant appeared interested. "That might be worth following up. Dark gave me the impression his missing woman has some issues with narcissism. Maybe the other guy had some mental issue."

"You think a bunch of crazies went off together?"

Lieutenant Sarkis shot him a scowl.

"Your guy have a name?" Blayze grabbed a napkin and the pen from his pocket.

"Lawrence Manke."

"And the woman?"

"Bobbi Bennett." The lieutenant shifted his gaze past a shelf of travel cups with forest scenery then back to Blayze with a frown. "Do you happen to know the guy who just came in?"

"Tim Hogan. He's the Chief Financial Officer."

Sarkis bobbed his head. Blayze couldn't tell if it meant something to him or not. "The woman is giving him a list of instructions on how to move up into the position vacated by Moseley."

They ceased their conversation while the lieutenant engaged in eavesdropping.

"At least you could let Slate know you're interested," she informed Hogan who appeared absolutely disinterested.

Blayze shrugged his eyebrows. From what he had seen Tim Hogan didn't strike him as CEO material. He refrained from voicing his impression.

"Do you know who the woman is?" Sarkis nodded toward the other table.

"No." It crossed Blayze's mind motive might be even more important in a disappearance than in a murder. He wondered if what he found at Ridinghood would amount to a motive for someone to disappear.

⚛

Arriving at her office Parish noticed the auditor had located his office without assistance. She moved to his door, noting he generally left it open. "Do you still have everything you need?"

He looked up from his keyboard with a grimace. "You have time to answer a couple questions?"

Rolling the plush white chair residing in the corner with a silver metal table to a position in front of his desk, Parish wondered what had made him banish the furniture to the corner. She refrained from asking since he didn't look that friendly. Two vertical lines appeared between his dark eyebrows.

Blayze leaned back in his chair, eying her. "I've found some oddities I hope you can explain."

Gazing at him with raised eyebrows she waited for the bomb to explode.

"For some time now, money is regularly withdrawn from the bank account, gone for a time, then reappears."

Parish realized he was watching her reaction carefully. Did he suspect her of embezzlement? "This is the regular corporate account as opposed to the payroll or investment accounts?"

"I have those account numbers and bank. No match to this number."

"Can you show me what you mean?"

Blayze moved his chair over to make room for Parish. She rolled hers around to a position beside him. He opened the accounting program to the corporate bank account and showed her the entries in question.

"I don't like the looks of that." She frowned. "I don't work with this as a rule."

"What does it look like to you?"

Was that a loaded question? "It appears the extra money in the corporate account that would normally be moved into an investment account is being diverted somewhere else." She sighed. "But if that were the case why does it return?"

"Who could answer that?"

"Honestly," she met Blayze's pale gaze, "I'm not sure anyone except the one who did it. You could check with Tim Hogan, the CFO, he manages the investment account. You could also ask Taylor Washington. He's the comptroller." She paused a moment then asked, "Did you think I had done it?"

She noticed a flush of color sweep up the auditor's high cheek bones. He took a deep breath but didn't answer.

"I'd have an awful lot to lose by fooling around with the company accounting. It would never be worth it, even if I was the kind of person so inclined." She shot him a defiant glance.

He scrolled for a time through the accounting in silence. "Okay. I'll consult those you mentioned. Also," he appeared to debate with himself. Was he going to take another shot at her? "I'm going to check routing numbers for payroll automatic deposits."

"Is there any way to find out what bank routing numbers go to which banks? It always seemed to me the bank numbers were similar for a particular area as if the number identified the bank's location."

He nodded. "Although it might relate to the bank's headquarters rather than branch location."

Parish stared at him, the intensity of his pale-eyed gaze, the hovering dark eyebrows. "Are you thinking someone has been embezzling from the company?"

"If the money didn't return so soon." He nodded. "This is a strange way to embezzle. Take the money then return it." He grinned at her. "Usually it's take the money and run."

"It sounds as if someone did run." She flashed him a smile. "They just forgot to take the money." She grabbed her chair and rolled it back to the little table. It might help to check with Midge about the other missing employees.

Instead of taking the elevator she made the longer trek to the stairs and up to the third floor where a tall double door in the curved portion of brick wall opened into the area housing human resources. Midge occupied a crescent shaped desk square in the middle of the room facing the doorway with a wall of windows behind her. Parish would have preferred a lower profile place to work.

She perched on the royal blue chair beside Midge's desk. "Mr. Pashasia will probably bug you for some employee information."

"He's done bugging you?"

"I'm chief suspect. He thinks I've been embezzling."

Midge put her elbows on the desk resting her chin on her hands. "You'd be the first one I'd suspect, too. You look too innocent to be true."

Ignoring the quip, Parish asked, "Have you checked on the absent employees?"

Most of the ones who are gone at the moment are legitimately on vacation or approved leave. Also they haven't been gone that long. The one Sally reported to the police, Lawrence Manke, worked in IT. I checked and he just left work one day and didn't return."

"How long ago was that?"

Midge frowned. "About six weeks."

"That long. Oh, I didn't realize it could be that long." Parish grimaced. "Truth is when they said Mr. Moseley had been gone a month I could hardly believe that."

"Poor Mr. Moseley," Midge assumed a mournful pose. "You didn't even miss him."

Parish rolled her eyes. "I'll send Mr. Pashasia over to see you. You can answer his questions better than I."

"Oh how nice. You're going to share." Midge rubbed her hands together.

"Don't complain when it doesn't turn out the way you want," Parish warned with a smile.

"Darling, things never turn out the way I want. But that isn't always bad." Midge shot her a parting cheesy grin.

◆CHAPTER FOUR◆

B layze watched Parish put the chair back and leave. Interestingly enough she didn't appear the least concerned about being suspected of embezzling. Yet he could still detect apprehension when she was with him. Whatever the cause he figured it didn't relate to a guilty conscience over embezzlement.

Her idea of checking bank routing numbers may at least narrow down possibilities where the missing money vacationed. Another question struck him, was the money vacationing or moonlighting? Would it be possible to use the funds to generate more money, then return the original capital?

Several problems arose in that regard. Banks tended to be touchy about large sums of money coming and going. The government held them accountable for keeping track of such things. An even bigger question plagued him, what sort of investment would produce enough return in the short run to make it worth the risk? Maybe someone just borrowed it to cover a cash flow emergency. However, the emergency was never quite resolved.

Blayze glanced at the time on the computer. He could use a cup of coffee. He had been introduced the afternoon before to the break room, although locating it again presented a challenge. According to his understanding of the building's anatomy it sat on the third floor above what would on the main level be the coffee shop. Once again deciding on the stairs rather than the elevator he followed the route Parish had taken him to get to the cafeteria. In the space where the circular stairs resided a set of double doors in the brick facade sat open allowing him to recognize the break room.

This room, done in platinum gray cabinetry with gray marble counters and backsplashes, was furnished in natural wood tables and chairs with burgundy cushions. A circular wall of windows framed the room through which he caught glimpses of the Port of Tacoma. A couple people sat at a small table near a window examining papers in front of them. Otherwise he found the room empty.

At the counter he fixed a cup of coffee, adding creamer with an ear to the conversation. However, it told him nothing. On his return trip he stopped at Parish's office. Since the door was open he entered. She looked up with a question in her expression.

"Could you direct me to human resources?" He noted her office furnished another variation in décor. Painted a deep subdued green it contained one wall of tall painted flowers as if growing in a garden, done in shades of pink, yellow and white.

"Sure." She rose. "I told Midge you might want to talk to her."

She directed their steps to the elevator, just outside her office. They took it to the third floor where they turned to the right and entered double doors in a curved section of wall. A plump woman pushing fifty, seated in a bright yellow chair, looked up when they entered. A trace of smile flickered across her oval face.

"This is Blayze Pashasia, with the IRS," Parish explained, to him she said, "This is Midge Melanckton. She manages human resources."

"How can I help you?" Midge asked Blayze as Parish left. She beckoned to the bright blue chair beside her desk.

Blayze hesitated slightly before taking the seat. Aside from a background in various shades of off-white, the room contained black desks and tables coupled with chairs in primary colors.

"Parish told me about your concerns regarding people missing from here." A trace of amusement twinkled in her gray eyes. "Those besides the CEO."

"I understand there are two, a man and a woman."

"Lawrence Manke, who worked in IT and Bobbi Bennett, who has worked in various spots around the company, most recently in purchasing."

"Leaving about the same time?" Blayze had the uncomfortable feeling people knew more about him than he did about them. That might not last long, his psyche inserted.

Midge shook her head. "Lawrence has been gone for about six weeks. But Bobbi only left about a month ago."

"No assumption they went together?"

Midge grimaced. "I wouldn't think so. I'd be surprised if they were even on speaking terms."

"Didn't get along?" Blayze found it difficult getting people to tell you what you needed to know. This woman appeared chatty enough if one could get her started, not one of Blayze's accomplishments. He found it easier frightening them into terrified silence.

"Oh, no, nothing like that. Bobbi only noticed people who could serve her purposes. I can't imagine someone in IT fitting that bill."

"Not computer savvy?"

"She wasn't anything savvy that required getting some work done." Midge clapped her hand over her mouth, "Forget I said that."

Blazye lifted an eyebrow restraining a grin. "Incompetent?"

"Lazy." Midge placed a hand on her desk, leaning toward the auditor. "Between you and me, for your edification . . . ."

He understood she was making a helpful confidence. He also realized side information could prove more valuable to the IRS as well as assisting Lieutenant Sarkis than his auditing would.

"Bobbi Bennett is related to the corporate execs. She is Slate Ridinghood's wife's sister-in-law's sister."

"So her position is guaranteed?"

Midge lifted her shoulders. "Not her position, just her employment."

He frowned. What did that mean?

"We have to keep moving her around so she doesn't disable one of the departments with her inactivity."

"She thinks she's getting promotions?"

Looking across the room, Midge grimaced. "I doubt she's fooled. I don't think she cares either."

"Or at least didn't care?"

Midge frowned.

"She's gone right?" Blayze watched for a reaction.

"You think she left because of her 'promotions'." Midge emphasized the word.

Blayze lifted his shoulders. "Just testing ideas. You expect she'll return?"

Laughing, Midge clasped her hands together and lifted a pleading gaze heavenward.

Smiling, Blayze figured from the sounds of it no one at Ridinghood missed Bobbi Bennett. "She worked last for purchasing?"

"You could talk to Odella Whitefeather. Bobbi worked for her."

"Would you say she was incompetent?"

"Before determining her competency you'd have to get her to do something. I'd say she wasn't intelligent but cunning. She knew how to get what she wanted."

"And not above doing what it takes?" Blayze suggested.

Midge gave him a thumbs up.

"What about Lawrence Manke?"

"That's a different story, but one I know less about. Since he was competent, accountable and caused no trouble I know very little about him. I believe Miguel considers him a loss to his department."

"Miguel?"

"Miguel Reyes, the IT manager." Midge laughed again. "What you need to do is have Parish introduce you to her Control Group."

Blayze frowned his question.

"You need to ask her about that."

⋙

At noon Parish paused at Blayze's door before heading to the cafeteria. "Would you like to go to lunch?" Unaccustomed to shepherding adult men she nonetheless realized they often struggled to navigate the building easily. Since she had responsibility for him she gathered her fortitude and offered the invitation.

"I'm to ask about your Control Group."

She smiled. "If we go to the cafeteria they may be there."

Blayze logged off the computer, placed a stack of papers in a folder he put in his briefcase, then rose to accompany Parish.

When they entered the elevator for the one floor trip, they were alone. Parish figured she should explain her group. "Just a bit of information regarding that group, several of the accounting managers have interesting heritage. The IT manager is Hispanic and German, the purchasing manager is Black and American Indian, and the Credit/Accounts Receivable manager is Arabian and Jew."

"Amazing." He frowned. "And you?"

"My mother is Italian and my father Greek."

Blayze appeared skeptical. "You look like a Swede."

Parish sighed. "Not all Italians are dark." Not wishing to make further explanations she asked, "And what about you?"

"Touché." He declared smiling. "French and Irish."

Reaching the dramatically flamboyant cafeteria Parish noticed Miguel and Odella at a black lacquer table in the middle of the room. Once she and Blayze had picked items for lunch they carried their trays there. Both Miguel and Odella gave Blayze a wide-eyed stare then turned to Parish for an explanation.

To Blayze she said, "This is Odella Whitefeather." She indicated the strikingly beautiful black woman with a heap of black curling hair and strong boned facial features. "She manages purchasing. This," she indicated the slim brown-haired man with fair skin and dark brown eyes, "is Miguel Reyes. He manages IT." To the two at the table she said, "This is Blayze Pashasia, IRS." She noticed the quick expression of surprise crossing the faces of the two seated then the skeptical look on Blayze's face. She felt like she had just pulled a rabbit out of a hat.

"Join us," Odella offered, motioning to the extra chairs.

"Thank you." Parish smiled.

When they were seated Parish explained. "I hoped we could run into you. Blayze is auditing our tax accounting, but he is also interested in people who have recently left the company without explanation."

Both Odella and Miguel frowned as if unsure to whom Parish referred.

"Lawrence Manke and Bobbi Bennett," Blayze put in.

"Ah." Odella's eyes lit. "Bobbi is easy to forget. It never quite seemed like she was here. And she wasn't in my department that long."

Miguel sighed. "We miss Lawrence, but he's been gone quite a while. It hasn't been that easy to replace him." He paused then something seemed to occur to him. "You're not looking for Mr. Moseley?"

Blayze appeared thoughtful, not responding immediately. Parish also wondered about his interest in the missing employees. Sometimes he appeared more interested in them than in the auditing. Or did he figure they were part of his tax discrepancy problem?

"I met the detective working to locate your CEO. He asked for assistance."

"Do you think Bobbi and Lawrence have something to do with his disappearance?" Odella asked, sounding incredulous.

"More like poking the woodpile to see what runs out."

"Bobbi left about the same time as Mr. Moseley," Parish put in.

"But Lawrence was gone quite a while before him."

Odella waved her fork. "One thing I'll tell you. If you want to find Bobbi your best bet is social media. She never did much in the way of work, but she was always very busy on Facebook."

Blayze glanced at Parish who met his gaze. She raised her eyebrows. She hadn't thought of that but undoubtedly a great place to look. He turned to Miguel as if wondering could that also apply to Lawrence.

Miguel shook his head. "Lawrence was a busy guy working here in the daytime and playing in a band at night. He had a lot going on to be very involved with social media."

"Nothing in his life induced him to leave?"

"Not that I know of." Miguel grimaced. "However, he did seem excited the last couple weeks he was here, almost as if he had some great expectations."

"Of?"

Miguel shook his head. "I have no idea."

When they had finished lunch and were headed back to the office, Blayze asked Parish. "You the third in your group?"

She laughed. "No, Alan Bernstein. He manages Credit and Accounts Receivable. But he has no disappearing employees."

⁂

At day's end Blayze stopped at the bar and grill where he had met the lieutenant a couple nights earlier. Located a few blocks from Ridinghood's Corporate offices on the way to his hotel he had found the restaurant convenient. The intense blue video screens and rose tone lighting was a little psychedelic for his taste but the menu was acceptable and the service reasonable.

Although not anticipating the lieutenant, after being shown to a booth toward the back of the restaurant and left with a menu he looked up to see Sarkis speaking with the hostess and pointing his direction. She brought the lieutenant to his table where the man thanked her and took a seat without waiting for an invitation.

"Driving by I saw you come in here," Sarkis explained when the hostess had given him a menu and left. "I thought I'd see if you'd come up with anything yet." He raised his eyebrows expectantly.

Blayze smothered a grin. "We could compare notes."

The lieutenant snorted. "You won't find much in my notebook.

The waitress arrived to take their drink orders.

When she had gone Lieutenant Sarkis removed a small notebook from his pocket and waved his empty pages. "So how about it? Have you learned anything?"

"Hard to say." Blayze sighed. "I've found accounting issues, but don't know if they're significant."

Blayze noted the lieutenant's eager expression. "Your missing band member, considered a valuable employee, worked in IT and went missing some time before that CEO. Probably not related."

Sarkis sighed. "However, that doesn't let me off the hook. I'm still supposed to find him."

"The woman may not have known the CEO, but disappeared about the same time. Apparently no loss as an employee. HR confirmed her personality issues."

The waitress brought their sodas and took food orders.

"I've talked to Manke's girlfriend. It sounds as if he enjoyed his work, was liked and respected by the other employees. The same in the band."

"Did she mention him being excited about some future prospect?"

Sarkis sent Blayze a puzzled glance. "His manager claimed Manke seemed hopeful regarding some future expectation."

"His girlfriend didn't mention that. I'd say she wasn't aware of it. Or at least didn't know what it was."

"When did he leave?"

"About six weeks ago now. According to this Sally, he had done his show with the band. She had a meeting with someone and couldn't leave yet so he told her he would see her at home. She hasn't seen him since." The lieutenant grimaced. "I talked to one of the bartenders who said he had stepped outside about the time Manke was leaving and saw him get in a car across the street and drive away."

Blayze gazed at the TV screen across the room. "What sort of meeting was the girlfriend having?"

"Apparently someone applying for a position with the band. She was assisting with the audition. I also asked if Manke had anything to do with that CEO. She didn't think so." The lieutenant sighed. "I got the search warrant for Moseley's house and had forensics there going over the place. It struck me as being rather sparsely furnished."

Blayze cocked his head.

"I had the feeling either he didn't live there all the time or he had moved some things out preparatory to disappearing."

"You think he disappeared on purpose?" That might give the accounting relevance.

Sarkis lifted his shoulders. "Could be."

"What about Manke's residence?"

"I've been there, but just to talk with his girlfriend. It's not like Moseley's where no one's home and you can examine things."

Blayze considered the lieutenant's predicament. "The purchasing manager thought you might locate the woman on Facebook."

"Ah! I need to get used to considering that. I don't do social media so it doesn't enter my mind. But I do have someone at the office fairly good at it. However, I suppose someone intent on disappearing wouldn't just post the fact on Facebook."

Blayze laughed. "Don't assume that. You can't believe how stupid people are."

"Oh, yes, I can. Most of my successful cases are due to stupidity. They have to brag. It's almost as if whatever they do is simply for the purpose of impressing someone."

"One wonders if the impressee is ever properly awed."

"Or do they think like us, how stupid can they be?"

◈CHAPTER FIVE◈

Climbing the stairs Parish considered whether failing to show up for work without an excuse, as had a number of Ridinghood's employees, qualified them as "missing". Failure to resign their positions amounted to the only corroboration. Back in the old days, as her father would say, that meant something. Not any more, not on either side of the equation.

She couldn't vouch for any of the missing. Two of them she hardly knew. In fact she barely recalled conversing with them, although they worked for two of her managers. She considered what she knew of Ian Moseley. Average height, he possessed the thinning hair of the over forty male. In fact, when she first met him he had the "going" bald look. Recently he appeared to have adopted "gone" bald, making it part of a macho image. One standout feature she recalled was his large green eyes. Made her think of a frog, although she doubted kissing this frog would produce a prince. In fact, except for the intense color of his eyes and a posture of detached arrogance, Mr. Moseley appeared so ordinary he would hardly be remarked in a crowd.

To the best of her knowledge he never knew she existed. She couldn't remember if he had ever even said, "good morning", which meant nothing as far as Parish was concerned. Most people rarely noticed her. Some she worked with on a regular basis greeted her, spoke to her, recognized her and gave her credit for her work. She doubted if those she did not work with directly even knew her. She realized she could feel bad about that. However, she tended to find it liberating. She could move about freely getting done what needed to be without other people's interference and agendas.

She had no doubt of her own competence or intelligence. Recognizing the first impression she gave was of an immature, naïve blondie amused her. She found it a useful disguise when she could not be invisible. Those with whom she worked directly knew better and generally respected her. For the most part her immediate superiors knew of both her understanding and proficiency to the extent she received appropriate raises and significant responsibilities. Having acquired this over an extended period of time working for the same company in a progression of positions fueled her great concern now. How would she fair if something happened to Ridinghood Corporation and she had to seek employment elsewhere? At this juncture with the media, the police and IRS focused on the company, investigating, she found herself consumed with anxiety.

Aware worry was not only unproductive but destructive she realized her best policy remained diving in, making every effort to assist whatever investigations existed to discover the truth and set Ridinghood free from threat. Consequently when she had checked with her group, making sure everything ran on track, the employees engaged in the tasks for which they had responsibility, she made a stop at the auditor's work area.

"Good morning," she addressed Blayze.

He looked up from his keyboard and blinked

"You mentioned yesterday you know the police lieutenant assigned to Mr. Moseley's missing person case?" She paused to verify he followed her.

He leaned back in his chair. "I ran into him the night Ridinghood announced Moseley was missing."

Parish stepped into his minimally furnished office. "Did he tell you about the case?"

Blayze grinned. "No, he asked me about it." His gaze questioned her interest. "I mentioned I was auditing here."

"Does he tell you what he finds out?"

"No." Blayze laughed. "He asks me what I find out."

Parish smiled vaguely. "So what do you tell him?"

"Are you concerned?"

"Not about what you say." She sighed. "I'd like to know what he's found out or what you have."

Blayze shrugged. "No much so far." He eyed her as if trying to determine the nature of her interest. "I've dealt with Sarkis in the past so he asked me to keep my eyes and ears open."

"Is it possible from things here to figure out where Mr. Moseley is?" That would be wonderful.

"Only if where he is relates to something here." Blayze pinned Parish with his gaze. "You know of something?"

"Besides my embezzling?" She lifted her eyebrows, suppressing a grin.

Blayze colored slightly, smiled, then became serious. "If he's responsible for embezzling then we might find something."

Parish had no idea if Ian Moseley would have been into embezzling. However she would willingly look into anything that might clear up Ridinghood's problems. "I have a lot to lose if something bad happens to Ridinghood."

"Can you access his office here?"

Parish considered. Presumably Mr. Moseley's office has been locked ever since he left. Could she get into it? She would have to secure the key. "I could try. We might need a good excuse."

"Besides suspecting him of embezzling?"

She grimaced. "If we could actually suspect him it might not be a problem but just a wild conjecture . . ."

Blayze folded his arms across his chest. "Let me work here a little longer. I'll see what I can find."

She left Blayze's area wishing she had paid more attention to Ian Moseley. Her work never brought her into direct contact with him and she possessed no desire to get to know him. In fact no one she knew had ever expressed a desire to get better acquainted with the man. However, she could check her assumption out with those in her acquaintance.

❧

When Parish had gone Blayze spent a moment considering her concerns. He could appreciate how she felt, particularly if she had a teen-age son. She might make a good ally in both auditing and assisting the lieutenant. He needed to avoid the mistake he made on a previous assignment, ignoring or intimidating the young accountant.

Just as the lieutenant came to mind he noticed Parish at his door with Sarkis in tow.

"There you are," Sarkis declared entering Blayze's territory. "I thought I'd take advantage of my search warrant and have a look at Moseley's office."

Blayze exchanged a glance with Parish.

"I'd appreciate your assistance. You might know more about what I find than I would."

"What about forensics?"

"Not a forensics issue at the moment."

Blayze beckoned to Parish. "If Ms. Stenopolis can join us."

The lieutenant turned to her then bobbed his head.

Blayze logged off his computer and put his papers back in his briefcase. Rising, he looked to Parish. "You're the only one who knows where we're going."

She led them from Blayze's space to the elevator next to her office which they took down one level. Turning to the right out of the elevator they proceeded through one of the Romanesque arches into an area containing a series of double doors. Taupe walls with white trim allowed the textured blue-gray rug to bring the focus down. The recessed wall to the left formed analcove of sorts. Beside each of the two sets of double doors engraved brass plaques identified the owner's name and position. Blayze noted the plaque to the right read "Ian Moseley, Chief Executive Officer". In each corner sat a cherry hutch behind a wide desk delineating a workstation. While one of these was unattended at the other Blayze noticed a woman with brown hair, pasty complexion and small beady eyes. Frown lines gave away her negative disposition. She eyed them with suspicion as Parish used a key to open the door. The woman appeared upon the point of objecting. Her brief hesitation allowed their entrance without interruption.

A large room, it possessed two sets of windows now covered by three panel drapes in shades of green and gold, emphasizing the gloomy interior of the room. The executive's desk sat to the left midway into the room with a large leather office chair behind and two smaller chairs facing it. Behind the desk ranged a row of low cabinets while to the left stretched another expanse of lower cabinetry, this with bookcases above, all in dark polished wood. On their right sat a living room style seating area with a lengthy sofa, a side chair, coffee table and two end tables. Above the sofa an enormous oil painting depicted the City of Tacoma in the late twenties much of which was unrecognizable to Blayze.

"Impressive," Sarkis muttered. "I should be so lucky." He turned in a circle observing the room. "Do you think we can get some light in here?"

Blayze turned to Parish. "Have you been in here before?"

She shook her head as she moved to open the drapes. The lieutenant switched on the overhead light, an elaborate brass chandelier.

"So you wouldn't know if anything is missing."

Parish met his eyes. "Generally speaking, however, some things should be here which if not is significant."

"Like?" The lieutenant challenged.

"The computer."

Instantly both men made a visual search of the room.

"You think the computer is missing?" Blayze asked.

Parish nodded. "I don't think it would fit into any of the cabinets and why would he put it there anyway."

Blayze started for the cabinets.

"Hold it," Lieutenant Sarkis stopped him. He tossed Blayze a pair of plastic gloves he dug out of his pocket. "Put those on." He had another pair he put on.

Together they opened cabinet doors proceeding across the back and along the side of the room. The lieutenant examined the drawers in the desk. Parish stood watching.

"No computer," Sarkis declared. "Why don't you come here?" he motioned to her. "Look in these drawers and tell me what you think." He opened each of the drawers while Parish looked on.

"Nothing personal."

"Is that the case here too?" Blayze asked as he went along the row of cabinets opening the doors again.

Parish accompanied him bending to observe the lower shelves and their content. "This is mostly corporate prospectus, financial reports, advertising materials." She lifted her shoulders.

"Looks like he made a run for it." The lieutenant declared.

Parish smiled. "Took the money and ran?"

"Looks like he ran, but take the money?" Blayze lifted his shoulders.

Lieutenant Sarkis wandered around the room examining various objects, brass and porcelain art pieces resting on the cabinets behind the desk, books on the shelves, magazines on the coffee table. He stopped finally at the desk and looked down at the desk pad and a leather box of loose note paper. He reached into the desk, grabbed a rubber band which he put around the box of loose papers and picked it up along with the desk pad. "I'm taking these with me." His tone of voice challenged objection.

Blayze considered the situation. "If he left intentionally will you quit looking for him?"

"That might depend on whether you find he took something along he shouldn't have." Sarkis turned to Parish. "Could you tell what he might have done with his computer?"

"Miguel might be able to, if you mean things he could have affected not just looked at."

"Miguel manages the IT department," Blayze informed the lieutenant.

He moved to the windows overlooking the small patch of park and stood. After a moment he turned back to Blayze and Parish. "You need to look for anything indicating he was operating illegally relative to Ridinghood's finances, business, etc. I'll give you time to see what you can find.

It looks suspiciously like this guy didn't all of a sudden disappear but had it planned. He appears to have taken away anything linked to him personally. His residence looked the same. If he planned to vanish, somewhere must be evidence of it. He couldn't instantaneously become thin air and float away."

Blayze turned to Parish. "What about that computer? Could he still get into the business with it?"

"I'm not sure. The PCs are hardwired. It would be easier for him to have something on a laptop he could use wirelessly."

"Check with your Miguel guy and find out what Moseley could do if he took the computer with him?" The lieutenant addressed Parish.

She nodded.

"How long will this office be kept like this?"

"I expect until some definite decision is made regarding whether he is returning or not."

The lieutenant peered over his spectacles. "I've looked in my crystal ball and it doesn't look like he's coming back."

◈CHAPTER SIX◈

When Lieutenant Sarkis had bid them farewell and Blayze had returned to his office, Parish remained to relock Mr. Moseley's. As she did so a shrill voice demanded, "What is the meaning of this?"

Turning at the sound she wondered who was being addressed. Doris Possum, a slight woman with light brown hair and a small pinched face stood with hands on her skinny hips glaring at Parish.

"What do you think you're doing?" she repeated.

Literal minded, Parish replied, "Locking the door."

"Where did you get the key? No one is supposed to be in that office." She held out her hand. "Give it to me."

Ah, the great high priestess. Parish recalled the rumors about Mr. Moseley's administrative assistant. "I'm returning it to Mr. Hogan. The police lieutenant was here with a search warrant.

Ms. Possum shot her an offended glance and returned to her desk. Taking a deep breath Parish continued to Mr. Hogan's office next door. She tapped on the door and at his invitation entered. A wide woman with a square face, short dark hair and intense hazel eyes sat in the chair facing him. The critical once over she gave Parish made her feel as if she was the harlot who helped the spies escape.

Approaching the desk Parish held up the key.

"Miss Stenopolis, this is my wife, Ellen Hogan." To the woman he said, "The head accountant, Parish Stenopolis."

"Nice to meet you." Parish smiled at the woman then placed the key back on Mr. Hogan's desk.

"Everything okay?" he asked with a glance begging her not to give him any bad news.

She could sympathize. "We have some things to check out first." That was the truth, she figured, saving him present anguish. What remained down the road wasn't predictable.

Before returning to her office she stopped at Blayze's. "What's the lieutenant going to do?" she asked him.

"Try to get something off that desk pad."

"From the impressions in it?"

"He might be able to see what was written there."

Parish studied the auditor a moment attempting to interpret his solemn expression. "Do you think Mr. Moseley disappeared on purpose?"

"Good possibility." Blayze maintained his sober pose gazing at her from beneath the dark eyebrows.

Parish lifted hers. "With the money?"

He laughed then became serious. "If money is missing I'll definitely think that." He sighed. "It's imperative to discover what that money's doing." Blayze moved over and with a wag of his head invited Parish to join him.

She grabbed the other chair and pushed it to a position next to his.

"Routing numbers identify both bank and branch," Blayze informed her.

"So when you found the money making trips what numbers did you have?"

"Account numbers, I believe." He logged into the accounting program and continued to a page listing banking and investment accounts and brokers.

"American Bank is the basic company bank."

"Can you tell if all these account numbers are American Bank?"

Parish took a notepad and wrote down the various account numbers listed. "Give me the keyboard a minute." On the bank's website she looked up Ridinghood's account and verified the numbers he listed were Ridinghood's, except for one set. For it no bank was listed and it showed no connection to the company. Examining the account number and comparing it she realized the number format did not resemble the others. "Okay," she said. "This account number doesn't connect to American Bank." She showed him the difference between the bank's format and that of the number.

"Can you find out what bank it is?"

She met his eyes. "Is this where the money goes?"

"You've got it."

Parish took a deep breath. "I'll see what I can do."

She rose and pushed the chair back to the corner. "Unfortunately Mr. Moseley was in charge of opening corporate accounts."

Blayze grimaced.

Returning to her office, Parish mentally sorted the possibilities for obtaining bank account information. Slate Ridinghood had taken Mr. Moseley's place, at least for the time being. She sighed. Might as well bite the bullet and check if she could see him.

She picked up her phone and put in the extension for his office.

"Well . . ." his administrative assistant was silent a few moments, "He's free right now but he has an appointment in half an hour."

"I'll come right away. "After grabbing her notepad with the account number Parish headed downstairs to the executive suite.

Mr. Ridinghood's office sat just beyond the reception area across from the interior designer's suite. Heading to his assistant's workstation, she glanced in the direction of Ms. Possum's desk, which she could not see from this location. She wondered what the woman did given her boss had been gone for a month.

Parish had seen Mr. Ridinghood's assistant around but had never officially met him. Probably a little younger than her, dressed for success in classic business fashion, dark brown hair and a fine-boned face he portrayed the ideal of an upwardly mobile professional. He frowned at Parish as if trying to recall her.

She gave her name then waited while he notified Mr. Ridinghood.

"You can go in." He opened the door to a light and airy office with off-white walls one of which was painted with oversized jungle leaves in green and gold, a carpet of pale beige and furniture in black and gold. The windows had no drapes. Not the sort of office she would have imagined for Slate Ridinghood.

He looked up as she entered and smiled at her. "What can I do for you?" The silver in his hair contradicted his otherwise youthful appearance.

"I've been working with the IRS auditor."

"Sit down." He beckoned to the chair facing his desk. "Have you found problems?"

"Actually we don't know. We need to identify a bank account number. I have the American Bank accounts, the corporate account, payroll account, and investment account. I don't think this is American Bank but I don't know where it is. We need to find out."

"Not even the bank routing number?"

Parish shook her head.

"Okay, what's the number you have?"

She gave it to him from her notepad.

"Let me see what I can find. I'll get back to you." He considered her a moment. "How is the audit coming? Is there anything else he's found?"

"Not relative to the accounting, but the detective in charge of finding Mr. Moseley was here. We examined his office. The lieutenant believes he left on purpose and isn't coming back."

Mr. Ridinghood narrowed his eyes, frowning. "What makes him think that?"

Parish sighed. She had misgivings about handing out too much speculative information. Nonetheless, Slate Ridinghood had the biggest investment of all in the outcome of both investigations. "There's nothing personal there. Plus . . ." She made sure he followed her. "his computer is gone."

"That doesn't sound good." He scowled, turning his gaze to the windows left of him which looked out on the miniature park running north and west of the building. "What was your name?"

"Parish Stenopolis."

"Okay, Parish, keep me informed."

❧

Leaving Mr. Ridinghood's office, Parish took the elevator to the third floor where the Information Technology Department was located. She found Miguel in conference with one of his programmers. He raised an eyebrow when he noticed her.

"I need to talk to you a minute when you're through."

He nodded.

She returned to her office where shortly Miguel appeared in the doorway. She beckoned to the chair facing her desk.

"You got a problem?" His voice held both concern and curiosity.

She smiled. "A problem would be wonderful. I have a whole pocketful."

His wisp of smile came and went.

"Mr. Moseley apparently took his PC with him when he left." She noticed Miguel's nod, which made her wonder how much he knew already. "Can he cause problems with it?"

"Not anymore." His dark eyes twinkled as he grinned.

"What do you mean?"

"We shut down his access to the company."

Had others known about Mr. Moseley's intentions before upper management? "When did you do that?"

"A few days after he left."

Parish frowned at Miguel. "Is that normal or did you have reason to suspect something?"

Miguel sighed. "One of my primary functions here is computer security. I have a set of criteria that when the server recognizes it relative to any one of the employees, it shuts down that employee's access."

"Did you know he took his PC with him?"

Miguel shook his head. "Not until you said."

"Did you shut down all his access?" She wondered about his laptop.

"Correct."

She sighed. That was good news. "Is that the case for Lawrence Manke and that Bobbi in purchasing?"

"Right. Bobbi didn't have much access anyway. Lawrence knew that would happen."

"Why would Mr. Moseley take his PC when he could get into the company with his laptop?"

Miguel narrowed his eyes. "Maybe getting rid of things was more important than accessing something."

"Oh, I hadn't thought of that." She nodded. "Get rid of the evidence?"

Miguel shrugged his eyebrows. "Something like that."

"Are there things you know about him other of us ignorant department heads don't?"

He grimaced rocking his shoulders. "I noticed things from time to time that made me suspicious, but I had no proof anything was wrong. Just things I questioned."

"Like?"

"When checking who accessed bank account information or looked at investment accounts his login showed up more frequently than seemed appropriate given his particular functions here. Had it been Tim Hogan or Taylor Washington I'd have thought nothing of it."

"Is that all?"

"Outside companies accessing his information seemed odd. Cookies that didn't make sense."

Parish frowned. "Okay, thanks Miguel. I may have the IRS auditor come and talk with you. He may have bank account questions related to the issues you've mentioned."

Miguel bobbed his head and departed.

Taking another trip to the third floor Parish stopped in purchasing to talk with Odella. Near her desk a teal velvet sofa sat in front of a wall of tall mullioned windows flanked by brass plant stands holding crystal table lamps.

"So what's your auditor really doing?" Odella shot the question with a glance up from her task.

Parish lifted her eyebrows. "You didn't believe what he said?"

She tapped her enter key and leaned back in her chair. "I thought it odd an IRS auditor would be interested in missing persons."

"I should think seeking tax evaders would often be looking for missing persons."

"You think Mr. Moseley was evading his taxes?"

"He could be, couldn't he? Actually I was wondering about Bobbi Bennett."

Odella frowned. "If she's evading her taxes?"

Parish laughed. "That too. Who would have known her well? Who might she have confided in?"

Odella stared across her group's work spaces. "That's a hard question. She talked a lot, but it seemed more like putting on a show than making confidences. She succeeded in making a couple in the department her minions. You could talk to them." She scribbled the names on a notepad, tore off the sheet and handed it to Parish.

She smiled her thanks and returned to her office glancing at the names Odella had given her. She was acquainted with the two, competent and accountable employees who, to her knowledge, faithfully performed their tasks. She realized how easily Bobbi Bennett could make them her minions. Neither would quickly refuse carrying out an assignment or doing something needing to be done. Both had worked in purchasing for at least a couple years.

Keeping the lazy and manipulative from taking advantage of the considerate and conscientious was one of those difficult management tasks? Parish needed to discuss Bobbi with them, gain some knowledge of how and why she disappeared, but without intimidating either of them.

A glance at her watch told Parish noon approached. She figured Blayze should know his way around by now and not need a guide or chaperon. However, the moment the thought crossed her mind he appeared at her office door.

"Going to lunch? I need to run some ideas past you."

She rose. "Okay."

They took the elevator up a level then climbed the circular staircase to the cafeteria where they proceeded through the line and made lunch choices.

"How about by the windows?" Blayze beckoned to where small tables sat next to windows framed by gold sheers pulled back to allow the view overlooking the Port of Tacoma.

The bright sunny day crooked a finger, urging Parish to escape the office and spend time near the sparkling blue water in the distance. Late August heralded the approach of autumn and the shorter cooler days. She doubted her readiness for the end of summer.

As if reading her mind, Blayze said, "Makes you want to play hooky."

She laughed. "Is that what our missing persons are doing?"

Blayze shook his head. "If it were only that simple. But . . ." he grimaced, "perhaps from a long term perspective. Your CEO might have worked out a life of leisure."

"The money?"

"More than that. The total absence of personal affects. That would take planning and need to be accomplished without fuss."

"Particularly the missing computer." Parish sighed. "Do you think someone knew about it?"

Blayze narrowed his pale eyes. "Was he close to anyone? Did anyone owe him a favor?"

"According to Ridinghood's Underground Press his administrative assistant has a thing for him." Parish shuddered imagining anyone having "a thing" for Ian Moseley. "Doris Possum. Her desk sits right outside his office. She's not only his administrative assistant, but features herself his girl Friday and the gatekeeper to his territory." Parish grimaced. "When I was locking his office after you left this morning she ambushed me, demanding the key I had."

Blayze eyed Parish then proposed, "Let's get to know her."

Parish regarded him with suspicion. Was this a subtle way of giving her an assignment? She knew Doris. It would be easier to chat with Jezebel after Naboath refused to sell the king his orchard. "I'll introduce you. You can see how far you get."

Blayze laughed. "You won't let me pass the buck."

Parish shook her head. "You'd probably have more success than I. She may transfer her allegiance to you."

Blayze rolled his eyes. "That sounds intimidating."

❦

Rising to leave the lunch room Parish noticed Jim Stanton and Elizabeth Bartholomew.

"I have a couple people I need to talk to," she told Blayze.

He nodded continuing to the elevator.

Jim worked with the supply inventory between the office and the warehouse. A trim man in his mid-forties with clear brown eyes and a ready grin, he reminded her of Mr. Rogers. Elizabeth was a friend of Jim's wife, which brought them together at breaks and office get-togethers. Although Elizabeth was younger her matronly appearance and sad eyes made her appear a decade older.

As Parish reached their table, Jim rose and moved a chair out for her. "You look like you need help."

"I do." Parish laughed. "You remember Bobbi Bennett?"

Both nodded.

Elizabeth observed Parish with her mournful eyes. "We're wondering if something happened to her."

"We haven't seen her around in a while," Jim continued the thought. "She hadn't said anything about going on vacation. Even then it's been so long I wouldn't have thought she'd have that much time available. I wondered if she was ill."

"Have you any reason to think she might be ill?" Parish grabbed his lead, glancing at each of them.

"Well . . .," Elizabeth began.

"She always had some physical complaint. You know how some people are. I never took it serious. She appeared healthy to me. In fact what she claimed doing when she wasn't at work made her complaints seem silly."

"Unbelievable," Elizabeth added.

"Like lies?" Parish asked.

Both of them shrugged.

"What did she do when she wasn't working?"

"It depends on the time of year. In the summer she went kayaking and hiking, in the winter she'd go to Snoqualmie skiing."

"She liked country dancing and would take her kids up to Northwest Trek," Elizabeth added.

"She's been gone for over a month now," Parish said testing their knowledge.

"Is that right?" Jim sounded surprised. "I knew it was more than the usual two weeks, but that long . . ."

"Is she on vacation?" Elizabeth asked.

Parish shook her head. "At least not according to Odella. I'll have to check for certain with HR." Although tricky Parish needed to ask. "Did she ever have any dealings with Mr. Moseley?"

"The CEO?" Elizabeth appeared shocked.

"The one that's missing? You think she might be with him?" Jim jumped to the conclusion.

"No, no," Parish raised her hand. "I was just checking to see if you thought she knew him. No one thinks she would be with him."

Jim grinned. "It would be rather scandalous. Ridinghood's CEO runs off with . . ." he stopped in mid-sentence as if unsure what to call Bobbi. "The truth is I wouldn't put it past her. Other things she always talked about were who she knew and all the who's who she did things with. I wasn't sure why she worked for Ridinghood when she knew so much and had so many connections."

Parish noticed Elizabeth frowning. "Did she ever introduce you to any of her connections?"

Elizabeth snorted. "I think a lot of it was wishful thinking, like playing the big shot trying to impress people. She's very status oriented. She's related to Slate Ridinghood some way."

"Would she have left to take a different position and not given notice?"

Both Jim and Elizabeth considered a moment then shrugged.

"I'd appreciate if you hear any gossip about her you'd let me know."

The three rose together and proceeded to the elevator.

"They still haven't located Mr. Moseley?" Jim asked as the elevator door closed on them.

"Not to my knowledge. Have you heard anything?"

"You know I heard someone in the warehouse joking he bought property in Puerto Rico and had left the country."

"Someone who knew him well?" Parish needed the information but feared drying up the line of communication.

Jim became thoughtful. "I don't remember who I heard say it. I think it was being passed along second or third hand anyway."

"Probably just a wild rumor," Parish agreed.

Jim and Elizabeth left the elevator at the third floor and Parish continued to the second. Her mind went back to Blayze's parting comment about Doris' interest being intimidating. Parish had difficulty imagining him intimidated by anyone. An impromptu inspiration took her to his office.

He looked up with raised eyebrows.

"Why don't you check routing numbers for banks in Puerto Rico?"

"You have a lead?"

"Just a comment someone made. Don't know who or how reliable it is. Could be wild conjecture, but it wouldn't hurt to check."

Parish returned to her office feeling a little better about things at Ridinghood. Examining her feelings to determine what gave her spirit the boost she realized several things. She no longer felt so alone in her concern for the corporation's future wellbeing. Others besides the owners took it seriously and were making an effort at problem solving. Blayze's active interest and pursuit of clues made her hopeful. She had ceased to feel the IRS was poised for attack. Even Lieutenant Sarkis tracked information without carelessly blowing the lid off everything. Obviously they remained a long way from any solution, but she no longer felt hopeless about it.

Wishing she had paid more attention to Mr. Moseley, she realized, probably like others, she had taken him for granted. One's fellow employees often came and went but one never expected that of the corporate officers. Wisdom suggested she search her experience and all the tidbits of conversation she had heard over the years for clues. If, as it appeared, Mr. Moseley was making plans over time for his departure then someone may have heard or seen something indicating that. Even something so simple as observing him remove things from his office one would not expect him to take away.

◈CHAPTER SEVEN◈

When his workday ended, Blayze wondered if Parish would be interested in having dinner with him. He preferred handling corporate employees with greater finesse than in a previous assignment where initially he had alienated at least one of those who could have been the greatest assistance to him.

She stepped out of her office as he left his and smiled at him.

"I was wondering," he said, "if you would have dinner with me."

She took a step back with a look of horror on her face, shaking her head. "I-I have commitments tonight."

Blayze stood dumbfounded.

"I . . . forgot something." She returned to her office.

He continued to the stairs and the main floor where he exited the building still trying to understand what happened. He had grown accustomed to intimidating people but not horrifying them.

As he walked toward his hotel his cell phone alerted him.

"This is Sarkis," the lieutenant informed him. "Would you have time to compare notes?"

"Sure."

"You mind the same restaurant as before?"

"No problem." Blayze felt a moment's irrational relief the lieutenant seemed neither intimidated nor horrified by the IRS."

"Ansgreth will meet us there, too."

Given his proximity, Blayze arrived before the other two. The hostess escorted him to a table near where he had met them the first evening. He ordered a glass of Merlot after informing the waitress he expected two others to join him.

Lieutenant Sarkis appeared with Dark Ansgreth and a third man, approximately the same size as Ansgreth, athletic build, brown hair streaked with blonde possessing the open countenance of someone sure of himself without being arrogant. Blayze would have tagged him one of the police scientists. However, Ansgreth introduced him as Sherman Bennett, husband of the missing woman. He was an engineer, however, which roughly qualified him as a scientist.

As soon as the three were seated the waitress came to take drink orders.

"Anything on that desk pad?" Blayze questioned Sarkis.

"Some numbers, didn't make any sense to me."

"I might get them to make sense."

The lieutenant removed a small pad from his pocket and searched its pages. He tore off a sheet and handed it to Blayze. "Providing you don't lose track of this and give it back to me."

Blayze put it in his wallet.

After placing dinner orders, Sarkis addressed Dark. "It appears that missing CEO made plans for leaving." He shifted his gaze to Sherman Bennett. "Is it possible your wife did the same?"

The man shrunk in his seat. "It looks that way, unfortunately."

The lieutenant waited for an explanation.

"She cleaned out all the checking accounts."

"Did she take personal belongings with her?"

Bennett stared into his beer. "That's harder to pin down." He glanced at Dark who nodded then continued. "According to my daughter she's been buying a lot of new things."

"Things?"

"Clothes, cosmetics, jewelry."

"So she took those things with?"

"If what my daughter says is the case. I haven't located any of the things Leslie says Bobbi bought. Also, very little of what she normally takes are gone. I think that's what concerned me to begin with before making any kind of investigation. She left things behind I would never have expected if she was joining her girlfriends somewhere."

"So what was your first thought?"

"Well, I accepted what she said. She was going for the weekend to Ocean Shores with some of her friends. She's done that before. Then when I found a bunch of money in the checking accounts missing I thought someone might have hijacked her."

"Would she have been an easy prey?" Sarkis asked.

Sherman gave a cynical snort. "She'd more likely be the one taking advantage. She wouldn't have been an easy target. She always had to be in control."

The lieutenant frowned his skepticism.

"She's a manipulator, able to get what she wants." He seemed to detect Sarkis' disbelief. "She could be charming."

"So you gave up the mugging idea?"

"It didn't make sense with what I knew of Bobbi. In fact, that might have been easier to live with than what appears to have happened."

"What do you think she's really done?"

"Left us, the kids and I."

"Premeditated?"

Bennett nodded. "Premeditated, pre-planned . . . the works."

"Why would she do that?"

Sherman Bennett shifted his gaze to Dark with lifted brows. The lieutenant turned to him.

"Some people's main purpose in life is having fun. If they've been raised in a home where their wishes are indulged, no great amount of responsibility, adulated and pampered, they expect other people's mission in life is making them happy. That particularly applies to their family. They don't want to grow up. They end up unhappy, self-indulgent, self-centered adults who can't understand why the world doesn't cater to their every whim. They have unrealistic expectations and an idealized perception of self. They can be charming and exciting to be around if you're expecting nothing more than a good time. However, on a permanent basis, expecting adult behavior and a realistic understanding of reality they are heck to deal with. Sometimes in seeking their lost childhood they leave their life, family, etc."

"Does that describe your wife?"

Sherman nodded.

Blayze's thoughts, listening to this description, shot to his doctor's advice regarding getting married to help him with his health concerns. As far as he could see getting married would only escalate health problems.

Lieutenant Sarkis sighed. "You realize it's not police business to keep track of people's runaway spouses."

Sherman nodded. "That's why I never reported her missing. After my initial concern I realized the greatest probability was she had simply left of her own free will."

Dark spoke up. "I suggested he speak with you. The other night when you were talking about your missing persons I recognized some parallels. The fact she also works for Ridinghood for one."

"That fact does interest me," Davy conceded. He turned to Sherman. "You definitely don't think her disappearance relates to Ridinghood?"

"It depends on how you mean that. No, I don't' think she ran off with Ian Moseley. On the other hand Bobbi had a number of connections to the corporation."

"Such as?"

"She's a shirttail relative, the owner's wife's sister-in-law's sister."

Sarkis groaned. "That's pretty shirttail."

"Nonetheless it guaranteed her employment."

Blayze noted Sherman didn't seem pleased with that arrangement.

The lieutenant must have noticed too. "You didn't approve?"

"She slid through life with little or no effort. It seemed to me if something she wanted could be a little difficult for her she might learn some self-discipline." Sherman ended on a note of frustration.

"Anything else besides being related to the owner and working there?"

"She was charming and social. She got around, people talked to her, she used information she acquired to advance her interests, maintain a following."

"What kind of relationship did she have with Ian Moseley?"

Sherman considered the question staring at the nearby television screen. "I suppose she had at least some dealing with him. She definitely knew who he was and had an opinion about him."

"Which was?"

Again Sherman paused to consider his answer. "She seemed both fascinated and disappointed in him. Undoubtedly his position with Ridinghood would fascinate her, but I doubt he responded to her the way she wanted, consequently the disappointment."

Sarkis leaned back in his chair. "I'll tell you what. I can't pursue your wife as a missing person, but given her connection to Ridinghood and the other two missing from there, I'll keep her on the list and note anything that might relate to her."

Sherman nodded his acceptance.

"At the same time I'll expect if you hear anything, particularly relating to Ridinghood, you'll let me know."

Sherman glanced at Dark. "I can do that. Thanks."

Once outside the building Parish paused a moment and took a deep breath. She realized her reaction to Blayze's dinner offer had shocked him. At the same time she had been shocked at his invitation. They had a comfortable working relationship. Why did he want to change that by making it social? How could she face him now in the morning?

She couldn't, no she wouldn't, explain her problems in relationships with men. She liked men, appreciated them, believed in them, enjoyed them. She was no feminist. She had a father, a brother, and a son. She loved them dearly. She had no problem with men in general or even particular men. It was having particular relationships with them. She did not want to date or have an affair or any such thing. Neither did she prefer an alternative lifestyle. She wanted none of those relationships with anyone. No one could understand that. They always made it an issue of rejection and took offence. She didn't reject the individual, she rejected the relationship. They could neither understand nor accept that. Ultimately she found her only recourse was allowing them to be offended and deal with the consequences. She sighed. So what would those consequences be with Blayze Pashasia?

It had been such a relief discovering his concern regarding Ian Moseley's disappearance; that he was working with the lieutenant in charge of the investigation. It had given her opportunity to observe, even participate, in the investigation up close and see, not only how it proceeded, but that it did proceed. What would happen how?

When she reached her car, she put in the digits for Midge. When she answered Parish asked if she was busy.

"Now that depends on what you mean." Midge laughed. "I'm hunting in the refrigerator for something to eat, watching the news on TV, washing a load of clothes, and let's see, I'm sure there's something else. Does that mean I'm busy?"

"Could you turn off the TV, let the clothes wash, quit hunting and join me at Applebees for dinner? Xavier is staying with a friend and I'm at loose ends."

"If I don't have to buy your explanation."

Parish sighed. "Are you assuming your psychologist persona?"

"Do I need to?"

"I'm taking the 5th."

"Coward."

"No argument."

"I'll see you in twenty."

Parish smiled as she backed her car out of its parking spot and headed for Applebees. Midge was the one person with whom she could discuss the problem. Not that she understood either, but she permitted Parish her emotions without attempting to argue her out of them or discount their validity.

Parish's parents would understand and allow her those feelings too, but they had also suffered through the difficult experiences landing her in this place. They could stand a break.

Caught in the after five o'clock traffic it took Parish twice as long to get to the restaurant as it would normally. Apparently Midge hadn't found it any better for they arrived at the same time. Crowded and noisy most of the time, the restaurant wasn't an ideal place for a chat. However, they managed in spite of traffic to arrive ahead of the evening rush allowing them to be seated immediately in a booth as distant from the bar area as possible.

After the waitress had taken their orders, Midge ventured, "My intuition tells me something happened after I left work today."

"Nothing important."

Midge leveled a scoffing eye at Parish. "Translated: important to you, but not to me?"

"I need some advice." Parish sighed and blurted out, "I've no doubt insulted Mr. Pashasia."

Midge waited for her to continue.

"I refused to have dinner with him."

"Oh, dear, that problem again." Midge stared across the restaurant at a noisy group in the bar. "You know, sweetie, some men may just want company at dinner with no ulterior motive."

Parish didn't respond. She had heard that before. She wished she could believe it. It had never been the case for her.

"Has he been paying you particular attention, acting like he's interested in that way?"

"No. He's been all business, which is why I was so shocked. He's the last person I would have expected it from."

"I suggest he's just out of town, at loose ends and interested in having someone to talk to at dinner."

Parish crossed her arms over her chest and glared at Midge.

"Don't give me that icy stare, lady. I'm not trying to line you up with him."

Parish grimaced. "I'm sorry." She sighed. "It was going so well. I really appreciated his interest in solving Ridinghood's problems. We had a good working relationship both regarding his audit and Mr. Moseley's disappearance."

"And now he's gone and spoiled it all by inviting you out to dinner."

"What am I going to say to him? He looked so shocked when I refused."

"I expect the worst of it was you looked so shocked when he invited you."

The waitress delivered their entrees. Midge took time to cut her sandwich in quarters and shake ketchup onto her plate. When she looked up Parish was watching her, waiting. "Do you honestly want advice?"

Parish took a deep breath, then nodded. "I don't think I can afford to screw this up. It doesn't affect just me. Others are concerned too."

"Try being straight with him. Tell him his invitation was a surprise. Tell him as far as you're concerned you had a good working relationship and want to keep it that way."

"But he'll want to know why I refused." Parish worked to keep the whine out of her voice.

"Actually he'll probably want to know if you would reconsider and have dinner with him. Would you do that?"

"If there's a way to make sure it's just dinner and nothing more."

"Tell him that."

"That's never worked before," Parish huffed.

Midge gazed at her with an expression of deep sympathy. "I know, sweetie. That's tough. You look like a cuddly little kitten. It makes people want to pet you."

"But . . ."

Midge interrupted. "I know, you're not. You're a full grown intelligent accomplished woman and you wanted to be treated with respect."

"It's just not fair. What did I ever do to deserve . . . ?"

"Nothing, it's not your fault. You didn't do anything to deserve being treated like Nicki quick trick. It's actually the fault of all those women who parade around declaring their power, dressing to expose everything they can and not even having the sense or capacity to say no. They have trained men to expect instant sex with no commitment in the name of being liberated women. There's nothing liberated about them."

Parish ate in silence, concentrating on her plate for a time.

"Remember, I've met Mr. Pashasia. He didn't strike me as the pushy I-have-my-way-with-women sort."

"I didn't get that impression either."

"Then why not give him a chance?"

Parish sighed. She felt a swell of tears rising and took a deep breath. "I have a seventeen year old son to prove that doesn't work for me. Every chance I've ever given someone they took advantage of me."

Midge sighed. "Maybe we can plan a strategy that provides a safety net. If you agree to have dinner with him, let me know. We'll work something out that keeps you safe. I'll be your invisible chaperone."

Parish laughed shakily, "Invisible?"

Midge rocked her shoulders. "Relatively speaking."

◆CHAPTER EIGHT◆

Blayze looked up as Parish appeared at his office door, still hesitant and apprehensive. If he jumped up and yelled "Where's the money?" he figured she would faint on the spot. However, he also realized her reaction would have nothing to do with missing money. He needed to exercise care, avoid being judgmental. He had jumped to a conclusion regarding her concerns. She had fairly cleared up the embezzlement issue.

At times he regretted his tendency to suspect everyone. Nonetheless, working for the IRS, that constituted a safer position than a more credulous viewpoint. Suddenly it hit him. She didn't fear Blayze Pashasia, the IRS auditor, her fear was of Blayze Pashasia, the man.

She took a few steps into his area and stopped. "I need to apologize for my ungracious refusal to have dinner with you." After a momentary pause she went on, "I don't date and your invitation was unexpected."

He smiled to cover his astonishment at her declaration. "I wasn't thinking about a date, just someone to have dinner with."

A half smile flickered across her face. "Midge said that. I jumped to a false conclusion."

"So, how about a non-date dinner with me?" He watched her expression with concern. "Like tonight?"

She took a deep breath. "Okay, if we can just go somewhere within walking distance."

"The bar and grill on Pacific Avenue? I eat there so often it's like my private dining room." He leaned back in his chair.

She laughed nervously. "Okay."

"I saw Lieutenant Sarkis there last night. He had some numbers from that deskpad of Moseley's. He couldn't make anything of them, so I asked for them."

Interest lit her pastel blue eyes. "Have you had a chance to check?"

"Not yet. I figured they could be routing or account numbers."

When she had gone, Blayze sighed considering his singular lack of success establishing friendly relations with the women in his investigations. At least she still spoke to him. He was honest. He hadn't considered a date, just someone to have dinner with.

And what did she mean she didn't date? At all? He struggled to believe that. Nonetheless, her horror at his dinner invitation returned to his mind. However unlikely, it must be the case.

He took out the slip of paper the lieutenant had given him. The numbers failed to line up with the routing codes for local banks generally beginning with 12. He also checked the account numbers he had for the company bank accounts. Those didn't match either or even appear similar. In truth he couldn't be sure the numbers related to bank accounts. He had to take care not to make them something they were not. However, neither did they resemble phone numbers.

Parish had said something about routing numbers for Puerto Rican banks. Why Puerto Rico he wondered?

He spent time investigating the bank numbering system both domestic and international. He learned the International Bank Account Number (IBAN) could have as many as 34 alphanumeric characters. The number Sarkis pulled off the deskpad had not near that. Did that mean he had only part of the number or an abbreviated version or did it not relate to bank numbers? The information indicated IBANs were often referred to as SWIFT codes and SWIFT had a website with information available.

On the internet Blayze located the SWIFT code for Puerto Rican banks which, since Puerto Rico is a United States territory, are considered US banks falling into the New York Federal Reserve District. Their routing numbers would begin the same as banks in New York. That didn't help since the number he had contained none of the Puerto Rican SWIFT code, so much for Parish's idea. He returned to his investigation of domestic banks. One thing he learned was the first two digits in the routing number related to the Federal Reserve District in which the bank is located with the next two digits refining it further. The number he had was not in the New York Federal Reserve District.

He reached for his briefcase and removed his check book to look at the routing number. The first two digits were 12. Next he looked at the routing number for Ridinghood's checking accounts. They also began with 12. To continue he needed a list of the Federal Reserve Districts with their associated numbers.

Time had moved swiftly. Suddenly it was lunch time. He considered checking with Parish but decided to take care of himself, not create issues.

Successfully reaching the cafeteria on his own, he arrived in the line behind a group of people who must be IT since he recognized Miguel among them. Miguel gave him a sympathetic glance, inviting him to join the group who had put together a pair of tables in the middle of the room.

"This is Blayze Pashasia, with the IRS," Miguel introduced him to his compatriots. "He's also assisting the detective investigating Moseley's disappearance."

Blayze noted the expressions of interest on the other faces in the group. Once he was seated the questions began. "Have they any idea where Moseley is?"

"I don't believe so," Blayze replied with a shake of his head. "Have you any idea?"

This took the young man by surprise, leaving him open mouthed.

"We never knew where he was when he was supposedly here," another in the group volunteered with a laugh.

Blayze wondered briefly what that meant. A smart remark? "Did he have much to do with your department?"

The group exchanged glances around.

"I think he was reasonably adept with the computer and internet, but not in any way that interacted with our department." One of the quieter participants furnished this information.

"Could one check his use of the computer not reflected in company records?"

Again they exchanged a glance around. Miguel answered. "I've been working on that, but haven't come up with anything conclusive."

"Anything suggestive?" Blayze pinned him with his gaze.

Miguel rocked his shoulders.

Blayze figured a chat with Miguel might be helpful, but not here and not now.

❧

Before logging onto her computer Parish climbed the stairs to the third floor where most of accounting was housed. After making her rounds of payables, receivables, credit and purchasing as she headed back toward the stairs, Odella hailed her. Stunning in a red and white silk blouse and black skirt, Odella grimaced as Parish approached her black lacquer desk embellished with brass in a room full of light, not unlike that of Slate Ridinghood. She envied Odella's dark beauty allowing her to be so striking in high contrast bold colors. Parish looked best in what she would have characterized as baby clothes, subdued colors and pastels.

"As I was leaving here last night something occurred to me." Odella leaned back in her teal leather chair as Parish took the one next to her desk. "You were asking about people here who spent time with Bobbi Bennett."

Parish nodded.

"Connie Evans."

"Bobbi spent time with her?" That was surprising.

Odella nodded. "Recently. I'm not sure how they got acquainted or maybe that's foolish since Bobbi has worked for almost every department here at one time or another."

Parish considered what she knew of Connie. "She invited me to one of those parties where you buy candles."

"Did you go?" Odella appeared surprised Parish had been invited.

"I did. It was all single women. What struck me they spent more time talking about men than whatever they were selling or buying." Parish frowned. "Were you invited?"

Odella shook her head with a cynical grin. "Obviously not since I'm married."

"Bobbi wasn't there when I went. I never went again." Parish wrinkled her nose. "I found it really uncomfortable. I like men but not in the way they were talking about them."

"I'm not sure how Bobbi got in with them since she's married and has a bunch of kids, but I heard her talking to one of the girls in my department about doing things with Connie. I got the feeling it was a bunch of single women hanging out together."

"That doesn't sound too healthy for a married woman."

Odella snorted. "No kidding."

"May I mention this to Blayze? He's been asking questions about her since that lieutenant also has her on his missing persons list."

"Sure, go ahead. I doubt if Bobbi is truly missing though. She probably wandered off like a loose puppy."

Parish returned to her office considering what it meant if Bobbi Bennett hung around with a group of single women. One thing she had forgotten to ask Odella was whether Connie still came to work. At her desk she made a quick call and verified that yes, she did.

Putting aside her questions regarding Bobbi and Connie, Parish plowed into her accounting tasks, becoming completely absorbed until she noticed a lull in the general area. Glancing at her watch she realized it was noon. She put in the digits for Midge's phone.

"Are you going to lunch?" she asked when Midge answered.

"I thought I'd hit the cafeteria today."

"I need to line up my invisible guard."

Midge giggled. "I'll meet you at the elevator."

Going through the cafeteria line, Parish noticed with relief Blayze had joined a group from IT.

She and Midge gravitated toward a tasseled and festooned alcove near windows at the opposite end of the dining room.

"So he asked you again?" Midge verified.

"I did what you told me, apologized for my attitude. We agreed to a non-date dinner at a real close restaurant."

"Was I right about his intentions?"

Parish cocked her head. "According to what he says."

"You're reserving judgment?" Midge nodded. "Okay, I get that. Give me a heads up when you're leaving and I'll follow at a discreet distance, staying invisible but available."

"You think I'm being stupid, don't you?"

"No, dear, I don't. Men don't look at me the way they do you. I was very happily married for years so my experience isn't the same. I know I can't judge you by my experience. I wish I could give you my experience so you would be happy and not so afraid but things don't work that way."

Tears came to Parish's eyes. She blinked them back. "I talked to Odella this morning about Bobbi Bennett. She says Bobbi was hanging around with Connie Evans and a group of single women."

Midge puffed out her cheeks. "Really. I wasn't aware of that." She concentrated on her salad for a time. "You know the problem with married women hanging around with single ones. They get a false idea about things. They see the freedom to come and go, the independence regarding money, and then imagine how romantic it could be. Except it's not. It's just lonely. You're in a boat all by yourself with no one to share the difficulties and no one to share the joys. Because the married ones actually have someone sharing their lives, even if they are resenting that person and any restrictions they live with, they don't know the emptiness of being alone. All they see are the advantages."

"You think that's the deal with Bobbi?"

Midge sighed. "Possibly, although even that requires some thinking. I'm not sure Bobbi ever indulges in thinking." She lifted a finger. "I'm not saying she's an idiot or incapable. There's a difference between being an idiot and being stupid. Idiots may be doing the best they can with what they have. Stupid ones could do better but fail to engage the brain so we call them idiots when in fact they're just foolish."

Parish laughed.

"You disagree?"

"No, no." Parish shook her head.

"Bobbi doesn't know there is anyone in the world except her. I don't think that makes her an idiot. But she is definitely stupid." Midge's eyes twinkled. "And if you think you heard me say anything, I suggest there's a big draft in here and that's all you heard."

After sliding papers into his briefcase and logging off the computer, Blayze proceeded to the door of Parish's office. She glanced at her watch and nodded. "I'll meet you at the stairs. I have to make a phone call."

That response certainly differed from the previous one. Nonetheless, he perceived the need for care. At least she bore no resemblance to that electronics manager he ran into at the last assignment. Shy and retiring he could deal with, aggressive females intimidated him. However, he revised his thought, Parish wasn't shy and retiring. Some problem lived there but it had nothing to do with bashfulness.

Her phone call didn't take long. She appeared at the stairs only a couple minutes after he arrived. After descending to the main floor reception area and exiting, they then skirted two-thirds of the building leading to the sidewalk along Pacific Avenue. Red, purple and yellow flowers bloomed profusely in the concrete planters surrounding the ornamental trees scattered about the tiny park on which Ridinghood's building sat. It was a beautiful afternoon, neither too hot nor too cold with bright sunshine and a light breeze.

"Are you originally from Tacoma?" Blayze asked as they reached 9th Street.

"I wasn't born here but I've lived here all the life I remember. How about you?"

"Wyoming. Like you I don't remember my life there. I was raised in Nevada near the California border."

As they stopped for the light Parish asked, "Is that where you live now?"

"No. I live in Salt Lake City."

After crossing the street, they continued to the bar and grill with which Blayze had become familiar since beginning the assignment with Ridinghood. The hostess escorted them to a table for four, midway into the restaurant. He let Parish lead the way on choosing beverages. She ordered a strawberry lemonade and he chose a soda.

When the waitress had gone Parish returned to their conversation. "So is it a lot different here than in Salt Lake?"

He smiled. "No ocean, no marine affects." Figuring work related issues were the safest topic he informed her, "The lieutenant's numbers don't relate to Puerto Rico."

She sighed. "Odella told me about a couple who work with Bobbi. When I talked with them the guy said he heard someone make a remark about Mr. Moseley buying property in Puerto Rico."

"But not who made the remark?"

Parish shook her head. "It was worth checking."

"It might still be. It's just those numbers don't hook up."

Their drink order arrived and they made dinner selections. Blayze kept an eye on the entrance to the restaurant somewhat fearful Lieutenant Sarkis would show up. Not that it would be a big deal if he did. He wasn't making an effort to spend time alone with Parish. He did notice the manager of Human Relations arrive. However, she didn't come their way, but was escorted another direction entirely.

Parish reclaimed his attention. "Odella told me about someone else who spent time with Bobbi Bennett."

Blayze lifted his eyebrows.

"Apparently she's been hanging out with a group of single women."

"I met her husband last night. He thinks she's left him and their children."

Parish grimaced shaking her head.

"Under the circumstances the lieutenant can't consider her missing unless she connects with Moseley's disappearance or Ridinghood somehow." Oh, oh, Blayze noticed Lieutenant Sarkis talking with the hostess and gazing around the restaurant. As soon as his eyes lit on Blayze and Parish, Blayze sighed. "We're getting a visitor."

After a glance at the lieutenant Parish turned to Blayze with a grin. "You're his five o'clock news."

Blayze leaned toward her. "Let's see what we can get out of him?"

The lieutenant charged directly to their table as if intent on an arrest. Without a word he dropped into an extra chair. "Well, we've located one of the missing persons," he declared.

"You don't look very happy about it," Parish observed.

"Hmmph! Now I have a murder instead of a missing person."

"Moseley?" Blayze asked.

"Naw, that Lawrence Manke."

"The IT guy in the band?"

Sarkis nodded. "Packed in a trunk in a moving and storage company's warehouse."

Blayze frowned. That sounded incredible. "How did you find him?"

"Smell. The guys in the warehouse noticed it and decided to find out where it was coming from. They pinned it down to this big trunk but couldn't get hold of the guy who put it in storage. So they called us. Apparently he's been dead about as long as he's been missing."

"So he was missing because he was dead?"

"Looks that way."

"How was he killed?" Parish asked.

Lieutenant Sarkis turned to her. "Shot in the head . . . execution style."

"Professional job?" Blayze suggested.

"Not necessarily." The lieutenant sighed. "But made to appear that way."

Blayze detected reluctance on the lieutenant's part to be specific.

The lieutenant turned back to Parish. "This means I need everything you have on Manke."

"I barely knew who he was. He worked in IT not accounting."

"Is there someone who knows more about him? Besides the girlfriend who I understand works for Ridinghood too."

"The best place to start is with Midge Melanckton, the manager of human relations. She has the official records. Also Miguel Reyes who was his boss."

Sarkis nodded. "Okay, I'll show up in the morning if you can introduce me to these people?"

Sighing, Parish nodded.

◆CHAPTER NINE◆

True to his word Lieutenant Sarkis showed up at Ridinghood just after Parish arrived at her office. "Okay, where's this Miguel guy?"

Rising from her desk Parish smiled at his impatience. She led him to the elevator which they took to the third floor. They crossed the brick lined hall to another set of double doors leading into a space decorated similar to purchasing in soft grays and blue-grays. However, while purchasing was flooded with light vertical blinds blocked the daylight from IT's windows making the computer screens more discernible. She spotted Miguel talking with one of his group at a desk in the middle of the room.

He looked up a question in his expression. After a word to the young man he came their way. "What can I do for you?"

"This is Lieutenant Sarkis. He's investigating Mr. Moseley's disappearance."

"I need some information." The lieutenant glanced around. "Is there somewhere more private we can go?"

"You can use my office," Parish offered.

The three returned there. The lieutenant and Miguel took the two square maple chairs facing her desk.

As she moved to leave, the lieutenant halted her. "No, stay. I need all the help I can get."

She returned to her desk and waited for Lieutenant Sarkis to begin.

"We've found your Lawrence Manke stuffed into a trunk in a moving and storage company's building," he announced to Miguel.

Miguel turned to Parish as if verifying the lieutenant's information. She grimaced nodding.

"He'd been dead about six weeks," the lieutenant continued. "So whatever he was doing with whom and talking about becomes important. I've been told he was excited about some future prospect. Do you know anything about that?"

"I wish I did." Miguel ran his hand through his hair.

"Was he involved with criminal gangs or drugs?"

Parish noticed Miguel's shocked expression.

"Not to my knowledge. As part of my group he was always on time, sober and straight. He did excellent work. I know he played in a club band in the evening. Who or what he might have met there I have no idea. I don't know that he ever talked about it here. Computer people and musicians have a great deal in common intellectually but not much in life style."

"Would there be anything on his computer?"

Miguel moved a grimace from one side of his mouth to the other. "Obviously the corporation is sensitive regarding confidential business records. His access to the company by computer was shut down as soon as he failed to show up for work. I can go through it and check for anything personal."

"I'd appreciate that. You'll let me know?"

Miguel nodded. "I can ask here if anyone knew anything about him outside work. I tried that at first when he didn't turn up but no one claimed any knowledge. It may be different now he's dead if someone was shielding him."

When Miguel had gone Lieutenant Sarkis grumbled. "That wasn't much help."

"Did you still want to see Midge Melanckton?"

"Can you get her in here?"

Parish texted Midge. "I have Lieutenant Sarkis in my office. He wants to speak to you here if you're available."

"Is this a command performance?"

"Absolutely." Parish smiled. She sent another text. "You think I have a police lieutenant in my office for the fun of it?"

"Well, I would, why not you?" Midge returned then added, "Coming."

When Midge arrived Parish introduced her to the lieutenant who informed her of Lawrence Manke's death.

"That explains that," Midge mumbled taking a seat.

"Explains what?" The lieutenant eyed her suspiciously.

"Why Sally isn't here today." Midge anticipated the lieutenant's question. "Lawrence's significant other."

Lieutenant Sarkis acknowledged her comment with a nod of his head. "She's being questioned."

Alarm leaped to Midge's expression. "I don't think . . ."

"At this point she's not a suspect," he assured her. "It's highly doubtful she'd have shot him execution style then stuffed him in a trunk."

"I could do that to some people. In fact I'd be glad to," Midge mumbled under her breath.

The lieutenant frowned at her.

She covered her mouth with her hand and gave him an expression of innocence. "But not Lawrence," she added.

"I need the basic employee information you have for him."

"You mean name, address, next of kin, that kind of stuff."

"His references, bank information, former employers, education."

"Boy, you want it all." Noting the lieutenant's continued frown she added. "I'll get that for you."

"Now?"

"It'll take me a little while to get it together."

"I'm going to chat with the IRS."

"I'll bring it to you there."

Nodding, the lieutenant rose and headed for Blayze's space.

"I feel bad about Lawrence," Midge said with a mournful expression. She smacked her palm on Parish's desk. "That really stinks!"

When Midge had gone Parish went to Facebook on her computer. What were the chances she could find something about Bobbi Bennett or even Mr. Moseley or Lawrence by checking there? She put their names into the search box. However, not being "friends" she could not access their information. She needed to find someone's page who was a friend and look there. Midge or Odella would have said something if they had any contact. One possibility came to mind, Connie Evans. Due to her invitation to Connie's sales party she was on Parish's list of "friends".

It took paging back a long way to find anything related to Bobbi Bennett. Nothing showed up at all relative to Mr. Moseley or Lawrence. Not that from Connie Evans she expected anything. She did find references and communication from Bobbi about going to Ocean Shores, including some pictures of her on the beach or at a hotel or restaurant. The pictures generally included someone else in a selfie shot of Bobbi. However, communication of that sort stopped about four to five weeks before.

As Parish scrolled through the subsequent pages she noticed that after a couple weeks of no communication from Bobbi posts from Ocean Shores began again. They weren't from Bobbi, at least according to the names, nor did the pictures show anyone resembling her. Nonetheless, Parish mentally filed it away wondering if she should attach any significance to them.

∽

"Is that right?" Lieutenant Sarkis said to his phone as he entered Blayze's office. "We'll see about that." After putting the instrument in his pocket he grabbed the chair in the corner and pushed it to Blayze's desk. Blayze leaned back, waiting.

"You want to know something." Sarkis plunked himself down in the chair. "Manke arranged to have his trunk picked up and moved to storage . . . after he was dead. Some trick, huh?"

Blayze laughed.

"You think that's funny?" Sarkis growled. "Try this. He went to his storage unit, packed himself into the trunk, then called the moving and storage company to have the trunk picked up and delivered to the building where his furniture is being kept, AFTER HE WAS DEAD." He peered at Blayze over his spectacles. "You think I ought to buy that dish of bull?"

"Who's selling it?"

"Good question. It's what my officer got from the moving and storage company. Their records show Lawrence Manke owns the furniture and boxes being kept at their warehouse;

that he called to have a trunk picked up at his storage unit and moved to that warehouse."

"And he signed for it?"

"Apparently."

"I hope I can get around that well after I'm dead."

The lieutenant snorted. "I checked with his girlfriend to be sure he actually did have things at that company's warehouse and she said he did. He had transferred some things there when he moved in with her."

"And you checked the signature?"

"My officer said it was one of those M-------- type." Sarkis made hand motions describing it. "Anyone could imitate it."

"What about the storage unit? Why would he have one of those too?"

The lieutenant stroked his chin. "I'll have to see if anyone checked that out. You get into those without anyone around as long as you have the key and the gates are open. Since the moving company verified picking it up there someone must have opened it for them or given them the key."

Blayze noted the lieutenant seemed to be thinking out loud. "How about some coffee?"

Sarkis glanced around.

"There's a break room," Blayze said with a wag of his head in that direction.

"Sure." The lieutenant rose.

Blayze ushered him across the hall to the elevator which they took to the third floor. "Have you made any progress on Moseley?"

"Beyond determining he left of his own free will?"

On the third floor they continued to the end of the corridor and into the break room.

Blayze handed him a cup indicating the coffee urn. "You've determined that?"

"With the information we have it seems logical." The lieutenant helped himself to coffee and some creamers.

"Will they quit looking for him now?"

"Under the circumstances we'll not be allowed to."

"Should you be?"

Sarkis paused a moment while Blayze fixed his coffee. "It's six of one half a dozen of the other. He should be free to come and go as he pleases. On the other hand he has a large responsibility to this company. It also depends on whether we find something fishy about his leaving." He raised his eyebrows and peered over his glasses at Blayze. "Have you found anything suspicious?"

Blayze sighed. "I've found suspicious things but no indication they're connected to Moseley." He motioned to one of the empty tables residing near the windows.

Once they were seated Midge approached with a file folder. "I've printed some of Lawrence's information for you. I hope this helps." She handed the folder to the lieutenant.

He nodded his thanks. When she had gone he opened the folder and looked through it. "Ah-ha, a picture." To Blayze he said, "I think I'll follow that whole transaction from beginning to end. We'll see how much he accomplished after he was dead."

Once the lieutenant had gone and Blayze had returned to his office, he took out the two slips of paper with numbers on them. He stared at the one on his notepad then the one on the slip he got from the Lieutenant. If he put the numbers together could he come up with something? If he used Sarkis' note would he find a bank with that for a routing number?

Starting with that assumption and the fact Moseley would have written it straight since he did it for himself and took the note with him, Blayze went to the Federal Reserve System website and the US map designating districts. Looking for a match for his first two digits 11 he found Texas and parts of New Mexico and Louisiana. That is, if his logic was accurate. He realized he could spend the whole morning on this and get nowhere.

The next two digits represented the location of the district office and following that the ID number of the bank. Next came the check digit which required the use of a calculation to determine the validity of the routing number. He meticulously followed the procedure outlined to validate the number and Voila! Supposedly he had a legitimate routing number. However, he still needed to find out what bank the second set of four digits represented.

He figured the quickest most accurate method of accomplishing that would be a call to his superior.

"Blayze, what can I do for you?"

"I need to identify a bank from its ID #."

"You found a problem?"

"That's what I'm trying to figure out."

"Okay, what's the number?"

Blayze gave it to him then waited on hold, wondering when he had the answer how to proceed.

"DC Maxim Hunter," Mr. Hornby said when he returned to the call. "This one in Dallas."

Afterward Blayze leaned back in his chair considering his options. Putting it to Parish was his best bet. He rose and went to the door of her office, once again noting the blatant femininity in her decor. Had it been her choice? It struck him suddenly she was not ashamed of being a woman. She made no effort to hide her femininity with men's apparel, aggressive behavior and false bravado.

She looked up, a question in her expression.

"I need some help."

She smiled. "Have a chair."

Accepting her offer he then placed the two slips of paper on her desk. "This," he pointed to the one from the lieutenant, "is a bank routing number and I think I've identified the bank. I'm guessing the other is an account number. Could you call Ridinghood's bank or do whatever you need to find out who owns that account."

"Can you leave those with me?"

He nodded, sliding them over to her.

❧

When Blayze had gone Parish found a message from Midge on her phone inviting her to her office. After checking to make sure she had no other urgencies to attend and what she needed to get done was under control she headed to HR's area.

Midge was on the phone when she arrived and waved her into the chair beside her desk. After Parish was seated Midge turned the monitor to her computer so that it was visible to both of them. She ended her call and set the phone down.

"I have a few moments in which I think we can avoid being interrupted. We're going on a virtual trip to Ocean Shores and look for Bobbi Bennett."

"And how are you going to do that?"

"With Google Maps." Midge shot her a smug smile. "I've learned she's probably still there. I've a feeling that she is up to no good."

Parish frowned. "Is there a real reason for this or are we just minding someone else's business? Lots of people are up to no good."

"I just have a feeling this is important."

Parish shrugged, watching Midge locate Ocean Shores on Google Maps and and get level with the street. It was possible to virtually walk down the street and see in the shop windows.

"You need to let me know if you see anyone that vaguely resembles Bobbi. In all probability she has changed her appearance. However, there are things we cannot change very easily like the way we walk or stand. Those are the things that make us the most recognizable."

Parish did not disagree with Midge's basic reasoning. However, in her opinion the likelihood of seeing Bobbi on Google Maps was remote. "I think you're making a false assumption regarding Google Maps. It takes still shots and although it might accidentally catch Bobbi in one of the shots it's not like it's live. And if you assume we have to recognize her from her movements it won't work."

Midge ignored her continuing to observe the scenes in Ocean Shores. Consequently, Parish concentrated on the computer with careful scrutiny. They moved along the street at a moderate pace. Not that many people were picked up by the camera. The streets were wide and the buildings distant from one another. Most people it caught seemed to be near vehicles.

Something caught her eye. "There!" Parish pointed to a man standing by a small SUV facing the camera.

Midge looked closer at the screen then gave Parish a glance with raised eyebrows. "Do you think . . ."

"I don't know why but there's something familiar about him."

"I'm going to zoom in." Midge brought the computer scene up close enough to see the details of the man's face. The man had a full head of hair in addition to a small goatee.

"There's something about the way he stands that seems familiar."

Parish focused on his face and in particular his eyes. Mr. Moseley may change many things about himself, but to change the color of his eyes, although not impossible to do was less likely than other things. There they were, the big green eyes. "It's Mr. Moseley," she declared.

Midge turned to her. "Are you sure?"

"Look at those eyes. He has those big green frog eyes."

"Do we dare tell the lieutenant?" Midge suddenly appeared unsure of herself. "What if we're wrong? I don't want to send the police on a goose chase."

"But we should at least give him a heads-up." Parish protested. She couldn't understand Midge's sudden reluctance.

"Maybe we should go and see if we could find them?"

Parish was shocked. "For what purpose? We're not the police."

"Would the police even believe us if we told them we saw him here on Google?"

"That lieutenant might. He seems to truly want help, especially with Mr. Moseley." Parish sighed. "But it could be bad if we're wrong."

"Which makes it even more important we go and check it out."

Parish cocked her head. "Are you serious?"

"You bet!"

❈

On her way home Parish recalled Xavier had another basketball game that night. She made grilled sandwiches for dinner and they left for the gym which was on the north side of Tacoma.

"What kind of game is this one?" she asked as they approached the parking lot to the neat brick building. Xavier resembled the southern Italian side of the family with dark hair and eyes but he also had the Greek god profile.

"AAU. Just regular."

Given his height and skills, he played in several different leagues. It had been one of the ways to keep him busy when he was younger and she was working.

After entering the building they went separate ways, Xavier to join his team in the locker room and Parish to the bleachers to watch with the other parents. She didn't recognize any of those present and was even uncertain which team they represented. She took a seat half way up on the aisle where she could leave without bothering anyone when the time came. Although the floor appeared regulation size, the room was small and crowded.

Watching while the boys warmed up and ran drills she paid no attention to the person who took the seat across the aisle until she spoke.

"What brings you here?" The woman with yellow blonde hair pulled into a knob at the top of her head leaned toward Parish.

Startled, she recognized Connie Evans. "My son is playing."

Connie's eyes widened in surprise which she covered with a laugh. "I didn't know you were married."

"I'm not," Parish declared in a tone she hoped would end the questions. "Do you have someone playing?"

"My nephew. My sister is out of town for work and her husband got caught in traffic so he called me to pick up

Stanley." She reached into the bag at her feet. "I'm having another party this week-end." She handed Parish a card.

Accepting it, Parish said, "I've had a lot going on lately, but I'll keep it in mind."

"What do you think about things at Ridinghood?" Connie leaned eagerly toward her. "Where do you think Mr. Moseley is?"

Parish's first reaction was to clam up. However, she realized Connie may have valuable information. "It's getting to be a zoo with the police and IRS both there investigating."

"What is the IRS investigating?"

"Just an audit."

Connie nodded, a skeptical expression in her brown eyes. "Nothing to do with the missing CEO?"

"Not yet at least." Parish noted the boys had left the floor for seats on the bench. "You know Bobbi Bennett is missing too?"

"Bobbi?" A number of expressions raced across Connie's face, surprise, skepticism then an ah-ha. "A bunch of us went to Ocean Shores about a month ago. We all came back together except for Bobbi. She said she was meeting another friend and staying a couple more days." Connie paused and frowned. "How long has she been gone?"

"Ever since that trip I think."

"Really!" Connie frowned, staring across the floor where the teams had positioned for the jump ball. "She was acting kind of funny, hinting about things but didn't make much sense."

"Hinting?"

"Like this fantastic plan she was all excited about. She didn't tell us what it was, just made suggestive remarks and wouldn't we all like to know what it was."

Once the boy's game commenced Parish turned to watch the play. Doing so she processed what Connie had said. Would Connie's information help in locating Bobbi? Another big question occurred to her. Would knowing anything about Bobbi and her whereabouts make any difference to Ridinghood and the investigation? Regardless, here was an opportunity Parish may regret if she didn't take advantage of it.

When the whistle blew she turned to Connie. "Do you know who she was meeting?"

Connie shook her head. "She never said. In fact, the way she acted I wondered if it was a man."

Parish grimaced. "Did she know Mr. Moseley personally?"

"That's right." Connie's eyes lit with a suggestive gleam. "He's been gone about the same amount of time." She sighed. "I wish I'd paid more attention. She had a habit of big talk, acting as if the whole world was just dying to hear what she was going to do next. It got kind of much at times."

"Would she have put anything on Facebook?" Parish also wished Connie had paid more attention.

"That would definitely be like her, but I haven't seen anything. Which now that I think about it is odd."

The boy's game resumed. Xavier was getting plenty of playing time which would make him happy. Parish wasn't aware of a Stanley on his team so Connie's nephew must be on the opposition.

"Would any of the others have heard from her or know anything about her plans?"

"Annabelle Elliott," Connie declared with excitement. "They do a lot together." She paused, casting Parish a suspicious glance. "Is the company trying to find her?"

"Several people are absent from Ridinghood without explanation. We're trying to eliminate the possibility they're connected." Something else occurred to Parish. "Where was she staying?"

"We were all at the Shilo Inn but I don't know if she was continuing there."

As the end of the game approached the score was close. They ceased their discussion to watch the play. The lead went back and forth a number of times before the final buzzer sounded. Xavier's team lost by two points.

"Do you happen to have a number for Annabelle?" Parish took a business card from her wallet and offered it to Connie. "I'd appreciate it if you hear any more about Bobbi if you'd let me know."

"Especially if she's run off with our CEO?" Connie laughed.

Parish smiled, nodding. "Especially then."

◈CHAPTER TEN◈

Blayze figured the painful pinch in out of town assignments consisted in occupying the weekend's time when the company offices were closed, a dilemma he frequently faced. Often he spent days exploring the city or sightseeing in the surrounding area. However, this was his third assignment in Tacoma. He had seen the glass museum, the waterfront, Dock Street, Point Defiance, and the art and historical museums. Undoubtedly he needed to move farther afield. His mind traveled to Parish wondering if she would want company doing anything, but given her previous reaction to his invitation he cancelled that idea. He was even tempted to go to the Villa where he had accomplished a previous assignment and check on Alexander. He would have balked if anyone accused him of being lonely, regardless of how well the description fit the situation.

He handled his laundry, paid bills, and put in his time at the hotel exercise area. He spent time reading a novel he had brought along and watching TV. Late in the afternoon he trekked over to a nearby coffee shop café where he purchased a sandwich and a latte. Noticing the local newspaper lay on one of the tables he sat there and perused it, looking for what if anything might be found on Ridinghood's case.

What he found was disappointing. Already he possessed more information than the paper made available. A couple items attracted his attention however. The news article made much less of the connection between Lawrence Manke and Ridinghood than Blayze would have expected. He wondered at the omission. Was it intentional or were the reporters unaware of the connection? Another item he noticed was the name of the nightclub where Manke played in the band. He scribbled it down on a scrap of paper.

Fighting the depression that hovered like an insistent mosquito, he wandered through Tacoma's downtown, mostly banks, office buildings, coffee shops and restaurants. When he returned to the hotel he went online to look up the club where Manke had played. It took time to locate not because it didn't give the address but because Blayze had to figure out exactly where that address would land him. Since it appeared to be the lounge accompanying a restaurant he figured he could do dinner and look at the other place where Manke worked.

He took his rental car from the parking garage and drove the short distance to where the restaurant sat along a finger of the sound reaching into the Port of Tacoma. Although it possessed a large parking lot Blayze spent time locating a vacant spot. He should have called for a reservation he realized as he left the car and continued into the wide low building. The front entrance presented a deceptively undersized image since, sitting above the channel, it spread out the back over the descent, occupying an additional level below the one on which he entered. The hostess counter sat in the dimly lit hallway leading to the back of the building overlooking the waterway.

He stopped at the counter where the girls perused the restaurant seating chart.

"Do you have a reservation?" One of them asked.

He shook his head.

"Would you mind eating in the lounge? The full menu is served there and you can be seated right away. Otherwise it's a long wait."

Since that suited his purposes ideally Blayze agreed. He was led to an angle in the hall where descending the stairs brought them to the lounge, also overlooking the waterway. To his left sat a J-shaped bar with stools. In front of him and to the right along the windows assorted tables ran all the way to the back wall. The stairs had descended into the middle of the lower level for behind them was the bandstand and a wood floor for dancing.

Blayze felt fortunate arriving when he did for even this level was filling fast. Directed to a table for two next to the windows he found himself in a spot not far from the bandstand. When left with a menu and word that his waiter would be with him shortly, he took stock of the other lounge occupants. It appeared many like him had failed to make reservations, rating seats in the lounge.

A tall young man dressed in black appeared at his table. "My name is Tony. I'll be your waiter. Can I interest you in something to drink?"

Possessed of ulterior motives and hoping to stretch his time long enough to see the band, he ordered a martini. "Is the restaurant always this busy?"

"There's some big exposition at the Tacoma Dome this weekend," his dark-skinned waiter with athletic good looks explained before departing to fetch his drink.

Blayze had waited until much later than he normally would have for dinner given his intention of catching the band. He had seen the sign on an easel in the hostess area indicating live music would begin at 9:00.

"Will the band be the one whose keyboard player died?" he asked Tony when he returned with his martini.

"Right. They got a new keyboard player to replace Lawrence."

"I imagine it takes a while to adjust to the group," Blayze tossed up.

"Lawrence was exceptional on the keyboard, played a wide range of music. This guy's okay, but he's not Lawrence."

"Did the business consider getting a different band?"

"There's a signed contract. Not easy for either side to back out."

Blayze considered the ramifications of a band member's death. Undoubtedly the affect depended on how much the group relied on the deceased member. He recalled Lawrence's girlfriend also played in this band. Working at Ridinghood he could have seen her. However, not having been introduced he wouldn't recognize her.

When his dinner arrived Blayze took time consuming it. He noticed the band arrive and watched them set up. There appeared to be five members including two women. One of the women apparently played guitar. The other had no instrument since the men played the other guitar, drums and keyboards. Observing the two women he tried to decide which would have been Manke's girlfriend. In so doing he noticed the one without an instrument perusing the audience pause as she reached him. Chances were she was the Ridinghood employee since he would have stood out there as the stranger.

Tony returned to his table. "How about dessert?"

"I'll have one of your spiked coffees." Blayze pointed to the one he wanted and Tony retired with his order.

As Tony left the woman Blayze had noticed, a short curvy brunette with blonde streaks in her hair, approached his table. Since a woman approaching him in a bar wasn't unusual he waited without assuming her interest.

Hesitant about speaking she took a deep breath and said, "You look familiar. You don't happen to work for Ridinghood?"

Much to his frequent regret, Blayze was not Mr. Charm and Sunshine. He was Mr. Precise. "I'm working at Ridinghood, not for them."

That left her at a loss for words.

Figuring if he were to get anywhere in this conversation he needed to bridge the gap. "Do you work for Ridinghood?"

She nodded with a sigh of relief. "Sally Stills, I'm in HR. I thought I saw you talking to Midge Melanckton."

"Possible. I'm auditing for the IRS." Blayze pointed to the extra chair. "Sit down, if you have time."

She perched there. "I saw you with that lieutenant. Did he tell you anything about Lawrence? Manke," she added, anxiety and dejection in her dark eyes.

Blayze grimaced. "No, he just asks me questions."

"About Lawrence?"

"And Ian Moseley."

"Oh." She sounded disappointed. "I thought maybe he would have told you something. He just asks me questions, too, and doesn't tell me anything." Her frustration made her breathless.

"What did you want to know?"

"How he died, who they think did it, why he was killed."

Blayze frowned thinking through the newspaper article he had read. He didn't want to give out confidential information and figured she should have seen the news. "I doubt they know yet who did it or why. He was shot. You know that already, right? I'm sure they've asked you if anyone would want to kill him."

She nodded. "Everyone liked Lawrence, the guys here in the band and at work. Even Mr. Moseley used to go to him to get information."

"Did he work with Mr. Moseley?"

"Oh, I don't think so. It sounded as if when Mr. Moseley had an IT question instead of going to Miguel he'd just ask Lawrence."

That's interesting, Blayze realized, it opened a possibility door.

Guitar chords came from the direction of the band's speakers. Sally stood. "I have to go."

<hr>

Saturday morning Parish got a phone call from Midge.

"How about a trip to Ocean Shores this afternoon?" She sounded chipper.

"Are you kidding?" With Midge she never knew.

"Of course not. It's a nice drive. We could have lunch."

"To the ocean beaches in summer weekend traffic. We might have to have dinner."

"We could do that too." Nothing daunted Midge.

"When did you want to go?" Parish mentally trekked through her day.

"ASAP or whenever you're ready."

Xavier had gone to his grandparents to help with the yard work and probably spend the day. Summer eased up some of her responsibilities. However, she felt reluctant to accompany Midge given what she figured her friend had in mind.

"I'll pick you up," Midge offered.

"Give me an hour."

As agreed, Midge arrived at ten o'clock sharp. Parish had managed a quick breakfast, prepping things for Sunday, and packing her handbag with a few in-case-of's. "We're coming back today, right?"

Midge raised two fingers in salute. "Scouts honor."

Once they were loaded into Midge's Outback and successfully wheeling down I-5 Parish asked, "So what are you really hoping to accomplish?"

Midge passed several cars then maneuvered her way from behind a slow moving semi. "I realize this is presumptive, but I feel compelled to go see for myself what's going on in Ocean Shores. First Bobbi Bennett goes there and doesn't return then we see Ian Moseley may be there. What does it all mean?"

"Maybe it doesn't mean anything."

Midge shot her a frown. "Just a coincidence?"

"Isn't that possible?"

"Of course it is, but I want to know that's the case," she huffed.

"Will you confront Mr. Moseley if you find him?"

Midge made a face but didn't answer. Parish wondered what she was in for. It would be different if they were the police, but two silly women.

In Olympia they left I-5 heading west on Highway 101 which quickly transferred them to Washington 8. At Hoquiam they changed to Highway 109 heading for Ocean Shores. The land gradually leveled off, changing from mountain evergreens to the sea grasses and shrubs inhabiting the coastal area. The sky, a clear bright blue, featured little clouds sailing by as if in a rush to see what lay beyond the Olympics.

"So what do you propose to do?" Parish cast a sideways glance at Midge as she succeeded in passing a garbage laden truck.

"Have lunch." She shot Parish a bright smile.

Parish rolled her eyes. "We're driving a hundred miles to have lunch?"

"Where's your spirit of adventure?"

"I put it in my back pocket and am sitting on it, so it won't get me in trouble," she huffed.

"Does that work?"

"No." Parish sighed. "Not when I have friends like you."

Midge remained quiet for a time checking the vehicle's GPS. "It sounds to me like a great many of Ridinghood's problems have transferred to Ocean Shores. I thought we'd have lunch, do a little shopping and see how they're doing."

"The problems?"

"You disagree?"

Well, that was a good question. In principle Parish was all for discovering what happened to Ridinghood's "problems". However, faced with the reality of confronting them she shrunk from the prospect. Horrors, I'm a coward! She took a deep breath. Okay, we do what we have to do. As crazy as she seemed at times, Midge was not crazy, foolish or ignorant. In fact, she was often inspired and with sufficient internal fortitude to follow through.

"If Mr. Moseley saw you would he recognize you?"

Midge lifted her shoulders. "A more significant question might be would he care?"

"Or even more important is we not let any of the 'problems'," Parish made quotation marks in the air, "know we recognize them." She emphasized the pronouns.

Midge shot her a sideways glance. "Do you think you can do that?"

Parish considered the question. "Under most conditions. Sometimes people surprise you, not because you recognize them when you don't expect to see them but because of something odd in their appearance."

They had reached the turn off from Highway 109 into Ocean Shores. As they approached the small town spread out before them in a simple grid with low rise buildings, wide thoroughfares and the inn, café and coffeehouse businesses common to a resort area.

"I think we'll cruise the main loop first. Look for a promising restaurant."

"There's a big restaurant with lots of cars around it." Parish pointed to a wide low building with big windows, surrounded by a parking lot nearly full of vehicles. "I imagine the large hotels have their own restaurants."

"Where they're staying is another issue."

"I talked to Connie Evans the other night. They stayed at the Shilo Inn when she was here with Bobbi."

"It might be worth checking that out."

Spotting a small octagonal building flaunting a seagull weathervane on its peaked roof and a painted wooden sign indicating it was a coffee café, Parish pointed. "There's a small one, but they might not serve lunch."

"I think we should try the one you spotted first."

After traveling the remainder of the street they were on and returning to the first avenue they had driven, Midge, following Parish's directions, swept into a parking spot to the side of the restaurant.

◆CHAPTER ELEVEN◆

Only moderately populated since they had arrived after the main lunch hours, the restaurant was arranged like the old fashioned family chain restaurants where the dining area included mostly booths. The hostess escorted Midge and Parish to a one along the wall. The décor featured sea shells, fish nets and pictures of exotic fish all done in soft neutrals and pastels. Parish found it a pleasant, peaceful atmosphere.

While being escorted through the aisles she checked out the other diners, a diverse assortment from young families to aged couples. All things considered she and Midge made the strangest pair there. Not conducive to invisibility. Nor did her perusal unearth anyone remotely resembling Ridinghood's "problems".

"I think this is a bust," she murmured to Midge as they were seated and left with menus.

"Oh, ye of little faith," Midge chided her.

A waitress arrived to take their orders.

Midge looked up from her menu. "I wish I'd paid more attention to Mr. Moseley."

"Would you have hired him?"

She shook her head. "The execs are done by the Board of Directors."

"You wouldn't have interviewed him?"

"Only for some special reason, which wasn't the case with Mr. Moseley."

"That's probably a good thing right now. At least he shouldn't recognize you."

Midge frowned at Parish, "What about you?"

She sighed. "He probably wouldn't know who I am, but he'd have seen me and may connect me to Ridinghood. On the other hand, I don't know that I've even had a conversation with Bobbi, not that she wouldn't have seen me. But you probably did interview her."

"Actually, I didn't," Midge grumbled. "She acquired the job through connections. However, she's acquainted with me from her various dealings with HR."

"So we need to be prepared not to acknowledge or recognize them if we see them since in all probability they will connect us somehow with Ridinghood."

"Are we able to do that?"

"It looks like our chance is coming." Parish nodded her head indicating someone behind Midge.

A man with flat dark hair, a bushy goatee, dressed in Dockers and a bomber jacket approached from the rear of the restaurant. Parish fixed her gaze on a young couple in the booth across the aisle, attempting to see the man's face without directing her gaze to him at all. As he came into position she transferred her gaze to Midge, passing over his face without changing her expression. He looked neither to the left or the right but kept his big green eyes focused in front of him, walking with arrogant indifference.

Midge lifted an eyebrow.

Parish nodded. "It looks like him."

"So the big question, what's he doing here?"

"And in disguise?"

The waitress returned to take their lunch order. When she had gone they sat for a time in silence.

"So if he's physically in disguise, does he also have a different identity?"

"That would be my guess." Midge frowned. "It would be helpful to get his new name."

Her expression made Parish think the wheels of how to accomplish that were turning. "We're going home tonight, right?"

Midge opened her mouth as though to contradict, but nodded. "I can't think how we'd get his name, unless we knew where he was staying."

Parish cocked her head and eyed her doubtfully. However, Midge's attention had been diverted to something outside the window. Glancing there she noticed the man she believed to be Ian Moseley standing beside a small Mercedes. Talking to him was a woman with fluffy chin-length hair, streaked with blonde and gray and over-toned with cranberry red.

"Doesn't look like Mr. Moseley's type," Parish commented.

Midge snorted. "I shouldn't think so. That's Bobbi Bennett, I'd swear."

Parish returned her gaze to the woman who chatted away, pointing to the Mercedes. "You really think so?"

"I've seen her plenty she's such a pain in the butt. I'd recognize her in a caftan and turban with a veil over her face." Midge dug the cell phone out of her handbag and aimed it at the window. She took a picture and then gazed at the results. "Not bad considering." She aimed again and took another picture.

Parish continued observing the conversation. She tried to determine if the Mr. Moseley person knew the Bobbi person, if that's who they were. The Moseley person looked haughty and defensive while the woman appeared excited and pushy. At about that time another woman came along capturing the Bobbi person's attention and they came toward the restaurant entrance. The Moseley person got into the Mercedes and left. Parish spent a moment memorizing the license number – SIRIAN.

"Okay, it's my turn to become invisible," Midge declared, grabbing the dessert menu tucked into a napkin holder and lifting it up in front of her face as if attempting to read something at the very bottom.

Parish watched the hostess lead the two women to a table in the rear and out of her vision. When they had passed she said, "You're safe. They're out of sight."

"If only we could have heard what they said." Midge grimaced. "It really makes you wonder what's going on here."

"Do you think they recognized each other?"

"It would be a kick if they didn't, but I'd surmise at least one of them recognizes the other."

"Bobbi knows it's Mr. Moseley?" Parish made the guess.

Midge nodded putting away the menu. "My guess is Mr. Moseley is hiding in some way. Bobbi is having a good time and for whatever reason has changed her appearance sufficiently to think no one will recognize her. I'd say she's playing a bit of a game with him."

"What's Mr. Moseley hiding from and why?"

Midge lifted her shoulders. "We'd know a whole bunch of things if we knew that."

"Would Bobbi talk to us if she knows who we are, but assumes we don't recognize her?"

"Now that's an idea." Midge grinned with excitement. "How could we find out?"

"It's hard given we'd have to act like we don't know her or where she works or anything to help us ask questions. Are we capable of that level of acting?"

"What have we got to lose?"

One of those questions a person learns the answer to when it's too late. Parish figured something was at stake, but at the moment she couldn't identify it.

"What we have to remember is she'll know us."

"We could take our lunch check to the cashier at the same time as she does. If she speaks to us we can play the role otherwise we'll know she is concerned we'll recognize her."

"Or that it isn't her." Parish countered. "They just came in. It may be a while."

"Eat slow."

They managed to string out their lunch, linger over coffee, and get the waitress to bring their check, putting them in readiness for their planned departure.

"Do you want to see my pictures?" Midge handed her phone to Parish.

She studied the phone images. As Midge had said, not bad considering that it was some distance away and through the window. At least it showed the general appearance of their disguises. She handed the phone back, noticing Bobbi and her companion approaching.

"Okay," Parish said, "here they come."

✧

After allowing the pair to pass Midge and Parish rose in a leisurely fashion and followed at a distance to the cashier. Parish concentrated on keeping her face in check focusing on Midge who had their tab. Midge kept her gaze fastened on the cashier. Once the other pair had paid their check and were moving toward the door the Bobbi person turned to her companion, Parish noticed the flash of recognition as her gaze glided past Midge. The other pair exited the restaurant while Midge paid their check.

"She recognized you," Parish said.

"Well, let's see what she does now."

The two stepped out onto the sidewalk surrounding the front and side of the building. The other pair stood near a mini car at the point the walk made a right angle. Midge's vehicle sat farther along at the end of the sidewalk. They moved in that direction.

"What are you going to say if she speaks to you?" Parish mumbled.

"It depends on what she says." Midge grinned. "Remember we don't know who she is and . . ." she gave Parish a pointed nod. "we shouldn't expect her to know who we are."

In the circumstances Parish figured Bobbi would not brave speaking to them. All she needed to do was avoid eye contact. However, she was wrong. As they moved past the pair toward Midge's car, the other two parted company. The Bobbi person came along side them and just as she moved slightly ahead she dropped her keys affectively in front of Midge.

"Oh, I'm sorry. How clumsy of me." She hesitated before bending to retrieve the keys allowing Midge time to pick them up.

The Bobbi person had her bag open, making as if she was rustling around in it. "Too many things in my hands," she said apologetically.

Midge handed her the keys. "No problem."

"Thank you so much," the Bobbi person bubbled. "Do you live around here?"

Parish figured it was a silly question, but Midge said, "No. We're just taking an afternoon drive on a nice day before fall sets in. Do you live here?"

The Bobbi person flashed a big smile. "Right now . . . for the time being."

"Have you lived here long?"

Parish wondered how long Midge could keep it up and not make Bobbi suspicious.

"Oh, not that long. It's lovely being close to the ocean."

"That's what we thought. Are there things to do you would recommend?"

"Oh, this is a lovely day for a walk along the beach. A couple really great souvenir shops are along the other thoroughfare." She waved her hand behind them.

"Thank you for the information." Midge was all politeness.

An awkward pause followed as if each thought it would be good to carry on the conversation but neither knew what to say next.

"Have a good day," the Bobbi person added and moved toward the vehicle next to them.

Midge and Parish continued to Midge's SUV. Once inside they looked at each other with raised eyebrows.

"Well, what do you think of that?" Midge challenged.

"Did she drop her keys on purpose?" Parish figured that was the case but the idea seemed incredible.

"Absolutely." Midge laughed. "She had to test her disguise."

"So, did we convince her she's successful?"

"I think so. But I had the feeling she wanted to push it further and make absolutely certain."

"You think she had doubts?" Parish would have had doubts, but she realized Bobbi had greater self-confidence, if not overconfidence.

"Not about us. I don't think we're the important ones she wants to fool."

"Who then?"

Midge lifted her shoulders. "I'd have a lot of answers if I had that one."

"Maybe Mr. Moseley, if that was really him."

Midge shook her head. "I have the feeling she was just testing him too."

Parish narrowed her eyes and gave Midge a skeptical look.

"I doubt if she would have approached him if she was unsure about fooling someone she knew."

Considering Midge's comment, Parish wondered who Bobbi wanted to fool. If she tested with fellow Ridinghood employees, maybe the whole point of her disappearance related to something separate from the company and others who had departed.

"You really have no idea who she's trying to fool?" Parish struggled to believe in Midge's absolute innocence. She always knew more than she admitted or confided.

She stared at the restaurant shaking her head. "I feel I should know something but I can think of nothing. What should we do now?"

"Try Bobbi's suggestion, look at those souvenir shops."

"Good idea." Midge started the Outback.

After exiting the restaurant parking lot they followed the traffic pattern to the other thoroughfare seeking the shops Bobbi had mentioned. A small strip mall induced them to park. Wandering through the shops Midge bought a tee shirt advertising Ocean Shores in a wash of blues, aqua, and sea green. Parish found a night light in gold and crystals in the shape of a lighthouse.

Leaving the last shop Parish grabbed Midge's arm and mumbled, "There he is again."

Midge carefully scanned the parking lot as they headed to her vehicle.

"Next to the little Mercedes."

The little sports car sat a couple spaces away from Midge's SUV creating the opportunity for another close up of the man Parish believed to be Ian Moseley. She put on her sunglasses and arranged her face in one attentive to Midge's conversation. Midge maintained a string of chatter regarding the shop they had just left, giving the appearance of being hardly aware of the man. Hoping her sunglasses successfully hid her gaze Parish took the opportunity to give his face a quick study. However, his affects for disguise and his sunglasses hid the most definitive aspects of his appearance. Although she believed this to be Ian Moseley, she couldn't be certain.

◆CHAPTER TWELVE◆

Blayze looked up as Parish entered his work space with the hesitant reserve to which he had become accustomed. However, he sensed a trace of excitement.

"Have a chair," he offered beckoning to the one in the corner.

She moved the chair into position. "Midge and I went to Ocean Shores on Saturday," she declared taking a seat.

Questions raced through Blayze's mind. "See anything interesting?"

"That Bobbi Bennett for one and possibly Ian Moseley."

Blayze stared. "Just hanging out?"

Parish laughed. "In disguise."

"But you recognized them?"

She nodded. "Bobbi for certain. I'm not sure about Mr. Moseley."

"Did she see you?"

"She dropped her keys in front of us so we had to talk to her. Midge believes she was testing her disguise to see if we recognized her." Before Blayze could ask Parish continued. "I think we managed to keep her from realizing we know who she is."

An astounding scenario. "So what's she doing there?"

"No idea. She also talked to the person I believe is Mr. Moseley. Midge thinks she was testing her disguise with him too."

"Did he recognize her?"

Parish shook her head. "I couldn't tell. She seemed pretty aggressive but he managed to get away from her."

"Did you tell the lieutenant?" What would Sarkis do with this information?

"I thought you might want to mention it. You're more likely to see him than me."

As Parish rose to leave someone passed by the opening to Blayze's office. She stepped into the corridor, attracting his attention.

"There you are. I have some information you requested."

"Have you met Blayze Pashasia, the IRS auditor?" Blayze heard her ask.

"No," the man said. "You mentioned you were working with him."

"In here." Leading him into Blayze's domain Parish introduced Slate Ridinghood, every inch the businessman with a pleasant but concerned expression.

"Blayze is assisting Lieutenant Sarkis in his search for Mr. Moseley. He's the one questioning bank accounts."

"It took me a while to get anything to match the numbers you gave me. Without a routing number it's close to impossible. Although I was lucky. I began with the larger banks and their usual routing numbers. This is apparently a Hunter account located in Dallas."

Blayze glanced at Parish who returned his gaze with lifted eyebrows. "Who owns the account?"

"The registered owner is a PR Investments which doesn't tell us much."

"Connected to Ridinghood?"

"It is not. That I could verify." Slate handed a piece of paper to Blayze upon which he noted the account number, the owner, and the address he found.

"Let me see what I can find."

"And let me know?" Slate confirmed.

"Certainly." Blayze nodded.

Slate left heading to the elevator.

Blayze typed the company name into Google's search box. "So Ms. Bennett left for reasons of her own not related to the company?" He resumed the conversation with Parish.

She perched on the plush chair. "That's Midge's conclusion. I'm keeping an open mind."

Google located the same address as Slate had given them but nothing further. Blayze tried several other options of acquiring information but came up empty. He explained, "This could mean anything from a legitimate business, parent or holding company to a shell."

"How can we find out?"

Blayze grimaced. "To have a bank account they must provide an EIN or a Social Security number."

"What paperwork might a holding company have to file?"

He leaned back in his chair. "An actual holding company has a raft of paperwork to produce, a simple LLC much less, depending on what the structure is meant to protect." He sighed. "Maybe I can get an EIN."

"Are you suspicious?"

"Absolutely. I need to see what goes in and comes out of this account."

"I have work to do," Parish declared rising.

When she had gone Blayze called his IRS superior requesting any information he could get hold of on PR Investments. It seemed the more knowledge they acquired the more suspicious circumstances appeared. Upon completing that task his mind traveled to the predicament Parish described in Ocean Shores. Another boatload of suspicion arrived in the wake of that revelation. Were they separate issues or connected? He lifted his shoulders. Too early to draw any conclusion and did he and Parish even possess the capacity to unravel it?

The situation was tricky. He definitely felt it necessary to inform the lieutenant of as much as he considered safe to securely communicate. However, the more he discovered the less it seemed the business of the police. Or even the IRS. Sarkis could not ignore the programmer's death, but did that connect to the disappearances? Blayze needed to continue his audit. Would that put a different spin on recent events?

Early yet, the disappearances, the red flag prompted audit, and the death of Lawrence Manke required they keep searching for whatever they could dig up in this situational graveyard without making any prejudgment as to relevance.

❦

Once Parish had her work on track she called Connie in credit. "What are you doing for lunch?"

"Eating." Connie laughed. "I brought my lunch. I thought I'd go outside."

"Could we get together? I need to pick your brain."

"Sure, meet you in the park? I'll be sure to bring my brain along."

Parish agreed, smiling.

Who knew Ian Moseley? Who had the inside track on the executive suite or was privy to chatter there? Strangely enough Mr. Moseley seldom rated a spot on the gossip slate, perhaps significant in itself. Wouldn't the executives be typical targets of rumor? Especially since chatty, name-dropping Bobbi Bennett had personal relationships with them.

However, the problem may be Parish, tending to excessive reserve which did not invite confidences. Her position in management posed another obstacle. Nonetheless, she figured somewhere in her brain resided things she had seen or heard that would provide clues. She leaned back in her chair and stared at the five foot peonies painted on her office wall. Nothing came to mind. In fact, attempting to recall gossip regarding Mr. Moseley brought up nothing.

As per agreement at noon she descended the stairs to the main floor meeting Connie coming from the direction of the elevator. She had braided her blonde hair and wore a light weight taupe pantsuit with a flourish of gold jewelry. Parish felt underdressed in her floral skirt and white blouse. She did wear the flower earrings she bought in Hawaii the previous year.

"How about we go around by the coffee shop? I'll get something for lunch." They discussed the basketball game as they followed the sidewalk around to the shop's main doors. "Would you like coffee or something?" she asked as Connie selected a seat at one of the wrought iron benches in the small park.

"Iced tea."

Grateful the order line was short, Parish ordered Connie's ice tea, a yogurt parfait and coffee for herself. Returning to the bench Connie had chosen she noted a fair scattering of employees lunching outdoors given the beautiful weather, many of them seated on the lawn.

"The building owner should put tables and chairs out here, at least for the summer," Parish observed as the pigeons trotted around seeking targets of opportunity.

"So what part of my brain are you interested in picking?" Connie asked once they were seated.

Parish grimaced, realizing how crude her suggestion sounded coming from Connie. "The part about Bobbi Bennett."

"What brings this up?" Connie removed a sandwich from her paper bag. "The fact she's missing?"

Parish debated telling her about seeing Bobbi in Ocean Shores, but decided against it. "Right. We're looking for any connection among those who are gone."

"Do you really suspect a connection between Mr. Moseley and Bobbi?" Connie smirked.

"It's not that I think there is," Parish explained, feeling a little foolish. "I'm just digging to see what comes up."

"I suppose there could be," Connie conceded. "Although I'd be more apt to consider a connection between her and the Ridinghood family since she's related to them."

"But only shirttail." Parish didn't figure hooking Bobbi up to the Ridinghoods would be particularly productive in solving the company problems, but perhaps she was naive.

"Right, but she might have some influence there, more than I think she'd have with Mr. Moseley."

Parish nodded. She could reason the same way. However, she needed gossip about Bobbi anywhere with anyone. "If she were somewhere in disguise, even Ocean Shores, who do you think she'd be hiding from?"

Connie glanced sideways at Parish. "Her husband?"

Parish acknowledged the comment with a lift of her eyebrows. "You think she's having an affair?"

"It's the most logical explanation."

Parish had to agree. "With whom?"

"You think it's someone at Ridinghood?" Connie sounded as if that thought had just occurred to her.

"Oh, not necessarily. Only if it is, it would really help to know."

"I've never thought much about it." Connie sighed. "She's worked in almost every department in the office so it could be anyone."

Parish stared at those gathered around the bench across from them, a group of both men and women colorfully dressed for the Pacific Northwest, a part of the country where nature's profusion of color offered no inspiration to the people who lived there. "Okay consider it from the other end. Are there guys you'd wonder if they're having an affair?"

Connie snorted. "Where do you want me to begin?"

Parish decided to tackle it literally. "In the executive suite."

"Of course everyone wondered about Ian Moseley." Connie laughed. "But really I don't think he was, except to the extent of leading on that administrative assistant of his."

"Leading her on?"

"He kept her on tender hooks. She was devoted to him. I heard rumors he made promises to her."

"Promises?"

Connie waved her hand indicating an assortment of possibilities. "You know the kind men make to keep a woman hanging on."

Parish wasn't sure she did know. Her relationships never got that far. "Do you really think he did?"

"Let's put it this way." Connie leaned toward Parish. "I think he told her whatever he needed to keep her where he wanted her. That what she believes he promised I doubt is the case. I think she believed more than he ever expressed. You know how we women are, get our hopes up over the smallest hint, blow it up all out of proportion."

Horrors, Parish thought, am I guilty of that? She shuddered.

Connie shot her a questioning glance.

"So did he have an affair with her?"

"I really don't think so. I think he may have hinted at the prospect but managed to avoid it."

"She's vicious about his office," Parish said, recalling Doris' animosity. "She caught me locking it up after the lieutenant came to examine it."

"I imagine now that he's gone anything to do with him is her private property."

"It makes me feel sorry for her."

"She wouldn't appreciate that at all." Connie laughed. "Someone I feel sorry for is Tim Hogan. Have you ever met his wife?"

"Once, just recently."

"If he's CFO at home his wife is the CEO. She treats him like he couldn't be more stupid. But, if she has enough time, she might be able to make something of him."

"Ouch," Parish shuddered.

"Mr. Hogan's someone I think would be ripe for an affair, but I've heard nothing to that effect."

Parish made a face. "I think I'd run away from home."

"It might not work with that woman. Believe me, I wouldn't want to be on her expendable list."

◆CHAPTER THIRTEEN◆

L ater than usual heading to the cafeteria Blayze met so many people returning he felt he had missed the party. Among them was Miguel whom he hailed. "I need some answers if you'd have time later."

"Sure," he agreed. "Your office or mine?"

"Mine, it's quieter."

Miguel checked his watch. "Two o'clock?"

Blayze nodded. In the cafeteria he grabbed a sandwich and coffee which he took back to his desk.

Mr. Hornby had sent a print-out of transactions on the bank account to which Ridinghood was depositing money. Blayze verified the amounts he showed leaving Ridinghood were arriving in the PR Investments account. However, as soon as Ridinghood's money arrived it left again for a third destination.

Sometime later an amount would return to the PR Investments from a fourth account. The original amount that left Ridinghood's bank would return there from that fourth account also.

Blayze gave an exasperated sigh. He ended up back where he started. Where had the money gone and what did it do while absent? Grabbing his phone he put in the number for Mr. Hornby.

"Blayze, you got my fax?"

"Right. It puts me back where I started. The money leaves this account, goes somewhere then part of it returns. Can you determine where it goes?" Blayze explained the sequence of entries and where to locate them on the printout.

Mr. Hornby sighed. "I'll see what I can find. Is this significant?"

"It's beginning to appear more significant all the time."

At two o'clock per agreement Miguel showed up at Blayze's office. He pointed to the chair in the corner which Miguel pushed to the spot facing him.

"So what do you want to know?"

Blayze leaned back. "You mentioned suspicious computer activity on Ian Moseley's part. Can you be more specific?"

Miguel eyed Blayze with a trace of suspicion. "Does this relate to your audit?"

Blayze considered. At this point he didn't know to what it related. He realized the two of them were facing off, each protecting the security of his work. Although he appreciated the necessity of proceeding with caution it remained critical they work together and not at cross purposes. However, he was considerably more adept at working alone and protecting his turf than sharing his endeavors.

"Does it matter to what it relates, the audit, missing persons, or even to some other activity threatening Ridinghood?" Blayze returned the pointed stare.

This paused Miguel's defensiveness. He hesitated momentarily. "Okay, I see." He sighed. "Moseley spent more time in the company bank account than seemed appropriate for his position. Also his ventures there seemed oddly timed, not in office hours."

"Any theories?"

Miguel grimaced. "Not really. It raised a red flag for my department but we wouldn't have the information to draw any conclusions." His dark eyes narrowed. "Do you have an explanation?"

Blayze snorted. "I keep running in circles and they may not even relate to Moseley." He explained the vacationing money and his efforts to determine who was moving it.

Miguel leaned forward. "If it was being done by someone in the corporation it would most likely be Moseley. I've had no indications of anyone else playing in the bank accounts, including the comptroller or Tim Hogan."

"Next question, does this relate to Moseley's disappearance?"

"Relative to cause or effect?"

"Either or." Blayze lifted his shoulders.

"I don't know if I can help you. You probably have all the information I have."

"But if you come across anything you'll let me know?"

Miguel bobbed his head. "I'll answer anything I can for you."

When Miguel had gone Blayze considered the conversation. More and more it appeared whatever took place in the bank account related to Ian Moseley. It also appeared he had left of his own accord, having preplanned it, making embezzlement a high probability. However, Blayze had found nothing indicating embezzlement as such.

He restudied the printout Mr. Hornby had sent him focusing on the ACH transaction removing the money from the PR Investments account. The name listed to which the money was transferred was an LLC along with a transaction number. He searched for a company with the name MIJ and Company LLC Investments without success. What did that mean? Presumably the money was sent to another bank account, which would require an EIN or Social Security Number. He needed to call Mr. Hornby again.

⚜

This time Blayze called the lieutenant. "Learned some things you probably should know."

"How about coffee at that shop in the corner?"

Blayze packed his paperwork, tidied his workspace, then headed for the coffee shop, taking the route outdoors and around the building.

Still beautiful, the day entertained a light breeze tickling the brightly colored flowers in the concrete planters where the lieutenant sat on a bench checking his cell phone. He stood as Blayze approached. In silence they proceeded into the shop and after ordering beverages took the table they had previously occupied near the windows. The sheers had been pulled into hiding behind the peach colored drapes, drawn completely open, allowing the sunshine in.

Eagerness lit Sarkis' eyes as he asked, "So what should I know?"

"Have you talked to Parish today?"

The lieutenant eyed him.

"She and that Midge from HR went to Ocean Shores. They believe they saw both Ian Moseley and that woman you're missing."

Sarkis gaped. "You're kidding."

Blayze shook his head. "In disguise."

The lieutenant sat back in his chair staring at his coffee cup. "But why?" He peered over his spectacles at Blayze. "You really think he's making a getaway?"

"It looks that way."

Quiet for a time, Lieutenant Sarkis frowned at the picture of coffee beans on the wall. "One thing occurs to me. There's a small airport out there. If he was looking to get out of the area he might try flying from there. Someone here looking for him might not check that small airport."

"Can he get out of the country from there?"

"He could get to another airport where he wouldn't likely be sought." The lieutenant lifted an eyebrow. "You think he's headed for another country?"

"I've been checking some traveling money. If I find it's out of country I'll definitely think that."

Sarkis grimaced at the coffee beans. "That Bennett woman was there too?" he verified. "In disguise?"

"Apparently."

"Maybe she's with Moseley."

Blayze sighed. "Didn't sound like it. Parish figured she was testing her disguise with him." A couple points suddenly merged in Blayze's mind. "I've been following the media coverage on Manke's murder. They never seem to connect it to Ridinghood."

"Ah," the lieutenant leaned back in his chair. "I agree that's odd, but we've avoided connecting the two as best we can." He gave Blayze a warning glance. "For various reasons."

Blayze took hint he wasn't to ask those reasons nor assist the media in making the connection.

Sarkis changed the subject. "I took that photo of Manke around to those storage places. He wasn't the one who ordered pickup of that trunk."

"You thought he was?" Blayze frowned. "Wasn't he dead?"

The lieutenant scowled at him. "The transaction was done mostly by phone. The guy at the storage units could describe the guys who picked up the trunk but they worked for the transfer company and only had orders and a key."

"No one saw who actually ordered it?"

"Presumably." Sarkis lifted his shoulders. "Although I guess one wouldn't expect them to."

"Was there anything at the lounge where he played to suggest a motive?"

The lieutenant shook his head. "The modus operandi suggests it would be difficult or impossible for a woman to accomplish . . . at least alone. Not that easy for a lot of men either. I'd expect to find at least a couple people involved."

Blayze considered the idea. "I also went to that restaurant bar where Manke played. His girlfriend recognized me from Ridinghood. She said something interesting. Moseley would go to Manke for assistance in IT rather than Miguel."

"You think that means something?"

"I'd see it unusual for a corporate CEO to go around a department head to seek assistance from one of his subordinates."

"You think Moseley was working with Manke?"

"That's rather a jump since Manke ended up dead. He couldn't have helped dispose of himself."

Sarkis gave Blayze a don't-be-stupid look. "But it might be worth keeping in mind where other things are concerned. Moseley's planned escape for one. Emptying his apartment and office for another." The lieutenant emptied his coffee cup. "I think I'll take a trip to Ocean Shores, although I might have to take one of those women along to make identifications."

◆CHAPTER FOURTEEN◆

After completing a number of analytical reports for Taylor Washington and feeling the need of movement Parish left her office for the break room and a cup of coffee. She found Midge there perched on a stool chatting with Odella. Both turned to her as if expecting an announcement by the Angel Gabriel.

"I was just explaining to Odella what we found in Ocean Shores," Midge said.

"Who would you think Bobbi was trying to fool with her disguise?" Parish asked Odella.

She narrowed her eyes in thought.

"Connie Evans seemed to think she's hiding from her husband."

Midge gave a hacking laugh. "If I were her husband I'd hide from her."

Parish fixed her coffee then moved to the windows overlooking the Port of Tacoma. It was one of those halfway days, sunny one minute, cloudy the next. At the moment the sun peeked through a break in the clouds like the earth's fairy godmother with her magic wand placing a golden glow on the waters of the bay. "Connie also thinks she's having an affair."

"Unfortunately that would make sense." Odella placed her cup on the counter and grabbed a packet of sugar. "But with whom?"

"I asked about Mr. Moseley, but she didn't think it would be him."

Midge laughed. "That's more than the wildest imagination could conceive."

"There you are," Lieutenant Sarkis declared entering the room with his customary abruptness. "You still haven't told me where to find my missing persons" he accused. "Although . . ." He peered over the edge of his glasses. "Rumor has it you've seen them."

"Well, yes," Midge grinned. "I think we have."

"How convinced are you?"

She glanced at Parish.

"We're more uncertain about Mr. Moseley than Bobbi Bennett."

"Does he have a better disguise?"

"Not necessarily. It's just that neither of us has spent that much time with him here and we only had a look at him there. We actually talked to Bobbi."

"I don't suppose you know what names they're using now?"

Both ladies shook their heads.

"Which of you wants to go to Ocean Shores with me and point out the people you saw?"

After a moment of shocked silence in which Midge and Parish grimaced at each other, Midge asked, "Are you serious?"

"Absolutely."

"Why don't you let us discuss it and see who has the greatest availability?"

The lieutenant appeared suspicious they were evading him. "You'll get back to me?"

"We will," Midge affirmed with a glance at Parish who nodded.

When the lieutenant had gone, Odella grinned. "I'm leaving you with your dilemma."

Parish could feel her shoulder muscles tightening as she considered the idea of accompanying the lieutenant. Midge watched as if she could read her mind. Parish thought ruefully, she probably could.

"Depending on when he wants to go, I have that conference in Spokane," Midge reminded her.

In Parish's head the argument raged. You actually have to put your money on your horse if you're going to back him, her intellect accused. But all the way to Ocean Shores with a man, alone, her emotions protested.

"Maybe you should see if Blayze would go. You wouldn't be alone with either of them." Obviously Midge read her mind.

"Okay," Parish mumbled reluctantly. "But I'll have to make arrangements with Xavier."

"I'll go if he doesn't hit my conference, but . . ."

"He'll probably want to go tomorrow or the next day and that's when your conference is."

Midge nodded.

Parish returned to the elevator feeling as though the life had been sucked out of her day. Exiting she noticed through Blayze's open door the lieutenant there talking with him.

She still had another report due within the next couple days. She began work on it, thinking she may end up with no time to finish before accompanying the lieutenant. As she worked her mind kept returning to the Ocean Shores trip. At least they would be doing something to solve the problems.

Perhaps they could still avoid a company disaster. She really didn't mind the lieutenant. He was brusque but kindly. He wasn't nearly as formidable as Blayze Pashasia, but she had also become accustomed to Blayze.

Her brother had once asked her if she thought she would ever get married. In all honesty her mind couldn't conceive of it. Just a personal, non-fellow-employee relationship with a man was close to unimaginable. Just about, but not quite. At times she felt she would enjoy having a man's friendship, someone whose company she enjoyed with whom she could do things, things that would be difficult with a girlfriend.

Romance remained another matter entirely, crossing boundaries her psychology refused to consider. She had barely reached the age a young girl could seriously consider romance and the thought of someday being married when her world had been shattered. Although one bad experience might not have ended her natural woman's desire to love and be loved, a couple ensuing close calls and a few nasty remarks had ended her thoughts along those lines. She had shut the door on that part of life and locked it.

Dinner with Blayze had worked out okay. He had been willing to abide by the limitations. When the lieutenant left she would ask if he would be willing to go to Ocean Shores. The three of them might get farther than one or two alone anyway. She wondered what advance preparation might make it more profitable. She recalled she still need to lookup Annabelle Elliott.

❧

"Have you found out what Moseley was doing with Manke?" Lieutenant Sarkis asked barging into Blayze's office.

Blayze frowned at him. "I haven't seen Miguel yet."

A what's-the-matter-with-you frown occupied Sarkis face as he grabbed the chair in the corner and pushed it to Blayze's desk.

He found the lieutenant's attitude annoying. "I haven't signed up with the police yet nor have you offered to pay me."

Sarkis wiped the scowl off his face and sat. "How's the audit coming?"

Blayze figured that must be his apology.

"Frustrating. I'm running around in circles. One bank account leads to another then another then another."

"Is that suspicious?"

"Absolutely. But I can't tell you if it relates to any of your problems."

"I've told your assistant and that Midge I need one of them to accompany me to Ocean Shores." He paused then continued. "I'm interviewing a few of your big chiefs today."

Blayze lifted his brows.

Sarkis took a slip of paper from his pocket. "Slate Ridinghood, Tim Hogan, Taylor Washington."

"Good luck." Blayze smiled.

Sarkis moved the chair back to the corner and huffed, "Same to you."

Blayze checked his messages, finding that Mr. Hornby had left a response to his last call requesting Blayze call him, which he did.

"I've checked the account for that LLC you asked about. I have an EIN for it, but no further information. I'll still do more checking. However, there is a lot of interesting activity in that account, including money leaving and returning. I'm faxing you a printout."

Blayze leaned back in his chair considering the message. As he contemplated the problem Parish appeared at the opening to his workspace and paused at the entrance.

"Can I help you?"

She took a few steps into the room. "The lieutenant wants either Midge or I to go to Ocean Shores with him. It will probably be me depending on when he wants to go. I wondered if you would be interested in going too."

Blayze stared at her processing the request. Given the situation he figured he could manage the trip even with his IRS commitment. However, he wondered why the lieutenant had not requested his company but Parish was. "Does the lieutenant know you're inviting me?"

Her demeanor suggested the frightened bunny standing very still to prevent detection. "No."

"Oh." He didn't know what to say.

"Does it make a difference?"

Strictly speaking? Blayze lifted his shoulders. "Not to me."

"Would you be willing?" Her expression was anxious.

"Sure, why not?"

She smiled.

"You're going to deal with the lieutenant?"

She nodded. "If he wants me to go he's going to have to take you too."

Blayze laughed. For all her gentle femininity she lacked no presence of mind or force of character. And, he realized, in the process she gave up not one iota of her charming womanhood. "Okay." He nodded then went on, "I'm waiting for a fax from my boss in Salt Lake. He's located that LLC account the money from PR Investments was sent to. It sounds as if the money continues traveling from there."

"What do you think that means?"

"Making a guess, whoever is doing this is taking the transaction as deep as he can go to discourage exactly what we're doing."

"Is it going to stop us?"

"I don't think he counted on the IRS. If he was just trying to keep someone at the company from tracing it, he might have discouraged them, but I have access to information regular people don't."

She nodded smiling. "I have a report to get done." With that she left.

Blayze stared after her. He still found her puzzling. He didn't think he had ever met a woman quite so difficult to understand. Why did she want him on the Ocean shores trip? Her face when he had asked her to have dinner returned to his mind. Now she was inviting him out. However, he doubted that was it. Somehow she still dealt with her fears. Ah, it hit him. She didn't want to accompany the lieutenant alone. She had selected Blayze as her protection. In spite of his brain's cautionary insertions, he felt pleased.

Someone Blayze had not met previously showed up at his opening with a handful of paperwork. After verifying his identity she handed him the fax that had come from Hornby.

Blayze laid the sheets out on the desk in front of him and examined the LLC account in detail. Money left that account for five separate destinations. He wondered if Mr. Hornby had noted those ACH transactions and would determine where this money was being sent.

He noted that the sum of three of the amounts leaving the LLC at one point was the same amount that had left Ridinghood for PR Investments and subsequently left PR Investments for the LLC. However, within the quarter each of those accounts returned to the LLC another larger amount. A short time later this larger amount left the LLC account for another ACH destination entitled RC Returns.

Blayze frowned. What was going on?

Subsequent to these transactions another smaller amount arrived in the LLC account from PR Investments and moved on to another account with the same basic name as the LLC. Going back to check on the PR Investments account Blayze noticed that the smaller amount arrived in PR Investments from the RC Returns account prior to being forwarded to the LLC.

He needed to determine the nature of RC Returns. Did it refer to Ridinghood Corporation? Or would investigation reveal only another layer of accounts?

Blayze sighed. It had to end somewhere.

❦

Connie had given Parish Annabelle Elliott's cell phone number. Since she agreed to meet with her, Parish arranged to stop by her workplace. Annabelle worked for a small printing company catering to local businesses in the downtown area.

The clouds had taken a break giving the sun a chance to monopolize the sky, making it a lovely late August day. Parish decided to walk since Annabelle's company was only a few blocks away. It felt good to let the breeze blow through her hair and hopefully her mind, clearing away the cobwebs. What she hoped to learn she didn't know, but she needed to listen carefully for whatever tidbits Annabelle made available.

The printing company sat midway through a block on Pacific Avenue. When Parish entered the shop Annabelle stood at the counter and waved cheerfully while waiting for her customer to finish the credit card process.

Parish had met Annabelle a number of times mostly in connection with Connie Evans. She was one of those people who inspired Parish with awe. She had seen the phenomenon a number of times. An adorable, bubbly, affectionate little girl who captured the hearts of all who came near her grew into a pudgy, garrulous, gossip of a woman in fashions by Omar the Tentmaker. That the woman never got over believing she was adorable never failed to amaze Parish. Her early life had infused her with such confidence in her charm and attractiveness that, regardless of what she later became, in her head she was still enchanting and desirable. She could almost make a person question her own eyes.

Parish studied a rack of greeting cards while waiting for Annabelle to be free, wondering what made it possible for some people to have so much indestructible confidence and others to have none.

"Okay, let's go." Annabelle grabbed a leather sack-like handbag and hung it over the well-padded shoulder of her tunic top.

They chatted about the weather and changes in downtown Tacoma on the way to a nearby coffee shop, which occupied the lower level of a triangle shaped building on a corner up the hill from Pacific Avenue. Filled with the aroma of brewing coffee, the shop contained a long counter case filled with attractive pastries. They each ordered a latte and Annabelle chose a piece of lemon pound cake. Recalling she had given up lunch to make this excursion Parish bought a scone. They found a table available in the point of the triangle offering a view of a section of downtown Tacoma.

"Connie told me to expect a call from you." Annabelle's eyes twinkled with anticipation. "She said you were looking for Bobbi Bennett."

Parish had considered how to approach the subject, wondering if she should mention seeing Bobbi in Ocean Shores. In the end she figured it best to let Annabelle lead the conversation and offer as little information as possible. "Connie said you were closer to Bobbi than others she knew."

"Bobbi and I went to high school together. I've known her since we were kids."

"Did Connie tell you she's missing right now?"

Annabelle nodded, smiling. "Which is nothing new. She goes missing every now and then."

"Really." Parish was shocked. "What do you mean by that?"

"Well, she gets bored easily. She's always chasing some butterfly." She waved her hand airily. "Something new and exciting."

"And you think that's the case now?"

Annabelle considered the bite of lemon bread on the end of her fork. "Connie said she's been gone since we went to Ocean Shores. That's a long time. She's usually just gone for a weekend or a week at most."

"So what would you expect she's doing?"

Annabelle laughed. "Chasing some guy."

Parish opened her mouth then closed it again. That left her wordless. "Are you kidding?"

"No, no." She shook her head, laughter still in her eyes. "We'd do that sometimes."

Parish stared. That was over the moon. Maybe she didn't mean it literally. Parish struggled at times being too literal minded. "What do you mean?"

"Oh, you know. Go to where some guy we knew was staying, like a trip out of town on business or . . ." Annabelle waved her fork.

No, Parish didn't know. She couldn't even imagine it. She concentrated on her latte trying to determine if she even wanted to know what Annabelle meant. "Single guys?"

"Mostly." She leaned across the table. "Actually I think there was someone in particular Bobbi was interested in. She kept dropping broad hints."

"Wouldn't she confide in you?"

"Generally." Annabelle appeared thoughtful. "You know now that you mention it, it's odd she didn't tell me. At the time I thought she was being coy, playing the tease-all-the-girls-with-tidbits thing, but she never did get specific. I forgot all about it."

"So, if she was interested in someone special, who do you think it would be?"

Annabelle covered her mouth, staring into the street. "I'm trying to think about the hints she gave out."

Parish licked her finger and concentrated on picking up the crumbs of her scone while waiting for Annabelle to think it through.

"One of the times we went for a long weekend in Spokane where there was a big business conference. We ran into a group from that conference at one of the hotel bars. If I'm not mistaken several of the men were from Ridinghood. Bobbi seemed to know who they were. Since I don't work for Ridinghood, I didn't know them and don't think I've ever seen any of them since."

"But you think Bobbi might have."

"She spent quite a bit of time that night with one of them. They seemed to hit it off. She was quite excited when we got back to our hotel."

"But you didn't find out who it was?"

She shook her head. "Bobbi was always doing something like that, always excited over some new project, new place to go, new restaurant, new outfit, new man."

Parish observed Annabelle's voracious but vicarious participation in the incident. "But you don't know if this person was from Ridinghood?"

"No."

Parish sighed. "When was this?"

Annabelle's gaze traveled over Parish's head then returned. "I can check at home I probably have it on my computer."

"Would you and let me know?"

"Sure." She eyed Parish. "But it might not have been someone from Ridinghood."

"I realize that, but it's still a place to start. I can check to see who from Ridinghood attended that conference. One of them may know something."

◆ CHAPTER FIFTEEN ◆

When it came time for a break Blayze stopped at IT on his way to get coffee.

Miguel beckoned him to his desk with a lift of his chin. "More questions?" He nodded to the oddly shaped gold chair beside his desk.

Taking a seat, Blayze considered his approach. "The lieutenant heard Ian Moseley would go to Manke with his IT questions instead of coming to you." He watched for Miguel's reaction.

Miguel narrowed his eyes gazing across his group. "I had the feeling that was happening."

"Manke never said anything to you about it?"

"Not strictly speaking. I think he tried some questions bordering on giving out information but he was cautious."

"You think Moseley requested his silence?"

Miguel gave a brief nod.

"Did you do anything about it? Or was it immaterial as far as you were concerned?"

"Initially I figured it was immaterial. I thought Moseley was just asking the first person in IT he came to. Something about it made me suspicious though." Miguel leaned back in his chair. "Manke seemed a little nervous about it as if he felt guilty."

Blayze lifted his eyebrows asking his question.

"That was when I started checking on Moseley's computer activities. I also started checking a lot of other people's activity in the company accounts."

"What do you think Moseley was doing?"

Miguel sighed. "It appeared he was moving money from the main account into an account for investing."

"Did you question that?"

"I wasn't in a position to. He is Chief Executive Officer. If he selects places to invest company money I don't have access to those accounts . . ." he paused and squinted at Blayze, "or any say about what investments he makes."

"Right. So you figured it was all on the up and up?"

"No." Miguel's deep brown eyes fired a frustrated glance at Blayze.

"I see." Blayze considered a moment. "One more question. Do you have the name on the account the money was moved to?"

Miguel shook his head. "All I have is routing numbers."

Blayze removed the slip of paper with the routing numbers he had been researching from his wallet and handed it to Miguel. "Is that the one?"

Miguel glanced at the note then opened one of his drawers and pulled out a file folder which he spread out on his desk. After a moment of comparing numbers he nodded.

"Okay. Answers one of my questions. It looks like we're on the same page." Blayze explained to Miguel his bank account research and what he had found. "This tells me who was moving the money?"

From IT Blayze continued to the break room where he found Parish with Lieutenant Sarkis.

"I understand you're going to Ocean Shores with us." Sarkis' eyes twinkled as he accosted Blayze.

Blayze glanced at Parish.

"Tomorrow," she said. "Does that work for you?"

Blayze lifted his shoulders and nodded. "No problem."

The lieutenant peered over his glasses at Blayze. "Did you talk to Miguel?"

"Right."

After they each fixed a cup of coffee Blayze led the way to his office. He took his chair and the lieutenant grabbed the one in the corner. Parish stood at the door poised to leave.

"I'd like you to stay," Blayze said to her.

"I'll bring another chair from my office." She left to retrieve the chair which she placed beside the lieutenant.

"So what did Miguel have to say?" Sarkis charged to the point.

"Moseley was the one moving the money."

Silence reigned as Parish and the lieutenant digested the information.

"However," Blayze continued, "that doesn't mean anything. He has the most right and responsibility to move money of anyone here."

"What about Manke's part in it?"

"Miguel realized he was working with Manke, but that doesn't prove anything either."

"So you're convinced everything is kosher?" The lieutenant pinned Blayze with a squint.

"No." Blayze scowled. "But we can't go charging in with guns blazing either." He glanced at Parish. "I'll keep following the money."

"I talked with your big shots today. That was a waste of time," Lieutenant Sarkis huffed. "How can they run a company when they know so little about what's going on here?"

Blayze noticed Parish smile. "Who did you talk to?"

"Slate Ridinghood for one."

"He's head of the Board of Directors. He's not usually in the office at all and normally has no responsibility for the day to day operations," Parish explained.

The lieutenant snorted. "What about Washington?"

"He's comptroller. He manages the operating budget."

"And Hogan?"

Parish glanced at Blayze before responding. "He's the one who should know something."

"Should I haul him in for questioning?"

"I wouldn't do that just yet," Blayze said.

Lieutenant Sarkis sighed and rose. He took his chair back to the corner. "I'll meet you two here in the morning." He left.

Parish shook her head. "He's not a happy camper."

"No." Blayze agreed. "But I doubt rounding these people up and corralling them would make him any happier."

❈

After completing her report Parish made the trip upstairs to HR. Midge sat in her bright yellow chair staring at a piece of paper in front of her and rolling her eyes. Parish took the chair beside her desk.

"I wonder if heads roll when the guillotine chops them off," Midge voiced her frustration.

Parish laughed. "You want to make some heads roll?"

"You bet!" She sat back in her chair with a sigh. "What can I do for you?"

"I met Annabelle Elliott at lunch."

Midge gave her a blank look.

"A friend of Bobbi Bennett's."

"Ah, learn anything?"

"Could you look up a conference in Spokane and see who from Ridinghood attended it?"

Midge peered at her with suspicion. "You have a date?"

"Not yet, but Annabelle is supposed to get it for me."

"Is something supposed to have happened there?"

"Possibly." Parish explained her conversation with Annabelle.

Midge stared over Parish's head with narrowed eyes. "Are we talking about Mr. Moseley?"

"Oh, not necessarily." Parish hadn't considered him since Bobbi's behavior they saw her with him in Ocean Shores would have cancelled that idea. "Does he go to those conferences?"

"Occasionally. Actually Tim Hogan probably goes more often, but even he wouldn't generally. It depends on what the conference was about."

"Annabelle wouldn't be able to tell me since she doesn't work for Ridinghood."

"What was she doing there then?"

Parish considered. "It sounded as if she and Bobbi were on a weekend jaunt. Even Bobbi may not be able to say what the conference was. Who else goes to those things?"

"It depends. If it's HR I go. If it's IT Miguel goes. If it's marketing their manager goes. If it's management any one or all of us may go, you included." Midge gave her a cheesy grin.

The upcoming trip to Ocean Shores flashed into Parish's head creating a pang of anxiety. She consoled herself. It shouldn't be so bad if they were able to make progress regarding the mysteries. "Could you send me a text with those pictures you took in Ocean Shores? It may help when we go tomorrow."

"Sure." Midge's gaze expressed concern. "Did you get things worked out okay?"

"I think so." Parish rose. "I'll let you know that date when Annabelle gets back to me."

As she stepped out of the elevator and turned toward her office Parish noticed Doris Possum appearing lost. "Are you looking for someone?"

After giving Parish a cursory once over the woman seemed to recognize her. She narrowed her eyes suspiciously. "That IRS auditor," she snapped.

Doris made Parish uncomfortable, actually more than uncomfortable. She feared any moment the woman would burst into shrieks of disapproval. She had seen Doris screaming at another employee once when she had been in the executive suite.

"He's here." Parish led the way to Blayze's office and ushered her in. "This is Blayze Pashasia." To Blayze, who looked up with a frown, she said, "This is Doris Possum, Ian Moseley's administrative assistant." She noticed the flicker of apprehension in Blayze's expression.

Mentally returning to her conversation with Annabelle she attempted to recall if she had ever seen Bobbi Bennett particularly attentive to any of the men at Ridinghood, or even if one of them had been so to her. Would it make any difference? Probably not, unless it was Mr. Moseley. However, she couldn't believe that. What occupied Bobbi's attention was probably immaterial.

Still half expecting to hear screams from Blayze's area, Parish wondered what Doris wanted from him. If she sought information, he was Mr. Taciturn. If she wanted reassurance he was Mr. Frigidaire. Maybe she was taking an opportunity to warn him off Mr. Moseley, which wouldn't work either.

Finishing up tasks needing to be done if she was to be unavailable for a day, Parish lost track of time. Looking up once she did notice Doris leaving Blayze's space. However, with only a glimpse she was unable to discern whether the results pleased the woman.

As Parish completed her report Blayze appeared at her door. "What did Doris want?"

He lifted one of his ominous eyebrows. "Difficult to say."

"Well, at least she didn't scream at you."

He cocked his head with a quizzical expression. "You expected her to?"

"She's known for being difficult to please . . . and vocal about it."

"I doubt anything I said pleased her." He sighed. "I figure she was warning me off Moseley. I told her as long as he wasn't involved in tax problems he'd be okay."

"Did that satisfy her?"

Blayze considered the question then shook his head. "No, but she changed the subject. She wanted to know how my audit was coming."

That was odd. Why would Doris care about the auditing?

"I told her no problem so far. True as far as it goes." He leaned against the door jam. "Would she still be in contact with Moseley?"

"Possibly." The thought had also crossed Parish's mind.

"Her questions would make more sense."

"Was she trying to find out if he was in trouble?"

Blayze grinned. "Or something."

Parish eyed him. "What did you tell her?"

"As little as possible."

"She put up with that?"

Blayze smirked. "You have to be careful threatening the IRS."

Parish laughed. "She threatened you?"

"She made a stab at it."

"I wonder if that means she still has contact with Mr. Moseley. Someone told me she believed he made promises to her."

Blayze lifted an eyebrow. "Did your person think he did?"

"She thought he probably gave Doris the impression he was interested in a relationship to get her assistance."

Blayze grimaced. "Could that explain moving things out of his office?"

"Ah." Parish hadn't thought of that. "Maybe."

Blayze straightened. "Well, I'll see you tomorrow."

◆CHAPTER SIXTEEN◆

Trekking from his hotel to Ridinghood Blayze considered the conversation with Doris Possum and then with Parish. Did this open a door to possibilities? Could Doris be Moseley's underground liaison?

The sun hung from the eastern sky like a fireball ready to drop into the sound. The forecast on his hotel television proclaimed storms from the south headed this way which undoubtedly accounted for the humidity. Probably a good day to head for the ocean beaches. With a little luck there would be a breeze.

From his conversation with Miguel the day before it seemed certain Moseley was connected to the traveling money. However, it may be legitimate, which meant he needed to keep digging and locate where the money ultimately landed. Since the amount leaving the corporate account returned in full, his task was to determine whether that money should have returned with company. That answer may lie in the amounts leaving the LLC for other destinations.

Arriving at his workspace he found new faxes from Mr. Hornby which he examined. Well, here we go again, he thought. The three amounts originally leaving the LLC went to three separate investment companies, well known and legitimate. The big question now, who owned those accounts?

"Ready to go?" Lieutenant Sarkis demanded from his office door.

Blayze sighed and slid the papers into a folder in his briefcase. He followed the lieutenant into Parish's office where she stood by her desk sliding the handles of her large handbag over the shoulder of a pastel blue blazer. Her eyes matched the blazer and appeared apprehensive.

The lieutenant led the way to the company parking garage where he had left his SUV.

Parish grabbed the handle to the back door. "I'll sit here."

Blayze turned to her. By rights she should sit in front. Noting the determined lift to her chin he opened the door for her and got in beside the lieutenant.

After leaving the parking lot and managing the onramp to the 705 spur to I-5, Sarkis announced, "I have the scientists going over Moseley's place today."

"Did something happen?"

The lieutenant shot him a sideways glance. "The last time they were there we figured he left then something happened to him. However, with what I know now it seems more likely he left intentionally, which changes what we look for."

"Have you learned any more about what happened to Manke?"

"We're still hunting for a murder sight."

"Obviously you checked the storage unit and his apartment."

The lieutenant huffed, "Nothing in the storage unit."

Blayze frowned. "Nothing?"

"Right, nothing." Sarkis pronounced the word as if it was a communicable disease. "Don't you think that's a little strange?"

Blayze waited figuring there was more.

"It may have been rented purely for the purpose of having the body picked up there."

"But then Manke couldn't have rented it."

"Right." Sarkis sounded triumphant.

Blayze wasn't amenable to falling in the lieutenant's conversational trap. He watched the landscape sliding by as they left the City of Tacoma, traveling through the military base and on to the state's capital. He recalled the conversation with Doris Possum. "I had a visit yesterday from Moseley's administrative assistant."

"That bundle of sunshine that stands guard over his office?"

"You've met her." Blayze laughed.

"If you could call it that." Sarkis shot him a scowl. "She figured she could forbid the police entrance to his office."

Blayze grinned. "Was she successful?"

The lieutenant gave him an admonishing glance. "What did she want from you?"

Blayze considered. "Make sure Moseley wasn't in trouble, I guess. Parish and I compared notes. We think she may still have contact with him."

The lieutenant became quiet navigating the interchange taking them off I-5 onto the highway heading west. Once accomplished, he asked, "Were they having an affair?"

Parish spoke up from the rear. "I don't think so, but the person I spoke with thought perhaps Mr. Moseley had given Doris the impression that was a future possibility."

"Is that right?" Sarkis sounded like he had the chicken by the neck. "I might have a chat with her."

Blayze contemplated his encounter with Doris. She struck him as obsessive regarding things within her private domain. She would be possessive of information, objects, people, i.e. Ian Moseley. Control would be a big issue for her, but Blayze failed to see what would give her any control over Moseley. Logically control would flow in the opposite direction, him over her.

The three lapsed into silence traveling Highway 101 briefly then Washington 8. Western Washington's unusually dry summer left the normally lush green landscape parched and brown in places. Some of the deciduous trees already showed signs of changing to fall colors.

Signs for Ocean Shores began to appear as they reached Hoquiam. The lieutenant addressed Parish. "Where would we expect to find Moseley?"

"We first saw him at a large restaurant in the middle of town. Later we saw him near one of the strip malls."

"It'll be close to lunch when we get there." The lieutenant turned to Blayze. "Think we ought to begin with something to eat?"

Blayze shrugged. He certainly wasn't up for missing a meal.

As they headed into Ocean Shores, Parish said, "Stay on this street. There," she pointed over his shoulder at the large restaurant on their left.

Again the parking lot was moderately full. He swung the SUV into the lot and they got out of the truck where they stood for a moment listening to the ocean. The roar of the rolling waters had struck Blayze with amazement the first time he ever saw the ocean.

❦

Glancing around as they entered the restaurant Parish recognized no one. She sighed. It was early yet.

When the hostess came to seat them, Lieutenant Sarkis indicated the area he preferred, a booth close to the windows with a reasonable view of the rest of the restaurant. He sat beside Parish with Blayze across from them.

Opening his menu, he turned to Parish. "Recognize anyone?"

She shook her head. "What are you going to do if he shows up?"

"I haven't figured that out yet."

Parish frowned. Flying by the seat of her pants didn't appeal to her. Watching people enter and leave she realized when she came with Midge they were in danger of being recognized. Little danger existed that either Mr. Moseley or Bobbi would know the lieutenant or Blayze.

The waitress arrived to take their orders. The men chose burgers with all the trimmings and Parish a BLT with salad.

As the noon hour approached the restaurant became busier. Retreating to silence the three perused the newly arrived. Occasionally Parish gazed out the window at a small set of shops across the side street and checked out cars in the parking lot.

The silence deepened once they received their orders. As time moved on the possibility one of the missing could arrive and someone would need to address the issue hovered. Parish figured that didn't include her. Her responsibility was identification which kept her alert to those inside the restaurant and out.

She noticed a white Prius, reminding her of the one Bobbi had driven previously. It left the strip mall across the street and entered the restaurant parking lot. Paying close attention she noted the driver had the red tinted hair she had seen on Bobbi.

Pointing to the car as it parked facing the window beside them, Parish alerted the lieutenant. As the driver got out, she declared, "That's Bobbi Bennett."

"Why don't you move over and sit by Pashasia?" The lieutenant stood in the aisle allowing Parish to move.

He sat on the edge of the booth keeping his eyes on the Bobbi person as she entered the restaurant and looked around in search of someone. Spotting an individual farther along from where they sat, she waved then headed that direction. Just as she reached their booth, the lieutenant stood blocking her path. "Why don't you join us?" He indicated the spot Parish had vacated.

Surprise then indignation flickered across her face. Before she could move the lieutenant flipped open his ID, still indicating the spot next to his. Surprise became fear and indignation turned to calculation. However she acquiesced and moved into the booth.

"What do you want from me?" she grumbled, her lips forming a pout.

"Just a few answers." Lieutenant Sarkis peered at her over his glasses.

Her dark-eyed gaze moved from Parish to Blayze then back to Parish where it remained a moment.

Parish figured she must look familiar.

"You're Bobbi Bennett?" the lieutenant verified.

A protest rose to her lips, but she paused then nodded. "Did my husband send you?"

The lieutenant ignored her question, asking one of his own. "Have you seen Ian Moseley?"

She opened her mouth a couple times without saying anything then hedged. "Not for a while."

"When was the last?"

Staring over Parish's head she calculated. "Last Saturday, I think."

The lieutenant glanced at Parish who nodded. "Where?"

Bobbi sneered. "Here."

"You haven't seen him since?"

She shook her head.

"Do you know what name he's using or where he's staying?"

"I think he was staying at the Canterbury Inn. We saw him there a couple times in the dining room, but I don't know any name other than his own."

"Have you any idea what he's doing in Ocean Shores?"

"The way he talked just on vacation. But I don't think he knew who I was." She paused then asked, "Are you going to tell my husband?"

"You think I shouldn't?"

"I'm not breaking the law." She appeared anxious.

The lieutenant did the maybe/maybe not motion with his hand. She frowned opening her mouth to protest but he made a stop motion. "I told your husband as long as you're not doing something illegal what you're doing is not police business. However, if I find you're involved in my investigation I'll haul you in."

Two little lines appeared between her eyes. Parish figured she didn't know whether to be pleased or upset. Did she even know what his investigation was?

Lieutenant Sarkis rose allowing her to leave the booth. She cast an apprehensive parting glance at him as if considering he might follow her.

"Well, what do you think?" the lieutenant addressed his companions. "Should I take her serious?"

"As far as it goes what she said is straight with what we saw on Saturday."

"You believe Moseley didn't recognize her?"

"I don't know about that. To my knowledge he wouldn't have seen enough of her at Ridinghood to know who she is, but she has other connections there that might have given him opportunities to know her." Parish sighed. "I don't think her disguise is so good someone who really knows her would be fooled. We weren't."

Blayze spoke up, "Would seeing her on Saturday have inspired Moseley to leave town?"

Lieutenant Sarkis frowned but didn't respond. After a time he asked, "Could you two manage another cup of coffee while I take a drive to confer with the local police?"

Blayze shrugged and Parish smiled.

When the lieutenant rose to leave Parish moved to take his place in the booth across from Blayze.

The waitress came by with the coffee pot and refilled their cups. They lapsed into silence gazing out the window at the activity in the parking lot and the shops across the street. Suddenly Parish noticed a shocked expression on Blayze's face. She examined the scene beyond the window looking for a cause.

At the curb where Bobbi's car had sat was a light green Prius from which two women were emerging. One was petite and blonde with a laughing face. The other was taller, with long curling dark hair and, although she too smiled, her expression betrayed a trace of melancholy. Blayze's gaze had fastened on them, following as they headed for the entrance to the restaurant.

The hostess brought them down the aisle where Parish and Blayze sat. Glancing at him she realized he still followed their progress but with an expression of mistrust. She watched his face as the trio paused near their table and the waitress arranged menus on the booth at an angle across from them. She figured his eyes had met those of the dark-haired woman before he looked away with a perplexed frown.

"Someone you know?" Parish ventured.

"Apparently not," he mumbled with a trace of bewilderment.

Parish cocked her head, asking her question with her eyes.

He ran his hand through his hair. "Either she doesn't recognize me or she's not who I think she is."

≋

Blayze stared at the Prius from which the two women emerged. He could swear she didn't recognize him . . . at all. He couldn't believe it. No way, it was impossible.

She looked good, as if nothing had happened, except for seeming more reserved than before. He hadn't seen her conscious since before the accident, still . . . he had gone to visit while she was in the hospital. But then she wouldn't know that. She hadn't acted as if she was trying to avoid seeing or speaking to him. She had looked straight at him without recognition, almost as if she thought he was flirting with her.

He turned back to Parish who watched him as if he was in danger of crumbling into a disjointed pile of body parts. He gave her a weak smile, shaking his head. "A strange coincidence, I guess." He noted the black SUV returning. "Sarkis is back."

They rose and after paying their check returned to the truck.

"I didn't get much out of that. Found out the airport in Ocean Shores is probably too small to accommodate Moseley, although he could possibly get a charter out of the one in Hoquiam."

"I think the corporation keeps a small jet at the airport in Olympia," Parish informed him.

"Is that right?" He eyed her. "How does one get access to that?"

She lifted her shoulders. "Maybe I can find out."

He nodded. "Do that." He sighed. "Although if he's trying to escape that might be self-defeating." He went on. "I managed to get a picture of Moseley at your office and gave that to the police here. They'll keep on the lookout for him, although he may be gone already."

"Midge took a picture of Bobbi and the man I thought was him on her phone while we were here."

Sarkis frowned. "Why didn't you tell me before?"

She shot him a frustrated look. "You never asked what he looked like."

"Do you have that with you?"

"On my phone." She took her phone from her handbag and after working with it a few moments gave it to the lieutenant.

He stared at it from several angles. "Not a great picture. I'm not sure this would help the police here." He returned the phone and unlocked the truck.

Blayze considered had he been in Moseley's shoes what he might have done to escape the area. It hardly seemed practical to use the company jet. "Wouldn't he be better off heading to Portland? Take a flight there to wherever he intended to go."

Sarkis acknowledged his comment with a nod. "I'm just trying to figure out what he's doing in Ocean Shores."

"Waiting for things to cool down," Parish suggested.

"No one was looking for him to begin with since no one figured he was disappearing."

"True," Blayze said, "but you could still trace his escape. You'd know when he left."

"We've done that." The lieutenant grimaced. "So did that detective Ridinghood had on him."

Blayze refrained from pointing out the obvious.

"I think you two should go shopping. See what you can find." Sarkis turned to glance at Parish in the backseat.

She laughed. "Will the county foot the bill for whatever we find?"

The lieutenant scowled at her. "Only if it's Moseley." He turned to Blayze. "I'll see what I can find out at the Canterbury Inn."

"Shopping is better on the other street," Parish informed him.

"I'll run you over. The Canterbury is close there also." Lieutenant Sarkis swung the SUV out of the parking lot continued a couple blocks, made a right turn, and dropped Blayze and Parish off at the corner.

Blayze turned to her. "Are you okay with this?"

She smiled. "I can always go shopping." After a pause she asked, "Do you think this is a waste of time."

He lifted his shoulders. "We have to waste time anyway."

For the next hour they wandered through the shops, hardware, t-shirt, souvenirs, a small grocery, a rather sparsely furnished coffee shop with various gift items for sale. They found a book store and a ladies' clothing store in addition to a shop selling kites and renting bicycles. Blayze bought an Ocean Shores sweatshirt. Parish also bought one for Xavier. The afternoon became hot and muggy. The ocean had failed to bring the breezes along with it.

"How will the lieutenant find us?" Parish asked when they had completed perusing that group of stores.

Blayze glanced at the time on his phone. "I have his number. I'll give him a call."

A few minutes later the lieutenant's SUV pulled up next to them. Once they were settled he turned to ask Parish, "Did you see anything interesting?"

"If you mean people," she replied, "no."

"How did you come out?" Blayze asked.

"With what I had for description I think I verified he had been staying there. A couple guests fit the time frame and more or less the description. I have both names but they have checked out since."

"But neither name was Moseley?" Blayze verified.

"I wouldn't have expected it to be."

"Do you think he has a full set of identification?" Parish asked.

"I imagine he has at least a driver's license and credit card. If he wants to fly commercial or internationally he's going to need more than that." After a pause, the lieutenant declared an ah-ha, "Maybe that's why he's hanging out in Ocean Shores . . . waiting for ID's to be made up."

"Is it that easy to get fake IDs?"

"It's easier than it ought to be," Sarkis huffed. "But fake or not it still takes time to get a passport."

◆CHAPTER SEVENTEEN◆

Returning from Ocean Shores the lieutenant had stopped at Bowerman Airfield in Hoquiam to check the possibility Moseley chartered a plane from there. Apparently that would not have been a problem but neither did it appear to have taken place. Officials at the field verified all the departing flights during the previous six weeks. A plane for Moseley was not among them.

Although the lack of progress and evident failure of the trip had not discouraged the lieutenant, he remained dissatisfied with his lack of information.

As soon as Blayze had arrived back in his hotel he made a phone call. "What's with Sylvia?"

Alarm sounded in his mother's voice. "What do you mean?"

"Do you know where she is?"

"She asked us not to contact her." His mother sighed. "She comes to visit now and then."

"Could she be here?"

"Where is here?"

"Western Washington . . . state." He had learned to anyone out of the area Washington meant D.C.

"Possibly, although I don't know why she would."

"I'll swear I saw her today. She looked at me as if she had never seen me before and had no idea who I was."

"Unfortunately that's possible." His mother sighed. "According to her doctors varying levels of memory loss is usual with severe brain injuries. Apparently she has significant blanks in hers, but they said some of that may return in time. She doesn't have complete loss of memory, just things here and there. She knows who she is and remembers most of the past, but some things are missing. It's kind of random." His mother paused as if uncertain about continuing. "Blayze, she has a completely different personality. Also common with that kind of injury."

"What do you mean completely different?" That sounded suspicious.

"She's no longer outgoing or aggressive or doing such extreme things. She's much quieter, more reserved."

That was hard to imagine. Sylvia was the ultimate, take charge, tell everyone what to do, ridicule if necessary to get what she wanted. She rarely let someone finish a sentence and always lived on the edge.

"She doesn't want anyone to contact her," his mother repeated. "She wants to get her head straight, she said, before she resumes old relationships. She's also changed her name."

"To what?"

"Elysia Sylvan. She's made it legal."

"Really," Blayze snorted sarcastically. "Do you think she's okay up here?"

"Was she alone?"

"No, she was with another woman."

"I think she's okay. Just let her be for the time being."

Blayze had no problem with that. Sylvia had driven home with lethal force her caustic remarks and stinging mockery. Her sarcastic jeers and perpetual efforts to maintain her superiority regardless of how emotionally bloody she left her victims, himself included, delivered him from any responsibility for her well being. Nonetheless, he did care about her and would not want to see her come to harm. However, that didn't appear to be a danger.

After entering Ridinghood's building and climbing the stairs Blayze stopped at Parish's office on the way to his.

She looked up from her computer.

"What kind of car does Moseley drive?" He noted her yellow sweater emphasized the blue of her eyes.

"A little Mercedes sports car with the license place 'SIRIAN'." Her expression questioned his interest.

"Does the lieutenant know that?"

She lifted her shoulders. "I haven't told him, but I assume he'd find that out for himself."

Blayze passed her a forced grin then continued to his area where the first thing he did was check his email. He found one from Mr. Hornby with the names of the owners of the investment accounts. He stared at them for a time trying to make sense out of them.

He considered his own investment accounts. Each had a bank account attached from which he could make withdrawals. In addition another bank account was attached to each allowing the investment firm a clearing account for use in buying and selling.

Each of the extra accounts Mr. Hornby identified had returned an amount of money to the LLC. Did each of them also send money to another account for the owner? Could this be the end of the line for the traveling money?

He probably needed to consult Mr. Hornby again. Before doing that, however, he figured it would be worth his while to decipher the account names. He had the feeling clues hid there.

He went to work immediately on the ownership of the two additional accounts to which the LLC sent money. One amount was fairly substantial, the other much smaller. He had the ACH transaction information which provided a code identifying, after a fashion, where the funds were being sent. One of the names was the same as the LLC. For the other he searched the internet for identification but came up empty. Contemplating the possible purpose of these he considered the likelihood they were phony names for private individual accounts.

If Moseley was using the traveling money for short term investments then returning the original capital to the company was this what those transactions would look like? He could move it through a series of locations to stop anyone from following the money. All that would make sense except for one thing. There were too many accounts. However, the big question remained, did the accounts belong to Ridinghood? A question he still couldn't answer.

His superior had agreed to use his position to obtain more names. Perhaps he would locate a lead.

When Blayze's phone announced a call he figured it was Mr. Hornby. Instead he was surprised to hear his mother's voice.

"Is where you are close to Seattle?" She sounded anxious if not actually frightened.

"Relatively."

"Do you know where Harborview Hospital is?"

She had alerted his suspicion. "Not specifically, although I've heard of it."

"Sylvia is there."

"What's she doing there?" With Sylvia you never knew. She could be windsailing at Discovery Bay, mountain climbing on Rainier, betting on the horses at Emerald

Downs, or in the hospital recuperating from head injuries in a car accident. That seemed to be her latest form of living on the edge.

"The police called me. She was involved in a hit and run. They airlifted her to that place."

"Again?" Blayze sighed, thinking it figured. "What name is she using?"

"Her IDs are all in that Elysia Sylvan name."

"What do you want me to do?" It wasn't the "no love lost" between he and Sylvia. He did care for her but generally that was a no win situation. He had reconciled himself to maintaining his distance.

"Go see her. If she needs help . . ." His mother paused. "Let me know. We can come up there."

"Okay." Blayze sighed. "I'll see what I can do."

Blayze put the phone down, Sylvia back in trouble again. So much for her personality change.

⚉

As soon as he set down the phone, Mr. Hornby called.

"I emailed you the information you wanted."

Blayze thanked him then informed him he had an emergency which may keep him away from his work for the day.

Figuring he ought to inform Parish he packed the paperwork into his briefcase then headed for her office. Her concentration was focused on her monitor when he entered. "I have an emergency of sorts to deal with today," he informed her. "You can text me if something important comes up." He gave her his phone number. "By the way, where's Harborview Hospital?"

She frowned. "In Seattle, just east of downtown, up the hill."

"Okay, thanks."

He could tell by the look on her face she had a raft of questions. The trouble was even if he wanted to answer them he couldn't. He probably had the same questions.

Having verified Harborview's general location, he figured he could get the car's GPS to direct him. Mid-morning by now the notorious congested Seattle traffic had eased allowing him to make the drive in reasonable time. Although a challenge, he managed to find parking and make his way to information where they gave him Sylvia's room number.

When he reached her floor, being traditional visiting hours, people roamed the corridor. Sylvia, the woman with long curling dark hair, shared a double room with a fair haired woman possessing head and arm bandages. Sylvia had some facial bruises including a small metal tent over her nose. Otherwise from outward appearances she fared better than her roommate.

She stared at Blayze as if thinking she ought to recognize him but couldn't put the name to the face.

"Are you Blayze?" her roommate asked.

He turned to her in surprise. "That's right."

"I'm Janice Colton. Elysia has been staying with me. I talked to her mother."

"Were you in the accident too?"

"It wasn't an accident."

Blayze stared at her. He turned to Sylvia or Elysia as she called herself. "Mom wanted me to check on you. She would come here if you wanted or needed her."

She frowned. "What's your name?"

171

A flash of anger grabbed him, but he recalled his mother saying she may not know him. "Blayze Pashasia." He figured he could play the game too. "What happened in this . . . non-accident?"

"We were in the bar at the Shilo Inn. When we came out some car came running right at us." Sylvia's gaze held bewildered disbelief.

"What kind of car?"

"A big burgundy Chevrolet," Janice put in. "I saw the Chevy symbol on the grill."

Blayze frowned at her. "You think it came at you on purpose?"

Both Janice and Sylvia nodded.

"Did you see the driver?"

Sylvia shook her head. "It shocked me to see it coming right at us."

He grimaced. "How long are they keeping you here?"

She lifted her shoulders. "They're still running tests. Plus I have a couple leg fractures."

"Tests for what?"

"Internal injuries."

Blayze realized Sylvia was sharing as little information as possible, unusual for the woman he knew. Generally she would gather as much attention as possible by giving blow by blow reports. He glanced at her roommate.

"They treated her for shock to begin, plus the fractures and a broken nose." Janice answered his unasked question.

He didn't fancy giving the ladies the third degree but he had a lot of questions and once he called his mother back she would have even more. "How about you?" he directed his attention to Janice.

"I have a broken shoulder and some cuts on my head, but I think I'm going home today." She touched the bandages on her head. "I'll keep tabs on Elysia."

"What should I tell my mother?"

"They're keeping me here for a while longer. I'll let her know when I'm getting out."

Blayze recalled his mother's comment "she comes to visit now and then". Although tempted to throw the comment up to her, he refrained. It wouldn't help anything. Addressing both women, he asked, "Have you any idea why someone would want to take you out?"

Shaking heads answered his question.

"When did this happen?"

"I lose track of time in the hospital." Sylvia consulted the opposite wall. "The night before last."

"Was there a police report?"

Sylvia glanced at her roommate as if she didn't know.

"Yes, there was."

"With the Ocean Shores police?"

Janice nodded.

◆CHAPTER EIGHTEEN◆

P arish looked up as Slate Ridinghood entered her office. "Good morning," she greeted him, wondering what bought him up from the executive suite.

He looked as if he had just stepped off the cover of *Money* magazine. "How is your auditor coming?"

"He's still working on those accounts we asked about. He believes if we find out where that money goes and why it may solve the auditing problems and some others as well."

"You're referring to Moseley's disappearance?"

Parish nodded watching Slate's expressions and wondering how he felt about it.

"You think he's mixed up with that money?"

"We know he's mixed up with it. The question is whether that's appropriate or not."

Slate looked as if he considered asking another question but changed his mind. "Keep me informed." He left.

Parish's thoughts returned to the restaurant the day before and the woman who elicited Blayze's shocked expression. Although he dismissed it as mistaken identity she didn't quite believe him. The woman must be a failed relationship since she had refused to recognize his presence. However, he acted as if she should have greeted him. Parish also wondered what his emergency was. Did it have to do with that woman?

She returned to her computer and concentration on her project. Looking up at one point she noticed Lieutenant Sarkis pass by. She smiled figuring he intended to hound Blayze again. However, Blayze was out of the office. Consequently in just a couple minutes the lieutenant returned.

He bobbed his head in greeting and parked on the chair in front of her desk.

"Can I help you?" He looked as if he had questions but didn't know where to begin.

"I wish." He sighed. "Where's your auditor?"

"He had an emergency."

"I got two names of people staying at the Canterbury who resemble that photograph. Both had checked out."

Something told her his plans were frustrated. Parish waited for him to continue.

"I've done everything I can to trace those two guys. I need to know which of them is Moseley. I figure if one of the names is phony the other wouldn't be. Eliminating the genuine I'd discover the name Moseley was using."

"That didn't work?"

"Hell, no." The lieutenant swept a lock of his hair off his forehead. "Sorry, I mean, no it didn't. As far as I can get both of them disappeared off the face of the earth. Now that don't make any sense."

Parish considered his predicament.

He went on. "I'm not hot to stir up trouble for some innocent guy who happened to be staying in the same hotel as Moseley."

"And you can't determine which of the names is an actual person with a real identity?"

The lieutenant snorted. "Have you any idea how many Michael Johnsons or Richard Matthews are in Washington State alone? Even if I eliminate all those the wrong age I still have too many."

"There must be some way to figure it out."

"If you get an idea, let me know." He rose. "If you see your auditor tell him I want to talk to him."

As soon as Lieutenant Sarkis left Parish's phone notified her of a text message. It was from Annabelle Elliott with the date of the Spokane conference.

At noon Parish took the stairs to the cafeteria. After selecting soup and a roll then looking for a table she noticed Midge sitting in the shadow of the elaborately framed windows overlooking the port. "May I join you?"

"Sure." Midge grinned at her. "You can update me on your trip."

Parish sighed. She didn't know if she had anything to tell her.

"Did you see Bobbi or Mr. Moseley?"

"Bobbi. She came to that restaurant again. The lieutenant forced her to sit down with us and answer questions. She verified Mr. Moseley was staying at the Shilo Inn. She had seen him there in the restaurant a few times. However, he seems to have disappeared again."

Midge cocked her head peering at her. "I'll bet he recognized Bobbi and was trying to avoid her."

"She seemed apprehensive the lieutenant would contact her husband. Initially she thought that was why he stopped her. He told her she was okay as long as she wasn't involved with Moseley."

"Could she be involved with him?"

Parish couldn't imagine Mr. Moseley working on something with Bobbi so how then would she be involved? "What do you think?"

Midge shook her head. "There are so many parallels between them it makes one suspicious."

"I got a message from Annabelle this morning. She gave me the dates of that conference in Spokane." Parish gave the dates to Midge, then she described the trip to Ocean Shores, what they found out and what they were unable to accomplish. "The lieutenant is frustrated regarding the names he got at the Shilo Inn. He's been unable to discover which of them is Mr. Moseley. Both names are too common."

"What were the names?"

Parish worked on recalling. "Michael and Richard, Johnson and Matthews."

Midge frowned at her. "I might look up Mr. Moseley's full name. Often when people change names they use their own initials."

"I'm sure Lieutenant Sarkis would be grateful."

"I can't promise it'll work. He may have been smarter than that."

Parish scoffed. "You think Mr. Moseley is smart?"

"Intellectually intelligent, not wise. Wise people appear much smarter than people who just have a high IQ."

Parish scowled expressing her skepticism.

"You disagree?" Midge grinned at her. "Mr. Moseley couldn't have made it to where he was in the company if he didn't have some positive qualities."

"I suppose, but it's hard to imagine what they are."

"I think he's basically intelligent, and crafty, too. He exudes that kind of self-confidence that makes people listen to him. He thinks he's something special even if no one else does which makes people take notice and give him credit, often for qualities he doesn't have," Midge put her finger in the air, "but thinks he has."

"I'm beginning to think there are a lot of people like that."

By early afternoon Blayze had made it back to Ridinghood, at least physically. Janice's disbelief their hit and run was an accident kept churning in his head. Sylvia was a drama queen. Whatever she thought had little credibility. However, her friend Janice seemed more level headed. Would it do any good to contact the Ocean Shores police? He figured if nothing else it would ease his mind. On the computer he looked up the means to contact them.

When he placed the call the receptionist referred him to one of the officers to whom he explained his questions.

"Their account appears accurate. It would have been difficult where they were found to get hit accidentally. One wouldn't drive a car through there fast enough nor would a speeding car likely go through there at all."

"Have you found who did it? Are you trying to?" Blayze didn't want to discount the police, but he didn't feel he could presume they were actively pursuing the driver.

"We're tackling it from the information they gave us. It's difficult. The driver had time to be completely out of the area before we were notified. The hotel called the ambulance first. They got hold of us once they realized the situation." The officer sounded defensive.

"They told you they thought the car was a burgundy Chevrolet?"

"Right. We've checked all the cars in the area matching that description, plus we've checked out ones in that color which could have been mistaken for a Chevrolet. Nothing so far."

"Have you any reason to think someone had it in for them?"

"We've questioned them and people who knew them. Rather, that knew Janice Colton. No one seems to know the other woman, Elysia Sylvan. Apparently she's here visiting from California. Although Colton has property here neither is particularly acquainted in Ocean Shores." The officer sighed. "The case remains open and will until we find out what happened, but so far we've gotten nowhere."

Blayze left his phone number, asking that they contact him if they learned anything. While he was at it he decided to call his mother.

As soon as she heard his voice she asked, "Did you see her?"

"She seems okay, at least according to the description you gave me."

"What do you mean by that?" she sounded alarmed again.

"What do you mean by is she okay?" Blayze grumped. "She acts like she has no idea who I am. It's difficult believing she remembers everything else and not me. That wouldn't make her okay in my book. Physically, she has a broken nose, some facial bruises, and a couple leg fractures. They're still doing tests to make sure there are no internal injuries. Her friend, Janice, who was with her, says she will keep watch on Sylvia and let you know when she's able to get out of the hospital."

"Do you know what happened?"

Blayze hesitated. He figured to explain the situation would worry his mother keeping her anxious when she could do little about it. On the other hand he realized she would want to know and feel betrayed if he kept things from her. "It wasn't an accident, mom." He explained what he had been told, informing her the police were working on it.

"Is she safe?" Anxiety sounded in her voice.

"Right now she's in the hospital. That's as safe a place to be as anywhere. I might suggest she recuperate in California with you."

As soon as Blayze ended his call Lieutenant Sarkis barged into his space. "You finally made it to work."

Blayze frowned at him. "When exactly did the County Sheriff's Department take over the IRS?"

The lieutenant opened his mouth, presumably with a retort, but closed it again. "I'm trying to figure out which of my two names could be Ian Moseley."

Leaning back in his chair, Blayze asked, "What two names?"

Sarkis pushed the chair from the corner to Blayze's desk. He took out his notepad and consulted it. "Michael Johnson and Richard Matthews."

Blayze frowned as he consulted his computer. "Michael Johnson?"

The lieutenant peered over his spectacles. "That name mean something to you?"

Blayze hedged. "It could. I've been chasing the ownership of a couple of bank accounts. One of them belongs to an M. I. J. and Company LLC."

Sarkis squinted at Blayze a moment then began scribbling on his notepad.

"If you find out any more about Michael Johnson, will you let me know?" Blayze asked.

Sarkis raised his eyebrows. "And you the same?"

Blayze nodded.

The lieutenant returned the chair to the corner and left with a decidedly preoccupied expression.

When he had gone Blayze leaned back and considered. If M.I.J. was Ian Moseley, alias Michael Johnson, who owned the other account? Was there a relationship between those accounts? It was time to bother Mr. Hornby again.

"I need the account transactions for RC Returns." Blayze said when his superior answered.

"Have you found something?"

"I may be getting closer to an actual person. However, I have too many accounts. I have to figure out if they're related."

"Do you have a name for the person you're getting close to?"

"Ian Moseley, the missing CEO of Ridinghood Corporation."

◆CHAPTER NINETEEN◆

Parish was considering Blayze's emergency when he stopped at the entrance to her office. "Did you resolve your crisis?" she asked as he paused in her doorway.

The waves in his hair fell over his forehead as he peered at her from beneath his dark brows. He grimaced. "No, in fact, it appears the Devil's at the door. Ocean Shores seems a dangerous place."

Skepticism narrowed Parish's eyes. She wasn't ready to buy that.

He leaned his shoulder against her door jam. "How about two women injured in a hit and run right in front of that Shilo Inn."

"On the street?" People were stupid sometimes, walking out in front of traffic especially when using the phone. That could happen anywhere including Ocean Shores.

"No, under the marquee by the front doors." Blayze cocked his head. "And it wasn't an accident."

Studying his solemn expression she noted the anger in his pale eyes. "You know the people involved?"

"The two women?" He nodded.

She took wild guess. "They came in the restaurant while we waited for the lieutenant?"

"Right, my sister and her friend."

"Your sister!" Parish tried to reconcile that with what she had seen of their encounter. "But . . ."

"You think IRS agents don't have sisters?"

Parish laughed shaking her head. "She looked like she didn't know who you are."

"Exactly." He widened his eyes. "Strange, huh?"

"You're teasing me." Parish was accustomed to people leading her on with strange stories testing her credibility. Her tendency to literalism made her a perfect stooge.

"I am not," Blayze declared. "That was my sister who looked like she didn't know me and according to my mother, she doesn't know me . . . anymore." Blayze moved to the chair in front of her desk, unbuttoning the jacket to his suit. "My mother called yesterday said my sister and her friend were in the hospital in Seattle. So I went to see them."

"And she didn't know you?"

"Right. She was in a bad car accident a couple years ago, head injuries, brain damage. According to my mother she remembers most things but not all. I'm one of those things she doesn't remember."

Parish was torn between laughing at the thought his sister might not want to admit being related to the IRS and utter disbelief. Repressing a smile she shook her head. "That's incredible."

He frowned as if he reading her mind. "What's more incredible, both those women believe the car who hit them did it on purpose."

"Do they live in Ocean Shores?"

"No. I'm not sure where my sister lives right now. The other woman, Janice, lives in Seattle."

"So there's no reason someone there should look to injure them?"

Blayze made a face. "I called Ocean Shores' police. They confirmed an intentional hit and run, but they haven't figure out who did it or why."

Parish could see Blayze's concern, although he also appeared frustrated and angry. "Are you going to mention it to Lieutenant Sarkis? He might be able to help. He may know people in other places."

Blayze lifted his shoulders and changed the subject. "I suspect that traveling money hooks to Ian Moseley."

"Was he embezzling?"

"Not strictly speaking. Probably investing it and not passing on the income. Undoubtedly illegal, especially relative to Ridinghood."

"Is that why he disappeared?"

"I don't think so." Blayze drew his eyebrows together. "I've traced those transactions back quite a few years. As long as no one knew about it there was no danger, no reason for him to disappear. It might relate to his disappearance but I don't think it's the cause."

"Then why did he leave?"

Blayze sighed. "I don't know. Finding that extra account owner may give me a clue." He rose. "And to that end I'd better go see what I can find."

In order to concentrate on her work Parish put Blayze's predicament out of her mind. However, it didn't stay there long.

Mid-morning Midge appeared in her doorway with a cup of coffee. She hoisted her cup. "Shall I bring you one?"

"That would be great."

Midge disappeared for five minutes returning with coffee for Parish, which she placed on her desk then took the chair in front. "I have Mr. Moseley's full name. Ian James Moseley. Does that help?"

"I'll have to check with the lieutenant or Blayze."

"I also checked that conference you gave me dates for. Alan Bernstein, Taylor Washington, and Tim Hogan attended."

"So which of them would interest Bobbi Bennett?"

Midge peered at Parish with a can't-you-guess expression. Parish shook her head.

"Why, all of them of course."

"That doesn't help," Parish huffed.

"I realize that, but you asked." She leaned back in her chair. "Maybe we should work the elimination method."

"Who would you eliminate?" Parish wasn't sure she could eliminate any of them.

"Taylor Washington."

Parish scowled at her.

"He's a good ten years younger and newly married which would probably only fuel her interest," Midge quipped with a mischievous grin. "He's awfully good looking."

Parish rolled her eyes. "Anyone else?"

"Well Tim Hogan appears a little frumpy for Bobbi's taste."

"So we figure it's Alan Bernstein, unless it wasn't someone from Ridinghood?"

Midge shrugged her eyebrows.

❧

Blayze considered whether informing Lieutenant Sarkis of his sister's situation would help. It probably wouldn't hurt although he had serious doubts it would accomplish anything either.

It seemed highly likely the lieutenant's Michael Johnson was Ian Moseley, alias M. I. J. but as he explained to Parish, he couldn't see that being a reason to disappear. How precipitate had Moseley's departure been? Could he find out? If the decision had been sudden what triggered it would be worth investigating. From all he had heard and seen at Ridinghood no one was aware of Moseley's activity, creating no cause for vanishing. He wondered if the lieutenant had other information.

It also occurred to him the administrative assistant may know how quickly Moseley made the decision. Considering what Parish had said about her, he wasn't sure he had seen himself in danger of being screamed at while she was in his office. However, she had definitely been in pursuit of information and displeased with his response. Would Tim Hogan, who occupied the office adjacent to Moseley have any idea? Blayze would have greater reason for visiting the Chief Financial Officer than the administrative assistant to the missing CEO.

Figuring he could use a cup of coffee he took the elevator to the third floor and the break room then to the main floor for a sojourn into the executive suite. Doris Possum eyed him like the snake poised for a strike. He allowed his gaze to pass over her without recognition as he stopped to speak to the woman at the desk outside Tim Hogan's office.

"Yes, he's in. I'll let him know you're here."

In a moment Tim Hogan appeared at the door and invited him into his quietly organized space. "What can I do for you?"

Blayze accepted the cream and black striped chair he was offered as Hogan took a seat behind his desk. "I have a couple questions regarding Ian Moseley."

An anxious expression passed over Hogan's face. "Have you found a problem?"

How much data should he pass on? His mission was acquiring information not giving it out. "That lieutenant bugs me with questions. I thought you might have some answers."

Tim Hogan frowned. "I have no idea where he's gone."

"Was he planning to go or did something happen?"

"You're asking what I think?" The man gave the impression he feared his next step would be into quicksand.

"Or know," Blayze nodded, suddenly suspicious of Hogan's concern.

Speculation flashed onto his face then disappeared. "I got the feeling he planned his departure."

"Something specific?"

"Not really, except I believe he was removing personal things from his office."

"Not business things?"

"No, no. Personal possessions."

Blayze wondered. "Like his computer?"

Astonishment flashed onto Hogan's face. "No. That belonged to the company."

"He didn't have a personal laptop here?" Blayze observed the man's confusion.

"Oh, well, he might have."

"You aren't aware his company computer is gone?"

"Gone? Really?" Hogan frowned.

"I was in his office with the lieutenant when they looked for it."

An idea lit his expression. "It might have been sent out for repair?"

Blayze hesitated, skeptical that explained the computer's absence.

"I was out there one day." Hogan beckoned toward the outer office. "Quite a while ago now, when someone with a tech company jacket was at Doris' desk. She had a big box he was arranging to take away. It could have been the computer."

"Did you ever see anything else being taken away like that?"

Hogan frowned then shook his head.

Blayze rose. "If anything occurs to you would you let me or the lieutenant know?"

"Sure thing." He bobbed his head seeming relieved to see Blayze depart.

Returning to his space he mulled over Hogan's responses. Had Moseley's computer been sent out for repairs or was Doris Possum helping him empty his office? Was she the owner of the other banking account? Perhaps gossip had it wrong. Maybe Moseley was planning to take Doris with him. Blayze smiled, screams and all.

At noon he stopped by Parish's office again. He needed to work through some things with someone and she was his best option. "You going to lunch?"

A frown crossed her face as she focused on him. She glanced at her computer. "It's time, isn't it?" She sighed. "Let me send a couple things here. I'll come by your office in a minute."

Blayze returned to his desk and checked a piece of paper that had arrived, a fax from Mr. Hornby. It regarded the RC Returns account for which the ACH transaction listed routing numbers in addition to the name RC Returns. As he considered possibilities for their significance Parish appeared at his door.

They continued to the stairs and ascended one level then made the trek to the circular stairs and up to the cafeteria. After choosing a sandwich Blayze motioned to a table for two along the ostentatious periphery of the room.

"I visited Tim Hogan this morning. I thought he might have seen Moseley moving things out of his office."

"Did he?"

"Ha! Good question. He mentioned seeing a tech person at Moseley's assistant's desk with a big box. He guessed it was the computer being sent out for repair." Blayze watched for Parish's reaction. "What do you think of that?"

"I don't think that's how computer repairs are handled." She frowned. "You think someone was actually removing his computer?"

Blayze made a forced grin. "Or something." Noting a surprised expression on Parish's face he turned to look at what she saw.

Lieutenant Sarkis stood at the entrance to the cafeteria looking as if he had followed the wrong road sign. She waved and turning again Blayze noticed the lieutenant headed their way.

❧

Lieutenant Sarkis appeared relieved to see Parish wave, making his way immediately to their table. He looked like a man with a purpose. Grabbing a chair from an adjacent table he took a seat. Parish and Blayze exchanged an apprehensive glance.

"So what's new?"

Parish smiled at him. "We thought you'd tell us."

He shook his head. "Nothing to tell."

Watching Blayze eye him suspiciously, she figured he also doubted the lieutenant's answer. "I believe that Michael Johnson name you have is the one Moseley is using."

The lieutenant gazed at him expectantly. "Are you going to tell me how you came to that conclusion?"

Parish spoke. "Midge found out Ian Moseley's middle name is James. She thinks he may have just rearranged his initials to come up with Michael Johnson."

"One name I keep running across is M.I. J. & Company," Blayze added.

"I can work with that." The lieutenant took out his little notebook and scribbled a memo.

Parish glanced at Blayze wondering if he would ask the lieutenant about his sister's accident.

He caught her eyes on him and shrugged. "Are you acquainted with the Ocean Shores police?" he asked.

The lieutenant frowned at him.

"A hit and run there injured a couple women. Could you find anything about that?"

"I might if I had a reason to." He eyed Blayze as if expecting a further explanation.

"Someone I know was involved."

Parish questioned Blayze's sidestepping which kept him from explaining about his sister.

"You think it has something to do with Ridinghood's missing persons?"

That surprised Blayze. "I wouldn't think so. Anything's possible I guess."

"Do you have names for the injured parties?"

Blayze grabbed a napkin wrote two names on it then handed it to the lieutenant who studied it a moment before putting it in his pocket. "We had another go at Moseley's house. Found some dried blood under a rug near the sofa." He shook his head at Blayze who appeared upon the point of asking a question. "We're having it tested. Don't know who it belongs to. Could be irrelevant."

"Have you figured out who rented the storage unit?"

"All I've found is who didn't rent it. Manke was dead so he couldn't have, although it's in his name. His girlfriend didn't even know he had a storage unit. She did know about the moving company storage." After a pause Lieutenant Sarkis said. "I'd like you two to do something for me."

Suspicion instantly leaped onto Blayze's face. Parish folded her hands and waited. She felt like Blayze looked.

"I thought if you two went there and rented a storage unit you could find out how the system works. Could someone actually obtain a unit without anyone ever seeing that person? You might chat with them, get more information that I can. They instantly suspect me of being the police."

Blayze snorted. "People instantly suspect me of being the IRS."

"Well the last I knew the IRS wasn't arresting murderers," the lieutenant huffed.

"Do you want us to actually rent a unit?" Parish asked.

"That would work best. Go through the whole process. You can be aware of the gossip a body was found in a trunk there. Be chatty."

Parish laughed, wondering how well the lieutenant knew Blayze if he expected him to be chatty.

Suddenly the lieutenant changed the subject addressing Parish. "Did you check on that airfield in Olympia?"

"I checked on the company jet. It's made a number of trips to California, but the best I can determine none of those would have included or even made it possible for Mr. Moseley to go. The airfield is like the one in Hoquiam, mostly charters and small private planes."

The lieutenant sighed gazing out the window near them. "For some reason I don't think he's left the country . . .yet." He shot a glance at Blayze. "Have you located your money?"

"Getting closer, but it doesn't appear to have left the country . . . yet."

"I think I'll send a detachment to Ocean Shores and the surrounding area. See if they can locate Moseley." He rose. "Let me know what you get out of those people at the storage units."

When the lieutenant had gone, Blayze turned to Parish. "I don't mind assisting the police, but I resent being treated as if they pay my wages."

"He is kind of bossy." Parish sighed. "Are you going to check out that storage unit?"

"What do you think? Do you want to do that?"

Parish couldn't say she wanted to do that. However, previously she had decided to cooperate if she wanted to protect the company and keep her job. Less apprehensive of accompanying Blayze since he seemed to stick strictly to business and treat her with respect she lifted her shoulders. "I suppose we could. Do we have an address?"

"I'll get one. Will you come with me or shall I come with you?"

"My car is in the parking garage."

Rising they headed for the stairs, dropping off their dishes at the busing station. Parish still wondered why Blayze wouldn't tell the lieutenant the woman in the hit and run was his sister. His whole attitude puzzled her. It wasn't that she thought IRS agents didn't have sisters. What she found difficult was imagining a sister having Blayze for a brother.

◈CHAPTER TWENTY◈

L ater in the afternoon Blayze called Parish to let her know he had an address for the storage unit. They agreed to leave directly from work at 5:00. The lieutenant failed to reckon that neither she nor Blayze were that chatty. Intimidated seeking information pretending to be something they weren't, Parish hoped Blayze would do the questioning. She had no problem with research and doubted he would either. However, actually interrogating people gave her empathy for Moses arguing with God by the burning bush.

Another concern, how much pretending was expected of them, a matter she addressed the moment she met Blayze.

He grimaced. "I expect Sarkis thinks we should pose as a couple. Anything else might be suspicious."

"Not that we won't be suspicious anyway." She shot him an anxious glance.

Blayze scrutinized her with his pale eyes, his brows drawn together. "Will this be a problem for you?"

She took a deep breath, meeting his eyes. "You'll do the talking?"

He nodded, grinning. "If you'll do the gossipy chatty thing."

They took the stairs to the main floor then proceeded to the parking garage and Parish's car.

"Where are we going?"

"Bridgeport . . . north."

Parish debated taking the freeway or using the streets. Given the time of day and the mess on the freeway she opted for heading up the hill on 15th then to 12th and cutting through the north end to Bridgeport. Even that route was slow with after five traffic.

Reaching Bridgeport they immediately recognized the storage units located on the side street. Parish drove through the open gate to the office. "Is it always open?"

"This gate only gets you to the office." Blayze pointed to where access for the storage buildings was blocked by another gate. "The other one probably requires a code."

Parish slid the car into a parking spot in front of the square two-story building. A fine drizzle hung in the air, but it was warm. From the small patch of lawn next to the building the scent of freshly mowed grass reached them as they approached the entrance.

Inside behind the counter sat a woman of indeterminate age, her dark hair pulled back into a ponytail. Her brown eyes registered boredom as she rose and approached the counter. "Can I help you?"

"We're looking to rent a unit," Blayze explained.

Parish noted the security camera aimed at them.

"Did you have a particular size in mind?"

Blayze consulted Parish with a glance.

She lifted her shoulders. "Not too large, big enough to store some boxes and a trunk." She noted a doubtful expression cross the woman's face and wondered if mentioning a trunk alerted her suspicion.

"About 5 x 10?" The woman addressed Blayze.

"That should work. Is it possible to get into it at any time?"

"Someone is in the office from 9:30 in the morning until 6:00 in the evening. It's possible to get a code for the main gate that can be used from 6:00 am until 10:00 pm."

"You do have outdoor security cameras?"

She nodded. "You're concerned about security?"

Blayze directed his pale-eyed scrutiny at her. "I have to transfer some valuables here. I understand there's been some funny business with one of the storage units recently."

"Someone stored a trunk here which was later picked up and moved. It turned out to have a dead body in it." She grimaced.

"Yuk!" Parish shuddered, bringing the woman's eyes to her with a smile.

"We had no idea what was in it."

"Did you see it delivered?"

"It was done after office hours. The security cameras did show the delivery, but it was a couple guys we know who hire themselves out to help people move things."

"Ah." Blayze nodded. "But it was moved out again?"

"It was." She appeared uncomfortable with Blayze's analytical gaze. "This time by a different couple guys who work for the transfer and storage company where it was eventually stored."

"So whoever it actually belonged to was totally anonymous."

"The police have been asking questions. I don't think they believe us when we say we don't know who it belonged to."

"That must be frustrating," Parish empathized with the woman.

She nodded at Parish. "They always want to know who rented the space. But I told them it was done online. They have the name of the person who rented it, but they said that was the body in the trunk." She lifted her hands in a gesture of frustration.

"Do you know who picked up keys to move things in or out?" Blayze asked.

"We have pictures of everyone on the security camera who pick up keys, but it doesn't tell for which unit."

"Have the police looked at that camera footage?"

The woman thought for a moment. "I know they looked at those for delivery and pickup. I'm not sure about key pickup. We couldn't tell them what day or time to identify the tape that person would be on."

"Sounds like you've done everything you can."

The woman sighed, nodding. "But I get the feeling they don't believe us."

"They may be frustrated more information isn't available."

Blayze finished filling out the paperwork and used his credit card to pay for the first month's rent. She supplied him with a gate access code and a means of opening the door of the unit they rented.

❦

Once outside the storage center office Blayze stopped to observe his surroundings. Although the pavement remained wet the drizzle had ceased. A light breeze pushed a gray mass across the sky.

"Shall we go see what we rented?"

"I can see the lieutenant's problem," Parish said. "Someone could easily have moved Lawrence there dead then later picked up and moved him again."

"One question though, how did they find out about the transfer and storage company space?" All the anonymous rental and removals attributed to Manke had been explained away by the receptionist. But getting into a managed storage area might require more finesse.

Blayze glanced at the envelope containing the key and code. B10 was their unit. He looked at the various buildings locked behind the additional gate. A, B, C, D, and E. B appeared to contain many smaller units, some with ordinary doors and others with small overhead doors. The one they had reserved possessed a narrow overhead door. He used the key to undo the company's lock then lifted the door. It was a clean, narrow room, half the size of a moderate bedroom with more than enough space for placement of a trunk with room remaining for other things.

Blayze walked around the area.

"I wonder how they thought of doing it this way." Parish stood in the middle turning around slowly.

"To answer that one has to know who 'they' are."

The quick glance she sent from beneath her bangs made him think she suspected him of knowing. Did he? Actually he had begun to formulate a theory about "them", figuring Moseley was somehow mixed up in it.

"Do you think Lawrence was killed here?"

"I'd have thought Sarkis would have found some evidence of it." Blayze moved toward the opening. "You ready to go?"

Parish followed him to the car.

When she started the engine it occurred to Blayze it was dinner time. Usually he would not hesitate suggesting a stop to eat, but now he waivered. She had developed some level of trust in him. Valuing her assistance he had no desire to sabotage it. He sighed, deciding on the bold move. "Are you opposed to stopping for something to eat?"

Again she flashed him the apprehensive expression. "Okay."

He withheld his grin. Had she decided on the bold move too?

"Where did you want to stop?"

"You know the area better than I do." Perhaps she would be more comfortable if she chose the location.

After a short hesitation she said, "There's a small Italian restaurant not far down Bridgeport."

They continued on Bridgeport, passing through a major intersection then making a left into a strip of businesses one of which was a small restaurant with a bold Italian name. The waitress seated them in a corner with windows both directions and handed them menus.

While Blayze studied his Parish took her cell phone and sent a couple messages. Recalling she had a son which included other responsibilities he figured she was managing those. When she had put away her phone and taken up her menu he said, "You sounded like you think I know who killed Manke."

She focused her large eyes on him with an intent expression. "Do you?"

He shook his head.

"But you have suspicions."

"I figure Moseley and Manke are tied together somehow and money is part of the deal."

The waiter arrived to take their orders. After the waiter had gone, Parish asked, "You believe Mr. Moseley is the one using the money?"

"I'm coming to that conclusion."

She frowned. "Were he and Lawrence in it together?"

Blayze considered. "I'd say Moseley played a lone hand."

Parish cocked her head. "Why didn't you tell the lieutenant it was your sister in that hit and run?"

Blayze opened his mouth then realized he didn't know how to respond. He hadn't taken time since they talked to Sarkis to examine his reluctance to confess his relationship to the accident. He seemed to be reacting more to his sister than about her. His mother could claim all she wanted that Sylvia had changed her personality, but he wasn't buying. To a degree he preferred detaching from any relationship whatever with the woman who was his sister. Somehow telling Sarkis would commit him in a way he did not wish to be.

He noticed Parish waited for his reply. "I don't think I have an answer to that."

She looked as if she didn't believe him.

"Don't misunderstand me," he added. "I love my sister."

"But?"

"I don't like her. I don't want to be connected to or responsible for her." How could he explain to Parish what he couldn't reconcile himself? Why had Sylvia been able to intimidate him so? He wasn't easily intimidated, although he had gained the ability to resist threatening personalities over the years through many tough experiences. He had learned that in truth bullies, male or female, were more afraid than the person they bullied and generally had far less power. He had gone from the boy browbeaten by his aggressive, unruly big sister to a man rarely threatened by anyone? However the black-haired manager of the electronics store in the mall flashed into his head. "Some women intimidate me," he confessed to Parish with a grin.

The look on her face made him think she didn't know whether to challenge him or laugh. She opted for the former. "That's hard to believe."

"Why?" Blayze decided on the offensive. "You appear intimidated by men."

She sighed. "I don't think it's intimidation per se."

"What then?"

"Hard lessons I've learned from experience. Men all seem to want to take advantage of me."

Blayze gazed at her realizing her appearance made her seem vulnerable. He had learned the inaccuracy of that impression, but recognized the danger she faced. "I'm sorry," he said.

"I've also learned not all men take advantage," she went on, "but I'm not good at determining which ones are which."

Her expression made him think she was attempting to determine which one he was.

"I only take advantage of women who blatantly advertise they want to be taken advantage of." That appeared to shock her. "You don't think women do that?"

Her expression was half smile, half disbelief. She laughed lightly.

"Some come on exceptionally strong." He grinned. "Hence, some women intimidate me."

She laughed then cocked her head and gave him a skeptical look. "I was under the impression that's what men wanted."

Blayze shook his head. "They want to capture the princess not have Jane club them over the head and drag them into the cave."

The look she gave him over her spectacles indicated the jury was still deliberating.

◆CHAPTER TWENTY-ONE◆

The dull gray sky hovered, presenting three possibilities, as Parish drove to work and parked her car. The gray overcast would remain for the entire day or it would grow more threatening, turn darker and eventually bring the rain. Or, the most likely, the sun would burn off the overcast and leave a beautiful late summer day. Parish figured she could use the same prognosis for her day. Best was to anticipate a beautiful late summer day.

Once she had her team on track and made certain her immediate responsibilities were under control she made a trek to the break room.

Midge was there ahead of her. "How did it go last night?"

"Fine."

"No ulterior motives?"

Parish shook her head.

"That's good, right?" Midge tipped her head and eyed Parish.

She sighed. "Yes."

"You say that as if you were looking for a pass and didn't get one." At Parish's shocked expression, Midge put her hands in front of her face. "Don't shoot. You're so solemn this morning I needed to make sure you're okay."

Parish rolled her eyes. "Could Lawrence have embezzled money from the company without anyone knowing?"

Midge frowned. "What brings that up?"

"Blayze thinks he was mixed up some way with Mr. Moseley. Since he traced some of that traveling money to Mr. Moseley I wondered if Lawrence was involved too."

Midge leaned against the counter staring into her coffee cup as if it held a crystal ball. "You'd be best off to ask Miguel. Lawrence would have been able to do that. His training and expertise was in IT. They can usually figure out how to manipulate things. But I also assume bank accounts, even specific financial information or the access to it is protected by layers of security. Of course, Lawrence could probably have gotten through that too. But those things show up and would be exceedingly risky unless you were a person normally trusted with the usual access."

That was an idea. "Who has the usual access?"

Midge's reflective gaze traveled over Parish's shoulder to the windows behind her. "Slate Ridinghood, and possibly some of the other directors but I wouldn't know which ones and Tim Hogan." Her gaze returned to Parish. "Taylor Washington may also, being the comptroller. You might want to ask Mr. Ridinghood."

Parish left the break room, having forgotten to get the cup of coffee she went for. She took the elevator down to the executive suite and Slate Ridinghood's assistant. "Is he in?"

"Yes, go ahead, I'll let him know."

When Parish reached the door Slate opened it for her. "Come in." He pointed to the gold upholstered chair facing his desk. "How can I help you?"

She paused a moment to take in the gold and green jungle print wall paper, somewhat out of character for Slate Ridinghood. However, she recalled this was only a temporary office for him. "I have some," she hesitated, "impertinent questions."

He frowned. "Regarding?"

"Something Blayze is working on."

"Sit down."

Parish sat in the chair Mr. Ridinghood indicated, admiring the view of the park outside. She could see patches of blue where the sun was breaking through the overcast.

"Like I said at the conference I'm open to questions, suggestions, gossip, whatever might help." His gray eyes were not only frank and open, but lit with perceptive alertness.

Parish plunged in, "Who here has the usual access to financial accounts? Not in the sense of accounting information, but in the line of company assets, investments, bank accounts?"

"What do you mean by usual?"

"Well, people who can access information or make entries in those areas without raising an alarm they're doing something they shouldn't."

She noted the quick flutter of expressions crossing his face including doubt, surprise, concern. "Is something like that happening?"

"Something is happening. Whether or not it's okay depends on who's doing it and who has the right to do it."

"Is this what your auditor has found?"

Parish nodded. "He believes he has identified one of the people involved but he's found more than one. Since it didn't alert Miguel it must be someone whose access wouldn't raise a red flag." She added, "Miguel caught Mr. Moseley's involvement."

Slate sighed. "Besides myself, Ian Moseley, Tim Hogan, and Taylor Washington there are a couple board members."

He mentioned two names Parish had heard before but didn't know. "Should I be doing something about this?"

"Blayze wants to investigate further before as he put it 'going in with guns blazing'."

Mr. Ridinghood's worried expression intensified.

"At this point I don't think it's causing harm to the company. In fact, I expect the activity itself has ceased."

Slate scrutinized Parish's face. "If there's something I need to do I'd like to know."

She nodded. "I know, but I don't think there is. First we have to figure out exactly what is going on. Some other more significant issues that don't specifically relate to the company are involved. To do something now without the whole picture may create a problem as far as those other things are concerned. Mr. Ridinghood, how much do you know about Bobbi Bennett?"

He rolled his eyes. "Is she mixed up in this?"

"Not that we know of." Parish emphasized "know". "It's more we're trying to eliminate her."

Slate peered at Parish with narrowed eyes. "If she could be she would be. You're aware my wife's brother, my brother-in-law, is married to Bobbi's sister." He leaned back in his chair. "She's what in old days we called a social climber. From what Dan has told me she and her sister were raised with the, at the time, new fangled idea that scolding and punishment damaged a child's psychology."

"What damages a child's psychology is not being scolded and punished," Parish mumbled.

"Exactly!" Slate smiled. "Bobbi's a perfect example. You learn self-discipline from being disciplined. Consequently she has none. She's like a child in grown-up clothes, running wild. Unfortunately for her and everyone else she has enough charm to get away with it."

"Sort of," Parish added.

Slate raised his eyebrows with a half smile. "Her family had no money or status, two things she is determined to get by whatever means she can."

"Sailing on Ridinghood's coattails?"

A comment Slate acknowledged with a bob of his head.

"Which means she can't be left off the list of people involved in Ridinghood's problems."

⧉

As soon as Blayze arrived at Ridinghood he returned to his pursuit of the traveling money. Mr. Hornby had sent account transactions for the next layer including the RC Returns account, with the comment information was becoming more difficult to access. Given the money in these accounts produced income, taxes remained an issue keeping the option of securing data alive for the IRS.

From what Blayze could see of the RC Returns account the larger amount of money moved directly and immediately to Ridinghood's bank account where it remained, at least for a time. The transactions also verified another smaller amount moving at the same time to PR Investments where, from other of his researches, he realized moved on to M.I.J. & Company Investments LLC then continued to a bank account with the same name as the LLC but without the "Investments". Similarly another even smaller amount went to a bank savings account but did not travel further. It remained there collecting interest, joined intermittently by additional sums which also remained to collect interest.

He leaned back in his chair, staring at his monitor. To him the smaller amount made more sense than the larger one. It might even have made sense as a Ridinghood account.

However, he didn't figure that was the case. Someone was building reserves. It could be Moseley, but Blayze's internal instincts wouldn't let him buy that. If not Moseley, then who? And did Moseley know about the other account?

As he stared at the monitor a shadow flickered above it. Blayze looked up to see Lieutenant Sarkis gazing at him.

"You have time for a chat?"

Blayze sighed. "Sure." He noted the lieutenant behaved with less assumptive self-assurance than previously.

Sarkis grabbed the chair in the corner and pushed it to the desk where he sat. Blayze watched him expectantly. "Parish tells me you're tired of being treated like a county employee."

Blayze laughed.

"She also told me one of the women in the Ocean Shores hit and run is your sister."

"Blabbermouth. Have you found anything out about that?"

"I talked to their police. They have a witness who confirms the car was a newer model burgundy Chevrolet. This person was in the hotel parking lot when it happened."

"He also thinks it was deliberate hit and run?"

"Right."

Sylvia was annoying, but Blayze didn't figure she deserved to be run over. He wasn't sure other people even found her annoying.

The lieutenant switched topics. "Did you learn anything at that storage facility?"

"As you probably found out picking up the body and delivering it to the storage unit would have been simple, including using Manke's name to rent it and do the moving. They employed a company that hires out to help people make that type of move." Blayze noted Sarkis' disappointment.

"We have a question. Did you check their camera footage to see who picked up the keys after it was rented? And did you check out the individuals hired to move the trunk?"

The lieutenant frowned, considering. "I imagine. I'll have to check with the team who took care of that."

"Another question. How did they get the moving and storage company's cooperation to pick up the trunk using Manke's name? Wouldn't they have had to provide some identification?"

"You think that would have been a problem?"

"Wouldn't you? Someone in the deal should have actually known who was or wasn't Manke."

The lieutenant eyed Blayze with a frown. "I got the analysis on the blood in Moseley's house."

"And?"

"Lawrence Manke."

For some reason Blayze had expected that. "So you think Moseley killed Manke?"

"I've put out the alert to have him picked up."

"But you still have no idea where he is?"

Sarkis shook his head. "I've alerted the police up and down the coast, but nothing. I've had my people here check with the hotels. At one point after he left Ocean Shores he spent a couple days at a resort in Moclips but he's gone from there. I've started them down the coast across that bay to Westport. However, he might have left the area entirely."

"To get away from this area in a big way he'd need to do it from SeaTac or Portland."

"Or Spokane." The lieutenant lifted his eyebrows testing the idea with Blayze.

"You're convinced he didn't drive?"

"We have word out on that Mercedes Parish said he was driving."

"He could have rented a car."

"Then where's the Mercedes?" Sarkis directed a pointed look at Blayze. "We've checked that too, along with rentals. So, you need to follow that money trail."

The lieutenant rose and put the chair back in the corner.

When he had gone Blayze leaned back again considering. Why would Moseley have murdered Manke? Because he had learned about the money deal? That seemed a stretch. All things considered Moseley had exercised great care in handling the money. He had stuck to the legal side of things as much as possible and still carry out his plan, whatever that was. It seemed unlikely he would risk committing murder. Of course, temper, panic, pressure of some kind could trigger an uncharacteristic response. Blayze had never met Ian Moseley. He had only his personal gut feelings with respect to the evidence left behind.

The other factor in the equation was Lawrence Manke. Once again Blayze knew too little about the man to make an accurate judgment but everything he learned contradicted involvement in something leading to murder. Accident was always possible in a death but not by a bullet to the brain.

❧

Parish returned to the break room for the coffee she had forgotten earlier when impulsively making the trek to Slate Ridinghood's office.

Odella stood by the counter stirring creamer into hers. "Midge told me you were interested in who attended the conference in Spokane last spring."

Parish paused in reaching for a cup to regard Odella.

"I went," she said. "It was Alan Bernstein, Tim Hogan and I. Taylor Washington was supposed to go but had a family emergency and couldn't."

"Did you see Bobbi Bennett there?"

Odella grinned, her big dark eyes twinkling. "Not at the conference, of course, but in the evening at the hotel lounge."

Surprised to find someone who had been on the spot, Parish struggled to line up her questions. "Did you notice what she was doing?"

"You mean throwing herself at Tim Hogan?"

"Really? Mr. Hogan?" Parish was shocked. She would have thought him the last one of the group to interest Bobbi. "What did he do about it?"

Odella gazed at the ceiling a moment. "I think the word is 'glowed'." She laughed at Parish's expression. "You can't imagine Mr. Hogan glowing?"

Parish smiled uncertainly and shook her head. That was like trying to imagine Jesus Christ sipping tea on a yacht in the Aegean.

"You're aware he has Mrs. Micromanager for a wife?"

"Someone told me that."

"Get him away from her and this company, he's a different person."

Parish frowned. "Different how?"

"Oh," Odella sighed. "More cheerful, has a sense of humor and an interesting perspective on things. He's freer, more open."

Parish tried to imagine a freer, open, cheerful Mr. Hogan. She failed. She also tried to imagine what he would have to do with Bobbi Bennett. "Do you think there's something going on between them?"

"Oh, definitely." Odella laughed again then became serious. "Why do you ask?"

Parish filled a cup with coffee. "You heard we found Bobbi in Ocean Shores?"

Odella nodded.

"We're trying to figure out what she's doing there. Her leaving coincided so closely with Mr. Moseley we thought they may be connected. However, from what you say it's more likely something to do with Tim Hogan."

"So your next question, does Tim Hogan have something to do with Mr. Moseley's leaving?"

"I . . . I hadn't really thought of it that way." Parish frowned working to put this new information in perspective. "Do you think that's the case?"

"No." Odella shook her head. "I don't think so. They didn't get along that well. Mr. Moseley was . . . hmmm . . .arrogant. Tim Hogan didn't need another arrogant micromanager in his life."

Parish felt as if she had her head buried in the sand box. Odella patted her on the shoulder as she took her coffee and left the break room. Parish moved to the windows overlooking the Port of Tacoma. The sun had succeeded in burning its way through the overcast to shine gleefully on the nearby buildings. Instead of mentally coming out of the overcast Parish had the feeling she was moving farther into it.

What difference did it make if Bobbi had a thing for Tim Hogan and vice versa? But why would that put Bobbi in Ocean Shores? Had Mr. Hogan been there too? Lots of questions, no answers.

Returning to her office Parish decided on a detour to Blayze's space. He was staring at the opening to his area when she entered.

They stared at each other a moment before anyone spoke. When they did they spoke at the same time.

"Have you . . ." Blayze began.

"Did you . . ." Parish started. "You first."

"Lieutenant Sarkis was here. He said the blood they found in Moseley's house belonged to Lawrence Manke."

"They think Mr. Moseley killed Lawrence?"

"That's the logical conclusion."

"But?" Parish detected doubt on Blayze's part.

"I can't get that to work." Blayze beckoned to the extra chair.

Parish retrieved it from the corner and moved it to his desk. "Why not?"

"It's out of character given how he's handled everything else. What would you say? You know him a lot better than I do. I've never even seen the guy."

"I didn't know him as you put it." Parish reflected a moment. "He was arrogant enough for something like that, but for the most part I just stayed out of his way."

"That's your usual modus operandi, isn't it?" Blayze lifted an eyebrow and speared her with his gaze.

She narrowed her eyes. "It's safer."

"Than?"

"Getting too well acquainted with someone who will only see you as someone to push around. If you keep a low enough profile they ignore you." Parish changed the subject. Talking about herself was never comfortable. "I ran into Odella. She thinks something is going on between Tim Hogan and Bobbi Bennett."

Blayze took a minute to digest the information. "Would that make a difference?"

"No. That's just it. Whatever Bobbi is doing has nothing to do with Mr. Moseley but rather with Mr. Hogan. So it's immaterial." Parish waved her hands in a gesture of frustration.

"Sarkis isn't going to be pleased with us. We keep exonerating everyone. He still has a corpse to deal with."

"Do you think he'll fire us?"

Blayze laughed. "He can't afford to."

⚜

As Blayze packed his briefcase to leave for the day his phone alerted him.

"This is Janice Colton."

He felt a stab of alarm. "Has something happened to Sylvia?"

"No, no. She's fine, at least she's still here in the hospital and they're taking care of things." Janice took a breath. "Something occurred to me about our time in Ocean Shores. I'd prefer to explain it in person if that would work for you. I'm at the hospital right now, but I live in South Seattle. I could meet you at the Starbucks on 320th in Federal Way."

"Okay. When?"

"Right now traffic getting out of Seattle would be a mess so 6:30?"

Blayze agreed to time and place which gave him time to grab dinner before making the drive. He wondered what Janice wanted to discuss, but figured advance concern was borrowing trouble.

Northbound traffic out of Tacoma was reasonable by six o'clock. Slightly ahead of schedule arriving at the Starbucks he was surprised to see she had arrived ahead of him. He nodded to her and went to order a latte.

Janice had chosen a table in the corner where she faced the counter. Her fair hair was pulled back from her face with a black headband. She wore an oversized light gray shirt with one sleeve hanging loose.

"How are you?" he asked taking a seat. He noted her bandaged shoulder in addition to the arm strapped to her side.

She shrugged then winced. "Okay."

"And Sylvia? Did she find out her test results?"

"Apparently she has internal bruising but nothing serious. They said she would heal on her own."

That would make his mother feel better. Blayze leaned back in his chair, waiting for Janice to explain their meeting.

She began hesitantly. "I've thought a lot about the night of the accident trying to figure out if anyone we saw or anything we did provoked the attack on us."

Blayze struggled to believe anyone would see her as a threat of any kind. Attractive in a gentle, nondescript way, she had a mellow but not necessarily timid personality. She seemed moderately sure of herself without being contentious. In fact he wondered what she saw in Sylvia.

"There was nothing so definite I could say it must be the cause. However, while we were in the bar we sat next to a table where two men sat."

Blayze nodded encouragement.

"From bits of their conversation I overheard it seemed they were sitting together simply because of how crowded the bar was. They didn't talk about anything personal, just business, politics, things like that. The bar was full of hoopla, people extra friendly all around. Something to do with a sports event gave the whole bunch something in common. We were out of it from that standpoint since we knew nothing about the sporting event. But, since everyone was talking to everyone else, the one guy at the other table started talking to us. He figured out we didn't know what was going on and explained it. He was an Ocean Shores resident so we asked him questions and he told us things about the area. When more people came in looking for places to sit he asked if they could sit with us to free up a table, so we agreed. They were friendly and didn't appear to have an agenda. The other guy didn't seem interested in us at all. He was polite, but distant, if you know what I mean."

Blayze listened patiently figuring she would eventually explain what this had to do with the hit and run.

"Later a woman came in. The bar was arranged with a big U-shaped counter. Tables ran along the outer edge. Our table sat near the end where the U turned." With her free hand Janice described a U on the table then taking her cup placed it in the position where their table would have been relative to the counter. "Since the guys had moved from their table to ours their backs were to the entrance and most of the U. When the woman came in she stopped suddenly and stared at the men, probably more at the quieter man, looking angry, really angry. She took an empty bar stool at the turn in the U and ordered a drink. Occasionally she would turn and glare at us. In the time we sat there she had a least three drinks."

"You think she may have been the person who hit you?" Blayze asked.

"We left before the men and she had left before us. I realize it sounds ridiculous but when the Ocean Shores police asked me to think about anything that might give them a hint. That's all I could think of." She crossed her free arm over her bandaged one and leaned back.

"What did she look like?"

Janice stared at the picture of a coffee plantation on the wall considering. "Short, not pretty. She looked mean and something in the way she sat made her look determined to act."

Blayze wondered what Lieutenant Sarkis would think of a description like that. "Would you know her if you saw her again?"

Janice grimaced. "I might. I couldn't say for sure."

"What about the guys?"

"One guy was big and blonde. He did most of the talking, real outgoing. The other guy had funny dark hair and really green eyes. He looked like he was putting up with the other guy for some reason."

Blayze frowned. "Green eyes?"

Janice nodded.

He wished he had Parish here. "Did they give you any names?"

"The chatty guy said 'you can call me Bob'." She smiled at the memory. "We teased him about that. He introduced the other man as Mark, or Mike, or Matt. Something like that."

Blazye grimaced. Had his sister and her friend accidentally gotten mixed up with Ridinghood?

◆ CHAPTER TWENTY-TWO ◆

As the workday ended Parish received a phone call from Midge. "What are you doing tonight?"

"Nothing in particular. Xavier is taking the car to a birthday party."

"How about a walk along the waterfront? I need to get in shape."

Parish laughed. Every other week Midge decided she needed to get in shape. Just before making it to the point her efforts would pay off she fell out of resolve. "What are you torturing yourself about now?" Parish had also observed every time Midge made the get-in-shape resolve guilt was harassing her.

"What makes you think I'm torturing myself?" Midge huffed. "I'm going to spiff myself up and entice that formidable auditor away from you."

"Then you'd better dress yourself up as a balance sheet."

"I can do that. Shall I pick you up or will Xavier drop you off?"

"I'll have Xavier drop me off but you need to give me a ride home."

"Deal."

At dinner Xavier brought up a topic that often plagued Parish. "Grandpa said he'd buy me a car."

"That's great, Xavier. Is he going to pay for the insurance?"

Xavier's expression went into frustration mode as he narrowed his dark brown eyes. "You already pay for my insurance to drive your car."

"Right. But adding another car of which you are the sole driver would double the insurance."

He tossed his black hair back from his face. "What if I pay my own insurance?"

"As things stand now if you want a car you're going to have to do that, in addition to paying for gas."

"What if I get an electric car?" He smirked as if pulling an ace from his sleeve.

"Great." Parish grinned at him. "But you're going to have to figure out some way to remember to charge it."

"Ooops." He took his cell phone from his pocket and examined it. "I need to take a charger with tonight."

Rising, Parish shook her head and removed an extra charger from the drawer in the hutch. "Try this one."

When she had finished clearing away their dinner Xavier declared he was ready to go. She handed him the car keys and grabbed a sweater. Throughout Xavier's childhood she had made a point of letting go gradually of things for which he needed to be responsible. She had seen mothers, especially single mothers, cling to their sons keeping them dependent in order to protect themselves from losing their companionship. She was determined to avoid that. He needed to grow up and move on to his own life. If he didn't she would consider she had failed as a mother.

They took Bridgeport then Jackson and Vassault to the waterfront. She had agreed to meet Midge at Commencement Park. Approaching, she noted Midge in front of her car in the parking area doing stretching exercises dressed in striped tights, shorts and a tee shirt. She waved to Xavier as he dropped Parish off.

Parish wore pink cut-offs and a white tee shirt with the sleeves of her sweater tied over her shoulders. In spite of the early overcast the day had become summer warm, what native Pacific North Westerners called hot. However, she was generally cold and evening cooled quickly the minute the sun hit the horizon.

"Are we going to run?" she asked Midge, observing her outfit and noting the exercises.

Midge scowled at her. "Are you kidding? I'd look like a bag of rubber balls."

Parish laughed, but said, "You're way too hard on yourself. What's making you feel guilty now?" They began a swift walk heading west along Ruston Way. The evening's cruising traffic filled the street.

"I had a chat with Sally Stills this afternoon. Recently, she has noticed a car hanging around her neighborhood she doesn't think belongs there. Ever since Lawrence was killed she has been jumpy regarding anything unusual."

"What did you tell her?"

"Feeling that way was probably normal under the circumstances. She shouldn't worry too much about it."

"So why are you feeling guilty?"

Midge stopped a moment to catch her breath. "It's a weird feeling I have I dismissed a cry for help. What do I know about what happened to Lawrence? Even that lieutenant doesn't know. What if someone actually is stalking her for some reason?"

"Do you know where she lives?" They resumed their pace.

"I looked up her address when I started feeling guilty. She lives in an apartment on Narrows Drive."

"Let's stop by and check on her on our way home?"

"I knew I asked you out for a reason."

Maintaining their stride, they passed several of the waterfront restaurants clinging to the rocks bordering the sound and the newer hotel braving the area. They met joggers and walkers in every state of dress and undress. A number of skateboarders and cyclists breezed past them, giving Parish the perception they walked a precarious thoroughfare. When they reached the last of the restaurants they turned around and headed back toward the car at a slower pace.

"I talked to Odella this morning. She said she went to that conference in Spokane."

Midge nodded. "I thought you just wanted to know about the men who attended."

"She was at the hotel bar when Bobbi and Annabelle were there. She said, and I quote, 'Bobbi was throwing herself at Tim Hogan'."

"Not surprising, I suppose."

"Really?" Parish found it amazing.

"Didn't Annabelle tell you she chases men?"

"You knew she was like that?"

"Not specifically, but it fits with everything else." Midge sighed deeply. "She has the brain of a teen-ager."

"And," Parish went on, "Odella said Mr. Hogan was, as she put it, 'glowing'."

Midge cast a sideways glance at Parish. "Now that surprises me."

On the way back to Midge's SUV they stopped at the refreshment stand and bought sodas. Midge checked her watch. "You think it's okay to stop by this late?"

"It's only 8:30."

"Maybe we can think of a good excuse."

"How about the truth?"

Midge frowned at Parish.

"You were feeling guilty you hadn't given enough credit to what she said and wanted to be sure she was okay."

❧

Midge headed her SUV west on Ruston Way then angled through the Ruston community. Trees, shuddering in the evening breeze, produced an infinitesimal hint of their preparation to change from summer's green to the burgundy of fall. Parish looked for addresses as they traveled Vassault which gradually turned onto Narrows Drive. "There it is." She pointed to a gathering of white trimmed gray apartments approached through a gate, open now. She watched for the apartment number. "Over there. You can park across from it."

Midge turned off the car. "Okay, let's go,"

"They must be townhouses." Parish noticed two stories but only an entrance on the main level. The lighted first floor gave every appearance of activity.

Midge pushed the doorbell button. Parish could hear it ringing inside the apartment, but no one answered the door. Midge rang it again. "Okay, now I'm getting worried."

Parish tried the doorknob and the door opened. "Should we?"

"I won't be able to sleep if we don't." Entering the apartment foyer Midge called out, "Sally, it's Midge. Are you here?"

Still no answer. They took a few steps farther into the hall. To the left over a half wall Parish could see a modest living room arrangement and beyond that the dining area with a wooden pedestal table and ladder back chairs. To their right was a closet. A few steps beyond was an opening into the kitchen.

"Oh, no," Midge breathed and charged in.

On the floor near the breakfast bar Sally lay covered with red splotches. Parish's first thought was blood but when she looked closer it was the wrong color and consistency. A pungent fruity smell filled the air. Midge knelt beside Sally speaking her name. Sally made no move while Midge put her hand on her chest and touched her face.

"She's still alive. Call an ambulance."

Parish took out her phone and put in 911. She gave the respondent the address and information. Turning around the room, she asked, "What's all that red?" She noticed nothing on the stove, so she hadn't been cooking. In fact, the only thing on the breakfast bar was a wine glass. A glance into the bottom verified it had held red wine. "Could she have had too much to drink and passed out?"

Midge stuck her finger in one of the wet patches on the floor, looked at it then sniffed. "If she did she spilled more than she drank."

"Where is the bottle?"

"The frig?"

Moving around the counter to check out the refrigerator, Parish noticed the bottle lying under a corner of the cabinet nearest the breakfast bar. "It's here under this cabinet." She bent to pick it up.

"Don't touch it. Leave it there."

At that moment the doorbell rang.

The first to arrive were the police. A young officer stood at the door a question in his expression.

Parish opened the door wider. "She's in the kitchen."

As Midge explained their concern and the stop to check on Sally the doorbell rang again. Parish opened the door for the emergency medical people who came in bringing their gear. They proceeded immediately into the kitchen and began their examination while the police officer continued questioning Midge.

"What made you think there might be a problem?"

"Sally was concerned someone was stalking her. She said a car had been hanging around her neighborhood that didn't belong here. It always looked like someone was in it. Her boyfriend was murdered recently so she's been jumpy. After I told her not to worry I started thinking maybe she really was in danger so we stopped to check if she was all right."

"And that's how you found her?" The officer maintained a neutral expression.

"We couldn't get her to wake up so I told Parish to call 911."

The officer glanced at Parish.

"There's a wine bottle there." She pointed to the item which looked as if it had rolled under the corner of the cabinet.

The officer moved into the kitchen and opened a couple drawers. He found the silverware and took a knife. Sticking it into the mouth of the wine bottle he lifted it off the floor. More wine spilled as he moved it to the counter.

Following a quick examination of Sally, the EMTs brought in a stretcher. After bracing her neck and stabilizing her head they moved her swiftly and gently to the stretcher then into the ambulance and took off with lights spinning.

The young officer had a notebook open. "Could I get contact information for you two? We may have more questions later on."

Midge shot Parish a suspicious glance. "Sure." She furnished her name, address and phone number.

After that he turned to Parish who did the same. "You might want to tell Lieutenant Sarkis about this," she suggested, which brought his glance abruptly up from his notebook.

"He's investigating the murder of this woman's boyfriend," Midge added.

"How is it you know her?"

"We both work for Ridinghood Corporation in human resources."

Another officer, somewhat older, entered the kitchen. "Nothing outside," he declared to his partner. "I've checked inside too. The only activity seems to have been in here."

The younger officer turned to Midge. "Do you know your way around this kitchen?"

She grimaced and shook her head. "What do you need?"

"A clean plastic bag." He indicated the wine bottle.

Midge went to work checking through the drawers then the shelves in the pantry where she located an assortment of plastic storage bags one of which she brought to the officer. "Are you going to lock up her apartment?"

The officers exchanged a glance. "Did the EMT's take her handbag with them?"

"I doubt it," Parish responded. "I didn't see it around anywhere."

The officer addressed Parish. "Why don't we go to her bedroom and see if we can find it?"

She followed as he headed for the stairs which sat to the right of the small foyer. On the second floor were two bedrooms and a bath. The bedroom to the left appeared to be Sally's, her handbag lay on the bed.

The officer picked it up. "I think they're taking her to Tacoma General." Once they were back in the kitchen he opened the bag and removed the keys.

The younger officer escorted the ladies out while the older one locked the apartment.

"Would one of you want to return Ms. Stills bag to her at the hospital?"

"I'd be glad to," Midge volunteered.

After a questioning glance from the older officer, the younger one explained, "I talked to Sarkis. He verified these two."

After surrendering the handbag to Midge the officers returned to their cruiser.

"You okay with a trip to the hospital before I take you home?"

Parish nodded. "We should find out how Sally is."

When they reached Tacoma General Hospital Midge maneuvered the SUV into a space in the parking building. Parish carried Sally's bag while they made their way to the emergency entrance.

A flurry of activity met them in the waiting area. All the reception stations were occupied with patients or family.

"We might as well wait until one is free. We probably won't get any information otherwise." Midge moved toward two empty chairs in the corner.

Parish followed. "What do you think happened?"

Midge grimaced, shaking her head. "It looked strange to me. It might help to know what injuries she has."

"Did the EMTs say anything?"

"They mumbled something about a blow to the head, which would account for her being unconscious."

"But you didn't see an injury?"

"No, but all I saw of her head was one side."

Parish retreated into silence watching the surrounding activity. Putting together everything she had seen at Sally's house her conclusion would be someone hit her with the wine bottle while it was open. That would explain the spilled wine and the bottle under the counter. However, who would do that and why? Nothing else there indicated anyone's presence beside Sally's.

"Come on," Midge nudged her. "There's a receptionist free."

They asked about Sally and were directed to the intensive care unit.

"That was easier than I expected." The look Midge gave Parish made her think it only increased Midge's concern rather than alleviating it.

"We probably haven't hit the blockade yet."

"Well, let's find the elevator and approach the blockade."

Leaving emergency they entered a hall where they found an elevator that took them to the right floor. Wall signs made it possible to find the intensive care unit where a nurses' station filled with computer monitors tracked patient progress. Checking the numbers on the rooms, Parish noted in front of Sally's number Lieutenant Sarkis stood talking with a man in a white coat.

"He made it fast," Midge mumbled as they approached the two.

"I understand you found her," the lieutenant addressed them.

"How is she?"

"Alive. But it's touch and go right now. She's had a terrific blow to the head."

The man in the white coat drifted away after a nod to the lieutenant.

"Now," Lieutenant Sarkis declared with a sharp glance at Midge, "it's time for you to tell me what you know."

She spread her hands open. "I'm not sure I know anything."

"How did you come to find her?"

Once again she explained the afternoon's activities that brought them eventually to Sally's apartment.

The lieutenant sighed. "The blow she got indicates someone tried to kill her or else that someone was extremely angry."

"Was she hit with the wine bottle?"

Lieutenant Sarkis turned a blank stare on Parish. "Wine bottle?"

"Did you go to her apartment?" Midge asked him.

"No, I came directly here."

"When we arrived there was wine spilled all over the floor and Sally. A bottle lay on the floor under the counter ledge," Parish informed him.

The lieutenant crossed his arms staring across the room. "Where's the bottle?"

"Your officer took it . . . in a plastic bag. We have Sally's handbag," Midge declared as Parish held it up.

Lieutenant Sarkis stared at the bag with a calculating expression. "Why don't you hang on to that? It'll probably be safer with you than anywhere else at the moment."

"Who would want to hurt Sally?"

"Now that's a reasonable question but one you should answer." The lieutenant directed his gaze at Midge as if expecting her to cough up the culprit. "Actually whoever killed Lawrence may have reason to eliminate Sally too."

"But you don't know who killed him either?" Parish verified.

The lieutenant made a face. "Moseley is probably involved in Manke's death somewhere, except we can't find him. However, I seriously doubt he attacked this woman."

"Is she safe here?"

"This didn't look premeditated, more like an angry attack. We'll keep it low profile so no one knows she's here. I don't think the media is aware of it. No reason to let them know anything."

Midge and Parish returned to the elevator which they took to the lobby, exited the building and returned to the car.

"I really feel guilty now," Midge declared.

"I need to go home." Parish figured Midge needed to deal with her guilt on her own. "I don't have time for another exercise routine."

Midge shot her a scowl. "You think exercise is my solution to everything?"

"No, just guilt."

CHAPTER TWENTY-THREE

While having breakfast at a small café down the street from his hotel Blayze considered whether he should call his mother and let her know what he had learned about Sylvia? He sighed. Probably, however, he would wait until he reached Ridinghood. He also considered contacting Lieutenant Sarkis. Would he see the same connection Blayze did relative to the hit and run? Or was Blayze reading too much into Janice's description of the men at the bar?

Having finished breakfast, an extra cup of coffee and paid his check, he picked up his briefcase and headed for Ridinghood. The beautiful day commenced with trails of white in the brilliant blue sky. Although persuaded this was the height of Pacific Northwest summer, Blayze could feel the touch of fall in the air. A chill not previously noted infringed on the sun's warmth. Stopping at a light he noticed a black SUV pull up to the curb next to him and roll down the passenger window.

"Care for a ride?" Lieutenant Sarkis called to him.

Figuring that would be strategic, Blayze accepted and climbed into the passenger seat.

"To Ridinghood?" the lieutenant verified.

"Right." Blayze set his briefcase at his feet and put on the seatbelt. "You any closer to finding Moseley?"

"No." Sarkis sighed, guiding the truck into the traffic lane. "Manke's girlfriend took a hit Friday night. That Midge and your Ridinghood assistant found her knocked out in her apartment. Looks like someone attacked her with a wine bottle."

Blayze considered the information. "Doesn't sound premeditated." It would almost make more sense if it was. He had met Sally Stills. She didn't strike him as someone who would provoke a sudden angry attack.

"Spilled wine all over the place."

"Who owned the wine?"

"It appeared the woman in the apartment was having a glass before she was attacked."

"Which means she wasn't expecting the company and the perp didn't come prepared to attack." So what did happen and had it anything to do with Lawrence Manke?

Sarkis grimaced. "It did look impulsive." He sounded as if that didn't add up for him either. "I've considered everyone I can think of and haven't even a likely suspect."

They had reached Ridinghood's parking building.

"I probably need to tell you something." Blayze had debated the advisability of sharing his conversation with Janice Colton. However, he continually returned to the possibility, strange as it seemed, it could relate to Sarkis' investigation.

"Coffee?"

Blayze sighed. He could probably fit another cup in.

After parking they headed for the coffee shop at the end of the building. Although the shop was busy most people were grabbing coffee and heading out leaving empty tables. They took their coffees to a window table overlooking Tacoma's port.

"Okay, shoot."

Blayze explained his meeting with Janice Colton, offering her description of the two guys at the table and the angry woman.

The lieutenant wrinkled his nose. "A mean looking woman and a guy with funny dark hair and prominent green eyes?"

Blayze pressed his lips together to keep from grinning.

Sarkis scowled over his spectacles at him. "You come up with winners, don't you?" He sighed. "You think it was Moseley?"

"I offer the information. I'm not speculating."

The lieutenant gazed out the window for a time silently. "Would you say the hook-up is between Moseley and this mean looking woman or between her and your sister, or your sister's friend?"

"Apparently, from what Janice said, Moseley never saw the woman since he had his back to her."

"Which means it was between that woman and your sister or her friend." Sarkis eyed Blayze as if seeking his agreement.

Blayze grimaced. "But means Moseley was still there, hadn't left the country."

"What about your money? Has it left the country?"

"Can't say yet. However, the money doesn't need Moseley's company to leave."

The lieutenant scowled. "But if the money left I'd think eventually Moseley would too."

Of course that was the logical presumption. Timing remained an issue. If the money had left the country that wouldn't mean the man had gone with it or was intending to within the short range. "If he has gone what provoked his departure?"

Sarkis shook his head.

Things had happened. Manke died and had been found, that Bobbi Bennett recognized Moseley in Ocean Shores, and, Blayze suddenly realized, an IRS agent had arrived to audit the company accounts. "Someone may be sharing in the proceeds of Moseley's little financial venture. Providing I'm correct in assuming the traveling money makes trips compliments of Ian Moseley, and inappropriately, two things bother me. I've detected a small portion of that money going a separate direction."

"And?"

"I haven't figured out who owns that account."

"Could that have precipitated Moseley's disappearance?"

"Only if it's something Moseley recently discovered and where it goes poses a threat."

Sarkis frowned. "But you don't think that's the case?" It sounded like an accusation.

"Well, it's possible, but a lot of things you want to lay at Moseley's door don't quite follow. Moseley has been extremely careful to stay just within the limits of the law or slightly outside. Nothing in what he has done, if it's him doing it, points to a man who blatantly disregards it."

The lieutenant eyed Blayze with frustration. "So you think we need to look for someone else?"

"Actually I think your best bet is to keep after Moseley. Somehow it's connected to him even if he's not the perpetrator.

❧

As Blayze returned to his workspace it struck him suddenly that if any relationship existed between what happened to Sally Stills and his sister it meant Sylvia was in danger. Did he have any reason to think the two incidents could be related? He needed to refrain from jumping to conclusions.

What even made him consider the possibility? Both were unreasonable attacks, unprovoked, at least as far as he knew. However, more differentiated them than made them similar. One was in Ocean Shores the other Tacoma. One was a planned attack, the other an unpremeditated assault. He took a deep breath. No reason appeared to make him believe they related to one another. However, in spite of his brain's logic he couldn't get the idea out of his head.

He grabbed his phone and put in the number for his mother. When they had exchanged greetings he asked, "Where is Sylvia now? Do you know?"

"Is she okay?" His mother sounded alarmed.

"As far as I know. I thought I'd have a chat with her."

He could hear his mother's sigh of relief. "I talked to her the other day. She said she was leaving the hospital and going to stay with her friend a while."

"Do you have that address?"

"No, but I have her friend's phone number." She gave it to Blayze. "You really should leave her alone."

"I understand what you said," Blayze grimaced, "but she needs to be aware of some things for her safety's sake."

"Is she in danger?"

"Not that I know of." Blayze emphasized the "know". "I just want to be sure she stays that way." Not that it worked with Sylvia, but he figured he needed to try for his own peace of mind. "You should have her come and stay with you a while."

"I invited her, but she didn't want to."

"I might give her some encouragement."

When the call ended Blayze figured he needed to take another day away from his audit to visit his sister, undoubtedly a fruitless effort. He checked the number he had for Sylvia's friend with the one his mother had given him. They were the same. When he called she invited him to lunch then gave him the address and directions.

He trekked over to Parish's office to inform her he would be out of the office again, probably the rest of the day. "My sister again."

Since he rode to work with the lieutenant he needed to return to the hotel. He dropped off his briefcase then got the car and headed for the I-5 freeway. Janice's directions took him off I-5 at the Kent/Des Moines exit heading west toward the sound.

Surprised to find her apartment situated in a large older home, converted into apartments, incongruent in the neighborhood, he climbed the stairs to the porch. An array of doorbells with names beneath rested next to the front door. He located the one for Janice Colton and pushed the button. Shortly the door buzzed and acting immediately Blayze entered the foyer. Since the number Janice had given him began with two logic said it should be on the second floor.

When he knocked it took only a moment before the door opened and Janice invited him in. "How was your trip?"

"Okay . . . fine," he mumbled taking in the room's arrangement, a living room with a coffee table surrounded by a sofa and chair seating area. Across from him an array of windows looked out on an angled modern building, presumably also apartments. Against the opposite wall to his right stood a large wooden armoire with shelves at the bottom containing electronic equipment. He surmised the cabinet doors hid the television. A comfortable room decorated with soft colors and good taste indicated someone cared for it. He focused on Janice. "Traffic was reasonable."

She smiled as if his comment was amusing. "Why don't you sit down? Lunch will be ready shortly." She glanced toward a door at the far right which Blayze figured must go to the kitchen. To his left three doors opened off a short hall.

"Sylvia's here?" He figured he ought to verify the object of his sojourn.

"She's fixing lunch." Janice perched on the sofa across from him.

Times like this Blayze wished he had developed greater social skills. It would help to be chatty. "So she's okay?"

Janice nodded. "I think she still has more difficulty recovering from her accident a couple years ago than from what happened last week. They said her fractures would heal on their own. She has a leg brace and uses a crutch."

At that moment the door to the kitchen opened and Sylvia appeared. She stared at Blayze as if trying to determine who he was. He returned her stare. They had the same naturally curling black hair and pale eyes, the same strong boned facial features. He wondered if she realized that or if still discounting him didn't know who the heck he was.

She leaned on a crutch allowing her braced leg to rest lightly on the floor. "Lunch is served," she announced.

Blayze and Janice rose to follow her through the hallway style kitchen to a small alcove where a round table with four chairs sat laid for lunch. After waiting for the ladies to be seated Blayze took a chair with his back to the windowed wall.

There were sandwiches with turkey, havarti, and lettuce, a salad, a bowl of chips and a dish of salsa. They each had a glass of water.

"I also have coffee available," Sylvia offered.

Blayze shook his head recalling he had already had more than his quota for the morning. Janice stood and helped herself to a cup and fixed one for Sylvia.

"So what brings you here today?" Janice addressed him. Sylvia regarded him with something akin to suspicion.

He grimaced. "I got to thinking about what you told me the other night regarding your encounter at the bar in Ocean Shores. I don't know if you're aware but the CEO of Ridinghood Corporation is missing. Someone spotted him a week or so ago in Ocean Shores but he has gone underground again and the police haven't been able to locate him. There's a possibility he was one of the men you met at that bar."

Janice widened her eyes. "You think so?"

"What difference would that make?" Sylvia frowned.

Blayze lifted his shoulders. "Maybe none, but a lot of problems have erupted at Ridinghood and I'm concerned you've accidentally gotten mixed up in them."

"So," Sylvia shrugged her eyebrows, "what difference would that make?"

He stared at his sister. He had grown up with that skeptical tone of voice, the cynicism and disapproval, the snappy rebuke. Did he really want to convince her, for her own wellbeing, to take care, find a safe place to stay temporarily? However, the look on her face arrested his doubtful self-interrogation. No scorn rested in her expression only the question, what difference would it make. Perhaps it was a reasonable inquiry.

"You've been attacked in a seemingly senseless hit and run. Last night another young woman was beaten over the head and is in the hospital. She worked at Ridinghood. So did her boyfriend who was found murdered."

"You think getting close to people from Ridinghood is dangerous?" Janice asked the question.

"I realize it sounds fantastic. It is fantastic. But a lot of what has happened seems to center around Ian Moseley, who I believe is one of the men you sat with at that bar and, as ridiculous as it appears, may be the cause of your incident."

"But how, why?" Janice lifted her hands in a doubtful gesture.

"If we knew that someone would be locked up and we'd end the danger."

"So what are you suggesting?" Sylvia eyed him with not only suspicion but antagonism. The hostility in her expression could fire up World War III.

Regardless, Blayze plunged forward. "Wouldn't it be better if you went to stay with Mom a while?"

Sylvia continued to stare at him as if the idea they shared the same mother was inconceivable. "Are you really my brother?"

Blayze rolled his eyes. "Have you ever looked in the mirror?"

"Just because you have black hair and blue eyes doesn't mean you're my brother."

He glanced at Janice wondering if she shared the same skepticism. Her expression contained only patient interest. He considered. Had he been injured in an accident and couldn't remember a person would he be so suspicious and antagonistic. He figured the least he would do is give that person the benefit of the doubt and attempt to verify the individual's claim. Sylvia rejected him out of hand. And his mother said she had changed. Ha!

He concentrated on his sandwich for a time as the three ate in silence.

"Is the problem relating to this person from Ridinghood you mentioned have a connection to money?" Janice broke the silence then glanced at Sylvia.

Sylvia gazed at him with her head cocked.

"We're trying to figure that out. It's likely, but we haven't been able to pin it down."

"So what do you want from me?" Sylvia demanded.

"I don't want anything from you," Blayze exploded. "Have you never been concerned for someone else's welfare enough to try to help that person avoid danger? You're my sister after all, whether you believe that or not. We have the same mother, a mother I'd like to save from further grief over you. Where do you get off with all this pretense of not knowing who I am? Remembering everything in your life except me?"

Sylvia sat back with wide eyes. She opened her mouth as if to speak and then closed it again.

"I don't think she's pretending," Janice put in quietly.

Blayze stared at Janice a moment. "Then what is her problem?"

She glanced at Sylvia as if for permission to speak. "She has been hounded ever since the accident two years ago with people trying to get money from her."

"Money?" He was dumbfounded.

"From the settlement."

Suddenly the light bulb flared. It never occurred to him Sylvia would have received an insurance settlement in her first accident. Of course, it made sense. It hadn't been her fault and she had been severely injured. "So she thinks everyone is out to extort money from her?"

"You can't imagine all the things they do, the schemes they come up with, the endless scams and harassment."

"Oh yes, I can," Blayze declared. "I don't work for the IRS for nothing."

"You work for the IRS?" Janice sounded astonished. "Sylvia never said . . . I guess she wouldn't since she doesn't remember you."

Blayze contained his scorn. "She really doesn't remember me?"

Janice nodded.

Sylvia shook her head.

"We also have a younger sister." He wondered if she also did not remember Luanne.

Again Sylvia shook her head and Janice nodded.

"Mom said you refused to stay with her."

"That's where all the harassment is. That's where people think they can get hold of me. I don't answer my phone unless I recognize the number but Mom doesn't understand."

Unfortunately Blayze could understand that. Mentally he trekked through what he had seen of Janice's apartment and living situation. It wasn't as if they were stuck out somewhere all by themselves. The situation alone may create some difficulties for any stranger trying to approach them.

"You realize then it's important you be aware of strangers and take precautions to keep yourself safe."

"I do that anyway."

"But this might not be anyone interested in your money. You could be in physical danger."

"For how long?"

Blayze lifted his shoulders. "I can let you know when matters are settled. But I can't tell you when that will be." He watched Sylvia assimilate what he had said.

Janice watched her too.

Speaking to Janice, Blayze said, "You're just as involved in this as she is."

Janice laughed. "But I can't go home to your mother."

Blayze smiled. "I'm not sure that's the case. Mom would be happy to have both of you."

"We'll be careful," Sylvia assured him.

◈CHAPTER TWENTY-FOUR◈

Aftera trip to the break room for coffee Parish stopped at Blayze's office. His curls spilled over his forehead as he examined an array of papers spread in front of him. He glanced up as she pushed the chair from the corner to his desk. He paused his study to sit back and greet her.

While taking a seat she passed a focused glance over the paperwork, which appeared to be banking information. "How did your trip go yesterday?"

He considered before replying. "Better than I anticipated."

"Your sister's okay?"

"Reasonably." He sighed. "I may be jumping to conclusions."

"Better than paying no attention to some real danger. Are you getting any closer to finding out where the money lands?"

"I suspect it's still moving." He snorted. "However, since the original amount ends up back at Ridinghood . . ." He lifted his shoulders.

"Which means there's no embezzlement?"

"As such. Although, I believe the money should return to Ridinghood with company. It's that 'company'," he made quotation marks in the air, "I'm tracing now. It seems to go a couple different directions. At the point it returns to Ridinghood from RC Returns two other amounts leave that account. One goes to PR Investments, then the LLC and on. The other, a smaller amount, goes to a different account entirely."

"Where does the larger amount go from the LLC?"

"To another LLC with the same name."

"And stays there?"

"Still working on that. What I really need to know is who owns the smaller account. If we assume the LLC belongs to Moseley, does he also own the small one or did someone figure out his scheme and cut himself in on the action?"

"Would that make a motive for murder?" Parish figured someone somewhere had a motive.

"It might if one, Moseley doesn't own the other account and two, if he knew money was being sidetracked."

She recognized Blayze's skepticism. "But you don't think he knew?"

"Right."

"Then it wouldn't be a murder motive."

He grimaced shaking his head.

Parish considered the possibilities. "What do you need to determine that?"

Blayze sighed. "Make sure Moseley owns the LLCs and PR Investments and that the larger amount of money is also his. Then, when and where does it stop moving?" After a pause he continued, "Then . . . does the smaller one belong to him and why two accounts. If it doesn't, who does own it?" Blayze scooped up the papers on his desk. "I have to get hold of my boss and more information."

Parish pushed her chair back to the corner. "So it's possible all this money moving may have nothing to do with the murder, or assaults either."

Blayze gave her a grim smile. "Exactly."

"Have you told the lieutenant?"

He admonished her with a glance from beneath his dark brows. "And get my head bit off?"

Smiling, Parish returned to her office. If they left the money out, what could be a motive for Lawrence's murder? She wasn't even sure what the motive would be if they left the money in, unless he was the one who owned the extra account.

Returning to her desk and her work Parish put the company mysteries out of her mind. She became absorbed in preparing an analysis, losing track of time. Hearing a noise she looked up to note Midge standing in front of her desk.

"You skipping lunch today?"

Parish glanced at the computer's clock. "That wasn't my intent." She logged off and joined Midge at the elevator for the trip to the in-house restaurant. After passing through the cafeteria line they found a table along the periphery overlooking a sundrenched section of the port and beyond that Dash Point.

"I had an interesting visitor this morning," Midge announced. "Ellen Hogan." She sounded like she had just struck the rock and produced water.

"Mr. Hogan's wife?"

"Correct." Midge spread mustard on her ham sandwich. "She was wondering where the people at the conference in Spokane are staying. She said Tim forgot to leave her the information for getting hold of him."

Parish frowned. That didn't make sense.

Midge laughed nodding. "Suspicious, huh?"

"Number one she should have her husband's cell phone number, two I thought the Spokane conference was last week, three what conference is he at then?"

"The answers are yes, yes and on vacation, not at a conference." Midge looked like she had not only managed water from a rock but produced it filtered, bottled and chilled.

"Is that what you told her?"

"Are you nuts? Of course not."

"So what did you tell her?"

Midge sighed. "I told her I'd have to check. So I made certain Mr. Hogan was actually scheduled on vacation and not in the office. Then I looked up the numbers for the hotel we stayed at last week when we were at that conference and gave that to her."

"Are you kidding?"

"What always makes you think I'm kidding?"

"The absolutely wild things you tell me." Parish scowled at her. "So what is going on?"

"Didn't you just tell me he had something going with Bobbi Bennett?"

All the things Odella had said came rushing back into Parish's mind. She realized she hadn't taken Odella seriously. "Do you really think he's with Bobbi?" She was incredulous.

Midge lifted her eyebrows and gave her a big cheesy grin. "Seems logical to me."

"Are we going to have another disappearing employee?"

"We might have another murder on our hands if Ellen Hogan finds out."

❧

After lunch Parish received a text from Annabelle Elliott.

"*I have something to show you*," Annabelle announced. "*Want to stop by the store after work?*"

Parish considered what Annabelle might have, then texted back. "*OK.*" Given the circumstances she couldn't afford to ignore her. At that moment she heard a familiar voice outside her office and glancing at the door noticed Lieutenant Sarkis standing in the hall talking to someone.

"We found Moseley's Mercedes," the lieutenant announced.

She didn't hear the reply, but presumed he spoke to Blayze.

"In a storage unit in Hoquiam belonging to a Michael Johnson."

Parish rose and went to the door of her office from where she could see she was correct. The lieutenant stood at Blayze's door.

"I'm coming to see you," he said when he noticed her. "I need a copy of that picture on your phone you think was Moseley. It seems we need all the help we can get."

"You think he's rented a car and left the area?"

"I figure he's rented a car. Left the area, I don't know. I wouldn't put my money on it one way or the other." After a pause to listen to Blayze, something Parish couldn't hear, the lieutenant continued with frustration. "We've checked every place in Hoquiam and Ocean Shores where you could rent a car and nothing. I've even checked to see if he owned another car which he is using."

"So you think he's still here?"

Lieutenant Sarkis bobbed his head. "'Here' being relative. I figure his plan is disappearing but for some reason he hasn't put it into effect." The lieutenant turned toward Blayze. "That's what I have you two for." He included Parish in his comment. "You're the ones who know him and have connections with the people he knows."

Parish figured that was an exaggeration. She didn't really know Ian Moseley or have any connections with him and Blayze had never even met the guy. She followed the lieutenant into Blayze's area.

"We figure you need to locate who allowed that trunk with Manke in it to be moved into that transfer and storage company. I doubt an anonymous someone could manage that."

The lieutenant frowned at Blayze. "I figured if we knew who rented that unit it would give us the person who made arrangements with the transfer and storage."

"Well, that was a bust, but it might work in reverse." Blayze shot the lieutenant a forced grin.

The lieutenant rose and excusing himself past Parish left.

She smiled at Blayze. "Well, you still have your head."

"I haven't told him about the traveling money yet."

Parish took advantage of extra time she had put in at the beginning of the month, leaving work early in order to stop at Annabelle's shop. The late afternoon sun made it hot, but the tall buildings created long patches of shade on the sidewalk as she walked around Ridinghood's building to Pacific Avenue and then to the print shop.

Annabelle was at the counter taking an order when Parish arrived. She wandered for a time reading store advertisements and observing the various services the shop offered. When the customer had gone Annabelle approached Parish. "I can't leave right now, but we could sit over there." She beckoned to a small round table in the corner with three chairs.

Parish followed her and took a chair. "What did you want to show me?"

Annabelle grinned like she'd figured out how to walk on water. Activating an electronic tablet she had grabbed on her way she brought up a Facebook account. After scrolling for a time with periodic stops to register a comment she located a picture which she enlarged and turned for Parish to see.

It took Parish a moment to focus properly and mentally register what she saw. The photo was a selfie of two people seated in a circular booth. The woman had dark hair streaked with blonde and over-toned with red . . . Bobbi Bennett. Parish had to concentrate to recognize Tim Hogan, unaccustomed to seeing him with a big smile and laughter crinkles in the corner of his eyes. "This is on Facebook?" She was incredulous.

"Daring, huh?"

"Idiotic, if you ask me." Parish frowned at Annabelle. "Are you aware of who the man is?"

She shook her head. "I don't know him but he's the one she spent time with in Spokane. You said you wanted to know who they were."

"Right." Parish nodded. "This is the Chief Financial Officer of Ridinghood Corporation. He's married to a very domineering woman. I doubt she'd find this photo amusing."

"Well, it's my private Facebook so who can see it is limited."

"You're not serious?"

Annabelle gave her a blank look.

"You think this won't be all over town in fifteen minutes?"

Annabelle colored slightly. "I don't think I've shared it with anyone but you."

Something occurred to Parish. "Did Bobbi tell you where this is or why she gave you the picture?"

"It's at the hotel restaurant in Spokane."

"The conference a week or so ago?"

"I accused her of keeping secrets from me." Annabelle nodded.

"She might have been better off keeping this secret. Would she have ulterior motives putting this picture on Facebook?"

"Like what?"

"Getting Mr. Hogan's wife to divorce him?"

Annabelle appeared shocked. "You think she would do that?"

"I don't know her. What do you think?" Parish emphasized the "you".

"She was awfully excited about something, like she had big plans of some kind." Annabelle paused then asked. "She still hasn't returned to work?"

Parish shook her head. "I wonder how Tim will feel about this. She may have ended his sojourn into the Promised Land and hers too."

"I doubt she had ulterior motives. I don't believe she thinks that far ahead."

Something about that made sense.

"She just really likes to show off."

Parish felt bad for Tim Hogan. He seemed to have already made one miserable choice. Now it appeared he was making an even worse one.

When Lieutenant Sarkis left Blayze considered the problem of Moseley's location. Since the police had located the Mercedes and the man owned no other vehicle they concluded he had rented a car. However, if intent on disappearing he could find that complicated. New IDs would slow law enforcement down but not eliminate the problem. Was a rental car his only, or even his best option? And if he did that would he not have been wiser to get away from the coastal area first?

What made Sarkis so sure Moseley had not left the area? He may have information he declined to share.

Mr. Hornby had sent information on the second LLC account to which Blayze had traced one of the two smaller amounts leaving RC Returns. At this point he figured wherever this money traveled it voyaged courtesy of Ian Moseley. The smallest amount interested him more, which the RC Returns ACH transaction indicated went to an FFT. Of the people Blayze had met in connection with Moseley and Ridinghood he could make no connection with those letters.

He had concluded the money leaving and returning to Ridinghood triggered the IRS audit. He had uncovered no other anomaly. Ridinghood's process was clean and straightforward, taxes handled according to approved accounting practices and paid within the appropriate time frames. That, however, did not back off the IRS. The traveling money needed to be located and accounted for within legal limits. Blayze couldn't do that yet. His gut feelings weren't evidence and even they only took him so far. He needed to haunt Sarkis. Maybe the lieutenant would be up for dinner again at the bar and grill.

"Sarkis," the man barked with a trace of suspicion in his voice.

Blayze identified himself. "Would you be interested in joining me for dinner at the bar and grill?"

Hesitation from the lieutenant alerted Blayze's suspicion.

"You want to take a ride?"

"Where to?"

"I need to revisit Manke and that Sally's residence. The scientists did the routine but I figure it might help to check it out myself."

After agreeing to be picked up on Sarkis' way, Blayze returned to the FFT problem, not that it got him anywhere.

Just after four o'clock Blayze received a text announcing Sarkis waited across the street on eighth. After packing his paperwork he exited by the staircase to the main floor where he left the building. Walking around to the sidewalk on Pacific he spotted Sarkis' SUV parked on the side street.

The lieutenant greeted him with a nod then directed his vehicle south on Pacific Avenue to eleventh and up the hill. They jogged through the streets heading west until they could see the supports for the Narrows Bridge rising above the evergreens backing the apartment complex. They turned into the drive.

As the lieutenant had been there previously he drove straight to a parking spot across from the apartment and they proceeded into the building. Stepping into the small foyer they were met with a stale bar-like smell. Blayze recalled the spilled wine. Little appeared changed since the night Midge and Parish had found Sally unconscious.

"Forensics has the wine bottle and glass." It seemed the lieutenant read minds. "I haven't heard if they captured any fingerprints beyond Sally Stills. Hers were the only ones on the glass. Those on the bottle were badly smudged but the guys were attempting a resurrection."

"What are you looking for in particular?" Blayze figured since all the forensic evidence had been accounted for they were just wasting time.

"Apparently Manke had some hot future prospect. I want to see if anything here indicates what that might have been."

Turning to the right they climbed the stairs. Two bedrooms sat one after the other with a bath across the small hall. Sarkis stuck his head in the first where a bed occupied the greater amount of space then continued to the next. In addition to a place to store and practice music it served as an office.

For a time they stood at the door while Sarkis perused the furnishings. In one corner sat a music stand and an amplifier along with a folding chair. Straight ahead was an old fashioned roll-top desk. An oak two drawer file cabinet kept it company. Bookcases lined the far wall with an assortment of books on a couple of the shelves. However, much of what was shelved were stacks of paper and magazines in addition to sheet music.

"Why don't you check out that bookshelf while I take a look at this desk?"

When the lieutenant rolled back the desk top Blayze noted in front sat a laptop computer. He removed it, placing it on the top of the file cabinet and seated himself in the chair. Blayze continued to the bookshelves where he gave the books a quick perusal. They appeared mostly novels which he guessed belonged to Sally. What attracted his attention and brought questions to mind were the magazines. One stack related to money, investing and economic issues. Another stack were travel magazines and cruise brochures. The third stack dealt with real estate in different parts of the U.S. and foreign countries. Considering this collection brought on the formulation of a theory. He began to see possibilities for the extra account for which he sought an owner. He turned to the lieutenant wondering what he had discovered.

In the lieutenant's hands were a couple items, one a check book and the other a small notebook.

"Is there money in the checkbook?" Blayze figured if amounts there matched the smaller amounts leaving RC Returns he would have the answer to his question. He approached the lieutenant who opened the register. Blayze peered around his shoulder.

Sarkis shook his head.

From what Blayze could see none of the amounts deposited matched the ones leaving RC Returns. They appeared to be wages and the outgoing amounts regular payments on bills. If this accounted for Manke's money then he would not be the one sharing Moseley's little project, which also eliminated some motive Moseley might have had to get rid of Manke.

Although not having bought the idea Moseley killed Manke Blayze had to admit disappointment finding him innocent of siphoning off Moseley's accumulation of extra money. However, it remained possible the money was in another account. Blayze struggled to give up the idea Manke had come on Moseley's scheme and wanted to cash in.

"He wouldn't have put the money in Sally Stills name?" Blayze consulted Sarkis.

"I'm not sure he could do that without her knowing anything about it and she didn't."

"Is she any closer to consciousness?"

"The hospital hasn't had anything to say either positive or negative beyond the fact head injuries can take weeks or months to heal."

"You're still keeping her survival confidential?"

"Right, both for her sake and strategically. It's safer if whoever attacked her thinks she's dead. Plus the perp may trip himself up with what he knows or doesn't know."

That sounded as if the lieutenant figured her attacker meant to kill her. "You think it was premeditated?"

The lieutenant grimaced. "It was a pretty vicious attack. Especially against a victim whom everyone says was easy going and peaceable." He moved the grimace to the other side of his mouth. "She may be the only person available to tell us who attacked her and maybe Manke also. She may hold the key to a whole lot of these mysteries."

As they prepared to leave Sarkis grabbed the computer he had set aside. "We'll see if this thing can tell us anything."

◆CHAPTER TWENTY-FIVE◆

On Parish's first trek to the break room she encountered both Midge and Odella with their heads together. Pausing at the doorway she considered whether she really wanted to know what they discussed. She had a pile of reports to get through and didn't need the distraction. However, she sighed and entered the room, heading straight for the coffee.

"Is she still unconscious?" Odella asked.

"As far as I know." Midge glanced at Parish as if expecting a further update.

She wondered if either had come across the Facebook picture of Bobbi and Mr. Hogan. Annabelle had said it was private. Parish's impression of the whole Facebook phenomenon made privacy not only impossible but contraindicated. Maybe they wouldn't recognize him if they had just come across the picture randomly. He certainly didn't look like the Mr. Hogan they knew.

Midge complained to Parish, "You look like a news reporter with a scoop trying to avoid us so you won't get one upped."

Parish frowned at her.

Odella grinned at Parish. "She's probably still trying to get over Bobbi Bennett and Mr. Hogan."

"Did you see Ellen Hogan this morning?" Midge asked.

"Here?"

"Right." Midge's raised eyebrows questioned what Parish thought of that.

"What's she doing here?"

"I didn't stop to find out. I didn't need to figure out any more answers to her questions."

Parish laughed. "You didn't answer her questions, you parried them."

Midge shrugged and explained her run in with Ellen Hogan to Odella.

Parish finished fixing her coffee and returned to her office where she plunged back into her reports.

Before she got very far Blayze showed up, stopping just inside the door. "Do the letters FFT mean anything to you?"

After consideration Parish shook her head.

"That's the routing information for my extra account besides the M.I. Johnson one."

"You think it's someone's initials?"

"What would you suggest?"

"Business lingo or a symbol for a special type of account." A hoard of ideas flashed into her head. Lots of businesses used letters to designate aspects of their operation.

He scowled, his dark brows hovering over his pale eyes.

"Flight From Terrorists, Future Financial Training?" Parish tossed up ideas.

"Forced Fiscal Temperance?" Blayze laughed stepping into her space. "Could be, I guess." He moved to the chair by her desk. "I accompanied the lieutenant to Manke's apartment yesterday. At first I thought I had found something, but . . . " He shook his head. "He has stacks of financial and vacationing magazines in his office. I thought they made him a good candidate for horning in on Moseley's money diverting scheme, but Sarkis found his checkbook. Nothing in it indicated having any extra money."

Parish considered the possibilities. "Maybe he hadn't gotten hold of the money yet."

"Right," Blayze agreed. "But then he wouldn't be the one with the account for FFT."

She sighed. "And it wouldn't be a motive for murdering him."

"But someone did murder him."

"And there must have been a motive."

Blayze frowned. "Maybe it has nothing to do with Ridinghood." He stared over her head a moment then returned his gaze to her face. "You wouldn't be interested in having a non-date dinner with me again?"

After a moment's consideration she smiled at him. "I think I'm free to do that."

"I thought I'd bug Sarkis. Get some helpful information, but that didn't work." Blayze rose. "I'll come by your office at five."

When Blayze had gone she considered his problems. She could see he was becoming discouraged. She could empathize. As far as it went she was just as discouraged except it seemed less and less the problems would adversely affect the company.

After returning to her reports she didn't get far before Lieutenant Sarkis tromped into her office and plunked himself down.

"How well do you know that administrative assistant of Moseley's?"

"By sight. That's all."

"You wouldn't want to get to know her a little better?"

Parish widened her eyes. "No." She shook her head emphasizing her refusal.

The lieutenant peered over his glasses at her.

"I stay as far away from her as I can. She goes into a shrieking tirade at the slightest provocation."

"I wouldn't mind seeing her in a shrieking tirade," the lieutenant declared thoughtfully, gazing over Parish's head. "I might learn something."

Parish almost laughed at the thought of Doris Possum having a tantrum and Lieutenant Sarkis taking notes. "Blayze might be up for your suggestion. Apparently she tried threatening him."

The lieutenant cocked his head like a bright-eyed bird. "Does she still have contact with Ian Moseley?"

"I believe if she is able to, she does."

"Sufficient she might know where he's gone?"

"If she still has contact I imagine she knows where he is. But if she knows anything about him at all it's a secret she guards with her life." While responding to the lieutenant, Parish noticed two women pass the open door to her office. She stared in astonishment.

The look on her face induced the lieutenant to turn around. "Doris, the one you were asking about, and Ellen Hogan, the CFO Tim Hogan's wife, just passed by the door."

"Where do you think they're going?"

Parish lifted her shoulders. "To see Blayze?"

❧

Blayze looked up as two women stood in the opening to his space. Behind them he noticed Lieutenant Sarkis. The one woman he recognized as Ian Moseley's administrative assistant. The other, a short square-built brunette with small piercing eyes in a perfectly square face, he didn't recognize.

Entering his area they glanced around as if looking for a chair. The only one available sat in the corner. Since he wasn't excited about the company he refrained from offering them a seat.

Doris Possum spoke first in a high pitch coercive tone. "Tell us where Ian Moseley is?"

"And Tim Hogan," the other woman added in a deeper, more forceful voice.

Blayze stared at them dumbfounded. "Why would I know where they are?"

"Don't play games with us," Doris snapped. "Ever since you came here funny things have been happening."

Frowning Blayze considered. In truth the funny things happening before he got to the company had brought him there. A glance at Sarkis told him the lieutenant hoped he would play it for all it was worth. Unfortunately the lieutenant wasn't aware of Blayze's ineptitude at conversational games.

"Where do you think they are?" He tossed the conversational ball back into their court.

They exchanged a glance.

"You're having them held on suspicion of some tax crime." This time it was the other woman who spoke. She sounded like a female version of The Godfather.

"Are they guilty of tax crimes?"

He could see by their expressions that shot a hole in their balloon. If they weren't careful they would provide the men a crash landing.

"You're with the IRS," Doris charged, as if working for the IRS was a crime in itself. "Ian was in Ocean Shores. So were you," she added, flint in her eyes. Apparently she decided to drop the tax ball.

Blayze cocked his head. "If I'm not mistaken lots of people are in Ocean Shores."

"After you left the men disappeared." Mrs. Hogan made it sound as if Blayze put a hex on them.

"And you think I'm to blame?" Blayze figured this conversation was just short of ridiculous. Obviously the women were scraping the bottom of the bucket in their attempt to locate the two men. "I may be bursting your bubble, but Lieutenant Sarkis has been working to find Mr. Moseley ever since he was reported missing to the police. I've been assisting, but we have no idea where he is."

From behind the women Lieutenant Sarkis spoke. "Maybe you could give us some helpful suggestions."

This produced a reaction not unlike an electric prod might.

"We could go downtown where I have some chairs and have a chat," he suggested.

The two women separated. Doris Possum narrowed her eyes as if so doing would put a hex on the lieutenant. However, Mrs. Hogan dissembled. "We're just trying to get some information."

"By intimidating the IRS?" Sarkis cast an amused glance at Blayze.

"No, no," Ellen Hogan protested. "It's just the last we knew he had seen Tim and Ian."

"How about it, Blayze? Have you seen either Tim Hogan or Ian Moseley recently?"

"I had a conversation with Tim Hogan a few days ago, here at his office. I've never even met Ian Moseley."

Doris Possum leveled a glance at Blayze that could have launched a hellfire missile.

Ellen Hogan graciously apologized. "Apparently we're mistaken. We'd appreciate it if you would let us know if you hear from them." She backed toward the opening to Blayze's area.

The lieutenant stepped aside allowing the women to depart. He turned to Blayze. "You were intimidated, right?"

Blayze laughed. "Oh, absolutely."

Lieutenant Sarkis went to the corner and moved the extra chair to Blayze's desk. "What do you suppose they thought they were doing?"

Blayze grimaced. "That's difficult to figure. I'd never met Hogan's wife, but that Possum woman should know very well I wouldn't have ever seen Moseley. I didn't come here until long after he had gone."

"I'd definitely say she has it in for you."

"So if I end up dead you'll know who to arrest?"

The lieutenant bobbed his head. "One person who'll be arrested on sight is Moseley. I've alerted the police here and all along the coast."

"You figure he killed Manke?"

"Evidence points that way. His house appears to be the murder scene. He's the one who made the arrangements with the moving and storage company to pick up that trunk." The lieutenant slid back in his chair. "I actually wouldn't have minded taking those two women downtown. I think that Possum woman knows more than she lets on. I wouldn't be surprised to find out she knows exactly where Moseley is."

"So what's she doing in here?"

Sarkis lifted his shoulders, shaking his head. "Probably an ulterior motive. Maybe they wanted to find out how much we know. It may be a diversion tactic."

"Trying to head people off Moseley's trail?" Blayze had to concede the possibility. "I'm not sure what Tim Hogan has to do with it though."

Sarkis grimaced. "Have you settled on a culprit for your money issue?"

"Moseley definitely appears to be the one moving the vacationing money. However, he operates so carefully within the boundaries of legality, it's hard to even accuse him of embezzling much less jump to the conclusion he committed murder."

The lieutenant scowled. "If you're exonerating him you need to furnish a replacement."

Blayze grinned. "I'll work on it."

◈CHAPTER TWENTY-SIX◈

After checking the time Parish closed her accounting windows, logged off her computer, tidied her desk and touched up her makeup.

Blayze appeared at her door promptly at five. "You're okay with the bar and grill?"

She nodded. "It's close. We can walk."

Sunshine greeted them as they stepped out of the building. Parish observed a number of people lounging on benches in the little park. When they reached Pacific Avenue she noted the heavy traffic moving slowly. She could hear it whizzing by on the I-705 spur.

"Maybe we should try the restaurant at the top of the Murano sometime," Blayze suggested with a sideways glance at Parish, pointing to the top of the hotel as it rose above the nearby buildings.

She didn't reply. She was as far out of her comfort zone as she could manage, although she had to admit acquiring a basic trust in Blayze and an appreciation for his company. She smiled wondering if Midge would give her credit for making progress. However, progress remained relative depending on the behavior of her companion. "Did you have a couple women visit this afternoon?"

Blayze gave a snorting laugh. "I'm still trying to figure that one out."

"How did they even get together?"

"An unlikely pair?"

"I'd have thought so, but maybe it's just unexpected." Sometimes her naivety prevented her from realizing connections people might make with one another. Perhaps it wasn't that strange for Ellen Hogan and Doris Possum to pair up.

"Ostensibly they were looking for a pair of missing men."

"I wouldn't have considered Mr. Hogan missing, but maybe . . . ."

Blayze cocked his head.

"Yesterday Ellen Hogan asked Midge what hotel the company was using for the conference in Spokane. But Mr. Hogan wasn't at a conference. That was the week before. He was on vacation this week."

They had reached the large wooden door of the restaurant. As Blayze held it open for her, he suggested, "Maybe she figured that out. She sounded as if she didn't know where he was."

Approaching the hostess stand they suspended their conversation. Having arrived early enough to be seated immediately they were led to a booth along the wall next to the windows and left with menus.

Parish waited to continue the conversation until they had placed their order. Once their waiter had delivered water and wine, then departed, she explained her conversation with Annabelle.

"On Facebook?" Blayze's sharp tone sounded torn between denouncing her a liar and laughing.

"I'm not kidding. I saw the picture. The only hope is the average person wouldn't recognize a happy smiling Mr. Hogan. I didn't right away."

"But that wouldn't apply to his wife."

"It might, depending on whether she ever sees him happy and smiling."

Blayze shot her a shame-on-you glance. "Sarkis thinks those two know where Moseley is." He lifted his wine glass staring at it thoughtfully. "I'm not sure they do. I detected a trace of desperation."

While the waiter served their entrees Parish considered Blayze's comment. In her experience Doris Possum always appeared a little desperate. Maybe she was. Her whole existence seemed to center on Ian Moseley, an attitude beyond Parish's comprehension.

"I'd put more than a penny on the line," Blayze offered when the waiter had gone.

Parish frowned.

"For your thoughts."

"Has someone ever been so important to you your whole life revolved around that person?"

Blayze laughed. "I can't keep a relationship together for longer than a couple years because apparently no one is that important to me."

She eyed him with suspicion. "I'm not sure any person should be that important to one. Makes the person your god."

His intense expression questioned her meaning.

"Maybe that never happens to men."

"I had a friend in college who felt that way about a woman. She didn't share his devotion, married someone else. He committed suicide." After a brief pause Blayze continued, "It was an outrageous waste. I don't think he'd have been happy with her had she married him. Sometimes we don't know when we're well off." After another pause he added, "You've never been desperately in love, as they say?"

Parish shook her head. "Never really got the chance."

The intensity of his scrutiny made her uncomfortable. He dropped his gaze. "Me, neither. Probably too self-centered."

"You don't seem so self-centered."

"You haven't got to know me well enough. I've been told I'm egotistical, self-centered, judgmental, arrogant and pig-headed."

Parish laughed. "Sounds like something a sibling would say."

"My sister probably thinks that about me, but it's me that told her that's what she is."

"You might get along with her better if you had nicer things to say."

"She might agree if she ever comes to the point of remembering me. Maybe I can start over since she's lost her memory."

Parish considered his sister's loss of memory. She knew nothing about head injuries and wondered what Sally Stills' head injury would do to her memory. Some hope existed if she recovered she would be able to identify her attacker. She put the question to Blayze.

"Sylvia's memory loss is random. Lots of things she still remembers, and is apparently recalling more all the time."

"So there's still hope," Parish summarized the conclusion then smiled at him. "Even that your sister will remember you."

The waiter returned to clear their plates. Both agreed it was better to skip dessert. When Blayze had finished with the credit card transaction he ushered Parish back to the sidewalk.

❧

Returning to Ridinghood's parking garage Blayze considered Parish's comment. He had in fact begun to believe Sylvia may be better never to recover her memory. Maybe as Parish indicated they could start over, have a better relationship. He had seen nothing to convince him of his mother's idea Sylvia's personality had changed. But with a fresh slate they could handle things differently, build better memories.

"You're certain they were actually targeted in that hit and run?"

"Evidence points that way." He still struggled with the idea. "Something else concerning me is they may have accidentally gotten mixed up in the Ridinghood deal."

"They wouldn't have actually had anything to do with it?"

Blayze shook his head. "I doubt they had ever heard of Ridinghood. Probably still haven't. No, it would have been purely a chance encounter." Climbing the hill to Commerce he explained the situation Janice had outlined for him in their meeting. "The big questions, who was the woman at the bar and did she attack them?"

"Could she have mistaken them for someone else?"

"Logical, however, I'd think she would have had enough time to realize that wasn't the case." He lifted his shoulders. "Something in the situation must be the trigger, but what? And nothing says she's the one who hit them."

They continued walking in silence. Although the sun hadn't completely dropped beyond the horizon, the air had cooled enough to make it chilly. Reaching the end of the block Blayze turned to Parish and asked, "Any theories?"

"One thing I'd question is did either of those men have a particular interest in your sister or her friend?"

Something about that rang a bell for him. He hadn't thought of it in those terms. Not that thinking about it did any good since he had no idea who the woman was or even who the men were except for the possibility one of them could be Ian Moseley.

Once they reached Parish's car, as she turned to him, Blayze moved her direction with intent then realized the mistake and stopped. He had been on the point of making a blunder that could have ended any further communication. She had taken a step back remaining at arm's length. He held out his hand, offering thanks for her company. She hesitated slightly before placing her slim fingers in his. Smiling, she indicated she would see him in the morning.

Walking back to his hotel he realized he had ceased to be confounded by Parish's viewpoint, but because she had lowered her guard he had begun to feel close to her and react accordingly. That would be an error in judgment, a costly error. He needed to remain as much on guard as she was. He could even empathize when considering his own perspective regarding his sister. Some experiences left an imprint on one's psychology.

Reaching his room his mind returned to the question of whether some relationship existed between the two men at the bar, Janice and Sylvia. Had they failed to be straight up with him? Going back to the conversation in Janice's apartment he struggled to buy their jointly hiding something so consequential. If one of the men were Ian Moseley then further examination of his life might be in order. With whom did he have non-business relationships? And who was the other man? Figuring he was in no position to determine either of those things, Blayze also concluded neither was the lieutenant. Who would be? He could pester his sister and Janice again, pressure them for more information on the two men. He wondered if any of Parish's gossipy friends would have an inside track on Moseley's outside acquaintances. Another consideration was Tim Hogan. Did he know more about Moseley's private relationships than he let on, either because of the man's confidences or because of gossip? If Hogan was hanging around with Bobbi Bennett, a name dropping, social climbing gossip, he may know more than he ever let on.

Since his only option was contacting his sister and Janice, once back in his hotel room he dug out the phone number he had belonging to Janice. He had no means of contact for his sister, undoubtedly by her design.

Either Janice recognized his number or his voice for she greeted him by name when she answered. "What can I do for you?"

"I'm wondering if what you told me about that meeting in the bar could be significant. Could that woman be your attacker?"

"But why would she?" Janice sounded as if the idea was incredulous. "We didn't even know her."

"It may have nothing to do with you or Sylvia, but something to do with the men instead." He tested a possibility. "Would it have looked to an outsider as if you were with the men?"

"Not just sitting there, but . . ."

"Their companions for the evening."

"I-I suppose it could. More relative to the Bob person and me. I don't think Sylvia said much at all and neither did the other man."

If Janice was correct it would move the situation farther from having any connection to Ridinghood than closer. It might explain what happened to Janice and Sylvia but nothing else.

"Did you get any idea the men knew the woman?"

"The one had his back directly to her. I don't think he even saw her there. The other guy was in a little better position if he looked to the side. Essentially his back was to her also, but not quite so directly. He could have swiveled a little and been able to see her."

"But you don't think he did?"

"No, I don't think so."

This conversation wasn't getting Blayze anywhere. "What about the woman? Did you get a good look at her?"

Janice sighed. "I could see her, but I was listening to the man and not really paying any attention except that she seemed angry, which I did notice, but the bar was dim and she wasn't close . . ."

"Would Sylvia . . . Elysia have seen more?"

"Do you want me to ask her?"

Blayze gave a hacking laugh. "Better you than me."

"If she has anything to say about it I'll let you know."

◆CHAPTER TWENTY-SEVEN◆

Blayze stared at Hornby's message. It had gone. The money had moved offshore, not as yet out of the United States, but nonetheless offshore . . . to Puerto Rico.

The printout of the second LLC account indicated almost the entire balance had gone. Checking the date he determined the move had occurred only a few days previous. Had the money landed or was it just making a stop before moving on? Undoubtedly it was time to give Sarkis a heads up. As he considered calling him the man showed up in his doorway.

Grabbing the chair from the corner he maneuvered it to Blayze's desk then cast a line. "Anything new?"

"Aren't you the great *Puhbah* who knows all things?"

Sarkis' face registered confusion.

"I've just learned the roving money I figure belongs to Moseley has moved to Puerto Rico."

The lieutenant eyed him with suspicion. "Why there?"

"It's a reasonable place to live if you like it warm, don't want to be on the continent, and have sufficient money to retire. It takes a lot less to retire there than here. At least to live with any comfort or style."

"You think that's what Moseley's doing?"

Blayze lifted his shoulders. "You tell me."

"Let's put some pressure on that administrative assistant. She may know."

Blayze rolled his eyes. "Get too close to her and she may put the pressure on you."

Sarkis snorted. "She'd better not try. I have leverage."

Blayze grinned. He entertained no confidence the lieutenant's leverage would prevent Ms. Possum's pressure. "Have you talked to Hogan?"

The lieutenant frowned. "I understand he's on vacation."

"In Ocean Shores I heard."

"What's with Ocean Shores anyway?" Sarkis exploded. "Maybe Ridinghood should move its headquarters."

Blayze laughed. "Have you checked? Maybe they have."

The look on the lieutenant's face wasn't encouraging. His gaze drifted over Blayze's head and remained there.

Blayze continued. "I think I saw him this morning when I was coming up the stairs, so maybe he's back."

"Let's have a chat with him? You can introduce me, I've never met the guy."

Frowning at the lieutenant Blayze wondered if he was serious. Sarkis' body language cancelled any doubt as he rose from the chair and paused as if expecting Blayze to do the same.

He ushered the lieutenant to the stairs down one level to the entrance foyer and into the executive suite. At the second archway they turned to the left and consulted Hogan's administrative assistant.

After being gone a moment she told them, "He'll see you now, but he's been gone for a while so he's quite busy."

Tim Hogan's expression reminded Blayze of the cornered rabbit and what made him so busy wasn't visible. His desk top was clear except for a couple sheets of paper.

His briefcase sat open on the floor beside the desk, but was nearly empty. "Sit down," he waved to the chairs facing his desk. "What can I do for you?"

"We're still searching for Ian Moseley. We understand you've been in Ocean Shores and wondered if you had seen him, since he was also there."

Confusion, surprise, and fear danced across his face. Had Hogan deluded himself his trip to the beaches went unnoticed?

"I – I," he made two attempts to respond then shook his head. "No, no, I didn't see him. I was only there a couple days . . . on business." His eyes questioned whether they would buy that.

Blayze kept his face expressionless and refrained from glancing at Sarkis.

"Your wife was here asking Pashasia where you were. She seemed to think the IRS had you locked up."

Hogan opened his mouth, then grabbed his handkerchief and began coughing. Apparently what he was going to say caught in his throat. After a couple minutes, he said, "I haven't seen Ian since he left over a month ago."

"So you weren't with him?"

"No." He shook his head. "No."

"Would you know if he's gone to Puerto Rico?"

Hogan's eyes widened in astonishment. "Puerto Rico! But what . . ."

"We thought you could tell us." Sarkis eyed the man. "He's never mentioned Puerto Rico?"

Blayze had the feeling this announcement came as a coincidental attack of emergency information requiring immediate attention. Hogan glanced at the papers on his desk, shot a look at his briefcase and then at the screen to his computer. Clearly he knew nothing about any plans

Moseley had that included Puerto Rico, but equally as clear, the knowledge meant something to him.

The lieutenant stayed in pursuit. "Could you guess how Moseley would travel to Puerto Rico?"

"Fly?" Hogan's voice squeaked.

"From?"

The executive's gaze moved back and forth between the lieutenant and Blayze. "Portland?"

At least he had the presence of mind to figure if the lieutenant was asking Moseley probably hadn't flown out of SeaTac.

Sarkis turned to Blayze. "Is there anything you want to ask?"

"Would you happen to know where Moseley does his banking?"

The blood drained out of Hogan's face turning him white. He shook his head.

Rising the lieutenant told him, "We may have more questions. We'll let you know."

Returning to the stairs the lieutenant asked. "What did you think of that?"

"He doesn't know where Moseley is, but if he's gone to Puerto Rico it's a first class emergency."

❧

Back in his office Blayze resumed his pursuit of the traveling funds, particularly the smaller amount for which he had not identified an owner. Could Hogan have discovered Moseley's plot and horned in on the project? Next question, if that were the case would Miguel have any evidence? It wouldn't hurt to trek up and see.

After locking his paperwork in his briefcase, Blayze headed again for the third floor where the accounting departments resided then proceeded along the brick lined hall to the double doors opening into IT.

Miguel sat in the far corner his eyes fixed on his monitor. He lifted his eyebrows as Blayze took the chair beside his desk. "What's up?"

"What entries have you for Tim Hogan in the financial accounts? Anything suspicious? I've just found out the bank numbers I've been chasing have moved to Puerto Rico. In addition to the ones I figured were being manipulated by Moseley I found another account. It appears to be derived from the ones he is manipulating. I'm wondering if it belongs to Tim Hogan."

Miguel narrowed his eyes. "I haven't noticed anything suspicious where Hogan is concerned. My guess if he was skimming off Moseley's proceeds it wouldn't show up here."

Blayze nodded. He figured that way too, but didn't want to overlook the elephant.

"What gives you the idea Hogan is involved?" Miguel frowned his skepticism.

"More than anything," Blayze realized suddenly, "his wife."

Miguel cocked his head.

Blayze explained the scene in his office the day before. "She has apparently hooked up with Ian Moseley's assistant who has been belligerently guarding Moseley's affairs."

"So where does Hogan's wife come in?"

"Rumor has Hogan out at Ocean Shores the same time as Moseley was seen there. His wife struck me as being more ruthless and astute, more determined. If she had any idea of Moseley's money scheme she would be all over Hogan to get his share."

"Blackmail?"

"No, no. I don't see him being able to carry that off, or even wanting to."

Miguel leaned back in his chair. "You're betting Hogan's wife pushed him into discovering what Moseley was up to and cutting in on it?"

"Someone is cutting in, at least as far as the evidence goes." Blayze grimaced. "But you think it's a stretch?"

Back in his office he realized the conclusion he had drawn from the two women's visit. Not necessarily sold on his hypothesis, he nonetheless considered it worth pursuing.

He considered the possibility Tim Hogan owned the other account moving a separate direction from the LLCs. The man had certainly been shocked out of his composure at their visit. What would it mean to him if Moseley had left the country, moving all the funds he had collected to Puerto Rico? How exactly would that affect Hogan if he had tagged onto Moseley's scheme?

From Blayze's perspective the money he had accumulated was totally separated from Moseley's. His plans should have no affect on Hogan and his accumulation. However, the accumulation would undoubtedly end if Moseley ceased his financial activities with the Ridinghood money. Did that present Hogan a problem? If his wife were the driver, his problem may be in relating to her ambitions.

Although Ms. Possum was more vocal and reactive, Blayze felt Mrs. Hogan possessed a greater level of determination combined with sufficient patience and persistence to employ stronger more effective methods. Ms. Possum had no control over anyone, but undoubtedly Mrs. Hogan had effective control over her husband.

Once again Blayze returned to his doctor's advice regarding getting married for his health. He remained convinced he would be far healthier disregarding his doctor's advice. A picture flashed into his mind of Parish requesting his presence on the trip to Ocean Shores. He pushed it out of his head.

◆CHAPTER TWENTY-EIGHT◆

Saturday morning as Parish finished her laundry and considered a trip to the grocery store she received a call from Midge.

"What's on your agenda today?"

"Not going to Ocean Shores," Parish declared in self-defense figuring Midge was anticipating another foray to the seaside resort.

"How about a trip to see Sally?"

"We're supposed to pretend she's dead."

"I have a bad feeling. I'd like to see for myself she's okay."

Parish sighed. She too was concerned about Sally. The last time Midge had a bad feeling there had been a good reason for it. However, Parish was unaccustomed to defying police instructions. "But the lieutenant said . . . ."

"We'll be careful, pretend we're there to visit someone else. One of Alan Bernstein's group had surgery. We can visit her."

Well, that might work. Parish considered her schedule. "When?"

"Two-ish?"

Since Midge lived closer to the hospital, Parish drove and picked her up. They continued to the hospital's parking garage. After inquiring at information and receiving the room number she gave Parish a big grin. "That's convenient, the same as Sally."

They proceeded to the crowded elevator. Undoubtedly appropriate, given it was visiting hours. Progress to the that floor was slow with a stop on every floor in between. An individual getting on at another floor caught Parish's attention. Dressed in scrubs with hair covered the person nonetheless seemed familiar. However, Parish was unable to even determine the individual's sex.

Once they reached the right floor and exited the elevator they checked the arrowed directions for the room they wanted. As it turned out a swarm of visitors crowded this woman's room. Consequently, Midge announced her presence, letting the group gathered know who she was, spoke a few moments to the woman in bed, wishing her well. They departed vaguely indicating they would return at a more convenient time.

"Now for Sally."

They headed to Intensive Care where the nurse's station sat in the center surrounded by individual patient rooms. Approaching the counter Parish saw the person she had noticed of indeterminate sex open the door to the room she recalled was Sally's.

Midge shot Parish an anxious glance. "Who is that?" she demanded in a louder than normal voice, causing the nurses at the station to turn in the direction Midge was looking.

One of the nurses immediately left the counter headed for that individual. "I need to see your identification. You can't go in there unaccompanied." Another at the station immediately picked up the phone and gave a coded message. "How can I help you?" she turned to Midge and Parish.

"I think you already have." Midge smiled. "We came to make sure Sally was alright."

The woman raised her eyebrows as if to ask who they were.

"I'm Sally's boss at work. I've had a bad feeling all morning about her and wanted to be sure she's okay. Who was that person?"

"I don't know. I didn't see any identification and the way he acted is suspicious."

"May we see Sally?"

The nurse turned to her companion who nodded. "I got hold of security. He said he would let the lieutenant know." She turned back to Midge. "Okay."

"Has she shown any signs of recovering?" Parish asked.

"She seems to be moving more which sometimes precedes recovering consciousness."

The nurse opened the door to Sally's room, ushering them in. Sally lay quietly, attached to less electronic equipment than Parish would have expected. She appeared to sleep quietly. Her color was good and her hair lay in curls around her head.

"Has anyone tried to see her?" Midge asked the nurse.

"Not officially, other than the police. You know they're keeping her survival unknown."

Suddenly the door opened and Lieutenant Sarkis strode into the room looking ferocious. His glance took in the patient, the nurse then shifted momentarily to Midge and Parish.

"Everything's okay?"

The nurse gave him an affirmative.

He wagged his head toward the door. "Can I talk to you two outside?" He followed Parish and Midge out of the room then demanded. "Did you see this person who tried to get in there just now?"

"I did," Parish volunteered. "He was in the elevator with us."

"He?"

She lifted her shoulders. "It could have been a woman. In surgical garb I couldn't tell."

The lieutenant frowned. "Why don't you describe him?"

Parish complied to the extent she could.

"Had you seen this person before?"

Parish considered. "He looked familiar somehow, but I couldn't even tell if it was a man or a woman."

"It wouldn't have been someone from Ridinghood?" The lieutenant focused on her as if by mental telepathy he could inspire her recollection.

"If it comes to mind I'll let you know."

"That person almost got in there," Midge charged him.

He grimaced. "We're doing everything we can to keep her safe."

❦

"That was a close call," Midge declared as they exited the hospital. "I can't tell you how much that worries me."

Parish empathized but what could they do? Her attempts to identify the individual went without success. Undoubtedly the harder she tried the more difficult it would be. Not that who it reminded her of had anything to do with anything.

"I think we should find out about that car in her neighborhood," Midge proclaimed on their way to the parking garage.

"Are you kidding?"

"There you go again. I'm never kidding."

"Someday I'll remind you of that." She took the keys out of her handbag. "So what are you suggesting? That we trump the police?"

"No, no, not that. It's just that they have limitations due to legalities."

"And we don't?" Parish shook her head. What fantastic scheme had Midge put on the front burner now?

"Well . . . I'm not sure, but the consequences for us aren't as great."

Parish rolled her eyes. "You figure an angel will break us out of prison?" she grumbled starting the car and backing out of her space.

Midge scowled at her. "Both Sally's neighbors and Blayze's sister report a burgundy car regarding the attacks. That's not like black, or white, or grey. I'll bet manufacturers don't even make burgundy cars every year."

She did have a point. "How do you expect to find out all those with burgundy cars?"

"We don't have to find out ALL who have burgundy cars, just ones who could possibly have attacked Blayze's sister and been in Sally's neighborhood."

"Okay, how are you going to do that? By the way, where are we headed?" They had exited the parking garage and were traveling south on Martin Luther King Way.

"If we go to my house, I'll fix lunch."

Since she had to take Midge home anyway Parish agreed. She made a right on Sixth Avenue and headed for her companion's house.

"The way I figure it," Midge addressed Parish's question, "they weren't random attacks. Somewhere is a connection to the victims, some motive, real or imagined."

"I doubt Sally had any relationship whatever to Blayze's sister or her friend."

"First," Midge wiggled her finger at Parish, "we have to avoid drawing conclusions we have no evidence for like assuming there's no link between these people."

Parish grimaced. "Okay. Then what?"

"We have to determine what the possible links are." When Parish opened her mouth to protest, Midge went on, "like Ridinghood."

"Ridinghood! But Blayze's sister wouldn't have any . . . ."

"How do you know?"

Blayze's concern that his sister and her friend had gotten mixed up with Ian Moseley popped into her head.

"It wouldn't be that hard to check out Ridinghood's parking garage to see if any cars match the description."

Parish shrugged. "Then what?"

"If we find one we can get the license number and have the Lieutenant locate the owner."

Once they reached Midge's house, Parish parked in the driveway to the small detached garage and they entered through the side door where Ezekiel barked as if holding off the Babylonian invasion single-handed.

"Can I help you with anything?" Parish offered.

"I'll give you the salad ingredients. You can work on that while I fix sandwiches."

While tearing lettuce and chopping vegetables, Parish considered Midge's plan. Although Midge's schemes worried her, she wasn't an idiot. What other avenues besides Ridinghood's parking garage might hold a clue to the burgundy car? She still found it difficult to include Blayze's sister in the equation. However, a chat with him might help determine other places to look. It crossed her mind to wonder if she had a way to contact him when they weren't at work. She also wondered what he would be doing on the weekend. It wasn't the same as if he were home in Salt Lake.

Midge brought her sandwiches to the table and took the plastic bags Parish had put the extra lettuce and vegetables in. After replacing them in the refrigerator she brought salad dressings and two glasses of water.

"So what's going on in that fair head of yours?"

"I've been thinking about other places worth checking for that car." They both sat down. "Do you think Blayze might have an idea?"

Midge focused on the lamp then shrugged. "It wouldn't hurt to ask him." She returned her gaze to Parish. "You could invite him out to dinner. He seems to like company."

Parish felt a stab of alarm at Midge's suggestion.

Midge waved her hands. "I'm kidding, I'm kidding."

"You said you never kid."

Midge gave her a sympathetic glance. "I'm sorry. I wasn't being flip. It would be a good idea to check with him. You two seem to have made peace."

Parish sighed. "We have in a way but that can be twice as dangerous."

"You can't go on being afraid of men the rest of your life."

She clamped her mouth shut and eyed her friend.

"You can't, you know. You'll regret it eventually."

"Like what I already regret?"

"No! Like putting your money under the mattress never risking to even get interest in the bank. Then a thief comes to your house, steals it and all you have left is regret for not even taking a safe risk. There are degrees of risk you know."

Parish didn't like this conversation. "I'm not afraid of men."

Midge rolled her eyes. "I mean something besides a business relationship, something like friendship even. You don't want to get twenty years down the road and realize how much you missed by not taking a chance."

This conversation was giving her a headache.

"It seems to me Blayze would make a safe risk as a friend."

"Bank kind of safety?"

"Right." Midge laughed. "Not like tossing your money into the high risk end of the stock market. You realize, he has as much to lose as you would, if not more, by mishandling his relationship with you."

Parish sighed. She wished Midge didn't always make so much sense.

∞

Blayze sighed, the weekend again. He should be able to wrap this assignment up shortly. Struggling with indifference about returning to Salt Lake, he realized it was even more imperative he return soon. After three assignments in the area he was feeling at home in the Pacific Northwest. He had made some friends, knew his way around, and something else. Something sat in a cloud at the back of his mind. Somewhere in that fog was something he didn't want to face. Somehow he knew if he did he would have even more difficulty leaving the area.

As he returned to his room from the workout area his phone alerted him. He glanced at the face and noted with some surprise the call was from Parish. "Blayze."

"I was wondering . . . ." she paused.

"Yes?"

"Midge and I were considering a way to locate that burgundy car that attacked your sister and might have been in Sally's neighborhood when she was attacked. We thought you might have some suggestions or information."

Ideas raced through Blayze's mind like a mouse in a maze. Might as well go for broke. "Do you want to have dinner?" He found he was holding his breath.

"Okay, that would be good."

"Will Midge come too?"

"No, she has somewhere she has to be tonight."

"Okay, my restaurant, say 6:00?"

Blayze doubted he could be much help to Parish and Midge. However, something did occur to him. Available information wasn't necessarily the issue but what wasn't there, more difficult to determine. Mostly a person sees what is there, if they see anything at all. They fail to recognize what should be but isn't.

He still had time to take a shower and dress before meeting Parish. He redid his shave and took care in choosing something to wear, refraining from considering what difference it made.

Given this came near to being his private dining room, the hostess recognized him, asking, "Your usual table?"

Parish arrived on time, charming in long, full-leg pants and a peasant style shirt tucked in. The look on her face reminded him of her apprehensive greeting the first day he met her. He leaned close enough to murmur, "I promise not to bite."

She flashed him a glance then laughed.

The hostess led them to his usual table for four toward the back of the restaurant. Chairs upholstered in rose vinyl with a table top streaked with teal reflected the strange psychedelic lighting.

"Is this one of Ridinghood's decors," he asked as they picked up their menus.

Parish cast a glance around. "You don't like it?"

"Makes me feel like I'm in the middle of a nightmare."

She studied him with an amused expression.

"You're thinking I am the nightmare?"

She laughed. "I feared that was the case the first day you came."

"And now?" He fixed her with his gaze.

The waitress arrived to take their order. When she had gone Parish returned to the question. "I'm hoping you can help be the solution."

"So what is Midge proposing?"

"She wants to find the car reported in Sally's neighborhood the night she was attacked and possibly your sister and her friend."

"She's decided they're connected."

"There are too many parallels to dismiss out of hand." Parish lifted her shoulders. "She's wants to check out the Ridinghood parking garage."

"She figures it's someone from Ridinghood?"

"You don't think that's the case?"

"On the contrary. That's the most logical assumption."

Parish shot him a surprised glance.

"You think she's wrong?"

She shook her head. "As crazy as Midge is, she's rarely wrong."

"So what are you looking for?"

"A burgundy car, that's all the information we have."

"I talked to my sister's friend after you called. All along they've sworn their attacker was a Chevrolet. Janice said she saw the symbol. She didn't see the driver because she thinks the windows were tinted. And it was night."

"That might narrow it down."

Blayze continued. "The big missing piece is motive. Why would anyone, specifically someone from Ridinghood, want to take out Manke's girlfriend, my sister and her friend?"

The waitress delivered their orders, a halibut filet with rice pilaf for Parish and pork chops with au gratin potatoes for Blayze. The meals came on platter style plates which included a green salad and toasted garlic bread.

"Weren't you concerned your sister and her friend had gotten mixed up with Mr. Moseley?"

Blayze nodded. "But I can't believe he's into murder, in spite of what the lieutenant thinks." He shifted his focus to the blue tinted television screens where one of the pre-season football games played on the set. "Most murder is committed for some kind of gain, or perceived gain, money, power . . . ."

"Or revenge," Parish added.

"Or sex. Can you hook any of those ideas up to Moseley?"

Parish opened her mouth then closed it again and shook her head.

"Obviously we've been considering the money angle, but from all I have seen, Moseley is taking the money. He doesn't have to murder anyone to get it and even if someone is pilfering from him, that individual doesn't have to commit murder to make his profit. I sincerely doubt Moseley would resort to murder to stop him, should he even know about him."

"Then what happened to Lawrence? You're good at eliminating possibilities. You need to suggest some."

"Makes no sense to me. It doesn't appear Manke was the one taking money from Moseley. I can't even be sure he knew what Moseley was doing. Why get rid of him?"

"And yet it appears that happened." Parish sighed. "Who do you think is siphoning off Mr. Moseley's money?"

"Initially I figured Manke. Now my bet is Tim Hogan, but I can't see him committing murder either. Why would he if all he has to do is skim a little off the top of the money Moseley does all the work to obtain?"

"And that wouldn't give him anywhere near a motive to kill Lawrence."

"I'm ready to throw money out the window as a motive."

"But power doesn't make any sense either. Mr. Moseley and Mr. Hogan already have the power at Ridinghood."

The waitress came to remove their plates. "Dessert?"

"You want to share something?" Blayze asked.

"I'll bring a menu," the waitress informed them.

"It's almost as if we made the whole thing up."

"Which might make sense if Manke wasn't dead, his girlfriend in the hospital with Janice and Sylvia recovering from injuries."

The waitress returned with dessert menus.

Parish opened hers and glanced down the list. "Why don't you choose? I'll have a couple bites." She sighed. "The one at Ridinghood into gossip is Bobbi Bennett."

"The woman Sarkis cornered in Ocean Shores?"

Parish nodded. "She's related to the Ridinghoods and is climbing rungs on the social ladder."

"And her rifle's loaded and aimed at Hogan?"

"To put it crudely."

"So she might have a motive."

"I don't think she has the brainpower or persistence to accomplish something like that."

"But," Blayze challenged her, "from what I've heard she's lassoed Hogan and has him making trips to spend time with her in Ocean Shores. You don't think that would take planning or persistence?"

"Well, put that way . . . ." Parish laughed. "But it wouldn't make any sense to murder Lawrence."

"Maybe we don't have the whole story."

When the waitress returned Blayze requested the apple tart with ice cream and two coffees. "Maybe we should discuss something besides murder," he suggested when the waitress had gone. "And money."

Parish smiled. "Have you made peace with your sister?"

Blayze rocked his shoulders. "She doesn't seem to know our other sister either, so it isn't just me."

"You have two sisters?"

"Shocking, huh?" He laughed. "One older and one younger."

When they had finished dessert and Blayze had paid the check they left. During their time in the restaurant the bank of clouds resting along the horizon had accomplished a trip across the sky and was currently dropping its load of moisture.

"Where did you leave your car?"

"On the next street." She pointed up the hill.

Blayze removed a small umbrella from his pocket. "Given the rains here and I usually wear a wool suit I keep one of these handy." He looked at her with raised eyebrows. "I'd share if you're willing to crowd a little."

Parish hesitated momentarily.

He opened the umbrella and with his left hand raised it above his head. With his other arm he drew her into a closer position so they both fit beneath its protection. "I promise to take smaller steps so you can keep up."

◆CHAPTER TWENTY-NINE◆

The moment she awoke Parish's mind returned to the night before. After unlocking her car she turned to thank Blayze. He leaned toward her to open the door still holding the umbrella. She smiled at him, wishing him a good night, at the same time feeling disconcerted by the intense expression in his eyes, darker now in the lack of light. She felt an inexplicable temptation to hug him. Conquering the temptation she quickly took her seat in the car and he shut the door. If that wasn't enough she spent the rest of the night tortured by dreams that threw together samples of relationships in her life.

Grateful for morning, she reclaimed control of her mind and returned to work. Here she might be safe from the distorted thoughts that attacked her. In her sleep Blayze stood beside a burgundy Chevrolet grinning with Midge's typical challenging expression while Ian Moseley leaned close to her whispering that Lawrence Manke had murdered Tim Hogan. Thinking over the ridiculous combination of distortions she almost laughed out loud.

"You going to share the joke?" Midge asked, pausing in her office doorway with two cups of coffee. Entering and setting one of them on Parish's desk she declared. "Bribery."

Parish eyed her with suspicion.

"Remember what we decided to do?" Midge admonished her with a look of reproach. "It's time to go to the parking garage and take a look at cars there."

Parish glanced at the clock. It was mid-morning. Probably most people planning to be at work for the day were there now. "On Saturday Blayze said he talked to his sister's friend. They're convinced it was a Chevrolet, with tinted windows."

"Tinted windows? Hmmm. However, I think we should check out any burgundy car there. No sense being picky."

Parish frowned. "It might take being picky to get the right one."

"In the end, but to begin we just need some possibilities."

Misgivings accompanied Parish as she followed Midge to the parking garage. But Midge was right. They couldn't just sit around and do nothing. Checking out the parking garage was simple and low risk.

The clouds and rain from the previous evening had gone, although sidewalks remained damp and the air cool. A fluffy fog hung about hinting at a beautiful day once it burned off. They had each brought along a notepad and pen.

"Let's start at the top and work our way down. Midge pointed to the stairs. "You saw Blayze last night?"

"We had dinner." Parish followed her companion up the stairs to the third floor of the garage. "I told him your plan."

"Did he have any new ideas?"

"I got the impression he's all out of ideas."

When they reached the third floor, Midge indicated with a wave of her hand she would take the north end if Parish would do the south.

"We're looking for anything burgundy?"

"I think that's best, although it doesn't sound as if it was a truck or large SUV. The trouble with what someone sees or remembers in a shocking emergency may not be accurate."

Parish began walking the garage aisles. Most vehicles were the colors Midge had mentioned earlier, black, white, grey, silver. A couple were shades of blue and one bright red one. No burgundy on her side of this floor. Midge found one large SUV on hers. They took the stairs to the next lower floor. On Parish's half she found a couple of the sub compacts, a KIA and a small Chevy in burgundy for which she recorded the license numbers along with the make and model. She noted that both had tinted windows. Midge found an expensive pickup with a canopy over the bed. No burgundy vehicles were on the main level in Parish's section. However, Midge found a Chevrolet crossover. It also had tinted windows.

"So what do you think?" Parish asked as they made their way back to her office.

"That crossover is a good bet. What about you?"

"It depends on how big the car is we're looking for. I found couple small compacts I got the numbers on. One was a Chevrolet."

"We should give our best bets to the lieutenant and see what he can do with them."

Parish retained her misgivings but agreed. In her office, Midge took her notes and wrote out a list for the lieutenant.

"If you see him you need to send him to me."

Parish returned to the accounting analysis on which she worked until it was time for lunch. Having brought a sandwich with her figuring to skip the restaurant she realized coffee would be good. She grabbed her handbag and headed for the stairs to the first floor. At the bottom she hesitated slightly wondering if she should go around outside instead of risking a run in with Doris in the executive suite.

You are such a coward, she accused herself. Taking a deep breath she headed into the executive's area. As it turned out Doris was not at her desk but she noticed Ellen Hogan leaving her husband's office appearing slightly sheepish, glancing around to see if she was observed. Noting Parish she straightened up and came toward her.

"Good morning Mrs. Hogan." Parish decided to be direct.

"Have you seen Tim this morning?"

Parish thought a moment. "No, I haven't. He's not there?"

"Not right now."

"Maybe he went up to lunch. You might want to try the restaurant." Parish maintained a neutral expression so as not to give away her suspicion Ellen Hogan was not looking for her husband.

"That's a good idea." Mrs. Hogan made a point of heading for the elevator.

Parish continued to the coffee shop door, turning slightly to check if Ellen Hogan actually took the elevator. Since she was no longer in sight Parish assumed she had.

Lieutenant Sarkis cruised into Parish's office just after lunch. "You need to come with me?"

She frowned at him.

"We're going to see Blayze."

She logged off her computer and rose. The lieutenant ushered her out the door and across the hall. A surprised expression flashed across Blayze's face at their entrance.

Lieutenant Sarkis pushed the extra chair over to the desk and signaled for Parish to sit then left the room without a word.

Blayze raised his eyebrows and Parish shook her head.

Momentarily the lieutenant returned with an extra chair which he placed next to Parish. "We need to talk." He sat. "We located Ian Moseley in Puerto Rico alias Michael I. Johnson. He's been arrested and is being returned to Tacoma."

"For murder?"

"That's what I need to talk about."

Parish exchanged a frown with Blayze. He shrugged his eyebrows.

"I have a dilemma." Lieutenant Sarkis declared with frustration, running his hand through his hair. "Moseley swears he's innocent of Manke's murder."

"You expected him to confess?"

The lieutenant made a face at Blayze. "He's been interrogated at length. The only thing he'll say, and I mean the only thing, is that he's not guilty. He's makes no objection to arrest, even after talking to his lawyer. They haven't requested bail only objected to being returned to Tacoma." The lieutenant lifted his shoulders. "I'd expect someone in his position to make a holy fuss at being held for murder. Call in the big shots to bail him out. He seemed perfectly contented to sit in jail as long as it was in Puerto Rico."

"Have they charged him with murder?"

"Right now he's being held as a material witness."

"But . . ." Parish protested.

Lieutenant Sarkis nodded to her. "We had a conference with his lawyer after he talked to him."

Blayze narrowed his eyes.

"Right, lawyers can't say much, they have to defend their client. However, we did get this guy to give us an opinion.

He honestly feels Moseley is innocent, although he believes the guy knows who did murder Manke."

"So why doesn't he just tell them?"

Sarkis inhaled deeply, frustration written all over his face. "The lawyer figures Moseley is more afraid of the murderer than the police."

Parish's mind jumped ahead. "He's afraid the murderer will kill him too?"

Lieutenant Sarkis shifted his gaze to her. "Which could explain why he's happy to stay in jail."

"So what do you want from us?" Blayze asked.

"You told me before you didn't believe Moseley was the murderer. How did you draw that conclusion?"

"Everything I've seen of Moseley indicates he operates quasi illegal, just barely beyond appropriate. Murder is way the other side of that. It seemed out of character. Plus I could see no motive. He'd have a lot to lose and nothing to gain."

"But why the heck protect the guilty person if he knows who it is?"

"Maybe he doesn't think the police will believe him. Maybe there's no supporting evidence." Parish put in.

The lieutenant scowled at her then turned back to Blayze. "What I need from you two is who could be guilty he's afraid of."

"Have you talked to Midge?" Parish asked. "She has something for you . . . and something she wants you to do."

"You made any progress in recalling who the person in the hospital reminded you of?"

She shook her head.

"So what does your friend want me to do?"

"She has some license numbers for burgundy cars in the Ridinghood parking garage. She wants to find out who they belong to."

"Is that right?" The lieutenant gazed over his spectacles. "She figures the person who attacked the Stills woman works at Ridinghood?"

"Not necessarily. It's just a place to start looking."

"She doesn't think the police are competent?"

"She figures your hands are tied by what the laws allow you to do."

"And she doesn't have any such laws to bother about?" A twitch in the corner of the lieutenant's mouth indicated he was suppressing a grin. "She may be right. I guess I'll go see her."

When the lieutenant rose, he grabbed the chair he had confiscated and left.

"Interesting." Blayze bobbed his head. "Very interesting. I never figured he'd come around to the possibility Moseley isn't the murderer."

"You think that's good?"

"It will get him closer to the real solution."

"Which is?"

Blayze shook his head. "I have no idea."

Parish rolled her eyes.

He asked her question for her. "How can I be so sure of the negative without having any idea of the positive?" Then answered it. "For some time I've been tracing Moseley's financial scheme. One gets an idea of how a person thinks. I just don't believe he thinks like a murderer."

"Just an embezzler?"

"Not even that. Just someone who knows how to work the system to accomplish his personal ends and stay relatively within legal limits."

"So you consider him innocent of any crime?" Parish frowned, frustrated at his *laissez faire* perception of the law.

Blayze pinned her with his forceful gaze. "You don't approve of my analysis?"

Was that what bothered her? Actually she couldn't fault his analysis. "You seem to approve of fudging with the law."

"And that might be okay, but not from the IRS?"

"I don't think it's okay from anyone. I realize it goes on, with almost everyone in one way or another, but I object to openly approving of it."

"For your information I highly disapprove of it." His eyes flashed. "He's a crook pretending he isn't. But based on that attitude I just don't think he's a murderer."

❦

Staring after Parish as she left his office, Blayze considered their conversation. He found her disappointment at his apparent lenience with the law confusing. People steered clear of him for fear of being accused of tax evasion, but felt it imperative he maintain an uncompromising attitude regarding the law. He felt fortunate he had never fallen into the pit of trying to please people or have them like him. He knew it was a pit. One many people tumbled into unaware of the impossibility of pleasing even one person.

He had to give Parish credit. She wasn't a people-pleaser either. As lacking in confidence as she portrayed herself, she seemed immune to popular opinion. He wondered why, given her gentle easy-going temperament. Something provided her an inner strength that maintained her independence of thought. Although still confused by her person and attitude, he had arrived at a great respect and appreciation for her, beyond which he refused to allow his thoughts to go.

He considered what she had said about someone trying to get to Sally Stills. Would that mean Sylvia and Janice were still in danger? Or was what happened to Sally separate from Sylvia and Janice. One big difference Sally probably knew her attacker. The girls did not. On the other hand, was the attacker aware they didn't know?

Considering what Sarkis had said about Moseley, Blayze figured he was definitely afraid of someone. But who? Who could possibly terrify him to the point he refused to fight arrest? And how long would that last? Did he have some plan or hope that individual would eventually be arrested? And convicted? It would be interesting to know if he would assist someone working to exonerate him. He might be Sarkis' best accomplice in solving the murder and possibly even the attacks. Had the lieutenant thought of that?

Taking Tim Hogan on as the possible owner of the FFT bank account, Blayze could still figure no reason to identify it by those initials. Nonetheless Hogan still seemed the most likely candidate. What would the man have had to do to siphon money off Moseley's accounts? Obviously his background and position in finance gave him appropriate credentials. Returning to the bank statements from Mr. Hornby in search of information tying in Hogan, his search brought up questions the answers to which only his superior had access. He made the call realizing it would take time for a reply.

A glance at his phone informed him it was mid-afternoon and he had missed lunch. Heading to the company restaurant he noted Parish was not in her office.

Considering evidence Sarkis had against Moseley for the murder, he figured one piece was the blood found in Moseley's house, another the disposal of the body. Did they have the weapon? It was as difficult to believe Moseley had nothing to do with it as to believe he committed it. What if he didn't kill Manke, but had seen him killed? Found the body?

To be the one who rented and arranged for the trunk storage he must know something. Was he protecting someone? If so, who? It seemed illogical to protect the murderer then be so afraid of that person he would prefer imprisonment. Somewhere remained a big hole in Blayze's information.

Reaching the top floor and the exotic restaurant he found it busy but not crowded. He grabbed a plate and continued through the cafeteria line before selecting a place to sit. The gaudy gangster style décor both fascinated and repelled him. It had been accomplished so exquisitely true to his imagination he had to admire the designer. However, he would feel more comfortable in something less ostentatious.

He selected a seat in an unobtrusive corner at a table for two squeezed into the angle of the building between windows. He noted, not cheerfully, the two women who had accused him of hexing Moseley and Hogan sat near the window just beyond his table. Due to the room's hexagonal arrangement the angle of their table to fit the space would not give them a direct view of him. They could see him if they tried, but one would have her back to him and the other would face off in a direction to his left. Not that it mattered, although he preferred to enjoy his lunch without being accosted. Nonetheless, he sat in an ideal position for overhearing their conversation.

He found Ellen Hogan, with a lower toned voice that carried well, easier to hear and understand.

"Do you know where Ian is? Is he still in Ocean Shores?"

The high pitch of Doris Possum's voice would have been difficult except for the area where they sat was scantily populated.

"He must be otherwise I would know."

"But you haven't seen him?"

Blayze didn't hear the reply but thought it impossible she could have seen Moseley given what the lieutenant had said.

"Apparently Tim was in Ocean Shores. I can't understand what he'd be doing there. Could he be with Ian?"

"Wouldn't he tell you?"

A glance at Mrs. Hogan told Blayze Hogan hadn't told her anything of the kind, but neither would she admit that fact.

"He must not have seen him," she voiced her conclusion. "I'm presuming Tim was there on some hush-hush business. I thought he was in Spokane."

"I'm sure Ian will get hold of me when he's ready to leave." This time Blayze could hear what Doris said. "We have plans and he just needs to work things out."

Really? Blayze wondered what that meant. Obviously Moseley had plans but did they include Doris Possum? Regardless, she figured they did. How would she react to learning he had been arrested?

"He's planning to leave Ridinghood?" Ellen Hogan verified her perception.

Blayze saw Doris nod.

"Tim will make a good CEO. They could bring Taylor Washington up to CFO."

Ah! There's Ellen Hogan's goal. Blayze had no idea if her plan was realistic or not. He wondered how her husband felt about it. He didn't strike Blayze as someone vying for the chief executive position. He also wondered to what extent Mrs. Hogan maneuvered and campaigned to get Tim into that position. Murdering Manke and attacking Sally seemed counterproductive of those goals. Unless, Manke represented some danger to Hogan.

"I told Lieutenant Sarkis about those license numbers you wanted him to check," Parish informed Midge, following her to the little window table. "He said they've arrested Mr. Moseley in Puerto Rico and are returning him to Tacoma."

Midge frowned, stirring her coffee. "I saw Ellen Hogan here with Doris Possum."

"Is it just me or aren't they an odd pair?" Maybe it was logical for the wives of two of Ridinghood's executives to be friends, except that Doris Possum wasn't Mr. Moseley's wife in spite of her ambitions in that direction.

Midge stared across the room with a grimace. "I don't know. It depends on what's drawing them together."

"The way they went after Blayze it must be their missing men, although Mr. Hogan isn't actually missing and at this point neither is Mr. Moseley." Parish recalled her earlier trip to the coffee shop. "I saw Ellen Hogan coming out of Mr. Hogan's office. She said he wasn't there, but looked surprised and embarrassed to see me. What do you suppose she was doing?"

"Looking for Bobbi Bennett?" Midge shot her a cheesy grin. "Checking if Mr. Hogan actually came to work? Applying for a job?"

Parish rolled her eyes. "For some reason I don't trust Ellen Hogan. Doris Possum is quite obviously fixated on Mr. Moseley. She figures, wrongly I suspect, that he is planning to take her away with him, but she's not being devious or subtle. But Mrs. Hogan . . . ."

"Maybe she's looking for evidence of his affair with Bobbi Bennett."

"You think she knows about it?"

"You're the one who said it's on Facebook?"

Parish turned to the window overlooking the Port of Tacoma. The late summer sun shed a mellow glow over the water and lit the orange cranes unloading ships in port.

"You do realize the plans Ellen Hogan has for Tim? He is going to take her to the top of the social ladder as the wife of the company CEO. She's probably making sure he stays on track." Midge shot Parish a you're-so-naïve glance. "By the way, what did the lieutenant say about the cars?"

"He'll come to see you."

Parish considered the situation at Ridinghood. If Ellen Hogan wanted Tim to become CEO she may need to get rid of Mr. Moseley but not Lawrence Manke. Or as things stood now she may need to get rid of Bobbi Bennett, but had no reason to attack Sally Stills. For Mr. Hogan it would be the same except he wouldn't do away with Bobbi. It seemed Mr. Moseley had no reason to kill Lawrence either. Even Blayze couldn't make that fit. If he was embezzling money all he needed to do was what he apparently did do, take the money and run. The fact Doris thought she'd be included in the trip was her fantasy. But even that wouldn't provide a motive to get rid of Lawrence Manke or Sally Stills. Parish knew of nothing to say Mr. Moseley was having any kind of relationship outside Doris. Not that Parish figured he was having a relationship with her either. Of course, things may be happening she knew nothing about.

What about Bobbi Bennett? Would it make sense for her to get rid of someone? Ellen Hogan maybe. From Parish's knowledge Bobbi wasn't looking to become the wife of Ridinghood's CEO or even the CFO, although she did have social climbing ambitions. Was there someone in this set of triangles they were overlooking completely?

Maybe, in spite of what Blayze thought, Mr. Moseley got rid of Lawrence because he had found out about the money moving scheme and attacked Sally because she was also aware of it. It may be as simple and straightforward as that. Were they making something complicated out of something quite simple?

Parish pushed all these concerns out of her head returning to her office and her accounting issues, which were enough of a problem for the time being. At the end of the day she exited the files she had open and logged off the computer. Descending the stairs she realized it was an evening she could stay home and get some work done there. As she reached the bottom of the stairs she noted a woman coming from the executive suite . . . Bobbi Bennett.

"Hey," the woman called to her.

Parish paused, uncertain whom she addressed.

"Hey," Bobbi said again coming to Parish. "You're the one who was with that detective in Ocean Shores. I heard they arrested Ian Moseley. In Puerto Rico."

A number of questions raced through Parish's mind. How did she find out? Was it general knowledge? Was it okay to talk about it? "I heard that too," she ventured tentatively.

"You don't know if it's true?"

"Where did you hear it?" Parish figured it was time to gain control of the questions.

"Tim said Slate told him." Bobbi's expression was suspicious. "He said Ian's attorney contacted Slate."

Parish frowned. That might make sense, although Bobbi appeared skeptical. "You don't think that's true?"

"What would he be doing in Puerto Rico? And why would they arrest him?"

Was Bobbi as ignorant as that? Were people truly unaware Mr. Moseley was suspected of Manke's death? "I believe the police have been searching for him in connection with Lawrence Manke's murder." Parish figured that was general knowledge, even if not for Bobbi.

"What! Are you kidding? That's impossible."

Parish stared at the woman. "You know who killed him?"

"No, but I know Ian wouldn't."

Parish sighed. Knowing Blayze would agree with Bobbi she wondered if it would be helpful to have her talk to the lieutenant. "Maybe you should tell Lieutenant Sarkis what you think."

"Was that the one in Ocean Shores?"

Parish nodded.

Bobbi looked as if she might do that.

◆CHAPTER THIRTY◆

The day began quietly uneventful, almost too much so. When Parish glanced at the clock and realized how much time had escaped it was nearly eleven. She rarely got this much done this quickly. She had not even gone for coffee. No Midge or Blayze or Lieutenant Sarkis came to interrupt her. She almost felt neglected. It crossed her mind to take a coffee break, but she decided to use the quiet and finish her reports.

Just before noon Midge dropped into the chair in front of her desk. "The lieutenant gave me the list of owners for those cars."

"And?"

Midge shook her head. "A barista from the coffee shop, the chef for the restaurant, Mr. Hogan's administrative assistant, and a name I didn't recognize."

"You don't think it's one of them?"

Midge sighed. "I know all those people and I can't imagine it being one of them, except the I-Don't-Know."

"What if it really was someone we don't know? What if the reason for the attacks is something we have no idea of? Remember, we really don't know what's going on." Parish sighed. "I ran into Bobbi Bennett on Monday. She heard from Mr. Hogan who heard from Slate Ridinghood that

Mr. Moseley was arrested in Puerto Rico. She didn't seem to know why he would be arrested. Are people that much in the dark?"

"I'd think the gossip would get around. But then Bobbi, chief of gossip, hasn't been here."

"She was adamant Ian would not have killed Lawrence Manke." As she spoke Parish noticed Blayze at the door. He hesitated as if unsure about interrupting. She beckoned him in. "We're just discussing what people here know or don't know about Mr. Moseley."

"And you concluded?"

"Amazing lack of knowledge."

Blayze took the chair beside Midge. "I overheard Mrs. Hogan and that Possum woman at the restaurant. They have rather fantastic ideas about where the men are and what's going on with them. Moseley plans to take the one with him when he leaves, except he left already." Blayze flashed a cheesy grin. "And she wasn't even aware of it."

Parish shook her head, wondering who Doris would scream at when she discovered that.

Blayze went on. "Mrs. Hogan thinks her husband was in Ocean Shores on some "hush hush" business for the company."

Midge snorted. "What kind of hush-hush business would this company have?"

"Are they really as deluded as all that?" Parish couldn't imagine being so obtuse and unaware. It was almost as if the two women were intentionally deceiving themselves.

Midge responded. "They're putting a front on for each other."

"But Doris Possum really thinks Mr. Moseley is going to take her with him. I honestly don't think she knows he left town."

"Well apparently he's back." Blayze grinned. He turned to Midge. "Who could frighten Moseley enough to keep him in jail? I wouldn't think he'd be concerned about Hogan or one of the women."

Midge wrinkled her nose. "You know if it weren't for Sally Stills, I'd think it doesn't have anything to do with anyone here. Your sister and her friend wouldn't necessarily have anything to do with Ridinghood." Midge fastened her gaze on one of the huge painted flowers on Parish's wall. "But Mr. Moseley's frightened of someone, right?"

"According to the lieutenant."

"Maybe he should put Moseley up as bait and set a trap," Blayze suggested.

"But if his fears are all in his imagination?" Parish didn't have much use for Mr. Moseley but it didn't seem appropriate to set him up.

Blayze addressed Midge. "Are you going to keep looking for burgundy cars?"

Midge nodded, glancing at Parish. "I just don't know where to search right now."

"We might try the parking lot at Sally's apartment."

"Or maybe you should take another shot at the parking garage. You might have caught the culprit absent."

Midge brightened. "That's worth a try."

❧

"What would Hogan's wife have to do with Moseley?" Lieutenant Sarkis barked in Blayze's ear.

Blayze was too stunned to answer immediately. "What are you talking about?"

"You know, that other woman besides Screaming Mimi."

"I know who you mean."

"Moseley's lawyer has just requested she be allowed to visit Moseley in prison."

Blayze waited. He figured there was more.

"Moseley refuses to see anyone at all without his attorney present."

"What about his administrative assistant?"

"Not her or anyone else as far as that goes . . . except this Hogan woman."

Offhand he could think of no reason to associate Moseley and Hogan's wife. He would have been inclined to question if they even knew each other. "Beats me." Recalling some questions he had, he asked, "Do you have the gun that killed Manke?"

"Yeah, it's Moseley's gun. They brought it back from Puerto Rico with him. No prints on it, but we did establish it's the murder weapon." After a pause, the lieutenant continued. "See if you can find out what the relationship is between Moseley and that Hogan woman."

Blayze groaned inwardly as the call ended. He wasn't hot to deal with either of the executive's women. Considering how to accomplish the task he figured it may be time for a chat with Slate Ridinghood. At the very least he ought to inform the man of his audit results.

After printing some information and placing it in his briefcase which he took with him, he left his office and descended to the executive suite. Slate's administrative assistant informed him Ridinghood was available. After a moment's absence the young man waved Blayze to the executive's office.

Slate rose to shake hands and motioned Blayze to a chair. "What can I do for you?"

"I thought I ought to inform you of the progress I have made."

Slate leaned back and waved a hand inviting Blayze to continue.

"It appears what triggered the IRS audit are actions taken by Ian Moseley." Blayze explained his investigation and what he had discovered.

"How certain are you about this?"

"As sure as I can be without a confession by Moseley." Blayze removed the papers he had printed from his briefcase and handed them to Slate. "These show the activity affecting the Ridinghood accounts. I've made notes to indicate the going and coming of the money. This is without bank statements from the additional accounts Moseley has and another account I located."

"I understand he's in custody for the murder of Lawrence Manke."

Blayze nodded. "I don't think he's guilty of that though."

Slate appeared surprised. "You know who is?"

"No, I don't even have a guess." Blayze explained his reasoning for exonerating Moseley. "Even his attorney and Lieutenant Sarkis have begun to doubt his guilt. However . . ."

Slate cocked his head, giving Blayze a skeptical look.

"Someone has been skimming off the top of the funds Moseley was collecting. I believe the one accomplishing that is Tim Hogan."

"Hell! A bunch of clowns I have here," Slate muttered bitterly.

Blayze sympathized. It couldn't be easy to hear the people with whom you had entrusted your business were crooks and possible murderers. "The good news is the IRS will completely exonerate Ridinghood, although we may need assistance in prosecuting guilty parties."

"As I have said I'm committed to seeing this through."

"I've just talked to Lieutenant Sarkis. He said although Moseley is unwilling to see anyone without his attorney and almost no one even then, he has requested to talk with Mrs. Hogan. Would you have any idea why?"

Slate folded his arms across his chest, scowling. "I'm aware she is looking to get Tim promoted, but I can't see what that would have to do with Ian Moseley, unless she's putting pressure on him to move Tim forward. That might explain why she would go to him but it wouldn't explain why he would want to see her, especially under the circumstances. There's a lot of office gossip, but I've never heard anything regarding Ian and Ellen Hogan."

Blayze cocked his head. "You're aware his administrative assistant thinks she has something going with him."

Slate nodded. "But I doubt she's anything to him beyond an administrative assistant. Are you done here then?"

"With the Ridinghood audit." Blayze nodded. "I'd like to hang around a bit. Both Moseley, and I believe Hogan, have some tax issues that interest the IRS. They'll be held accountable for their illegal profits. In the end Ridinghood may want to prosecute for recovery." Blayze lifted his eyebrows to question Slate's reaction.

He sighed. "Let's wait and see how things shake out."

Blayze left Slate's office comfortable with his corporation report but frustrated at learning nothing for Sarkis. He wondered if in the end there was anything to discover.

Heading through the executive suite to the elevator Blayze noted Moseley's administrative assistant at her desk on the phone. Although facing his direction she appeared absorbed in her call. Could the lieutenant get anything out of interrogating her?

❦

Returning from the company restaurant Midge said to Parish, "Why would Mr. Moseley want to see Ellen Hogan?"

"No idea. Blayze said he's afraid of someone, but apparently not Ellen Hogan. Maybe he's heading off problems while he's safely in jail."

Midge scowled. "I suppose if he can't resolve his fears he'll just have to sit there or be prosecuted for a murder he supposedly didn't commit."

"And if he didn't do it, who did? Ellen Hogan?"

Midge turned a speculative eye on Parish. "You don't think that's possible?"

"You do?"

She shrugged. "Maybe." When they reached the door to Parish's office, she asked, "You want to take another run through the parking garage after work?"

Parish sighed. "Sure." It wasn't that she didn't want to help or thought Midge's idea was off base. In some ways she was just tired of the strain. She had to remind herself that so far they had kept the problem from being Ridinghood's. And of course it wasn't her problem or Midge's. She needed to be thankful for those things.

Sitting at her desk she considered what or who would so frighten Mr. Moseley he would prefer jail. If it was someone whose knowledge could convict him of the crime it might seem logical, but he was already chief suspect with a fair amount of evidence backing it up. It sounded more as if he feared bodily harm.

Mid-afternoon she made a trek to the coffee shop where she ordered an Americano and chatted with the barista. Returning to her office through the executive area she could hear Doris Possum's shrieking voice. However, it wasn't coming from Doris' work area but from farther along the corridor.

"They arrested him!" she shrieked. "Arrested Ian! How could they? What has he done?"

Wondering at whom she fired this tirade Parish passed into the interior designer's area. Here Slate Ridinghood had set up his office. It was his young administrative assistant at whom Doris shrieked. The young man stood petrified, a look of stunned horror on his face. Parish slowed her pace considering a quick retreat but considering Doris' defenseless victim she continued into the battlefield.

Hope lit the young man's eyes as he noticed Parish. "I-I don't know. I hadn't heard he was arrested." He turned to Parish.

"I heard he's being held for Lawrence Manke's murder."

Doris sputtered, her voice rising octave by octave, "That's ridiculous. Ridiculous! Absolutely ridiculous! Can't Mr. Ridinghood do something?"

Too whom could she divert the woman's attention? "You need to talk to the lieutenant in charge of the investigation," Parish told her. Hadn't he expressed a desire to see Doris having a fit?

The woman paused, her gaze shifting to Parish. "Where is he?"

"He was here earlier talking to Blayze, the auditor."

This caused an eruption of expressions on Doris' face. Parish watched with fascination wondering what went on in her mind. The result was a wordless woman who turned on her heel and marched back to her workspace.

The young man swiped his hand across his forehead. "Thanks for the rescue," he said with an embarrassed laugh.

"I avoid her like poison." She smiled at him. "She's obsessed with Mr. Moseley."

At five Midge appeared at her door again, dressed to leave with her handbag over her shoulder. Parish logged off her computer then grabbed her purse and followed. They didn't talk while crossing through the small park to reach the parking building. Although it was just barely quitting time the garage was quickly becoming deserted.

"Why don't we start on top again," Midge suggested.

They climbed the stairs and together walked through the parking aisles. Again only the large burgundy truck was on that floor. They descended the stairs where on the side of the garage facing Commerce Avenue four people stood behind a burgundy sedan chatting. From what Parish could see it was Ellen Hogan, Doris Possum, Bobbi Bennett, and Connie Evans. What a gathering!

She glanced at Midge to see if she noticed. Midge grimaced in return. They descended one more floor to the main level.

"I wonder which one owns the car," Midge said.

"Maybe none of them. We should wait and see if one of them leaves with it."

"Where's your car?"

"Over there." Parish pointed to the wall near the north exit from the building.

"Mine is up on that floor."

"That might be a more strategic one to watch from."

"But it's too close to where they're talking. I don't want to put them on alert or get involved." Midge glanced around the parking area. "Maybe you could move your car closer into the middle."

They got into Parish's car and she moved it between two SUVs to face where they could observe both exits. They could hear vehicles moving in the area above them.

"You watch one direction and I'll watch the other."

While they observed a succession of cars came down the ramp. Parish noticed the Prius followed by the burgundy truck and a white Camry. When the cars were all out of the garage, she asked Midge, "Did you see who it was?"

Midge shook her head. "All the cars coming down had tinted windows."

"Oh, I forgot that."

"Well, so much for that idea." Midge grimaced. "Was the burgundy sedan a Chevrolet?"

"I didn't notice."

"We could be making the circumstances fit the situation. The car may not have belonged to any of them."

When Parish arrived at home she noticed her phone blinking a message.

It turned out to be a text from Annabelle Elliott. *"Just saw another post from Bobbi regarding Ellen Hogan. She's been invited to visit Mr. Moseley in jail."*

Parish frowned. Was that the discussion at the parking garage? If so Bobbi made a fast post. Didn't want someone to beat her to spreading the news? She had to wonder how much information Ellen Hogan or Doris Possum would share with Bobbi Bennett. And where did Connie Evans fit in that group? She had difficulty imagining them sharing anything, even a discussion of the weather.

"Say anything else?" Parish texted back.

"Only inferred couldn't imagine what Mr. Moseley would want with her."

"Could you guess?"

"Is it true?"

"Apparently."

"No."

Parish had a bad feeling about the parking garage meeting. Regardless of times recently she had seen Doris and Ellen together she still had difficulty imagining what they had in common. Adding Bobbi and Connie to the mix only heightened the incredibility. She could easily imagine Bobbi playing games with the other three, entertaining herself at their expense. However, she could also envision Doris and Ellen discounting Bobbi as a foolish kid, although in all likelihood Bobbi was not that much younger than them.

She wondered what Ellen made of Mr. Moseley's desire to see her at the prison. Maybe it was only odd to Parish not to people who knew them better.

Before retiring for the day she went to Xavier's room and spent a half hour chatting with him. She even posed her questions anonymously. He had no insights either. Too restless for bed she turned on the television and cruised through the channels. A street scene with the police and ambulance flashing lights made her pause. A line of type ran across the bottom of the screen. "Hit and run on Tacoma's north side leaves one woman dead."

Parish perched on the edge of her sofa, watching the scene.

A news reporter following police as they interviewed bystanders in the vicinity caught a young man in a Starbucks apron. "I was wiping tables when I heard a squeal of tires."

"Did you see the car?"

He shook his head. "I think it was gone by the time I got there."

Examining the surrounding buildings at the scene Parish attempted to determine the location. North side the type had indicated. From her recollection it appeared to be the Proctor District.

She grabbed her phone and called Midge. "Take a look at the television, channel five."

"What for?"

"Just do it."

"Yes, ma'am."

Parish continued searching the background checking the cars she saw. In the camera's sweep of the area she noticed a burgundy sedan parked on the street farther along the block. Not that it meant anything. The whole block was lined with parked cars.

"You think it's someone we know?" Midge asked.

"The police won't release the victim's name until the next of kin have been notified."

◈CHAPTER THIRTY-ONE◈

After arriving at Ridinghood Parish made the trek to Midge's office where she conferred with an employee. Making hand signals Parish invited her to her office. Midge nodded.

On her way downstairs Parish met Lieutenant Sarkis who turned around and followed to her space.

"Have you seen the news?" He stood in her doorway looking fierce. Not waiting for a reply he continued. "Ellen Hogan was killed in a hit and run last night."

Parish blinked. "Ellen Hogan!" She was stunned. "I saw the news, but they didn't say who it was."

"Mrs. Hogan. What do you think of that?" the lieutenant glared at her as if she were the guilty driver.

Parish had no idea what to think. She shook her head.

"Does your buddy know . . . Pashasia?"

"I haven't seen him yet."

The lieutenant waved a come-on and headed across the hall to Blayze's office.

He observed Lieutenant Sarkis apprehensively from beneath his dark eyebrows. "This looks rather official."

The lieutenant snorted. "I wish." He grabbed the chair by the little table and pushed it to the desk. "You need another chair for this room." He beckoned Parish to be seated and left to return with another chair on which he sat. "Did she tell you?"

Blayze turned to Parish with raised eyebrows.

"Ellen Hogan was killed last night in a hit and run."

"What do you make of that?" The lieutenant peered over his spectacles at him.

"What should I make of it?"

"Maybe someone didn't want her to talk to Mr. Moseley," Parish suggested.

"Who knew besides you people?" The lieutenant looked fierce again.

Recalling the scene in the garage Parish wondered if it had any relevance. "Last night Midge and I saw her with Bobbi Bennett and Doris Possum in the parking garage."

"Doing what?"

"Standing there, chatting."

"You think she told them about her pending visit?"

"That's possible isn't it?"

The lieutenant scowled. "I can't seem to stay ahead of gossip around here."

"Maybe you should check with Bobbi Bennett," Parish said. "She's big into gossip and broadcasts it on Facebook."

The lieutenant stared at Parish as if his brain had left on a mission. "I really hoped to get something out of Moseley's visit with Mrs. Hogan."

"What are you going to do now?" Blayze asked.

"Haul a few people in for questioning," the lieutenant barked as he rose and picked up his chair."

When he had gone Parish sighed. "The way he looked I was afraid he'd come to get us."

Blayze lifted an eyebrow. "For spreading gossip?"

Midge was waiting at Parish's office door when she left Blayze. "What's up?"

"Did you watch the news last night?"

"That hit and run?" Midge cocked her head. "So who was killed?"

"Ellen Hogan."

"What!" She stood speechless her mouth open. "Great Jehoshaphat! What a lousy break. And you think it may connect."

"Wouldn't you?" Parish moved into her office and dropped into her chair.

Midge perched across from her. "But why? I can see Ellen doing the hit and run but the victim?" She waved her hand in front of her face, a gesture of bewilderment.

"Did she know something?"

"And someone had to eliminate her?"

"The lieutenant was here. He's upset about gossip getting in the way of his investigation."

"He thinks gossip got her killed?"

"No, well, maybe in this case. Everything gets around before he has a chance talk to people. They know it all ahead of time. He has no advantage of surprise." Parish sighed. "I got a text last night from Annabelle Elliott. She said Bobbi posted the fact Mrs. Hogan was to see Mr. Moseley on Facebook."

"Someone needs to tie her up. Maybe she isn't as innocent as we've given her credit for. It might help to check out everything she's put on Facebook." When Parish opened her mouth Midge continued. "You could do it with Annabelle."

When Midge left Parish considered the idea. It could help and it wouldn't hurt. She called Annabelle and explained, offering to bring lunch if she could be free then. Checking the clock she realized she better get her work done.

At eleven-thirty Parish climbed the stairs to the in-house restaurant where she picked out a couple lunch boxes to go. When she reached Annabelle's place of business the store was empty. Annabelle motioned toward the little table where they had sat before. Parish set up their lunches while Annabelle located her tablet and brought it over.

"So what are we looking for?" Annabelle worked to bring up Facebook.

A good question Parish realized. Was it just something regarding Ellen Hogan or did they need to check for anything regarding the Hogans and Bobbi Bennett, even Doris Possum? She expressed her uncertainty to Annabelle.

"Well, let's see what we can find."

Parish pushed her chair over to sit next to Annabelle and watch her scroll through her Facebook posts. She paused at one, indicating for Parish to read it, the one broadcasting the proposed meeting between Mr. Moseley and Ellen.

"If the lieutenant is ever in doubt about how the word gets around I'll have him come here and you can show him these posts."

"Would this mean anything to someone not connected with those people?"

Parish sighed. "I'm not sure we know who is connected or interested, except Bobbi Bennett obviously."

"But why is she so interested?"

"Well, where Ellen Hogan is concerned, you remember she's having a little fling with Ellen's husband."

Annabelle continued to scroll. "Okay, look at this." She pointed to a post posing the question, "Is dear Ellen having an affair with Ian Moseley?"

Parish stared open-mouthed at the screen. Could that be?

After returning to work from Annabelle's shop Parish took the elevator to the third floor and proceeded immediately to Midge's office.

Midge looked up with surprise. "You look like someone just told you the sale is over and you missed out."

Parish perched on the blue chair with a sigh. "Would you think it possible Ellen Hogan and Mr. Moseley were having an affair?"

Midge scowled at her. "You're putting me on, right?"

"I just came from Annabelle Elliott. She found a Facebook post suggesting that. Could we have been so focused on Bobbi Bennett and Mr. Hogan we ignored his wife?"

"We didn't ignore her."

"But we figured her whole ambition was getting her husband into the position of CEO. Maybe she had another idea for becoming the Chief Executive's wife."

"Marry him?" Midge clasped her hands on her desk staring into space. "Do you really think that's possible?"

"No," Parish declared, "but then I can't image Mr. Moseley with anyone."

"What you're actually trying to imagine is whether Ellen would be interested in being his wife."

"That's worse. I could more easily imagine him being interested in her than the other way."

"As it stands she's not going to be anyone's wife anymore. How does that make any sense?"

They remained quiet for a time while Midge made entries on her computer and Parish considered the question. Who could want to get rid of her? Tim Hogan and Bobbi Bennett were possibilities, but she had a hard time imagining either one having the internal drive to pick someone off with a vehicle. She could see one of them planning and executing murder, but less violently. Poison perhaps.

⚛

When Parish and the lieutenant had gone, Blayze considered the death of Ellen Hogan. Was it significant? Even premeditated and connected what could it mean?

While finalizing his IRS reports, Blayze received a call. With some surprise he noted his sister Luanne's name on his phone.

"What are you doing in Tacoma, Blayze?"

"Auditing, what else? Just finishing up a job. Where are you now?"

"TDY at JBLM. Mom said you've visited with Sylvia."

Blayze snorted. "If you can call it that. How long are you here for?"

"The week is all."

After arranging with Luanne to meet later for dinner, Blayze picked up the fax lying on his desk and gave it a onceover. It might do the trick, he thought, although it required more perusal than he was up for at the moment. He slid it into a manila envelope to take with him, having decided to leave work for the rest of the afternoon and get some personal things done.

Stepping out of his office he noticed Parish with a preoccupied look of consternation on her face.

"Something new?"

She shook her head. "Just more gossip. I'm not sure I even believe it. Bobbi Bennett intimated on Facebook Ellen Hogan and Mr. Moseley were having an affair. Seems rather farfetched to me."

"So why post it?"

"What could she hope to accomplish spreading gossip about Ellen Hogan and Mr. Moseley?"

Blayze gave her an admonishing look. "Isn't she the one having an affair with Mrs. Hogan's husband?"

Blayze and Parish continued together down the stairs to the taupe and teal foyer. Oblivious to the consequences he said, "I'm having dinner tonight with my little sister. You could join us if you like, at my personal dining room, six-thirty."

"I'll need to check with Xavier to see what he has going."

Blayze smiled, wondering briefly if she had given up her fears of him. No apprehension lay in her expression as she considered his invitation. He couldn't help but hope she had begun to trust him. It flashed into his head he needed to take care to be worthy of it. "The invitation is open. Come if you can, even just for coffee. If you don't make it I'll assume you're tied up."

Leaving Ridinghood's building he noticed a black SUV at the curb. "How about a ride?" Lieutenant Sarkis called from the truck's lowered window. Sarkis appeared considerably discouraged. Not that he blamed him.

"This Ridinghood tangle gets more complicated every day. I wouldn't be surprised to learn your accounting assistant is having an affair with Slate Ridinghood himself."

Blayze shook his head. "I can guarantee that's not the case."

Sarkis shot him a suspicious glance.

"She doesn't even date."

The lieutenant was skeptical. "Weren't you out with her the other night?"

"She agreed to have dinner with me, not a date, after considerable negotiation."

Sarkis laughed. "On the whole that would be advisable for all Ridinghood employees. It might prolong their lives."

"So this whole murder thing relates to affairs people are having?"

"We've gone through Manke's background with a fine tooth comb, all his connections, employment history. I couldn't have done anymore if I was working on a high level security clearance – and nothing. The same with that girlfriend of his."

"They'd both qualify for a high level security clearance?"

"You might have to overlook cheating on their taxes or late payments on their credit cards."

"What about the hit and runs?" Blayze figured several things were happening at the same time, each confusing the issue where the other was concerned.

"All things considered they make no sense at all. I can't even connect them to Ridinghood or Manke's murder. I wouldn't think your sister and Ellen Hogan even knew each other. Much less someone from Ridinghood knew both of them. I think I need to look at this from a completely different angle." After a pause, Sarkis asked, "What about the money thing?"

"So far as I can tell that's Moseley's deal. It might involve Tim Hogan too, if he's the one piggybacking onto Moseley's scheme."

"Are you in a position to confront Hogan and find out?"

Blayze grimaced. "I can give it a shot."

The lieutenant pulled his vehicle into the parking lot at Blayze's hotel. "You'll let me know?"

"Right." Blayze waited for the lieutenant to exit the lot then headed for the side door. Part way there as the lieutenant's SUV moved into the street he noticed a sedan enter. Once in the lot the driver accelerated heading directly for Blayze. In that what-the-heck-are-you-doing second it took him to recognize the impending danger time slowed to a crawl. Although his mind centered on the action required to preserve his life he nevertheless observed the face of the vehicle's driver. Eyes narrowed and blazing with focused intent and lips compressed with determination were the last things he saw before making a dive for the sidewalk. However, his leap didn't remove him quite far enough from the sedan's path. The vehicle's fender struck him throwing him against a sign post implanted in a concrete base. As his head struck the concrete he heard a screech of tires then lost consciousness.

◆CHAPTER THIRTY-TWO◆

Climbing the stairs to the second floor Parish heard Lieutenant Sarkis voice. Turning she saw him in the foyer below. He glanced toward the executive suite and then up the stairs as if uncertain where to go. Seeing Parish he began the climb to where she waited mid-stair.

"Anymore gossip floating around?" He peered at her over his glasses.

"I heard speculation Mr. Moseley was having an affair with Ellen Hogan."

"Are you kidding?"

"Not about the gossip, but I'm not sure I believe it. And Doris Possum had a shrieking tirade about Mr. Moseley being under arrest. I told her to talk to you."

The lieutenant considered. "Where would I find her?"

Parish pointed. "On the main floor toward the end before you get to the coffee shop."

He moved to return down the stairs, stopped and turned back to Parish. "Who's spreading the gossip?"

"Bobbi Bennett."

"How come she knows it all?"

Parish shook her head. "She might be manufacturing it."

Lieutenant Sarkis snorted. "Have you any idea how to get hold of her?"

"Tim Hogan? She has a thing going with him."

The lieutenant rolled his eyes, wagging his head. "Ridinghood needs to clean up its morality, probably be healthier for everyone."

Continuing to her office Parish considered the lieutenant's point. Not that she figured it would ever happen.

Noting the closed door to Blayze's office, she realized with an unexpected pang that when his assignment at Ridinghood ended she would miss him, a hard admission to make even to herself. There was no real solution for it. Remaining at the company would not be an option and expecting him to stay in town irrational. However, the thought made her aware she had accepted him as a friend, significant progress for her in relationships. She wondered if Midge would give her any credit.

Wrestling her emotions all the way home, Parish would love to meet Blayze's sister. On the other hand the whole set up was dangerous, not that she didn't trust Blayze. She would not even need her invisible guardian. The danger was no longer external it was right inside of her. No amount of running away or avoidance protected one from the dangers that live within.

Even once she had arrived at her apartment and verified Xavier was having a quick dinner and heading out to meet a couple of his friends at the gym, she hesitated. However in the end she heaved a sigh and got her car out. After leaving it in Ridinghood's garage she walked to the restaurant.

Once there she noted a young couple waiting for a table in addition to a brown-haired woman with dark horned rim glasses consulting her watch. Parish checked her phone. It was 6:35. Undoubtedly Blayze and his sister were already seated. Glancing around the portion of the dining room she could see she failed to spot them.

She approached the hostess stand. "I'm looking for Blayze Pashasia. He should have a woman with him."

The young hostess frowned then checked her map of tables. "Ah, Blayze. He has a reservation but hasn't come yet." She pointed to the brown-haired woman. "She's waiting for him too."

Parish turned to the woman figuring she must be his sister. "You're waiting for Blayze?"

The woman's expression registered surprise, but she nodded.

Parish introduced herself and explained. "He's usually not late. Just before leaving work he invited me to join him and meet you." A bad feeling attacked her, but she shook it off. "He only lives a few blocks from here."

By unspoken agreement the two took chairs in the waiting area. "I'm Luanne Fraser. Do you think I should call him?"

"That's a good idea." Parish reminded herself there was no reason to be concerned. The fact Blayze was a little late didn't necessarily mean anything.

Luanne tapped an entry on her cell phone and they waited. After a time she shook her head. "He's not answering."

The bad feeling escalated. "This is really unlike him. I don't feel good about it."

"Do you know where he's staying?"

"His hotel is about half a dozen blocks from here."

"Let's go see if he's there?"

Parish nodded. She wouldn't feel good until they found him. "I'll tell the hostess what we're doing. If he comes here she can tell him." She led the way south on Pacific Avenue then up the hill to where the hotel sat. Approaching the lobby she noted a police car leaving the parking lot.

"Do you know what room he's in?" Luanne asked.

"No, we'll have to ask at the desk."

"They might not be willing to tell us."

Parish sighed. "Let's see what we can do."

Once the attendant was free Luanne asked if he knew what room Blayze was in."

A look of concern came over the young man's face. "Blayze . . .Blayze Pashasia?"

"That's right."

Fear crept into Parish's mind as she watched the expressions on the attendant's face. Somehow she knew the answer wouldn't be good.

"Who are you?"

"His sister."

"He's been taken to the hospital. He was in an accident in the parking lot."

"What hospital?" Parish asked.

"TG."

Luanne turned to Parish. "Is that far?"

Parish shook her head.

"My car is here if you can direct me."

Parish followed Luanne to her car near the restaurant. On the short drive to Tacoma General and the hospital parking she wondered what could have happened. Alive in her mind was the death of Ellen Hogan.

"Oh, no," Parish murmured as they entered the emergency waiting area. There stood Lieutenant Sarkis. "This doesn't look good," she mumbled to Luanne.

The stormy expression on the lieutenant's face faded somewhat as he noted Parish and Luanne. He came to them.

"They told us at the hotel Blayze was in an accident in the parking lot." Was it more than an accident Parish wondered. "This is his sister, Luanne Fraser."

The lieutenant focused on her with a grimace.

"Where's Blayze?" she asked.

"In surgery."

Parish was suspicious. "What happened?"

"I don't know. Maybe another hit and run. No one seems to have seen what happened. A guy who arrived to check in at the hotel found him on the ground outside by the building unconscious."

"But why Blayze?"

"Why anybody?" The lieutenant grumped. He turned to Luanne. "Does someone have something against your family?"

Her eyes widened.

"You realize this is the second one injured in a hit and run." He paused. "Are you going to be here a while?"

"If we can find out what room he's going to be in."

"Let me see what I can do." The lieutenant left them for the reception desk.

Parish watched him speaking with the triage receptionist then turning to point at Parish and Luanne. "Are you able to stay?" she asked Luanne.

"Yes, in fact, I don't think I could leave under the circumstances. What about you?"

Parish nodded. "I'll stay as long as I can."

When the lieutenant returned he told Parish, "they haven't assigned a room as yet. They'll let you know when they have."

"How is he?"

The lieutenant snorted. "Broken bones, internal injuries and a possible concussion, at the very least."

"Will he be okay?" Luanne appeared stricken.

"They're cautiously optimistic. I'm going back to the hotel to see what I can find out."

❦

Scenes circulated in Blayze's head. He stood under the marquee at the Shilo Inn in Ocean Shores watching a sedan move aggressively toward him. At the wheel sat Satan with a sinister grin and red eyes. "Wrong picture," he mumbled. In another he sat in the bar at his customary restaurant with Tim Hogan examining a bank account statement. "Yours?" He shook his head then moaned. The dreams began again. Parish had her hand on his forehead asking if he was okay. "Yeah, I'm okay." She removed her hand and moved away. "Don't go." She paused, looking back at him. He reached out toward her. She asked what happened. "Satan attacked." He grinned.

He drifted into deeper sleep and was quiet. Suddenly, as if surfacing from a dive, his eyes opened to the glare of florescent lights in the midst of a white ceiling. His analytical mind systematically searched the surroundings, soft green walls with black moldings, black metal furnishings, gray plastic receptacles with bright red warning labels. A television projected from the opposite wall on a metal arm registering no picture or sound. In the corner to his right a brown vinyl recliner resided near a wall of windows. A woman in the recliner sat reading, a woman with long curling black hair.

He closed his eyes again. Hospital, he thought, that's where I am. At least I hope that's where I am. He could think of less desirable possibilities. He attempted to shift his position. "Auk!" That's a no go. Head injuries, he figured from the electric shock movement produced. Bringing his gaze in closer, he noted a cast on his leg and another on his arm. Could be worse. Of course, he realized, it actually might be worse. He wasn't the authority in this case. He was alive and could still think for which at the moment he determined to be grateful.

Reopening his eyes he glanced at the woman in the chair. "Sylvia?"

She looked up. "You're conscious." She set her book down, and with her crutch rose and approached the bed. "How are you?"

"I doubt I'm *au courant* on that."

A smile flickered across her face. "How do you feel?"

He lifted his shoulders. "Maybe you should tell me how I am."

She grimaced. "You're pretty banged up. But since you're conscious and seem able to think straight you'll probably be okay. Eventually."

He laughed a little, which shot pain to his head again. "Patience, my man, patience?"

"Do you recall what happened?"

He closed his eyes again. He saw the Chevrolet symbol on the approaching burgundy sedan. He saw the fender he had been unable to avoid, the bit of chrome, the headlight, and eyes fired with determination. "Hit and run?"

"Apparently." Sylvia frowned but the look in her eyes appeared far away and perplexed. "Did you see who it was?"

"Satan at the wheel." He grinned at her frustrated expression. He saw who it was, but couldn't reconcile what he had seen with his logic. And at this point given his head injuries he wouldn't trust his recollection.

She tried again. "Did you recognize the person?"

"Not someone you know." At least he didn't think she knew the person.

"So it wasn't the one who attacked Janice and I?"

Blayze sighed, closing his eyes. "Probably it was." That created the problem in his logic. If he could make sense of it he wouldn't hesitate to say, but it made no sense.

"But . . . why?"

"That's what I have to work out." He opened his eyes. "They didn't catch anyone?"

Sylvia shook her head. "No one saw it happen. A guest of the hotel found you when he came to check in. They called the ambulance and the police."

"Does Lieutenant Sarkis know?"

Sylvia frowned. "There's a guard at the door. You have to produce IDs and get special clearance to even come in this room. Someone is protecting you from another attack." She regarded him intently. "Why would someone want to get you? Or Janice and I?"

"I don't know. I'm trying to make sense of it." But thinking was hard. His head ached. He closed his eyes.

It seemed only an instant before he reopened them, however Sylvia was gone. He could hear voices from just outside his open door. The clock, residing to the right of the television, informed him it was four hours later. Someone closed the door eliminating the sounds.

What element was missing? Why the hit and runs? And how was his family involved? If the attacks were against his family, why attack and kill Ellen Hogan? Somehow there was a connection.

In the midst of his ruminations Lieutenant Sarkis entered quietly, moving like a lynx approaching his prey fearful of alerting his victim. He gazed at Blayze apprehensively. "How are you?"

Blayze grinned. "You expect me to answer that?"

"What happened?"

In the process of lifting his shoulder and shaking his head he recalled the painful probability and halted. He closed his eyes a moment without responding.

"Problems with your memory?"

"Logic. Can't trust my memory." Jumping to conclusions especially in a police matter could cause untold problems. However, without them it may be impossible to resolve.

The lieutenant glanced around then looked in the closet where he found a folding chair he brought to the bedside and sat. He regarded Blayze for a time before asking, "The burgundy Chevrolet?"

"If my recollection is accurate."

"Could this be a family issue and nothing to do with Ridinghood?"

Was that possible? He frowned. He certainly didn't make friends auditing for the IRS. Sylvia had been involved in another accident which was costing someone a lot of money; or more particularly their insurance company. He didn't know enough about Janice to speculate. The problem with that was Ellen Hogan and Satan behind the wheel. He didn't want to lead Sarkis astray. "Unquestionably related to Ridinghood."

"Okay, that's something."

◈CHAPTER THIRTY-THREE◈

Blayze's accident circling endlessly in Parish's mind made getting her work done difficult. She and Luanne had remained at the hospital the night before until he had been returned from surgery and the lieutenant had established a guard on his room. The hospital attendants brought him there with bandages on his head and casts on his arm and leg. He had been unconscious whether because of head injuries or the anesthetic for surgery she couldn't say, but it left her and Luanne with nothing more they could do so they had gone home.

Luanne intended to alert Sylvia to share the vigil in his room. Parish would visit him once she had finished work for the day. Her hourly prayer was for his healthy recovery. Her mind kept drifting to the accident, if such it was. She couldn't help but wonder if he qualified as another victim of the hit and run driver. Would he even know? The variety of victims had grown so diverse determining a culprit became continually more difficult. What motivation could tie all these people together?

Restlessness kept her watching the clock, for what reason she couldn't say. However, when it reached eleven she determined going to lunch might relieve some of the stress. Closing her office door she noticed Lieutenant Sarkis headed directly her way.

"You leaving?" he asked.

"Going to lunch."

"You mind company?"

They took the stairs to the third floor, crossed to the circular staircase and continued to the company restaurant. It was quieter than usual Parish realized probably due to the early hour. After proceeding through the cafeteria line they took their trays to a small table along the room's periphery.

"Have you seen Blayze?" she asked the question foremost on her mind.

"I had a little chat with him earlier."

"He's conscious?"

"Relatively." He cocked his head, giving Parish a searching look. "I think his brain's okay. The doctor said he should recover completely."

Parish sighed with relief bringing a perceptive smile to the lieutenant's face. His smile produced a warning twinge her consciousness ignored in her concern. "Did he tell you what happened?"

"Another hit and run apparently."

"Did he see the driver?"

"You know," the lieutenant grimaced, shaking his head, "I think he knows who was driving, but refuses to say. He seemed unsure he wasn't dreaming it up. However, he did say it was definitely related to Ridinghood."

"You thought it might be something else?"

"Well, with the hit and runs including him and his sister I figured it could be something else entirely."

Parish nodded her comprehension.

The lieutenant sighed. "I'd like to hang around here until I could collar someone and pack him off to jail. Obviously that won't work."

"So what are you going to do?"

"I want you to see what you can get out of him."

She sat very still her mind racing through the possibilities. Number one, would Blayze even tell her something he refused to tell the lieutenant? Number two, if he told her and she immediately repeated it to the police, wouldn't she be guilty of betrayal? Number three, if betrayal mean they saved another person from being injured, killed, or something worse would the sacrifice be appropriate? And number four, why would she consider betraying Blayze a sacrifice?

The lieutenant watched her as if he could read her mind. He probably could she thought ruefully. Was she really that transparent? "I'm not sure he'd tell me anything different than you."

"I realize that. But it's worth a try. This whole thing keeps escalating."

Which could be really bad for Ridinghood.

"I can see what he has to say."

When they finished lunch and returned to the third floor Parish bid the lieutenant a see you later at the door to Human Resources where she noticed Midge watching her. She went to Midge's blue chair and sat.

Her friend leaned forward with an expectant expression. "What's with Lieutenant Sarkis now?"

Parish hardly knew where to begin.

"It must be pretty awful if you're having that much trouble talking about it."

Parish sighed. "Blayze is in the hospital after what we think was another hit and run."

"You're kidding." Midge frowned, shaking her head. "No you're not. Is he badly hurt?"

"Apparently he'll recover. The lieutenant thinks he knows who hit him. He wants me to talk to him."

Midge stared over Parish's head grimacing. "You realize none of this makes any sense if you put it all together. Who would want to take him out, his sister and then Ellen Hogan? Not to mention Sally Stills, although she's not a hit and run."

"You think they're separate issues?"

"No! Somehow it's all related in spite of how illogical it seems."

"I'm thinking it all started with Lawrence Manke's death?"

"So what was he doing that brought all this on?"

"All I can think of is what he wasn't doing. He wasn't part of the money scheme, at least according to Blayze. He wasn't having any inappropriate relationships with any of these people. As best we can determine he was being totally proper at work and with the band. Why would anyone kill him?

"And attack Sally?"

"How would anything he was doing or not doing have anything to do with all the rest of these people like Blayze, his sister, and Ellen Hogan?" Parish stood up. "It's a mystery to me."

"Do you think Blayze knows?"

Parish shook her head. "I think if he knew he'd tell the lieutenant."

When Parish reached the hospital after work she went directly to the room where she and Luanne had left Blayze.

She gave her name and ID to the security person on duty. Once inside she saw that Blayze was asleep. However, in the corner Luanne sat with her laptop open apparently working.

She smiled when she saw Parish who went to sit on the window ledge near her.

"How is he?" Parish observed the sleeping man with apprehension.

"Not bad. He's only awake for short periods of time, but seems to be okay when he is."

"Has he told you what happened?"

Luanne shook her head. "When he's asleep he groans and occasionally makes smart remarks about Satan. If you know someone by that name or who he thinks that is . . ."

Parish sighed and shook her head.

Luanne closed her laptop. "Are you going to be here a while? I need to get something to eat."

"Sure, go ahead."

When Luanne had gone Parish wandered to the bed and stared down at Blayze. The portion of his dark hair free from bandages lay across his forehead making his ominous eyebrows less threatening. It made her smile to think how vulnerable he appeared now. Gone was the formidable auditor. As she moved to return to the chair by the windows she heard her name and turned back to the bed.

"Don't go," he said.

"Are you awake?"

"No, I'm talking in my sleep."

Parish rolled her eyes.

"There's a folding chair in the closet," he informed her.

She went to the closet and brought the chair to his bed. "How are you doing?"

"Okay as long as I play dead." He grimaced. "My head aches. At least I know it's still there."

"How long do you have to stay here?"

"No one's mentioned that yet. It's mostly my head. I'm sure if it was just broken bones they'd chuck me out."

"Lieutenant Sarkis thinks you know who hit you."

Blayze eyed Parish. "I don't trust what I remember."

"Accident?"

"Well, if what I recall is correct it was an attack not an accident."

"But why?"

"If I could figure that out I might trust my memory."

"Has it occurred to you it might need to be done in reverse?"

"Have you considered what kind of an accusation I'd be making? It wouldn't be just me the person would have responsibility for but my sister and killing Ellen Hogan."

Parish sat down. "What makes the person you think or," she grimaced, "dreamt about so difficult to imagine as the guilty party?"

Blayze's gaze drifted to the blank television screen then gradually back to Parish. "No motive. In fact I can come up with more motives to preclude this person's guilt than affirm it."

She gazed out the windows across the room, which from the height at which they sat and the fact the hill descended to the port beyond gave only an expanse of blue sky with streaks of white cloud. "What motives would make sense to you?"

"If we start back at Manke's death, which may not relate to the hit and runs of course, he would have needed to present a threat to someone or done something for which they were making him pay the price. He would have had to know something threatening someone or present an obstacle to what someone was doing, or want part of the action."

"The action being Mr. Moseley's money scheme?"

"I believe he knew about that, which may have got him in trouble." Blayze attempted to shift his position bringing a startled look to his eyes and a grimace. He smiled sheepishly. "Head's calling the shots these days."

"Can I help you with something?"

He glanced around him. "That pillow there," he pointed to one sitting at the bottom of his bed. "Could you give me that?"

Parish grabbed the pillow and brought it to the head of the bed. Considering the expression of pain she had seen on his face, she asked, "Where do you want it?"

He began to motion with his bandaged arm, stopped and grinned again. "Under my head."

She studied him with apprehension. "Can you do that without hurting yourself?"

"I'm not sure I actually hurt myself. It's just painful. I can bear it for a minute."

Glancing around she said, "Do you think if I raised the head of the bed a little it would make it easier? If you lifted your head I could slide the pillow under."

"Let's give it a shot."

Parish bent down and found the button to raise the bed, which she did very carefully keeping an eye on Blayze's expression. Then she took the pillow and as Blayze made a move to raise his head closing his eyes with a wince she put her hand under his head for support and slid the pillow into place.

He leaned back with relief and smiled. "Thanks." His eyes held hers a moment before she resumed her seat.

She returned to the subject under discussion. "But you've said you don't think Mr. Moseley killed him."

"Right, I don't."

"So where does that leave you?"

"Nowhere, that's what I mean. If Manke's dead why attack Sally Stills? And how would any of that relate to the hit and runs?"

"Then you think the hit and runs are a separate issue from what happened to Lawrence?"

He grimaced but said nothing.

"If, as you have said, Mr. Hogan was tapping into Mr. Moseley's money scheme maybe the hit and runs have to do with that."

"But my sister?"

"And you?"

"Well, I might fit that deal if the whoever is aware I've figured out about the money. But then why is Moseley afraid?"

"I think I'm going to have a headache."

Blayze patted the bed. "There's room for you too." After noting the look on Parish's face, he hastened to add, "Just kidding, sorry."

A noise behind her alerted Parish to someone entering the room. Luanne had returned.

"You're awake," she said approaching them.

Parish rose. "I need to get going."

"Come back again." Blayze grinned.

❧

Blayze watched Parish leave his room with a feeling the sun was disappearing behind a cloud, an unpleasant sensation. Returning his gaze to his sister he noted her gray eyes watched him with a trace of amusement laced with concern.

"She's a pretty little thing. You need to be careful."

"Don't I know it," he muttered with a hint of bitterness.

"You don't think she's interested in you?" Luanne sat in the chair Parish had vacated.

"She's not interested in anyone."

Luanne frowned. "You mean . . ."

"No." He sighed. "She's been through a lot. She has a seventeen year old son."

"Her? She hardly looks more than seventeen herself."

"I didn't get off to a very good start. I started to accuse her of embezzling."

Luanne laughed. "You really do have a way with the girls."

Staring at the television he considered a question. "How would you deal with her?"

His sister gazed at him with sympathetic concern. "First of all with someone like that you have to be very certain you want to deal with her. You could cause a lot of problems, hurting her a great deal by starting something you decide you don't want to finish."

Blayze sighed.

Luanne tipped her head her gaze still piercing. "Are you interested?"

"I find it difficult keeping her out of my head."

"I'd say you're in trouble." Luanne gave him an anxious look. "It might be good for you to get out of town quick."

Both turned to the door as voices there attracted their attention. Blayze could see Lieutenant Sarkis talking to his guard at the door.

"You're looking better," he observed after closing the door and approaching the bed. "Are you better?" He glanced at Luanne.

"Not sure. This is my sister." Blayze introduced them. "My other sister, not the one in the hit and run."

Lieutenant Sarkis nodded to her. "We've met, while you were in la-la land. Maybe you can get him to tell us who hit him." He turned to Blayze. "I ran into your accounting buddy. She said you wouldn't tell her."

Luanne moved to the recliner near the windows leaving the chair by the bed free for the lieutenant who promptly sat down.

"I've been thinking," Blayze said, "I'll make you a deal."

Lieutenant Sarkis eyed him with suspicion. "What kind of deal?"

"I'd like to talk to Moseley alone, no lawyers, no police, just him and I."

The lieutenant raised his eyebrows. "And what would you hope to accomplish?"

Blayze shook his head then grimaced closing his eyes.

"That's your side of the deal, what do I get out of it?"

"I might be able to tell you who attacked me with the car."

"Might? I need more than might." The lieutenant gave him a stern look over his spectacles. "Let's say will."

Blayze concentrated on the television again then shifted his gaze back to the lieutenant. "If you could refrain from going off half cocked. It would be easy to jump to an erroneous conclusion and cause a whole lot of problems."

Sarkis scowled at Blayze.

"I have an idea but I may be way off base."

"But you did see who hit you?"

"Maybe."

"Maybe nothing. You saw who hit you."

Blayze lifted his shoulders carefully.

"Have they said when they're letting you out of here?"

"No."

"If we delay this too long the perp may get away," Sarkis pleaded his case.

Blayze gave him an admonishing look. "Not this time."

Sarkis turned to Luanne. "Have you seen his doctor around?"

"He was in earlier today. He may come again around six."

"See if you can get an idea of when they're going to let this guy out."

Luanne smiled at him with a brief nod.

"Get some rest," the lieutenant admonished then left the room.

Something had occurred to Blayze while discussing the case with Parish. He figured it was worth testing the idea with Moseley. Gazing across the room at Luanne he considered it. He was tired he realized after so much company. His headache was better, but still there.

He closed his eyes. When he opened them again it was three hours later. Luanne was gone and Sylvia sat in the recliner in her place.

"Would you go through what you remember of the hit and run in Ocean Shores?"

Sylvia rose and approached his bed. "But . . ."

"I know, you've been all through it a dozen times. I may have recognized who the driver was."

"Someone you know?" Sylvia seemed to have lost some if her belligerence and the mocking twist of her lips had gone.

Blayze remained nowhere near buying her changed personality but her recent civility was a welcome relief. "Sort of." He grimaced. "I can't make any sense of it though."

"Would I know this person?" Apprehension returned to her face.

"I don't think so. That's one of my big problems. If I left you and Janice out of it I could make it work."

Taking the chair Sarkis had vacated Sylvia carefully went back through the incident in Ocean Shores.

"Have you had any new insights?"

She gazed over his head at the various apparatus on the wall. "Not really. Since we're pretty certain now it was an intentional hit and run I've tried to think of things that might relate. I've considered those two men we sat with at the bar, but they were both there when we left to my knowledge."

"What about the not so talkative man? Could you describe him?"

"Average build. He never stood up so I don't know how tall he was. He had kind of funny hair and a mustache and goatee."

"Could you see what color his eyes were?"

"At times they looked dark gray and sometimes green depending on the lighting." She frowned. "But I still think they were in the bar when we left."

"Did you leave directly from the bar to your car?"

Sylvia paused to consider. "We might have stopped at the ladies' room first."

"But you don't remember for certain?"

"I could say yes and make it fit my memory or I could say no and make it fit. After what happened I'm not sure I'd trust my memory."

Blayze nodded. He could relate to that.

◆CHAPTER THIRTY-FOUR◆

Blayze sat in the folding chair beside his bed, his leg in the cast stretched out in front of him. The doctor was releasing him from the hospital with numerous cautions regarding his concussion. Just getting prepared to leave had been exhausting. However he figured it might be more emotional than physical. He had acquired a dilemma given his need for crutches because of his broken leg, but an inability to use them with a broken arm. Feeling helpless did nothing for his state of mind. That combined with his other issues sucked away his energy leaving him depressed. He kept reminding himself he was still alive and in all probability would eventually completely recover. He had every reason for thankfulness not depression.

His dilemma did not confine itself to managing with his broken appendages. He had determined the cause of Ridinghood's problems and with little effort could finalize the responsibility for that. A different IRS department from his would manage the enforcement of taxes due leaving it Ridinghood's responsibility to end the inappropriate use of funds, which formed a criminal act outside the IRS jurisdiction. However, a significant number of issues remained unresolved, not the least of which was the hit and run attack on himself.

A noise outside his door attracted his attention. A nurse came into his room accompanied by one of the hospital attendants bringing a strange wheeled device resembling a tall scooter.

"This is your new leg," the nurse informed him cheerfully.

They assisted him to stand then demonstrated how kneeling the broken leg on the seat of this device he could move about with reasonable safety and little strain on his broken arm. It would have been a piece of cake without the broken arm. Nonetheless it made mobility possible with his limited useful body parts. In the midst of his becoming acquainted with this new mode of locomotion Luanne appeared at the door.

She smiled. "That should work."

One advantage of his new transportation device, he escaped having to be taken down to the car in a wheel chair. Once they had made it to the front entrance, Luanne left him. While she retrieved her car he mentally addressed the question she had put to him. What was he going to do now? He needed time to determine how well he could manage in his current physical condition. Thankfully the hotel had an elevator. He figured he could manage somehow. He had no interest in staying with Sylvia and it wouldn't work with Luanne in her military situation. Returning to Salt Lake offered no better solution given he would still need to manage alone. It occurred to him as Luanne's car pulled up next to the curb Dr. Cheung's advice about getting married might have some advantage here.

"What do you want to do?" Luanne asked the moment they were settled in the car.

"Home is the hotel right now. I expect to hear from Lieutenant Sarkis if he took me serious about Moseley."

She cast a dubious glance his direction with evident concern. "You don't think someone will try to take you out again?"

"Well they can't run over me in the hotel."

Luanne shook her head. "Running over you isn't the only option."

"So far that seems to be the only one this individual uses."

Once back in his room he found he was exhausted. After securing his new transportation device close to his bed and placing his phone on the stand he lay down. The sound of his phone's tune gradually penetrated his conscious, waking him. He was amazed to discover the late afternoon sun slanting through the opening in his curtains. Checking the time he found he had been asleep for six hours.

"Blayze," he said to the caller.

"This is Parish."

His brain jumped to alert mode. "What can I do for you?"

"I wondered if I could take you out to dinner."

Blayze laughed. "Turnabout is fair play?" He realized he could feel the pangs of hunger attacking. "I'd be grateful . . . if you let me put it on my expense account."

"Charge the IRS?" She laughed. "Do you have any diet restrictions?"

"I don't recall them giving me anything like that."

"And if you didn't like the restrictions you'd conveniently forget about them?"

Blayze laughed. "I might, but I really don't believe they gave me any."

"I'll come by for you in about half an hour."

Tempted to make something of Parish's invitation, she was put up to it or she actually cared for him, he determined to be grateful, regardless of the reasoning, and not look his gift horse in the mouth.

By the time Parish arrived he had managed, with considerable difficulty, a shave and a change of clothing. However, the prospect of freedom and some normalcy in life again helped him maintain a positive attitude.

"How do you like my little vehicle?" he demonstrated his scooter. "I feel silly, but it's better than helplessness."

"It's great." She inspected him with brows drawn together. "Luanne is concerned about you. She's not sure you're safe from another attack."

Ah, Blayze thought, that was the reasoning. Luanne enlisted Parish's assistance to watch out for him. Although he felt a pang of disappointment he didn't care to examine, he reminded himself to be grateful she was willing to accept the responsibility.

"Are you okay with Italian again?"

"I'm your captive, what can I say?"

She smiled at that.

From the hotel they headed north to Sixth Avenue and from there to what the banners announced was the Proctor District.

Fortunately the waitress, observing Blayze's handicap, led them to a quiet table in the corner of the busy Italian restaurant where he could stash his scooter and have room for his broken leg. Parish noticed his stoic expression while enduring the necessary arrangements for being seated.

After placing their order, she took a deep breath. "Will your attacker try again?" She noticed his surprise at the question. "That's right. You know who it is. But still . . ."

He lifted an eyebrow. "Won't it be worse now?" He smiled ruefully. "To be honest I hadn't considered that, but you're right. The person definitely has a motive now."

Parish felt a stab of alarm, suddenly stung by the nature of his vulnerability.

He watched her with a poignant gaze that confused her. "Would you care?"

She was shocked. "Of course I'd care. I wouldn't want to see something awful happen to you."

"But would you care . . . ?" He emphasized the last word watching with a strange light in his pale eyes. His dark brows still hovered ominously.

She opened her mouth but before she could speak the waitress returned with their drink order. When she had gone Parish asked, "Are you any closer to a motive?"

He smiled. "I've been too tired to think about it. I keep falling asleep before I get anywhere."

"Is this person you won't name that far out of the picture?"

"You realize what the accusation would be – premeditated murder done execution style." Blayze grimaced. "Three hit and run attacks and one personal attack with a wine bottle."

"Maybe there isn't just one person or one motive."

"I've considered that, but it doesn't help. Obviously the person I've seen is responsible for the hit and runs." He sighed. "Why don't we talk about something else?"

Parish remained silent at a loss for another subject.

"Do you ever think about traveling?"

"I'd love to travel, but I've never had the freedom or finances."

"Where would you go?"

"Anywhere." She laughed. "Mostly historical places on the east coast and Europe." After a moment she asked, "Do you travel?"

He grimaced. "For business, which isn't the same as traveling for pleasure. I get tired of it, but for leisure it could be good. I'd enjoy historical places in Europe."

While the waitress served their entrees Parish noticed a couple familiar faces. When the waitress had gone she leaned toward Blayze. "See those two women in line to be seated?"

Blayze looked to where she indicated then frowned. One was the blonde with the overlay of Kool-aid red, the other was a short heavy woman with a bubbling expression of amusement. "The one looks familiar. Who's the other one?"

"It's Bobbi Bennett and her friend Annabelle Elliott."

Blayze continued to frown gazing at the two as they were escorted to a table in a corner of the restaurant.

Although not inclined to believe the hit and run attacker was a woman Parish watched Blayze's reaction and continued interest in the pair.

"When did she come back from Ocean Shores?" he asked.

"I saw her a few days ago at Ridinghood. She stopped me to ask if I'd heard Mr. Moseley was arrested in Puerto Rico. When I told her I had, she asked what for. She was adamant he would never have killed Lawrence."

Blayze tipped his head giving Parish a speculative look. She went on. "You know he didn't do it, right?"

"Pretty much."

"And who did?"

He sighed. "Maybe that too."

"Maybe?"

"I don't have a motive"

"And without the why you won't tell anyone?" She scowled at him, huffing in frustration, "You'll let someone make you the target instead."

His gaze shot to her face with a trace of hopefulness.

Parish met his gaze with exasperation, pausing confused at his expression then looked away.

"I've asked Sarkis for an opportunity to talk with Moseley alone. I believe he knows who is doing all this and why, or I might be able to figure out why from talking with him."

Their entrees arrived diverting their attention for a time. Parish mulled over what Blayze had said while noting the two women at the other table from time to time. They appeared to be having an amusing girl's night out, laughing and talking as if they had not a care in the world.

When she returned her gaze to Blayze he was watching her.

"Why is the why so important?"

"Because I can't trust my memory. You have no concept of all the crazy ideas that race through your head when you're semiconscious.

Parish figured she did know, at least in a small way. She had woken from sleep after a series of impossibly illogical dreams with no comprehension of what put those thoughts into her head especially in that arrangement.

◈CHAPTER THIRTY-FIVE◈

Sitting in the hotel breakfast area Blayze noticed Lieutenant Sarkis' black SUV pull into the parking lot. Had the lieutenant cleared it for him to visit Ian Moseley? Sarkis hadn't been excited about the idea. Blayze had some doubts he would make the effort. Would making those arrangements even be possible? He had no idea of the requirements for visiting prisoners, especially those held for murder.

Sarkis looked him over as if he were an interesting specimen for analysis.

"Coffee, Lieutenant?" he motioned to the coffee bar across the room. "I'd get some for you, but . . ."

Sarkis grimaced at him then went to fix coffee. When he returned he pulled out one of the chairs, taking care to avoid Blayze's broken leg, and took a seat. "Have you changed your mind yet about telling me who ran over you?"

Blayze shook his head. "Have you arranged for me to see Moseley?"

"Ten o'clock you see him." The lieutenant glared. "Then you see me." It sounded like a threat.

"Alone, right?"

Sarkis nodded. "I put a tail on the Bennett woman and that Hogan character."

Blayze blinked his surprise.

"I don't want have to bring one or both of them back from Puerto Rico."

"You expect them to leave the country?"

"Apparently that's the idea with all this traveling money. First the money travels then the people. It looks as though Ridinghood's employees either die or getaway."

"Maybe it's the other way around. If they don't getaway they die."

Sarkis snorted. "I haven't told Moseley I'm bringing you to see him. His reaction to visitors hasn't been appreciative. We're letting him assume he's meeting his attorney."

Blayze nodded his understanding and acceptance.

"Are you ready to go?"

Blayze made a mental inventory of what he needed to take with him. "I should get my briefcase. I might have to prove some things to him."

When he returned Sarkis gave a doubtful glance at the scooter then led the way to his vehicle. Given it was Blayze's right leg and left arm that were broken, he was able with the handle to hoist himself into the passenger seat while the lieutenant stowed his scooter.

It was a short drive to the building where Moseley was being held. When they had successfully passed through security, the lieutenant led the way down a hallway of busy people on various assignments who observed Blayze with a curious glance. Arriving at a small room set aside for the use of lawyers and their clients, the lieutenant left Blayze indicating he would bring Moseley.

The man Lieutenant Sarkis ushered into the room was somewhat shorter than Blayze had imagined him. Without the hairpiece and goatee, as Parish's picture had shown him, Moseley appeared both younger and more distraught.

With his head clean-shaven and the large green eyes sunk into a shadow beneath his brows one could see the toll his adventures had taken. Blayze wondered if he had any regrets, that is, outside the accusation of murder one.

He eyed Blayze with a perplexed frown as the lieutenant introduced him.

"Sit down," the lieutenant beckoned to the chair across from Blayze. "Mr Pashasia has some questions for you. I'll let him explain."

Moseley hesitated briefly before cautiously accepting the chair. Once the lieutenant had departed he gazed at Blayze with suspicion. "And who are you?"

"The IRS auditor investigating Ridinghood's tax accounting."

Moseley's expression didn't change but he lifted his shoulders as if to ask, what are you doing here?

Blayze studied his companion while determining whether to start at the beginning or jump to the end. "I've come to persuade you to tell us who murdered Lawrence Manke."

Moseley's suspicious frown leaped from surprise to confusion. "They've determined I murdered him."

"Did you?"

"No."

"But you know who did?"

Moseley said nothing. His expression returned to suspicion. He crossed his arms over his chest.

"In auditing Ridinghood's accounts I discovered the problems that alerted the IRS came from money being sidetracked into a different account from which it was subsequently put into investments. The investment income was shifted off to another location while the original sum returned to Ridinghood. Ridinghood paid taxes on their income but not on the additional amount earned in the investments. An attempt was made to give the appearance those accounts belonged to Ridinghood. Consequently the IRS viewed the whole matter as if Ridinghood was hiding the proceeds of their investments."

Moseley lifted his shoulders as if to say, what has that to do with me?

"I've traced those transactions to the point I could see they in no way attached to the corporation. Some individual manipulated them. The process of elimination brought me to you . . . and Tim Hogan."

"Hogan!" The moment the name escaped, Moseley realized his mistake and attempted to return to his expression of indifferent suspicion.

"Apparently he discovered what you were doing and from your investment account has been siphoning a little off the top." Blayze could see this had taken Ian by surprise. He had been unaware of Hogan's activity. "Putting all this together, how carefully you manipulated those accounts then returned the original sum to Ridinghood, I couldn't see a murderer. Apparently Manke discovered what you were doing, but all you had to do then was pack up and leave the country, as you did. Killing Manke would have created an unnecessary complication. You didn't strike me as someone who indulged in unnecessary complications."

Ian's gaze left Blayze, drifting off to the corner of the room. Blayze called his attention back. "Your behavior since you were arrested in Puerto Rico has led your attorney, the lieutenant and I to conclude, although you did not commit the murder, you know who did."

After giving Moseley time to respond Blayze continued. "You're the only person with a motive and with what evidence the lieutenant has you'll be convicted of first degree murder unless . . ." Blayze gave Ian another chance to respond then went on. "A couple nights ago I was attacked by someone in a burgundy Chevrolet sedan. I believe I saw the driver. I've had time to consider this person may have been the one who killed Lawrence Manke and Ellen Hogan."

Moseley frowned, "Ellen Hogan?"

"They didn't tell you?"

"They said I wouldn't be able to see her."

"Because she's dead, killed in a hit and run attack."

A flash of fright passed over Ian's face. He put his hands on the table and stared at them as if fighting an internal battle. His shoulders sagged. "I thought maybe she could help me." He returned his gaze to Blayze. The suspicion was back. "If you know who did it why don't you tell them?"

"If I'm wrong I'll have gotten someone into a lot of trouble they don't deserve."

"What if I tell you and it isn't the person you think it is. I'll still be in trouble in jail or out."

"I'm sure Sarkis can manage some kind of protection for you. Send you back to Puerto Rico?"

Moseley stared at his hands again for some time. Blayze waited patiently.

"Okay," Moseley capitulated, "you've got the money part. Lawrence found out about it. He thought he could do a little blackmail so he let me know he knew what I was doing. He demanded a certain amount of money for his silence to which I agreed. I'd be out of the country before he could hit me up for more. He came to my house the night he died to pick up the money.

Ian sighed. "I had made a fatal error. My administrative assistant had been helping me move things out of my office in preparation for leaving the country. She was there the night Lawrence came. Stupidly I'd allowed her to think she'd be coming with me." Moseley grimaced and took a deep breath. "I hadn't taken her interest seriously enough. Lawrence sat on the sofa and I was in a chair across from him. She was standing next to a lamp table at the end of the sofa. I kept my revolver in a drawer in that table." He shook his head. "I don't know how she knew, but she reached into the drawer took the gun out, put it to Lawrence's head and fired."

"Doris Possum?"

Ian nodded.

After Ian Moseley had been returned to his cell, Lieutenant Sarkis took Blayze to his office. Once they were seated, Sarkis demanded, "Okay, now talk. Who are we dealing with?"

"Doris Possum."

"Screaming Mimi!" The lieutenant narrowed his eyes, studying Blayze as if he thought he was putting one over on him. "This is for real?" He scowled. "She was in the car that attacked you?"

Blayze nodded. "She shot Manke." He explained what Moseley told him about the murder.

After calling in an order to have Doris Possum picked up, the lieutenant turned back to Blayze. "What in the heck would she do that for?"

"Protecting her man? Keeping what she believed was her future intact?"

Sarkis wiped the hair off his forehead. "So why come after you?"

"Same thing. I'd figured out the money scheme."

"And your sister?"

"Jealousy. She probably thought Sylvia was making time with Ian, threatening her control of the man. And probably the same thing with Ellen Hogan."

"And with Sally Stills?"

Blayze grimaced. "I don't know. Could be any one of the three, Manke's blackmail accomplice, she knew about the money scheme, or jealousy."

"And the trunk set up? Who managed that?"

"Moseley, protecting himself. He used Doris, but knew, just as things have turned out, she could get him into a lot of trouble."

The lieutenant stared into his coffee cup and huffed, "So will we end up with a plea of insanity?"

"I don't think they could make it stick. She definitely has a warped sense of right and wrong, but I don't believe she's technically insane, just obsessed."

"Well, I'd better get you back to your hotel." He rose. "I expect I'll be tied up the rest of the afternoon."

After the lieutenant dropped Blayze off at his hotel, he realized he was tired again. His recovery still had a long way to go.

He woke to the sound of knocking on his door. A glance at the clock told him he had slept for another four hours. Managing to get to the door and open it he was so surprised to see both of his sisters there he simply stared at them.

"Can we come in?" Luanne asked.

Blayze moved out of the way.

"We figured we'd come see how you're doing," she explained, giving him a careful once over.

"Take you out to dinner," Sylvia added, maneuvering her way around him with her crutch.

"Sit down." He waved at the two chairs accompanying a small table near the windows.

Luanne turned the chair at the desk around so that it faced the inside of the room, making it easier for Blayze to sit. Then she joined Sylvia at the table.

"So what have you got to say for yourself?" Luanne grinned at him.

"Have you gotten any further in figuring out who did this?" Sylvia asked.

Blayze sighed. "I talked to the guy they've arrested." He addressed Sylvia. "I believe he was the quiet man at the table with you in Ocean Shores. I don't think he knew anything about what happened to you. It seems the woman on the corner at the bar was the one in the car that attacked you. She's the one who attacked me." He went on to explain the traveling money, the attempted blackmail, and Doris shooting Manke. He continued adding Moseley's escape to Puerto Rico, the attack on Sally Stills, on Sylvia and Janice, and on Ellen Hogan.

Sylvia scowled. "What was her problem anyway?"

"She's obsessed with Ian Moseley."

Rolling her eyes Sylvia declared, "She's some kind of howling witch."

"Did they get her?" Luanne asked.

"The lieutenant is having her arrested." He addressed Sylvia. "I believe this clears up the matter where you and Janice are concerned."

"As far as this accident is concerned."

"What are you going to do now?" Luanne asked him.

Blayze shook his head. "I don't know for sure. I have to finish reports for Ridinghood and get them straightened out with the IRS. I'll probably have to testify at the trials."

"Will they be tried together?"

"Hard to say. There are at least two separate crimes. The murders and assaults plus the money deal."

"Will they let the Moseley guy out of jail now?"

Blayze grimaced. "It might depend on whether they charge him with being an accessory after the fact for covering up Doris' crime. And then it might depend on whether the police believe he is actually innocent of the first murder. I don't believe he'll be charged with the assaults since much of the time they were committed he wasn't available."

Sylvia glanced at her watch. "Let's go get something to eat."

Luanne stood up. "We've found an enticing restaurant we want to try, an Argentine steakhouse with great reviews." She glanced at Sylvia's crutches and Blayze's scooter. "You two are a pair. The restaurant will think I'm bringing in the orthopedic unit.

◆CHAPTER THIRTY-SIX◆

Parish made a trip to the bank on her lunch hour. Returning to her office she entered the main floor foyer where she noticed a couple people from the sales department observing something in the executive suite corridor. Curious, she paused beside them. Coming toward them were two uniformed police officers and between them handcuffed was Doris Possum.

"Will I be able to see Ian?" She was asking as they reached the foyer.

The two young officers ignored the question.

Doris sent a glance Parish's direction with a puzzled expression. She appeared neither upset nor alarmed, just confused. Obviously she was being arrested, didn't she realize that? Undoubtedly they had given her the standard warning and with handcuffs it seemed conclusive. Surely she didn't think this is how they would take her to visit Mr. Moseley.

Parish climbed the stairs puzzling over the situation. Why was Doris being arrested and what did she think was happening? Instead of stopping at her office she continued to the third floor and Midge's office. Finding Midge absent, she continued to the break room where she found her conversing with Odella.

"Where have you been?" Midge accosted her. "I've been looking all over for you."

"Bank. Did you see they've arrested Doris Possum?"

Both Midge and Odella stared as if she had just informed them Congress cancelled the Fourth of July.

Before Midge could get a word out, she said, "And for your information, no, I'm not kidding." She explained the scene in the foyer.

Midge and Odella exchanged a glance.

"I wonder what that means. Have you seen Blayze? Or the lieutenant?" Midge asked.

"Not today."

"I got a call earlier. Sally Stills came out of her coma."

"Did she say who attacked her?" Odella asked.

Midge shook her head. "From what the nurse said, Sally wasn't saying much at present and they're not pressing her."

A sudden look of surprise on Midge's face made Parish turn around. Lieutenant Sarkis stood in the doorway.

"We were just talking about you," Midge said.

The lieutenant peered over his glasses at her. "I'm hauling one of your employees off to jail."

"I could give you a couple names I'd be glad to see you haul off," Midge mumbled before asking, "Who?"

"Moseley's assistant, Doris Possum, two counts of murder and three of assault." His expression challenged Midge to object. "She won't see the light of day again for a very long time, if ever." He paused as if giving them time to react. "I thought I'd inform you before I give your chief the news."

"We appreciate your consideration," Parish said and meant it.

He bobbed his head and departed, ostensibly headed to the executive suite. His leaving left behind a stunned silence.

Midge shook her head. "Doris Possum?"

Odella laughed. "Who would have figured?"

"So she's the one who attacked Blayze?" Parish asked.

"Three assaults? Undoubtedly."

Parish sighed her relief, realizing as she did so it was doubtless a dangerous sign. After fixing a cup of coffee she returned to her office. She found it difficult to keep her mind on her work. Thankfully Xavier had another basketball game that night which would help divert her attention. She decided to leave work early and pick up fast food for their dinner.

※

In the quiet of early morning Blayze considered his situation. All things considered he was as well off here in Tacoma as he would be anywhere else. Of course, he could go home to his mother, but that presented other problems. She lived in a multi-level with no elevators. At least here he could get around by himself. Doubtless he would need to be available for the prosecution of Ian Moseley and Doris Possum, if not also Tim Hogan. However, if he went home to Salt Lake he could fly back for those occasions. He could also get around on his own there.

Being honest with himself, he didn't want to leave Tacoma. Unfortunately he had failed to get out of town soon enough. He realized in the half-light of dawn something had happened to him he had never experienced before. He had fallen in love. He had said, "I love you," before. And he had meant it. Somehow this was different. Never before had he experienced the anxiety, the painful longing, the intense excitement. He had little doubt "falling in love" was an acute, destructive, debilitating disease for which there was no antidote. What was even worse heartbreak wouldn't support a cast that could help it heal.

He sighed. What were his options? He could stay in Tacoma and hope. Maybe Hornby would give him another assignment in the area. Or would it be better to bite the bullet and get away? He wasn't sure he would have a choice.

Getting dressed these days was considerably more complicated and time consuming. Once he had accomplished that and managed breakfast he put a call into his superior, realizing he hadn't let Mr. Hornby know the recent developments.

"Blayze, haven't heard from you in a while."

"I've been indisposed. I got caught in the tangle here at Ridinghood and was attacked by an irate driver. Spent a couple days in the hospital, have a couple broken bones."

"Sheez, are you all right?"

"I will be eventually. I'm a little handicapped at present. Probably need to take some time off. The audit results completely exonerate Ridinghood, but I'll probably have to testify in criminal actions here. The IRS will need to prosecute also. I'll send you the reports and all the necessary paperwork."

"I might have another job in that area, if you'd be interested. You wouldn't need to report for a couple weeks."

"That might work. I'll let you know."

When he ended the call Blayze figured he should make a final appearance at Ridinghood and conclude his dealings there. While considering how to manage the trip his phone alerted him. Parish's number showed up on the screen. "What can I do for you?"

"Before I reported to Mr. Ridinghood I wanted to be sure you're done here."

"I am, but I need to make a trip over there to be sure I have everything out of that office and give the final word to Mr. Ridinghood. You wouldn't be up for picking me up?"

Parish laughed. "Sure. Are you ready now?"

"I'll wait for you downstairs."

Blayze hung his briefcase strap over his shoulder then took his scooter to the elevator. Waiting in the registration area he kept an eye out for Parish. When her small car pulled into the lot, he managed the side door.

Blayze presented two opposing appearances; one the immaculate businessman in his well-fitted suit, the other the invalid struggling to manage. Parish felt somewhat at a loss to help him without discrediting him. Determining quick effective assistance making little of the circumstance was best. She opened the passenger door and the hatchback, then grabbed his scooter and stored it while he seated himself.

Belted in and before starting the car she turned to him and asked, "Are you okay?"

"Might depend on what you call okay."

A trace of defensiveness and some sadness belied his business-like appearance. Confused by this and his comment she turned to the task of getting them to Ridinghood. Once there she retrieved his scooter while he got himself out of the car.

When they reached the foyer he turned to her. "I'm used to taking the stairs. Presumably the elevator comes down this far."

She smiled, directing their steps into the executive suite. "Do you want to see Mr. Ridinghood first?"

"Good idea. Why don't you come with me? You may need to pick up the pieces when I'm gone."

Slate's administrative assistant smiled at Parish as they inquired about the executive and were ushered into his office.

Alarm charged into Slate's expression when he looked up at Blayze.

Blayze laughed. "Auditing has become a somewhat dangerous profession."

Although smiling with his lips Slate registered misgiving with his eyes. "Sit down."

"I've come to pack up my things and get out of your hair. Ridinghood is off the hook with the IRS. Moseley will be prosecuted for the financial finagling and possibly Tim Hogan as an accomplice after the fact. He might just rate a fine and a blemished record. Doris Possum is on the hook for everything else."

"I understand they arrested her here yesterday."

Blayze nodded.

Slate appeared bewildered. "I appreciate everything you've done here. I never figured I be grateful to the IRS. I could use a few more people like you on the company roster."

Blayze laughed. "But it's not your accounting people giving you problems."

Slate nodded with a grimace. "I need a whole new executive team."

Blayze and Parish rose.

"Well thanks again and take care of yourself."

Parish walked with Blayze back to the elevator which they took to the second floor and the office Blayze had occupied.

"You'll handle having me taken off the computer?" He asked her.

She nodded. "I'll talk to Miguel." After a pause, she asked, "Are you going back to Salt Lake right away?" When he turned to her she noted the sadness and defense were back in his expression.

"Maybe not right away." His eyes pinned her from beneath the ominous eyebrows. "Does it matter?"

It did matter. She wished it didn't, but it did. "I've gotten used to having you around."

"Do you think we could be friends? Maybe do things together once in a while?"

She met his eyes confused by the hope she saw there.

"My boss may have another assignment in this area. I have to be around for the trials so that may be convenient."

"Really? That would be good."

"You think so?"

"Yes."

"I may need someone to help me get around. I can't drive a car now and walking won't get me too far."

She laughed. "I can be your chauffeur."

"I'd appreciate that." He held his hand out palm up. "Deal?"

She placed hers in his. "Deal."

Printed in the United States
By Bookmasters